DYING TO RECALL

A Medical Thriller Series Book 2

Chris Bliersbach

Smashwords

CHAPTER 1

D r. Steven Caron's lifeless body hung in his office, dealing a severe blow to the crusade against AlzCura Pharmaceuticals that he agreed to join one week earlier. He had been a principal investigator of AlzCura's clinical trials for the Recallamin vaccine, now successfully marketed to tens of millions worldwide as a cure for Alzheimer's and a preventative for those carrying the Alzheimer's gene. AlzCura had tapped Dr. Caron as their regional investigator for Central Maine. Caron, a neurologist, a few years removed from medical school, was eager to grow his practice. So eager that he gladly accepted AlzCura's support to grow his practice from an office in Campion to outreach clinics in Ramsey, Namahoe, and Farrisport.

Dr. Caron had met with Jackie Deno, Curt Barnes, and District Attorney Will Wydman at the Farrisport Inn and formed the Table of Four. As they learned at that meeting, Dr. Caron's eagerness and AlzCura's greed resulted in some shady financial arrangements, as well as some less than professional behavior on Dr. Caron's part. Dr. Caron had revealed AlzCura's unconventional research protocols that he claimed kept harmful data out of AlzCura's clinical trials, thereby assuring their vaccine's approval. At the meeting, a repentant, Dr. Caron, had pledged his desire to stop living a lie and, regardless of the cost, joined the group bent on exposing and stopping the AlzCura juggernaut. Now, however, he was dead.

Rebecca Klatz, Dr. Caron's Office Manager, was the first to find him. Pulling into the parking lot an hour before the office opened, she was surprised to see his red BMW. Dr. Caron was perpetually late and never early. Rebecca immediately grew concerned by his uncharacteristic punctuality.

"Well, what's this, Dr. Caron? Turning over a new leaf?" Rebecca called out as she walked down the hall and stuck her head into Dr. Caron's office.

There was no one in the office or nearby to hear her screams. The sight of his pale body, his blue protruding tongue, and the smell of urine and feces assaulted her senses in a way that would repeatedly haunt her in the coming months. Stumbling out of the office and gagging, she made it to a phone and called 911.

"911, what's your emergency?"

Before she could mouth the words, Rebecca vomited. The 911 Operator read the address on her screen and, hearing the caller vomiting asked,

"Are you sick? Do you want me to send an ambulance?"

Finally done depositing her half-digested breakfast on the office floor, Rebecca tried to cough out the address.

"Ma'am, I have your address. Do you want me to send an ambulance?"

"Yesssssssssssssssss."

"Are you choking?"

Finally, regaining her voice, Rebecca nearly screamed, "No, it's not for me. Dr. Caron has hung himself. Send someone now."

"An ambulance and the police are already on the way, ma'am. Have you cut the body down?"

"Noooooooo, I can't even look at it," unable to believe she

was even asking her that question.

"Is he dead, or do you think he can be saved?"

"Why are you asking me so many questions? Send the fucking ambulance!"

"Ma'am, the ambulance is on the way. Try to relax. I am just trying to help you save him if you think he can be saved."

"His tongue is sticking out, and he's white except for his blue tongue. There are piss and shit all over the place. He's fucking dead, do you understand?"

"I understand ma'am, try to calm down. I was just trying to help. The ambulance and police should be there shortly."

While the record would show that it only took 8 minutes for the ambulance to arrive after 911 received Rebecca's call, it seemed like 8 hours to her. The EMTs and police arrived simultaneously, and seeing the scene, agreed that no rescue was possible.

The police approached Rebecca. "Ma'am, we'd like to ask you some questions."

Rebecca, struggling to maintain her composure, said, "I just found him this way."

"I understand, but we need to investigate whether he committed suicide or if foul play may be involved."

The officer's suggestion that this may be something other than a suicide sent Rebecca's mind reeling.

"Was he depressed or more stressed recently? Suffer any major disappointment? Or did his behavior change radically in the last few days or weeks?"

"Not that I'm aware of. He's been the same old' Dr. Caron. If anything, he has seemed less stressed lately."

"Do you know if anyone was mad at him? Any angry patients or family members who may have threatened him? Maybe someone in the office who may have been mad at him or someone who was recently fired?"

"No. Dr. Caron's patients loved him. He bent over backward for his patients. As for the office staff, Dr. Caron was a perfectionist, so he wasn't always the easiest person to work for, but I can't imagine anyone wanting to kill him."

"Has anyone been fired or resigned recently?"

"No. The last person to resign was a year ago, and she was one of our Medical Assistants who went back to school."

"Was he married? Was he having any marital difficulties that you know of?"

"Yes, he's married, and I really can't say I know anything about his relationship. He didn't talk about it much."

"And how was your relationship with Dr. Caron? Did it change recently?"

Rebecca, realizing the officer was now exploring whether she could have been a part of this, decompensated.

"What? You think I did this?" she blurted as tears began to flow.

"No, ma'am. These are just the standard questions we need to ask," the officer tried to say in a matter-of-fact tone.

"I made the 911 call. Why would you think I did this?" she screamed, attracting the attention of the other police officer. As if on cue, the pair of officers switched roles, with the questioner taking his leave while his partner seamlessly took over.

"Ma'am, my partner didn't mean to upset you. I'm sure you understand that we are just trying to get as much information about what happened as possible."

Rebecca was sobbing and inconsolable, and the officer motioned to have one of the EMTs stay with her. At the same time, he and his partner surveyed the scene from the office door.

"See anything suspicious?"

"Nah, looks pretty straightforward to me."

"Why would a doctor choose to hang himself? Don't you think they would have access to more effective and less messy ways to kill themselves?"

"Yeah, and you'd think he'd know that death wouldn't come quick, dropping only a couple feet. He kicked and struggled for a while, judging by the scatter of the shit in the room."

"Yeah, it also looks like he kicked over some things on his desk. What are we missing?"

"Looks like his computer is on. I'll glove up and check the scene some more before we call this a suicide. Check on the woman and see if she's notified the doctor's next of kin."

The officer pulled out a pair of gloves and stepped cautiously into the office, traveling along the edges so as not to disrupt or cover up the indentations from foot traffic on the carpet. Approaching Dr. Caron's desk, the officer noticed a stack of files, journals, and papers knocked on the floor. At first, he surmised that the doctor must have kicked this stack off the desk in his struggles. Then he realized that the rest of the desk still had many stacks that appeared untouched. Given the location of the fallen stack on the desk, it seemed unlikely that he would have only kicked over that one pile. He jiggled the computer mouse, and the computer screen sprang to life. What he saw made him call out to his partner and grab his radio simultaneously.

"Dispatch, we need Crime Scene Investigators to our location ASAP, over."

"Roger, I will send CSIs ASAP, over."

CHAPTER 2

Curt spent the weekend following his dinner with Jackie, Dr. Caron, and DA Wydman, trying to reconcile the commitment he made to the group. He was apprehensive about its' impact on his home and work life. Before he could even think about authoring a letter to AlzCura, he needed to make some decisions and difficult choices.

He pretty much knew he would have to resign as a partner of Jackson & Barnes, the healthcare management consulting firm that he helped build over the last ten years. The stakes of going up against AlzCura were just too high. He could not risk having the pharmaceutical company taking aim at Jackson & Barnes should they use a "scorched earth" approach in retaliation, as DA Wydman had bluntly intimated. Curt estimated that between Callis' life insurance, his investment accounts, and selling his stake in the consulting company, he could probably wage this war and still provide for his kids for the next two to three years. He could probably pick up a few consulting gigs here and there to augment his finances if the fight looked like it would extend beyond that. If he and the group were successful in proving their case against AlzCura, the likely settlement he would receive would dwarf the amount invested in the battle. If, being the operative word. Any way he cut it, he was taking a substantial professional and financial risk.

The immediate impact of leaving Jackson & Barnes on the

kids would likely be positive. He'd be a stay-at-home parent. If they didn't want to ride the bus, he could drive them to school in the morning and pick them up from school in the afternoon. Heck, he could even volunteer in their classrooms from time to time if Caitlin or Cade wanted him to. Sure, there would be times when the kids might have to take the bus or have Jordan's mom watch them after school, but those times would be the exception, not the rule. If anything about his decision to take on AlzCura was reassuring, it was that he would be able to be more available to his kids. He decided to hold off, telling Caitlin and Cade about his meeting with Jackie. There would be time for that in the future. He clicked off the light on his bedside table, eased back into bed, and slept soundly despite the enormity of the decisions he would set in motion the next day.

"Good morning, LB. How was your weekend?"

"Just peachy boss and yours?"

"Interesting."

"Oh? How so?"

"I'll have to tell you later. Is Sam in?"

"No, but I expect him any minute. Do you need time with him today? He's free until 10, and then he's booked solid."

"Yes, I'll meet with him first thing. Thanks."

Curt started walking to his office but was interrupted by Loribeth.

"So, you're just going to leave me hanging about your "interesting" weekend?"

"I'm sorry, LB. I promise, as soon as I've met with Sam, I will tell you all about it."

"You better."

He turned to walk to his office, and as he closed the door, he felt tears well up in his eyes. He walked into the office knowing what he needed to do but hadn't counted on the emotional upheaval his decision was going to cause. Sam and LB were family. What seemed like an academic decision when he walked in was now beginning to feel like a painful divorce. They were so supportive of him through the whole ordeal, and now he was going to leave them. Worse, he was there for them during rocky times in their lives. He realized that a significant part of his life and identity was bound up in his relationship with them. He wasn't so sure anymore if he could step away. As his resolve was disintegrating, a knock on his office door interrupted his thoughts.

"Good morning, partner. LB tells me you needed to meet with me?" greeted Sam poking his head into Curt's office.

"Sam, come on in."

"What's up?"

"I don't know where to begin, Sam. I was pretty certain I knew what I needed to do after this weekend, but now I'm not so sure."

"Well, LB told me you said you had an interesting weekend. Maybe you should begin there?"

Curt briefed Sam on the dinner meeting and the decision the group made to pursue the truth about AlzCura and the vaccine Recallamin.

"Phew, taking on a pharmaceutical company won't be easy."

"I know Sam, and I don't want my decision to impact Jackson & Barnes adversely. I'm afraid that AlzCura will try to tarnish our reputation and even try to destroy our client base. I couldn't live with that. Making this decision and having them attack me is one thing. Having them attack you, LB, and everyone else in the company is another. I think it best that I leave the company."

"Wow, glad I'm sitting down."

"I know Sam, I'm sorry."

"Don't be sorry, Curt. You need to do what you need to do. I understand. I don't want to lose you, but if I were in your shoes, I'd probably do the same. Let's discuss this for a moment, though. What if we dissolve the partnership, and I kept you on as an independent consultant?"

"I don't know, Sam. That's mighty generous of you, but I'm just worried that they will go after anyone and anything I'm associated with. Besides, I will have to devote a lot of time to the effort against AlzCura."

"Part-time then, you name the hours. I certainly don't want to lose your skills entirely. If the water gets too hot with AlzCura, and it looks like our consulting arrangement may reflect poorly on the company, we can always dissolve the consulting agreement. What do you say?"

Sam's proposal successfully struck a compromise between Curt's need to assure his decision didn't harm the company and his need to continue to have a relationship with his partner of 10 years and his trusty assistant. Drawing an income, even if only part-time, also wouldn't hurt.

"It's a deal."

"Great. Well, not great, but better than seeing you walk off into the sunset. What are we going to tell LB?"

"Oh, I'm not looking forward to that."

"She'll understand, eventually."

"Thanks, that's reassuring. Perhaps we should tell her together?"

"Good idea, let's call her in."

LB entered Curt's office, apprehensive. She had a radar that tipped her off the moment Curt characterized his weekend as interesting. It was also rare that the two partners would call her into the office.

"I don't think I'm going to like hearing about your interesting weekend Curt," LB said, anticipating bad news.

"Sit down, LB. It's not that bad," Curt started.

"But it's bad. I knew it."

Over the next 30 minutes, Curt and Sam tried their best to let LB down easy and build her back up. Unfortunately, any disruption to their decade-long relationship felt like the earth had moved out from under her feet. It wasn't until they realized that they all had bunched up bundles of tear-soaked tissues in front of them that the scene struck them as funny.

"Look at us. Single-handedly giving an economic stimulus to the tissue-making industry," joked Sam, whose mind always thought about the economic impact of things.

That broke the tension, and the realization that Curt was still going to have some connection to the company made LB relent.

"Frankly, the only reason I'm crying is I don't know who will bring me my hot chocolate on those cold winter mornings," ribbed LB.

"We'll write it into his consulting agreement LB."

"Good, and if he fails to deliver, we can fire his ass."

The somber office transitioned, and after hugs all around, the weight of Curt's decision didn't seem as heavy as it had been an hour earlier.

"This just might work," Curt said to himself after Sam and LB exited his office.

CHAPTER 3

The last thing Jackie expected from her trip to Maine was that she would be coming back from it allied with Dr. Caron. It had taken a lot for him to admit his mistakes and decide to come clean. For this, Jackie respected him. Curt had been right in inviting Dr. Caron, and the information he could provide would be invaluable to their cause.

On the flights back from Maine, Jackie cataloged all the things she needed to do in preparation for the upcoming battle. First, she needed to come clean herself and talk with her parents. She had yet to tell them about her dismissal from Alz-Cura, Stu's preliminary autopsy results, or the crusade against her former employer that she was embarking upon. As upside-down as her life was now, she knew that it would likely get worse before it got better. She would need their support, and she knew that they would initially feel hurt that she delayed telling them.

Second, she had to determine how she was going to afford to fight this fight without a job. One of the terms of Jackie's termination was the immediate sale of her shares of AlzCura stock. Although she only participated in the stock purchase program for less than two years, she received a tidy $25,000. This was dirty money to her, and she was happy to reinvest it towards the crusade against AlzCura. Then there was Stu's life insurance. They increased their life insurance policies to

$250,000 each when Jackie became pregnant. Her most significant expense was the mortgage on the house, and she pondered whether to put the house on the market. The thought of selling it pained her, but she needed to be practical. She didn't need a big home with a big mortgage. She resolved to call the realtor to see if it made financial sense to put her house on the market. She was quite sure her parents would offer Jackie the option of staying with them, but Jackie needed her own space. Oddly, the Village Square apartment that she and Stu had been so eager to move out of now seemed like the perfect option.

Third, although foremost in her heart and mind, was Ashley's welfare. If the finances held out, being able to stay home with Ash was a blessing. At 7-months old, Ashley's daily routines were well established. Jackie reasoned that much of her work could be done during Ashley's morning and afternoon nap times or after her early evening bedtime. As Ashley was starting to crawl and babble, it wouldn't be long before she was walking and talking. Jackie relished that she would be able to be there when Ashley reached these developmental mileposts.

Finally, she needed to find a good employment lawyer. One of the first shots across AlzCuras' bow was going to be appealing her termination using AlzCura's internal appeals process. She fully expected this appeal to fail but would then be prepared to file a wrongful termination suit. Jackie didn't want her job back, but she and the group had agreed that these steps would accomplish several things - expose the company's deceit, tie up some of AlzCura's attention and resources, and restore Jackie's spotless work record. This was a crucial strategy in exposing AlzCuras' questionable employment and research practices to attract the attention of the Food & Drug Administration and perhaps the Equal Employment Opportunity Commission. If their strategy worked, AlzCura would have a whole alphabet soup of Federal agencies investigating them. They knew they would need the firepower, and the sooner they could bring these agencies into the mix, the better.

Arriving at the airport on Saturday night, she decided to wait until the following morning to have her heart-to-heart with her parents. Arriving at her parents' home and seeing Ashley hold out her little arms when she recognized her mother was like heaven for Jackie.

"Awwwwww, Mommy missed you sooooo much," she said, scooping Ashley up and drowning her in kisses.

"Well, I hope these weekend trips don't become a habit, or I'm going to give your employer a piece of my mind," Jackie's mother warned.

Although this would have been a perfect segue for Jackie to inform her parents, she was tired and stuck to her original plan to speak with them in the morning.

"Don't worry. I doubt it will happen again. This was just a special situation."

"Yeah, well, that's how they getcha," Jackie's father replied. "All of a sudden, every situation is special."

"Thanks for taking care of Ash. How was she?"

"She was a little angel, as always. It won't be long before she has Nana and Papa running circles around here, though. She's got crawling down to an art, and we're going to have to beef up baby proofing the house. You should let your father help you do the same at your house."

"Thanks, Mom, that would be good."

"So, will we see you at 10 o'clock Mass tomorrow?"

"We'll be there. Maybe we could go to Momma's afterward for brunch?"

"Your Dad and I are always up for that!"

"Ok, see you tomorrow at church."

Jackie couldn't have choreographed it any better. She successfully sidestepped her parents' ire with her employer and set up a potential time and place for her to break the news. She reasoned that divulging this news after church and in a public place would likely curb any histrionics.

Jackie was anxious to get Ashley back to the house and sleep in her own bed. She pulled into the garage and thought about Stu as the automatic garage door opener he installed did its work. She hadn't counted on this prompting his memory, and her heart sunk in sync with the door's closing. Her tears began to flow as she picked Ashley out of her car seat. As she approached the back door, her sinking heart suddenly did an about-face and lodged in her throat. Shattered glass and the back door stood ajar. Momentarily paralyzed, she tried to determine what she needed to do. Her impulse was to run to her parents' house rather than take time to bundle Ash into the car. Instead, she opted for the phone. With Ash in one arm, she reached with the other to pull out her phone. She punched in the numbers.

"911, what's your emergency?"

"Someone has broken into my home."

The 911 operated confirmed Jackie's address and instructed her to stay out of the house, find a place to hide, and stay on the line. Jackie moved into the shadows of the shed, one of Stu's household projects, after they had moved into the house. Oddly, she found some comfort standing next to the shed as if it were Stu himself.

"Why don't I hear sirens?" Jackie asked, wondering what was taking so long.

"This is a silent response, ma'am. They don't want to scare the intruder away. They should be there soon. Where are you hiding so that I can inform the officers."

"We're beside the shed in the backyard."

"We?"

"Yes, I have my 7-month old daughter with me."

"OK, don't move and try to keep your baby quiet."

"She's asleep."

"OK, good. You will probably not even hear the patrol cars pull up. They will park their cars and walk in. Tell me when you see them."

Almost as if on cue, two officers appeared on the backyard walkway. Jackie couldn't believe how quiet they moved as both officers were substantial human specimens. They entered through the back door, and Jackie braced herself for potential gunfire. Beams of light danced through the house, and the only thing Jackie heard was the officer's.

"Clear," said one voice.

"Clear," said another.

All in all, four officers entered her home - two from the front and the two from the back. After all the officers had shouted "clear," an officer appeared in the back door.

"Ma'am, it's all clear. You're safe. You can come out now."

Jackie took a couple of unsteady steps out of the shadow of the shed, and suddenly, the whole world seemed to be spinning. She saw the officer moving quickly towards her and then nothing.

CHAPTER 4

"Jeezum, Crow! You can't be serious." DA Wydman couldn't believe that Dr. Caron, likely the best witness against AlzCura, was dead.

"Yes, sir," said Inspector Adams. "DCPD just called the CSI team and me in, and I'm standing here in his office. He's deader than a doornail, sir."

"Obviously, DCPD thought there was something suspicious about it. What have you figured out so far?"

"Not much. PD found some graphic pictures of Dr. Caron in compromising positions with a cute blond on his computer and a pile of files knocked off his desk."

"I'm assuming the blond isn't his wife?" DA Wydman surmised. "He did tell us last week that he had done some things of which he wasn't proud."

"No, his Office Manager told us his wife is a tall brunette."

"Have you spoken to the wife yet?"

"No. I'm going to finish up here and then go speak to her at her house."

"Any idea who the blond is?"

"Not yet, but from the pictures, it looks like they may have been in a hotel. They also look like they were into asphyxiation sex."

"Jeezum, what whack jobs. Well, that throws a wrench into things. Could his hanging be sex play gone awry?"

"Maybe, but I doubt it. He's fully clothed, and judging on the limited height from which he fell, he would have struggled for a few minutes before he died. I would think if it was sex play, his partner could have easily righted the chair for him."

"Did he leave a suicide note?"

"We haven't found one yet."

"Has the Medical Examiner arrived yet?" DA Wydman questioned.

"No, but I heard that Dr. Corpisen is on the way."

"OK, good. Continue your investigation. I probably don't need to tell you, but we need everything in that office bagged, tagged, and brought in. I need every phone call, email, text, post-it note, or tweet he may have made in the last week. If this wasn't suicide, it could be a nervous Pharmaceutical company silencing their biggest potential problem."

"Will do, boss."

DA Wydman heaved a sigh as he ran his hands through his thinning hair. The group had agreed at their dinner meeting that each would assemble the evidence against AlzCura and review it with him. His meeting with Dr. Caron would not be happening. His only hope was that whatever evidence that Dr. Caron may have had was still available. Maybe he was overreacting. Perhaps the stress of what Dr. Caron did was too much. Maybe this was just a straightforward suicide. Perhaps the pictures on his computer WERE his suicide note. He would have to wait until Adams completed the investigation for answers. In the meantime, it was a fatal blow to their case against AlzCura, regardless of what caused Dr. Caron's demise. He reached for the phone and called Curt.

"Curt, it's Will.

"Hi Will, what's up?"

"Bad news. Are you sitting down?"

"Yeah."

"Dr. Caron is dead."

The silence from the other end of the phone was deafening.

"Curt? Did you hear me?"

"Yeah, I can't believe it. How did he die?"

"It looks like he hung himself in his office, but we're investigating to make sure it's a suicide. One thing is for certain; the good doctor was into some crazy shit."

"How's that?"

"Well, I can't say, open investigation and all. Let's just say he participated in some dangerously unconventional behavior. I really can't say more."

"I can't believe it," Curt repeated, not immediately able to wrap his mind around the news.

"Listen, I think you should get in touch with Jackie and let her know. Maybe this was just Dr. Caron committing suicide. Maybe not."

"What are you saying?" Curt said, still trying to recover and think clearly.

"I'm saying it wouldn't hurt to be a little extra cautious and aware. This could be AlzCura's way of trying to stop our crusade before it even begins."

"Whoa, are you saying they may have killed Dr. Caron?"

"No, I can't say that, but there is some suspicion around his hanging. All I'm saying is that we should all be careful," said the DA trying to modulate his warning so as not to spook Curt further.

"You got me a little nervous there, Will."

"I'm sorry, Curt, I didn't mean to upset you, but I just got the news myself. I'm a little rattled myself."

"Well, I appreciate your call, although it probably won't make me sleep any better tonight."

"Well, I'll be an insomniac right there with ya partner. You got my cell phone number. Call if you need."

"Thanks, Will. I will call Jackie and let her know."

"Good, sleep tight."

"Gee, thanks, Will. I'll call you if I learn anything from Jackie."

Curt hung up the phone, and immediately the fears crept in about his decision to join Will, Jackie, and Dr. Caron in their effort to expose AlzCura. If they were bold enough to drive Dr. Caron to suicide, or worse, murder him and make it look like a suicide, what were they willing to do to him? What were they willing to do to his kids? He almost called Will back and told him he was out but then thought better of a knee-jerk reaction. He reached for his phone to call Jackie but then realized that he was late in picking up his kids at school. They had grown accustomed to his chauffeur service back and forth from school in the last week, and he enjoyed the feeling of being a more attentive parent. Curt vowed to call Jackie later that evening. Instead, he hopped into his car and drove to pick up his kids at school.

CHAPTER 5

"Why, doctor, you told me I'd only feel a little prick," Margo pouted, employing a verbal device usually reserved to prepare patients for how the Recallamin injection would feel.

"I'm sorry, Margo, but I had to use a bigger needle," Dr. Sheridan quipped from behind her as he withdrew and zipped his pants.

Margo pushed herself up from being bent over the back of his office couch and pulled her skirt down. "Excuse me a minute," she said as she made her way toward Dr. Sheridan's executive-size bathroom. "I think your syringe had an extra-large dose in it, ya know."

"Well, I wanted to be sure you were properly vaccinated," he chuckled, making his way over to the wet bar to refill his crystal tumbler with Scotch. He eased into the leather chair behind his massive desk, kicked his feet up, and momentarily tried to relax and lose himself in the view from his penthouse perch. Neither the sexual release nor the Scotch could calm him.

"When you said you wanted to debrief me, ya know, I had no idea," Margo winked at him as she emerged from the bathroom.

Playtime was over, and Dr. Sheridan got to the point. "Did

you get what we needed?"

"Most of it."

"Most is not all. I knew we should have,"

As Dr. Sheridan was about to launch into a tirade, his office assistant's voice came over the intercom announcing that Ms. Baker was there to see him.

"Send her in."

Cheryl Baker breezed in, gave her daughter a quick hug, and saw that Dr. Sheridan was about to decompensate.

"Asa, don't worry," she started.

"Don't worry? How in the hell am I supposed to not worry? I knew we should have just torched his office."

"Oh yeah, that wouldn't have looked suspicious at all. Asa, think. He has three other offices. What were we going to do, torch all four offices?"

"I guess not."

"Asa, didn't your debriefing with my little Alexis here put you at ease? We need to stick with the plan."

"So, Margo disappears?"

"Yes. We fire ditzy, fuck me Margo and magically send my little baby to our Paris office to charm the pants off those grabby French physicians. Literally."

"Oui, oui, Docteur. Voulez-vous voir mes actifs?" said Alexis in perfect French as she stood, placed her arms on the desk, and leaned over, accentuating her breasts.

"See, she's a natural."

"Yes, maybe, but I don't speak French. What did you say?"

"Yes, yes, doctor. Would you like to see my assets?" replied Alexis.

Dr. Sheridan blushed uncharacteristically.

"Why Asa, you haven't seen or touched my daughter's assets, have you?" Cheryl questioned in mock indignation.

"No, mommy," Alexis cooed in a little girl's voice. "Dr. Sheridan just injected me with a vaccine he said would be good for me, ya know," as she moved one hand under the back of her skirt and rubbed her left butt cheek.

They all erupted in laughter.

"What about Jackie?" Dr. Sheridan asked, interrupting the gaiety.

"I think we've taken care of that problem too. Asa, you need to relax and do as I always say."

"Just sell the drug," Dr. Sheridan said in his best Cheryl Baker imitation.

"Good boy. Now say goodbye to Alexis, I mean Monique Deuvolet, and I'll see you tonight for my vaccination."

"What? No ménage a trois?"

"I thought you didn't speak French?"

"Some of it must have rubbed off on me when I was vaccinating Margo. Or was that Alexis or Monique?"

"Sorry. You'll only get to vaccinate this old broad tonight. Alexis will be on a plane."

"What a shame. I'd recommend another dose for her, just to be on the safe side."

"She has 15 minutes. I'm going to see what Anthony discovered at Jackie's." She kissed her daughter, wished her a safe flight, and bid them adieu.

Dr. Sheridan got up from his chair and rounded the desk where Alexis sat. "The doctor recommends that the second dose be oral."

Sliding from her chair to her knees, Alexis slowly tugged at his zipper. "I wouldn't think of going against the doctor's orders, ya know."

CHAPTER 6

The light was blinding her, and she felt lost. She heard and felt the rumble of a diesel engine. She tried to move her arms and legs but couldn't. Suddenly, the bright light in her eyes subsided, and the silhouette started to come into focus along with the surroundings. She began to panic. She was in a tiny space, unable to move with someone hovering over her that she couldn't quite make out.

"Relax, ma'am," said the dark shadow hovering over her. "My name is Ronald. I'm an EMT, and you're in an ambulance outside your home. You fainted."

Jackie stopped straining against the restraints that were holding her down, and Ronald's face started to come into focus.

"Fainted?"

"Yes. Thankfully, the police officer caught you and your daughter before you fell to the ground."

"Ash? Where is Ash?" She panicked again, renewing her struggle against the restraints.

"Relax, ma'am. Your daughter is fine," placing a reassuring hand on her shoulder. "We took care of her until your mother arrived."

"My mom? How did she find out?"

"Your cell phone, ma'am. The entry 'Mom' in your phone directory was a dead giveaway. I hope you don't mind."

"No...is she here?"

"Yes. Do you want to see her?"

"Yes, can I get out of here?"

"No, I want to be sure you're OK before we let you go. I'll have her join us here. When your vitals return to normal, then I will remove the IV and the restraints and let you go."

"OK."

Ronald radioed his partner and instructed her to bring Jackie's mother and daughter. Moments later, the back door of the ambulance opened. The other EMT assisted Doris Selaney, who was cradling Ashley in her arms, up into the back of the ambulance.

"Jackie, what happened?" Doris asked while bending to kiss her daughter on the forehead.

"I don't know, Mom. They said I fainted," as she once again strained to at least pull her arms up to return her mother's affection. Ash started to whimper.

"Can you please take these straps off me? I promise I won't try to escape," she directed towards Ronald. Sensing her growing frustration, Ronald moved to release the straps across her legs and chest.

"OK, but let me help you up slowly. I don't want you to have an orthostatic event."

Jackie, not knowing what Ronald was warning her of, waited for his assistance. She thought to ask him to elaborate, but as she reached an upright position, the urge to hold her daughter took precedence. She held her arms out, rewarded with her little bundle of joy.

"Oh Ash," Jackie cooed and kissed her. Ash squinted due to the transition from the darkness of night to the bright lights that illuminated the inside of the ambulance. Her whimpers turned to wails.

"Can you turn down the lights some?" she asked Ronald, who almost immediately flipped a switch dimming the back of the ambulance. As their eyes began to adjust, Ash's crying subsided, and Doris, still not comprehending what happened to her daughter, resumed her questioning.

"Jackie, I'm so concerned. Are you sick?" she said, turning to Ronald to see if he would divulge any information.

"No, Mom," Jackie responded. "I'm not sick. I don't know what happened." As she strained to reconstruct the moments before things went dark, patches of memory returned.

"I remember calling 911 when I saw the house was broken into. Then I was hiding by the shed. The police came, and," she then turned and looked at Ronald. If on cue, he filled in the gap in their knowledge.

"The police officer said that he called to you. You stepped away from the shed and started to wobble. He ran and caught you just as you were about to fall. The police called us, and that's how you got here."

"What is this?" asked Jackie, pointing to the intravenous line in her arm.

"D5W," Ronald shot back.

Jackie's expression communicated that his answer didn't register.

"I'm sorry. It's just a sugar-water solution. Dehydration can cause fainting and low blood pressure. I'll check your BP and remove it after your visit."

Satisfied with his explanation, Doris once again jumped in, rattling off a series of questions aimed as much toward Ronald as her daughter.

"Are you OK? Did someone check Ashley? Who could have done this?

"Mom, I'm fine. Relax. I'm still trying to piece things together."

"The baby is fine. We checked her. Except for missing her Mom, she is fine," added Ronald.

Doris started to relax and suddenly recognized how cramped the back of the ambulance was with three adults and a baby.

"Let me take Ash. We'll wait for you outside. You can stay with us tonight."

Not wanting to give Ash up, she looked up at Ronald. "Can I get out of here? I feel fine."

"You can hold your baby. I want to do another set of vitals, and if everything is fine, you'll be good to go."

Doris exited the ambulance, and after a few minutes, Jackie emerged from the back of the ambulance with Ashley. She wasn't prepared for the scene outside. A cadre of police officers combed the area in and around her home, flashlights aglow cutting beams of light in the darkness. Some neighbors came out wondering about the commotion and late-night light show. Jackie felt uneasy, as if the invasion of her privacy was continuing. It was bad enough that someone broke into her home. Now she felt naked and exposed and just wanted everyone to go away so she could return to the warmth and safety of her home. She realized that her home, however, wasn't safe. The reality of her situation started to wash over her. No Stu. No job. Her home was invaded. She felt alone and anchorless. Had a burly police officer not made his way towards her, she may have thought herself into another fainting episode.

"Ma'am, I'm Officer Todd. You may not recall, but I caught you as you were going to the ground."

"Thanks, Officer, you're right. I don't recall."

"As you can see, we're still busy investigating. Do you and your husband and baby have a place to stay tonight?"

The question struck her as insensitive until she realized that the officer had no way of knowing about Stu. Not up to explain, Jackie answered him.

"Yes, we can stay with my parents," gesturing towards them with her hand.

"Good because it's a mess in there. We'll be sure to secure the area and your home when we're done," he said as he handed her his business card. "Call me in the morning. I want to go through the house with you and your husband if you wouldn't mind. It will help us understand and document what may be missing."

"That would be fine. Do you have any idea who may have done this?"

"No, ma'am. Other than the broken window, we're still investigating," he lied, not divulging the ominous message spray-painted in the baby's room. Officer Todd felt that she probably had enough stress for one evening. There would be an opportunity the next morning to explore who may have such a vendetta.

"If you don't mind, ma'am, where do your parents live?"

"Just down the street a bit."

"I'll need the address, please." This caused Jackie to wrinkle her face with suspicion. Before she could ask, he added, "Just procedure, ma'am. I want to put it in my report to document that we assured your safety."

Jackie's curiosity quelled, she gave him the address.

"Thanks, ma'am. If you don't have any questions, I would suggest you go and get some rest."

"Thanks, Officer Todd. I'll call you in the morning."

Jackie and Ashley accompanied her parents for the short walk to their home. Once inside, she placed Ashley into the crib that was still in Jackie's childhood bedroom - a fixture from when Jackie had stayed there, coma-like, after Stu's death. She felt dirty, like the act of the intruder somehow left invasive germs all over her. She decided to take a hot shower, hoping to wash away the feeling and perhaps relax enough to get some sleep. As the water pelted her back, neck, and shoulders, she felt some of the grime melt away. As she stepped out of the shower, a sudden wave of exhaustion overtook her. She had all she could do to dry off, slip into a T-Shirt, and make it over to the bed. Curious to see if the police were still in front of her home, she peeked out the window blinds. To her surprise, there were none, but there was one directly across the street from her. She snapped the blinds closed, lay down on the bed, but couldn't sleep. She was tortured by questions about why the police were outside her parent's home.

Why were they here?

Was it just Officer Todd assuring her safety?

If so, why didn't he say he would be stationing police outside her parents' home?

Could he have found something in her house to cause concern for her safety?

Maybe the police cruiser was checking the address and not stationed there.

Did AlzCura know about her trip to Maine?

She sat up and cracked the blinds again to see if the cruiser was still across the street. It was. Now for sure, she knew she wouldn't get any sleep.

CHAPTER 7

C harlene Caron answered the door cautiously, surprised to have a visitor this early in the day.

"Can I help you?" she said, opening the front door just far enough to show her face.

"Mrs. Caron?"

"Yes?"

"I'm Inspector Adams," he declared, holding his investigator identification up so she could see. "I need to speak with you. May I come in?"

Charlene Caron's expressive face had always been easy to read. Her look of surprise turned to one of distress. "Is something wrong?" she asked, starting to tremble and unable to move to open the door further.

Seeing that she might decompensate right there in the doorway, Adams softened his tone. "I'm sorry to startle you, Mrs. Caron. I think it would be more comfortable for both of us if we could discuss this matter in your home."

His empathetic tone momentarily propped her up. "I'm sorry. Come in," she offered, finally opening the door and letting Inspector Adams into the expansive white marble-tiled foyer. Adams was familiar with homes in this neighborhood occupied predominantly by doctors and lawyers. No matter the lengths to which homeowners here went to build palaces of extravagance, it always shocked him. Dr. Caron's home was no different. A grand stairway worthy of royalty ascended to the second floor. Although the day was just dawning, the brightness inside the home was striking. The open architecture, the oversized windows, and thick, pristine white carpeting lay like a blanket of snow. A white baby grand in one corner and white furnishings formed a blizzard of white contrasted only by the gold piano casters and the colors that erupted from the stunning artwork framed in white wherever wall space permitted. Adams marveled at how all the whiteness matched so perfectly. The home screamed purity.

"What a beautiful home you have, Mrs. Caron," Adams remarked.

He knew that in seconds, he would either shatter the world of an unsuspecting spouse or detect the telltale signs of a spouse who was only acting as if her world was shattered. In his years as an investigator, the difference between the two was stark. To Adams, the fakers were like listening to a band whose drummer had no sense of rhythm. The next 10 seconds would likely tell him more than the following 10 minutes.

"Thank you," she said in a rehearsed manner as if she would have been surprised not to receive the compliment. "Please, have a seat. Would you like some coffee?" she offered to try to sound hospitable even as the apprehension in her face gave away her true feelings.

"No, thank you," Adams said as he eased uncomfortably into a white upholstered living room chair that looked too white and too expensive in which to sit. The thought of having a cup of coffee amongst all this whiteness almost made him shutter. Although Dr. Caron wasn't a surgeon, Adams felt like he should have been garbed in a sterile gown with surgical booties to cover his shoes. He fought through his growing discomfort with the virgin whiteness around him.

"I need to speak to you about your husband."

"OK," she said as her body language showed she was trying to hold on to the last vestige of sanity that remained.

"I'm sorry, Mrs. Caron, but your husband is dead," he said, trying to strike a balance between empathy and the blunt reality that would provide the fuel for a response that would tell him whether her response was genuine or fake.

His words fell with a thud, and he waited for her response. Charlene Caron's face fell, and her body reacted as if his words had punched her in the stomach. She seemed to be crumbling before his eyes. To Adams, it seemed like minutes from her implosion to the time she was able to open her mouth. In a flash, he knew she wasn't involved in her husband's death. A genuine reaction to bad news involves clear facial and body language, a beat or two before the person verbalizes anything. Fakers didn't have the facial or body language changes, or their words preceded their facial expressions or body language. Before Charlene Caron was able to speak, he cursed himself for not thinking of having someone from the Victim's Advocate Service waiting in the wings.

"How did,"

Those were the only words she was able to get out before the tears erupted and some primordial sound emanated from deep within her. Adams controlled his urge to offer her immediate comfort, waiting to see if she would recover enough to finish her obvious question. Suddenly a wave rolled up from her middle, overtook her, and caused her to pitch forward and vomit violently onto the previously unspoiled carpet. Falling to all fours, she continued to deposit the remains of her cheese, sausage, and red pepper omelet with orange juice breakfast she swallowed only minutes before. Her retching continued until she produced nothing but the racking pain and staccato gags of dry heaves. Adams couldn't restrain his empathy any further. He went to comfort the woman whose world was turned upside down. These moments were what he hated most about his job, but oddly, they were also the moments that fueled his passion for the job. Giving bad news sucked. Finding the guilty party and bringing them to justice was most gratifying. Unfortunately, he wasn't sure there was any guilty party to bring to justice in this case. Perhaps he wasn't done shattering Charlene Caron's world. He couldn't imagine having to tell her now how her husband was found and that they also found sexually explicit pictures of him with a blonde. As he kept one arm wrapped around her as she continued to gag and heave, he radioed dispatch.

"Dispatch, this is Adams, over."

"Go ahead, Adams, over."

"Send a VAS representative to the Caron residence immediately, over."

Receiving confirmation that a Victim's Advocacy Service person was en route, Adams went to the kitchen and retrieved a wet dishtowel. Charlene Caron was trying to make her way back into her chair, and he assisted her and gave her the damp towel.

"Thanks," she managed as she wiped her face.

"I'm sorry, Mrs. Caron," Adams stepped carefully around the collage of color seeping into the carpeting.

"What's a VAS representative?" she asked.

"Oh, a Victim's Advocacy Service representative," he replied and then immediately regretted saying so.

"Victim?" she paused as a quizzical look crossed her face. "Did someone kill my husband?"

"We're not certain, ma'am," trying to stall on more details until the VAS representative arrived. "Perhaps you'd like to freshen up a bit before we continue?" he asked, hoping to buy some time.

"No, I'm fine now. Why aren't you certain? How did he die?"

Adams stammered, knowing that there wasn't any hope of waiting for the VAS representative and no delicate way to break the news. "He was found hanging in his office, ma'am."

"Hanging? No," she shook her head as her momentary composure melted into tears of disbelief. "Steven would not have done that."

Adams paused briefly, trying to determine if her denial was the type most people have when first hearing terrible news.

"Why don't you think he would do that?" he said after she regained her composure.

It was almost as if her knowledge of the mechanism of his death injected strength and resolve into her.

"My husband would be the last person to hang himself. He had so much going for him. So much he was looking forward to…" she trailed off as the reality of his death hit her again.

"I'm sorry," as she buried her face in the towel, her shoulders jerking in time with her sobs.

"I understand," Adams consoled, shooting a glance at his watch. It seemed like hours since he radioed for the VAS representative, but to his chagrin, it had been more like 2 minutes. He started to curse himself internally for such a rookie mistake. Everything associated with first the Darius Scott investigation and now Dr. Caron's death had been one frustration after another.

"You said you weren't certain about someone killing my husband. Why?"

Her recovery and the direct question didn't allow Adams any choice. He would have to push the snowball down the hill and deal with the potential avalanche it would create.

"Can I ask you some questions first?" he asked, hoping to squeeze additional information out of her before divulging news that would be more devastating.

"Yes, but I don't know why you can't just answer my question."

"I understand. The fact is, we are not sure about whether someone contributed to your husbands' death. My questions may sound odd and even insensitive. I assure you, they are standard questions designed to help us investigate your husband's death. If someone did cause your husband's death, we want to bring them to justice."

"OK," she said as her face implored him to go on.

"Can you tell me about earlier this morning? How did your husband seem before going to the office? "

"He seemed fine. He was focused and anxious to get to work."

"Was that a change from his usual behavior?"

"No. He goes through phases like that. He latches on to something that interests him and then immerses himself in it. I suspect he was excited about another research protocol."

"Has your husband acted depressed lately or been under unusual stress?"

"No. if anything, he has seemed happier and less stressed of late."

"When did that change occur?"

"In the last week. My husband has a very busy practice, and up until last week, I think the pace was getting to him."

"What changed?"

"I don't know. It was as if a cloud had lifted. He was more energetic and happier. He started doing things around the house that he had never done before. It was like he was a brand-new man."

"How would you describe your relationship with your husband?"

There was no way of asking this question innocently, and the reaction to it in almost all cases was predictable – fury.

"You're not saying that I had something to do with this, are you?" as she looked at him warily, and her face flushed red.

Adams knew that if he didn't interject a calming reassurance here, he could lose her.

"No, Mrs. Caron, I just want to understand your relationship, his state of mind, events that could help us investigate why this happened."

Adams' intervention was successful. The wariness left her face, and she let down her guard.

"Our relationship is great," not yet able to speak about her husband or their relationship in the past tense. "Being married to a doctor isn't always easy, but Steven recognized that and would always make it up to me. He took me on his business trips when he could. We went to Paris last Fall," she brightened as if the thought had transported her there momentarily.

Adams recognized that she was speaking of the conference Dr. Caron was attending when he first attempted to meet with him about Darius Scott. It lent credence to what she was saying.

"I don't mean to sound indelicate, but I need to ask you about your physical relationship with your husband."

The statement hit her like a cold slap across her face.

"Inspector Adams, I hardly think that's pertinent," she said, trying to maintain a sense of dignity and not give in to feelings boiling up inside her.

"I know it doesn't seem appropriate to be asking such personal questions, but it could be pertinent."

"Our sex life was fine," she said curtly. "We had no problems in the bedroom Inspector Adams. Now can you tell me why you think someone may have killed my husband?"

Her patience was wearing thin, and Adams knew he had only one more question to ask before he could respond to her question. It wouldn't be an easy question to ask, and it would be an even harder question to answer. He glanced at the front door, hoping the VAS representative would finally arrive. His hope was to no avail. He had no choice but to ask his question.

"Mrs. Caron, I will answer your question, but I need to ask you one more very personal question. I assure you, it is pertinent to our concerns about your husband's death. After you answer it, I will tell you everything I know."

Her eyes told him to proceed, but her body language said she was growing increasingly uncomfortable.

"Did you or your husband participate in any unconventional or dangerous sex acts?"

He saw her struggling to maintain her composure. Her eyes flashed fury, and her fists clenched and unclenched. Her cheeks flushed, her chin trembled, and tears spilled over and down her face.

"I don't understand why you're doing this to me," she cried. "No, no, Steven and I have a very normal sex life. Nothing weird. Nothing dangerous. Now please, can you answer my question?" she pleaded, erupting into another round of body quaking sobs.

"Mrs. Caron, we found photos of your husband with a blonde woman on his office computer," he broke the news as gently as possible.

"With a blonde woman? What do you mean?"

"Sexually explicit pictures."

Charlene Caron was stunned, unable to reconcile what Adams had just said.

"I can't believe that. There must be a mistake."

Adams knew that her denial was the only thing keeping her from losing it entirely. He wondered if he would be able to calm the tsunami when that denial dissolved. Where the hell was that VAS representative, he thought.

"I'm afraid not, ma'am."

She shook her head, and her body looked to be crumbling again under the weight of the emotional insults she had to endure.

"Who is she?"

"We don't know, ma'am. We haven't shown them to anyone."

She sat motionless with a far-off stare that didn't seem to be focusing anywhere in particular. She seemed wrung out of emotions, and her perfect stillness made her appear almost like a wax figure. A minute passed, and Adams was beginning to worry that he had damaged her.

"Can I see the pictures?" she said suddenly.

"Are you sure you want to? I don't want to upset you any more than I already have."

"Inspector Adams, if I can identify the woman, then you won't have to parade those pictures around to others. That at least may save some shred of respectability to my husband's reputation and our marriage."

Adams was stunned. Charlene Caron may have looked like a shell of herself, but her mind was still sharp as a tack. Her concern for her husband's reputation and the marriage, even amid the news he gave her, showed an unfathomable depth of love.

From his portfolio, he pulled out an envelope.

"Are you sure you want to see these, Mrs. Caron? We can do this another time."

"I'm sure. Thank you for your concern, but I can't believe Steven killed himself, even if he did have a fling."

Adams approached and handed her two of the least offensive pictures from the envelope. The reality broke her near-catatonic state and sprung forth a renewed river of tears. Her head fell forward as she handed the photos back to Adams.

"I don't know who she is," she managed to say between sobs.

"I'm sorry, Mrs. Caron. Is there something I can do or someone I can call for you?"

"No, no, thank you. I'll be fine," she said unconvincingly as her shoulders once again rose and fell to the beat of her cries.

"The VAS person may arrive soon. Do you want to see them?"

"No, that won't be necessary. Thank you."

His professional training quelled his human desire to give this broken woman a reassuring hug. He placed a hand on her shoulder and, with the other, offered her his card.

"If I can do anything or if you think of anything that may help, please call me."

"Thank you, Inspector Adams; I will."

"I'll let myself out."

As he exited the White Palace, the VAS Representative was making her way up the walkway.

"You're too late. We don't need you anymore," he said as she approached.

"What?"

"I took care of it. She doesn't want to talk to you. Thanks," he said, barely able to keep himself from adding "for nothing."

He got into his car, slammed the door, and knew that this investigation was going to be as frustrating as the Darius Scott investigation had been.

CHAPTER 8

C urt arrived at Caitlin and Cade's school and waited in the car in his customary space. Moments later, they exited the school, accompanied by the school principal. He had about 20 seconds to surmise what trouble they must have gotten into before the trio arrived.

"Dad, Principal Taylor, needs to speak with you. We didn't do anything wrong," Caitlin said as she hopped in the car with her brother. Curt exited the vehicle, and the two exchanged greetings.

"I'm sorry for this impromptu meeting Mr. Barnes, but I just thought I'd inform you of a call we received just 30 minutes ago. Perhaps it was nothing."

"Please, tell me."

"Well, we received a call from a man who claimed to be your brother Robert Barnes."

"BB called?" he asked incredulously.

"No, you see, the caller identified himself as Robert Barnes."

"That's odd; he never refers to himself as Robert Barnes."

"Exactly. We know that too because you put 'BB Barnes' down on the approved alternate contacts card we have in the office."

"So, what did he say?"

"He said you were busy, and he was going to pick up the kids today. He also said he needed to pick them up a little early for dental appointments."

"What? They don't have any appointments today," he said as fear crept into his stomach.

"When we told the caller that we didn't have a Robert Barnes on the approved contact list, he hung up."

"Did you say anything to Caitlin or Cade about this?"

"No, I didn't want to concern them unnecessarily. Instead, I asked them to come down to my office under the guise of just checking on how they were doing. They seem to be doing great, by the way."

"Thanks, but this is concerning. Let me call BB and see if he called."

Curt pulled out his cell phone and punched BB in his contacts list. After a couple of rings, BB answered.

"Hey, bro, what's up?"

"BB, did you call the kid's school today and say you were going to pick them up for a dental appointment?"

"Huh? Are you taking that Ambien again, big brother? I wasn't supposed to pick them up, was I?"

"No, BB. Listen, I'll have to talk to you later. I'm talking with the kids' school Principal right now."

He ended the call and looked up at Principal Taylor with concern.

"It wasn't him. Did you happen to get the phone number of the caller?"

"Unfortunately not. The caller must have call blocking."

Curt glanced at his kids through the windshield and was thankful that they had cranked up the radio and were bouncing around to the music. Had they been observing the interaction with their Principal, they would have likely noticed his concern and fear that had grown to immense proportions.

"I'm worried. What do you suggest we do?"

"I understand your worry. I will notify Security and your kids' teachers so they are aware. I would also suggest that we only allow you to pick them up. If you need someone else to pick them up, give a note to your kids to give to us. We will call you to confirm the note. I will station extra monitors in the pick-up area. If you'd like, I could have someone escort them to your car. We could notify the police, but without any way to identify the caller, I'm not sure they would be able to do anything."

"OK, that sounds good. Let's skip the escort or calling the police for now. That would spook the kids. I don't want to upset them."

"We'll take good care of them, Mr. Barnes."

"Thank you, Mr. Taylor," he replied, extending his arm and shaking the Principals' hand.

Curt eased into the driver's seat, ratcheted down the volume on the Taylor Swift anthem that was playing, and tried not to let the overwhelming fear he felt show.

"What did Principal Taylor want to talk to you about?" said Caitlin.

"Just how proud of how you are both doing at school."

"Yeah, at first we thought we did something wrong," said Cade.

"Then when we got there, he was all like: 'How do you like your teachers?'" said Caitlin.

"Well, that was nice of him," Curt said with as much genuine enthusiasm as he could muster.

"Yeah, Principal Taylor's a good guy," Cade punctuated.

Thankfully, his kids were oblivious to the ominous secret

that was rolling around in Curt's brain. If the news of Dr. Caron's death just an hour ago wasn't concerning enough, this latest revelation hit right at the heart of his world. He tried to imagine that these events were coincidental, random, and unrelated, but his rational mind kept refuting this conclusion. If AlzCura was attempting to orchestrate an effective counter-attack to the crusade that the Table for Four had planned, they couldn't have scored a more significant victory than eliminating Dr. Caron and threatening the safety of his children. He knew he needed to speak with Jackie, Will, and BB, but those calls would have to wait until he got the kids to bed. Although not his strong suit, he would have to act as if nothing was amiss for the next few hours.

The drive home proved to be easy as Caitlin and Cade were in an unusually happy and animated mood. They serenaded him, singing along to songs on the radio and played "I Spy." Seeing kids at the playground and filled with energy, they pleaded to go directly to the playground. Not wanting to squelch their bright mood, he allowed them to go to the playground and lugged their backpacks up the three flights of stairs. Pausing at the third-floor landing to watch them prancing merrily around the playground, he had almost forgotten his concern about the call. That is until he turned and walked the remaining distance to the door of their apartment. A note was stuck in-between the door and the frame. He pulled it out, opened the tri-folded paper, and read the single sentence printed in large, bold font.

How was Caitlin and Cade's dental appointment?

Curt almost choked on the fear that now seemed to grab his throat and squeeze. His heart raced, and he turned to make sure the kids were still at the playground. He felt paralyzed between yelling to the kids to come to the apartment, racing down to the playground, and checking to make sure the apartment was safe. Whoever the caller was, he knew where they lived. Worst of all, the person that left the note could have been involved in Dr. Caron's death. This made the caller and the note that much more threatening. He tried to consider his options, but his mind could not focus as fear overtook him. He was shaking. For a moment, he was glad that the kids had not accompanied him to the apartment. If they had, they would have seen the note and his fear. His relief was fleeting, replaced with the fear of now being 50 yards away from his children. Recognizing that he needed to do something, he looked to make sure Caitlin and Cade were still on the playground before opening the apartment door. His hands were trembling so badly that it took a few attempts to get the key in the lock. He opened the door cautiously and half expected to find it ransacked or some crazed psychopath on the other side. Instead, everything looked in place and untouched. He steeled himself against his fear and entered the apartment. Tossing the kids' backpacks on the couch, he did a quick walk-thru. Satisfied with his inspection, he left the apartment, locked the door, and ran down the stairs to the playground.

"Dad, what are you doing here?" Caitlin chided.

"Can't your Dad have some fun too?" he asked, trying to sound nonchalant despite the fact his heart felt like it was going to beat right out of his chest. Caitlin laughed. His act was believable so far.

"Come and push me, Dad," Cade yelled from the swings.

"Be right there."

He glanced up at the third floor and saw a man walking down the outside balcony that fronted the apartments and ran the length of the building. Curt caught his breath as the man seemed to pause near their apartment. The man then proceeded past their apartment and instead went into the neighboring unit. He then realized it was his elderly neighbor, a retired schoolteacher, out walking Booboo - his equally elderly Beagle. Booboo was almost blind but had not lost his acute sense of smell. As Curt breathed a sigh of relief, he wondered if his neighbor's pause was Booboo recognizing an unfamiliar scent. What he would give to be able to learn the identity of the person Booboo, a blind Beagle had detected.

"What's wrong, Dad?" asked Caitlin, who recognized the concern that crossed her father's face.

"Oh nothing," Curt returned his attention to the playground. "I thought I forgot to lock the front door and then remembered that I did."

This explanation seemed to satisfy Caitlin. He then made his way towards the swings. Thankfully, Cade was more interested in his own entertainment than in examining his father's emotional state. Curt took up his position behind Cade and pushed him repeatedly until Cade was swinging as high as gravity would allow.

The reprieve allowed him to form a plan in response to the day's events. Calling BB would be the most difficult. He debated how much he should tell his brother. On the one hand, he felt he should tell his brother the whole story. On the other hand, he didn't want to cause his brother to have even greater concern for him. He would call BB tonight and arrange to meet him on the weekend to tell him the whole story. He would resist his brother's inevitable attempts to drag more information out of him this evening.

Calling Will and Jackie would be less stressful. In fact, it might be therapeutic. He would call Will first and end his stressful day calling Jackie. As he pondered the conversation they would have, he replayed the hug she had given him at the Inn. His imagination was so vivid that he could almost smell the perfume that had lingered on his collar.

"Daaaaad!" Cade called out from across the playground.

Curt didn't even realize that his son had stopped swinging, traversed a good distance, and was now trying to get his attention to push him on the merry-go-round. He interrupted his momentary daydream and walked over to oblige his son's wishes. Getting the merry-go-round up to speed, he returned to the fantasy, seemingly the only haven left for him. He decided to go on this crusade for Calli. Now, if he were to continue what now seemed like a dangerous journey, Jackie would likely be the reason. Seeing her determination to right the wrongs that AlzCura perpetrated inspired him. She was bravely forging ahead despite losing her husband, potentially jeopardizing her promising career, and all while raising a baby. If he didn't have her as a model, particularly now that the crusade may have turned deadly, he would have ceased any interest or effort to try to expose the pharmaceutical giant.

"Time for dinner and homework," he called.

"Awwww, Daaaad," was their predictable response.

"Come on, we've had a good time," he tried to convince them even though most of the time, he felt tortured by a new menacing and invisible enemy.

They tramped up the stairs, and Curt couldn't help but feel a sense of foreboding as he once again went to unlock and open the door. If not for Caitlin and Cade's continued cheerfulness and energy, he felt like he would have crumbled under the fear and pressure. While he put frozen chicken nuggets and French fries in the oven, the kids washed up. They then moved to their backpacks and the daily process of transmitting graded work and a flurry of notices, newsletters, and other correspondence. Except for the occasional posting of artwork on the fridge, or marveling over a paper with an excellent grade, or signing a permission slip for a field trip, most of this avalanche of paper was quickly dispatched to the recycle bin.

Backpacks relieved of all past work and paperwork, both kids marched to their rooms to deposit their evening homework on their desks. Although the worrying events of the day were never far from his consciousness, Curt was observant enough to realize that Caitlin and Cade had fallen into comfortable and constructive routines. The words of Principal

Taylor echoed briefly in his head.

"They seem to be doing great, by the way."

However, the threat that he now may have brought upon them thwarted any opportunity for him to feel a sense of pride. The oven timer dinged, and as if trained by Pavlov, his kids appeared at the kitchen counter minus the salivating. In addition to the fried food fest, Curt placed a small stack of lettuce topped with Ranch on their plates as a nod to some semblance of healthy eating. Squeezing out large doses of ketchup onto their plates, the kids began to devour their meals. Except for a stray fry that escaped the pan, Curt couldn't get himself to eat. He grabbed a diet soda out of the fridge and, in short order, was cleaning up the remains of dinner.

After helping Cade complete his homework and reviewing Caitlin's, they all spent an hour watching TV. Whatever they had watched engaged the kids' attention, but Curt's mind was working overtime. He began to think about whether they should move or whether he should tell Will and Jackie he was out. Bedtime routines began, and while he went through the motions, read stories, and sang Cade the National Anthem, his thoughts continued.

When the kids were finally asleep, he was able to start making the calls that were on his mind for hours.

"Hi, BB."

"I was beginning to wonder whether you were going to call me back."

"Yeah, I'm sorry. I wanted to wait until I got the kids settled in for the night."

"What's up? You had me worried."

"What's up is that someone made a prank call. It was probably just some kid, but the school and I aren't taking any chances. We've developed a plan, and the Principal is beefing up Security procedures and keeping an eye on Caitlin and

Cade."

Curt was trying to strike a balance between concern and confident self-assurance so BB wouldn't feel compelled to ask too many questions. He would tell BB the whole story eventually, but he didn't want to have to tell him tonight over the phone.

"Wow, that's messed up. Who would do such a thing?"

"Yeah, it is, and I wish I knew. The good thing is that I will be able to drop them off and pick them up each day, and the Principal, Security, and all the kid's teachers now know to be on the lookout."

"Do the kids know anything?"

"No. No sense in getting them upset."

"Yeah, that's probably smart."

"Hey, listen, little brother, I have to make some business calls yet tonight, but do you want to connect this weekend? Maybe your ball and chain will let you free for one evening, and we can grab dinner and some drinks."

"Like old times?"

"Yeah, just like old times."

"Sounds good, but if Melissa ever heard you refer to her as my ball and chain, she'd make me divorce you as my brother."

"Did I say ball and chain? I meant your better half."

BB laughed. "Now that's the truth. Talk to you soon, bro."

Curt hung up and heaved a sigh of relief. He successfully navigated the conversation with BB but realized that the stress of the day was getting to him. He had a splitting headache, and the tension in his shoulders made him wish Calli was there to walk on his back like she used to do. Neither Caitlin nor Cade were heavy enough to dig their heels into his bound-up muscles as Calli could. Instead, he took a couple of Tylenol and decided to take a hot shower before calling DA Wydman. The shower was marginally helpful, and if the Tylenol was going to help, it hadn't helped yet. He pulled out a bottle of Maker's Mark that Sam gave him for Christmas. Ever since his bender at The Lost Loon, when Chelsea rescued him, Curt shied away from drinking alcohol. Tonight was different. He needed something to take the edge off. He poured two fingers of the golden liquid into a glass, took a healthy slug, and punched DA Wydman's number in his contact list.

"Hi Curt"

"Hey, Will, sorry to call you so late."

"No problem. It's been a hell of a day."

"You're telling me. You don't know the half of it," Curt countered, taking another gulp of his drink.

"What? Did you call Jackie?"

"No. I didn't get a chance to yet."

Curt recounted what had happened after Will's call that postponed his call to Jackie, including the school receiving the mystery call and the note left at his door.

"You're shitting me."

"It's the god's honest truth, Will. I almost called you earlier to tell you to shove this crusade up your ass," Curt replied colorfully, as the smooth heat from the aged whiskey was loosening his tongue.

"What changed your mind?"

"Well, I'm still on the fence to tell you the truth. I want to talk to Jackie. Have you learned anything about Dr. Caron's supposed suicide?"

"Just that his wife doesn't believe he would have committed suicide. The Medical Examiner has his body now, and I have an investigator sniffing around. We should know more soon."

"Why doesn't his wife think he wouldn't commit suicide?"

"Well, Curt, I'm in kind of an uncomfortable situation. I really can't go into any great detail with you regarding an active case."

"I understand."

"Suffice to say, nothing definitive has surfaced yet."

"Let me ask you this," Curt said, draining his glass. "Do you think the person who called the school and left me the message could also be involved in Dr. Caron's death?"

"That's a good question, Curt. Do you still have the note?"

"Yeah."

"Have you handled it much?"

"Just to open and read it."

"Do me a favor. Put it in a plastic bag if you have one. It's a long shot, but maybe the person who left it at your door also left fingerprints."

"Okay."

"Even though the Principal said the caller had call blocking, I'm going to ask for phone records. Maybe our Forensics folks can learn something. And Curt…"

"What Will?"

"Stay in the game. We need you. I know you're worried about your kids, but the fact is that you're in this whether you want to be or not."

"What do you mean?"

"You're a threat to AlzCura regardless of whether you pursue this or not. You could declare that you're not going after them until the cows come home, but why should they trust you? They won't risk their billions, if not trillions, of profit on your word."

He didn't know if it was the alcohol clouding his judgment, but this seemed to make sense.

"OK, Will. I'm still in. I'll call Jackie. She's going to be blown away when she hears what all has happened."

"I'm sure she will be. Keep her in the game, Curt. If we need to, we can get together. After today, that may be a good idea."

"OK. I'll call you tomorrow."

They hung up, and Curt was feeling the full effect of the emotion of the day combined with the Tylenol, shower, and whiskey. He went to lay down in his bed, and before he could make his call to Jackie, he fell asleep.

CHAPTER 9

J ackie tossed and turned all night. What little sleep she may have gotten was light and restless. Still, she woke up disoriented - trying to recall where she was and why. Finally recognizing her childhood bedroom, she padded over to the crib where Ashley's angelic face conveyed a sense of serenity that was diametrically opposed to her growing dread. She was not looking forward to the day. She almost didn't want to go into her house to see how the contents and the memories may have been disturbed, destroyed, or stolen.

She could hear her parents downstairs in the kitchen. Their conversation merely muffled tones punctuated by the occasional clatter of a plate or pan. Her dread evolved to include the discussion she would have to have with her parents. She had lots of explaining to do, and none of it would be easy. She longed to be back in the days when she woke up with Stu's arm draped protectively over her. They would follow a comfortable morning routine, and it didn't matter what challenges the day would bring because they had each other. Stu could cure virtually every care by merely wrapping an arm around her or lifting her spirits with his incurable optimism. As a tear fell from her face, the smell of bacon wafted into the room, and Jackie's stomach growled. Realizing that the only sustenance she had in the last 12 hours was the IV of sugar water Ronald the EMT gave her, she forced herself to get ready for the first hurdle of the day. Breakfast with her parents.

As if on cue, Ashley stirred in her crib and began to babble. She was growing up too quickly. She had graduated from total dependence to an increasing ability to interact and control the environment around her. Jackie started to supplement her breastfeeding with a bottle and baby food. Her babbling grew progressively more like talking. All these changes were bittersweet. Each new developmental step came with the dueling emotions of joy and despair. On the one hand, Jackie was happy and amazed to see Ash's transformation from a baby to a toddler. On the other hand, she was disturbed by the changes and depressed that Stu was not there to see his daughter's transformation.

"Well, there's my two angels," announced Doris as Jackie made her entrance with Ashley in her arms. "How are you feeling today?" she asked, giving Jackie and Ashley a quick buss on their cheeks.

Although Jackie knew the innocent question was out of her mother's genuine love and concern, it somehow felt like the beginning of an inquisition.

"We're fine, aren't we, Ash?" Jackie responded, employing a strategy of trying to deflect attention away from her by calling attention to her daughter.

Hearing her name, Ashley smiled and laughed. For added effect, she held out her arms, begging grandma to hold her. Jackie's strategy, aided by Ashley's actions, gave her a reprieve from the inevitable conversation that would follow. Doris placed a full plate of scrambled eggs, bacon, and breakfast potatoes in front of Jackie and took Ashley into her arms.

"There's my little girl," Doris cooed. "Are you hungry? Do you want Nana to feed you?"

Ashley's attentive gaze, and smiles in response to Nana's questions, communicated her assent. Nana placed her in the highchair and busied herself preparing Ashley's breakfast.

Jackie wasn't one to eat a big breakfast, but after a couple of small forkfuls, she realized she was famished.

"Where's Dad?" she asked between bites.

"Getting ready for church, I imagine."

"Oh yeah," Jackie responded, realizing that she completely lost track of the day. Without a job, the differentiation between weekdays and weekends ceased to exist. Not to mention, the trauma of finding her home broken into had somehow changed her experience of space and time.

"Have you told your boss about the break-in? I hope they don't expect you to come to work tomorrow."

The question caught Jackie off-guard and only amplified how, in the dark, she had kept her parents over the past couple of weeks.

"No, I haven't, but I'm off tomorrow," she lied, wanting to wait until she could break the news to both of her parents.

"Well, that's good, at least. You know, if they hadn't sent you on that trip, your house probably wouldn't have been broken into. It makes me so mad. I know you love your job, but sometimes I wish you just had a normal job."

Jackie could tell that she wasn't going to be able to play this charade much longer. She vowed to tell them the whole truth and nothing but the truth, but for now, she needed to protect them from the truth a little longer.

"Maybe it's a good thing I was gone. I'm concerned about what they might have done to Ash and me had they broken in while we were there."

"Good point. I never even gave that possibility a thought. Maybe I should be thanking your employer."

"Listen, could you take Ash to church? I'm going to meet with Officer Todd and go through the house this morning."

"You sure you don't want us to come with you?"

"No, Mom, I'll be fine. It will be more helpful if you can keep Ash. Once I'm done, we can get together."

"OK," her mother sighed.

Jackie polished off the rest of her breakfast, kissed Ash, and hugged her Mom. As she made her way out of the kitchen, she pulled Officer Todd's card out of her jean pocket and punched his number into her phone. They agreed to meet in front of Jackie's house in 10 minutes. Not wanting to chance the possibility of more questions from her mother, she left the house and crossed the street to the park. The park hadn't changed much since she learned to play basketball and volleyball there as a little girl. She took a seat on one of the swings adjacent to the basketball court and allowed her mind to drift to her grade school days when she and her friends would gather there almost every day after school. They would often play until their parents called them home for dinner. Sometimes they would even skip dinner and play until it was dark. She smiled, reminiscing until she saw Officer Todd's cruiser pulling up in front of her house. Her mental vacation was over, and she walked the short distance from the park to where Officer Todd now stood. She couldn't help but notice his physique, which grew more hulking as she approached. Even in his uniform, you could tell that he had muscles upon muscles. Despite his imposing figure, he had soft, friendly eyes.

"Good morning Officer Todd."

"Good morning, ma'am."

"You can call me Jackie."

"In that case, you can call me Barrett." When Jackie didn't immediately respond, he added, "I know, my names seem reversed. A lot of people call me Todd. I answer to just about anything," he chuckled.

"OK, Barrett. What am I going to see in there?" she nodded towards her house.

"Before we begin, will your husband be joining us?"

Jackie had forgotten that she had avoided telling Officer Todd about Stu the previous evening.

"Oh, I'm sorry, Barrett. My husband passed away recently," choosing to avoid the more stark and final sounding died. "I should have told you last night, but,"

"I understand, Jackie," he interrupted, "And I'm sorry."

"Thank you," she replied as the awkward and uncomfortable moment passed. "So, what am I about to see?"

"I'm afraid whoever broke in ransacked the place pretty good. There are a few broken things and one thing, in particular, that has us concerned."

"What's that?"

"How about we go in, and I'll show you?"

"OK," she said with apprehension.

Entering through the front door, it looked like a giant had picked up the house and shook it like a snow globe. Things that formerly resided in drawers or on shelves now covered the floor. Overturned furniture and displaced couch and chair cushions told the story of someone looking for something. A few knickknacks lay broken on the floor.

"Do you notice anything missing?"

"No, not yet. He certainly was looking for something."

"I was wondering if he took a computer. There's a printer over on that desk, but no computer."

"No, I have a laptop that I took with me on my trip."

They moved into the kitchen that looked equally tossed. Drawers and cabinetry stood open, and most of their contents were dumped unceremoniously on the floor. The dinnerware and glassware survived.

"Nothing missing here," Jackie announced. She was starting to feel a sense of relief. While her home was a disheveled mess, nothing yet was missing. They made their way upstairs and started with Jackie's room. It looked like a clothing bomb had gone off. Clothes were scattered all over. Jackie blushed to see some of her more risqué underwear and nighties openly on display. The contents of her jewelry box were tossed. She was certain that the diamond earrings and necklace Stu gave her would be missing. Oddly, as she accounted for the jewelry scattered about, absolutely nothing was missing. She couldn't believe her good fortune.

"Wow, I thought for sure this stuff would be gone."

"Yeah, we were pretty surprised to see it still here too. So, you think it's all there?"

"Yep, I don't see anything missing. What was this guy after?"

"I don't know, but I want to prepare you. I think the next room may be difficult for you."

Jackie looked at him, startled. "You mean in the baby's room?"

"Yes, ma'am."

She followed him hesitantly into Ashley's room. She was first surprised to see that, unlike all the other rooms, nothing seemed to be out of place. Then to her horror, she saw what Officer Todd must have been referring to. Above Ashley's crib and across the wall in black spray-painted letters was a menacing two-word phrase

"Goodbye, baby."

Suddenly, Jackie felt light-headed, and luckily, Officer Todd's beefy arm and shoulder were close enough for her to lean and prop herself against. For the second time in a day, he rescued her from falling.

"Easy," he said, reaching his arm around her shoulders and pulling her in.

Jackie disintegrated into tears, and her knees started to

buckle. Officer Todd guided her to the rocking chair and, with strong hands, settled her in. He grabbed a box of tissues and handed them to her.

"I'm sorry, Jackie, I knew this would upset you. Heck, it upset us when we found it."

"What does it mean?" she asked even as she was starting to formulate a good idea.

"That's what we want to know too. Is there anyone who has a grudge against you? Someone who may be jealous that you have a baby?"

She tried to wrap her head around the possibility that Alz-Cura could be behind this. She wondered if they somehow found out about her trip to Maine or the pact with the Table for Four. It didn't seem possible, given the precautions they had taken. The evidence in the house was irrefutable. This was a warning, not a burglary.

"I don't know," she answered. "I was just let go from my job, but I can't imagine they would be behind this," she said, even though the more she learned about her former employer, the more cold-hearted and cutthroat they seemed. But breaking into her home and spray painting a threat? That seemed extreme. She couldn't reconcile it.

"Is there anyone in particular there you think we should speak to?"

"No," she fired back a little too loudly and urgently. "I mean, no," she said, softening her tone.

"Forensics did find several sets of fingerprints, and they are processing them now, but it will take some time before we have the results. It would help with the print identification process if we had a set of your prints. Do you mind if I fingerprint you today?"

Giving her consent, Officer Todd went to his police cruiser to retrieve the fingerprint kit. As she waited for his return,

Jackie's mind swirled, thinking that some of the fingerprints they would find would be Stu's. The realization that she was sitting amidst dozens of invisible impressions unique to her husband hit her hard. As Officer Todd returned with a small tackle box in hand, a tear fell, forming a rivulet down her cheek.

"I'm sorry, Jackie. I know this must be hard for you."

"What about Stu?" Jackie blurted out as a tear fell streaking down her other cheek.

"Stu?" Officer Todd asked with a quizzical look on his face.

"My husband. Wouldn't they have found his fingerprints too?"

"Maybe," Officer Todd said, recovering from his momentary confusion.

"How will they know which ones are his?" Jackie looked pleadingly at Officer Todd.

"They may not know unless his fingerprints are on record."

"Stu was not a criminal," she replied bluntly, as her sadness was about to be replaced by anger.

"I'm sure he wasn't Jackie," he reassured her. "Many companies fingerprint their employees now, so the database of prints includes more than just fingerprints of people who have committed crimes."

"I'm sorry. I didn't know that."

"Why would you?" Officer Todd replied as he removed the supplies from the tackle box and started taking Jackie's prints.

"Stu worked for the Department of Transportation," she offered as she pressed an inked finger onto a card.

"Then his fingerprints are on file. State employees have their fingerprints taken."

After completing the fingerprinting procedure, Officer Todd handed Jackie towelettes to clean the ink off her fingers.

"Has there been other break-ins like this in town?" Jackie queried.

"No, ma'am. Break-ins are rare, and when they do happen, the motive is theft. We usually find the electronics and jewelry gone."

The more she thought about it, the more it looked like a message from her former employer. Nothing was stolen, and the message in Ashley's otherwise untouched room was unambiguous. If she continued her crusade against them, they would find a way to take her baby away from her. She couldn't let her mind even consider all the ways they could take Ashley away. They hit the one spot where Jackie was vulnerable – her baby. She suddenly felt like she needed to be with Ashley.

"I need to go back to my parents' house," as she rocked up and out of the chair.

"You sure you're OK?"

"Yeah, I'll be fine. Thanks," she said shortly, with only one thing on her mind now.

"And you're sure that nothing is missing?"

Barrett, the formerly friendly and reassuring officer, now seemed like an annoyance delaying her return to Ashley.

"Pretty sure. I'll know better after I clean up," she said as she walked with determination out the door and down the steps.

He finally caught up with her as she was exiting the front door. "You'll call me if you do find anything missing, right?"

"Yep."

His words no longer had the power to stop her as she traveled down the front porch steps.

"Is there anything I can do to help?" he said, left standing helpless at the front door.

"Nope," she called, now well into a power walk.

"I'll have extra patrols monitor the house," he called.

"Thanks," she said and dismissively waved her hand without turning around. She doubted she would ever spend another night in the house. How would she ever feel comfortable again in her home? How would she ever be able to lay Ashley down in that room again? Whatever magic Stu, Jackie and Ashley created, whatever security they felt being in the house, now exorcised by an intruder and two ominous, spray-painted words.

When she arrived at her parents' house, their car was gone. She had entirely forgotten that they would be at church with Ashley. She considered driving to the church but thought better of it. She needed to make a plan and pull herself together before she faced her parents. Fighting through the urge to find and hold Ashley immediately, she forced herself to consider her options.

Give up and give in. She could walk away from this crusade right now. Stu was never coming back regardless if she ever was able to prove Recallamin caused his death. She could find a "normal job," as her mother said, and spend more time with Ashley. She wouldn't even have to tell her parents about her termination, the questions around Stu's death, or the pact she made to try to expose her former employer. If Recallamin were causing deaths, eventually, it would be discovered. She didn't need to be the trailblazer and risk her future or Ashley's welfare. She could move to a small apartment, AlzCura would leave her alone, and life could be easy again.

Stand up and fight on. She could use this event as a signal that she and the Table for Four were on the right track. Why else would AlzCura go to these extremes? Where there is smoke, as the saying goes. And perhaps the break-in wasn't related to AlzCura at all. In which case, she would be discontinuing the fight for an unrelated reason. She could restore order in her house, defiantly stay there, and continue to fight the good fight. Perhaps they could save hundreds, maybe thousands of lives. She could come clean to her parents and tell them everything that she had been keeping from them.

Lost in her reverie and still flip-flopping her options, Jackie didn't hear her parents return from church with Ashley until they paraded through the front door.

"Oh, you're home," exclaimed Jackie's mother. "I thought you might still be at your house. How bad was it?"

Caught unprepared and not wishing to raise their concerns, Jackie had to think quick.

"Actually, not bad at all," she lied. "A few things knocked over, but surprisingly nothing was stolen."

"Well, that is surprising," her father replied. "Do the police have any idea who might have done it?"

"No, but judging from the lack of damage and nothing stolen, they think it just might have been some kids out for some mischief," she lied again.

As her parent's questions started to come rapid-fire, Jackie rethought her earlier doubts about returning to her house. Right now, she would rather be there than playing 21 questions with her parents.

"You know what, Mom & Dad, I think I'm just going to take Ashley home for her nap and put the house in order."

"We can come over and help," her father suggested.

"Oh, Dad, that won't be necessary. There isn't much to do. Why don't you and Mom go out to the movies or to Momma's for brunch?"

"Oh, I'd like to go to Momma's," purred Jackie's mother. "Jack, do you think we can splurge and have mimosas with our carrot cake pancakes."

"I'll let you have the mimosa. I'm the designated driver, dear," he replied.

Jackie picked Ashley up, hugged her parents, and started the short walk back to the house. With each step closer to the house that she used to call home, she wrestled with overwhelming fear. Then, slowly, she felt something arising from below - a wave of emotion, a distant voice from within, imploring her to fight on. The voice grew, "You can do it, Boo," and then it was as if Stu was right there with her. Stu always believed in her and always encouraged her. She reached out, expecting her hand to touch his face, but it just continued through the emptiness. The voice, his face, they seemed so real. Then he was gone, and she knew what she had to do.

CHAPTER 10

Returning to Dr. Caron's office, Inspector Adams saw that the CSI team and Dr. Corpisen, the Medical Examiner, had arrived. A police barricade stood at the entrance of the parking lot to allow in only authorized personnel and redirect patients who would not be having their appointments. As Adams entered the office, it was humming with activity. Photographs of the office were taken, and agents were dusting for prints. Adams conferred with the CSI team leader, who updated him on the investigation. Several sets of fingerprints had been found, and agents were preparing them for analysis back at the forensics lab. Dr. Corpisen, with assistance from a CSI agent, was carefully lowering Dr. Caron's body to the floor and preparing the body for transport and autopsy. A gaggle of office staff sat quarantined in an office waiting to undergo questioning, including Rebecca, Dr. Caron's Office Manager.

Inspector Adams took up residence in Rebecca's office, and one by one, interviewed Dr. Caron's staff. The interviews painted Dr. Caron as a demanding perfectionist who generally treated his team well but occasionally would bark when things didn't go as planned. He wasn't abusive, but he wasn't warm and fuzzy either. His receptionist, Medical Assistant, and Physician's Assistant all respected him, and none seemed to have an ax to grind. Although they were upset by the events of the day, you couldn't say they were distraught. Like Dr. Caron's wife, all of them noted that he had an increased sense of purpose and contentment in the last week. He seemed more energized, which was saying something because they all marveled at his stamina before this past week. Inspector Adams explored their knowledge of Dr. Caron's professional and personal relationships and demeanor but waited to share the incriminating photos with Rebecca. Not learning anything out of the ordinary, Inspector Adams called for the Office Manager.

"Hi Rebecca, I'm sorry to put you through this. I know you've been through a lot already today."

"Thank you, Inspector Adams."

"I just want to ask you a few questions, standard stuff."

"I understand," she said, dabbing at her eyes with a crumpled wad of tissues.

"Did you notice anything unusual or different about Dr. Caron lately?"

"Yes. He seemed more at ease and somehow more driven."

"Why do you think that was?"

"I have no idea, but we all loved it around here."

"No signs that he was depressed or suffered a loss or lack of self-esteem."

Rebecca managed a chuckle, "One thing you could never accuse Dr. Caron of is a lack of self-esteem. Quite the opposite, he seemed happier and less stressed out."

"How was your relationship with Dr. Caron?"

Rebecca started crying. When she managed to pull herself together enough, she answered. "It was good. I think I understood him better than most of the staff. When he would get upset with me, I never took it personally. I knew that he just had the patient's best interest at heart."

"How was Dr. Caron's relationship with others?"

"His patients just love him," pausing, she corrected herself. "Loved him. He would always take time for them. That's why he was always late."

Inspector Adams paused, remembering the times he visited Dr. Caron's office and had to wait forever for him.

"What about his relationships with the staff, colleagues, others?"

"Dr. Caron, in small doses, was charming and friendly. His colleagues quickly accepted him, which is saying a lot since he's from away. He was supremely confident, and at times, I think his ego may have rubbed people the wrong way, but most people liked him. I think some of the staff wished that he would have been more appreciative of their efforts, but they didn't dislike him. The crew we have now works hard. It wasn't always that way. Some of our former staff didn't have strong work ethics. They probably didn't like him or me, for that matter."

"Anyone, who you think could have done this?"

"What?" she paused, not sure she heard him right. "You think someone could have staged this to look like a suicide?"

Having not answered his question, he tried again.

"Yes, do you think any former staff could have been mad enough to do something like this?"

"No, Inspector Adams. I can't believe anyone could have done this. Why do you think someone did this?"

"I'm not at liberty to say. To your knowledge, was everything alright with things at home?"

"I think so. Dr. Caron didn't talk much about his personal life, but Charlene would pop in every so often, and they'd go to lunch together. She would always bring in homemade cookies or pie for the staff."

"So, you're not aware of any difficulties or marital problems?"

"No, everything seemed fine. As I said, he didn't talk much about his marriage or his home life."

"Rebecca, I'm going to show you some photographs. They may be disturbing to you. I would appreciate it if you didn't discuss them with anyone afterward. Do you understand?"

"Yes," she responded as the mere mention of disturbing photos made her start to tremble.

"I want you to tell me if you know the woman in these pictures?" he said as he dealt out the photos and placed them in an array in front of Rebecca.

"Oh my God," she cried, and tears brimmed in her eyes. "Oh my," the words stuck in her throat, and she turned her head away, unwilling to look at them. "Please take them away. I know who she is."

When Adams collected all the photographs and returned them to their envelope, Rebecca cautiously turned her head back, fearful of being assaulted by the images again.

"I can't believe it," she swallowed and looked away again as tears continued.

"You said, you know the woman. Who is she?" he prompted.

Turning back to face Inspector Adams, she tried to find her voice.

"Mar, Mar," she stammered and stopped trying to fight another bout of tears. "Margo from AlzCura," she finally blurted.

The mention of the pharmaceutical company threw him for a loop.

"Do you have a last name?"

"No. She was just a fill-in for Jackie, our regular rep who was on maternity leave. I'm sure the company can give you her last name. I can't believe it," she started but then stopped and just shook her head.

"Tell me what you know about Margo."

"Not much. She only visited once. I can tell you that we didn't like her."

"Why not?"

"She wasn't like Jackie. Jackie is smart, professional, and responsive. Margo was just the opposite. I can't believe Dr. Caron would even," she couldn't finish the sentence.

"Do you have any idea where or when these photos were taken?"

"She visited last fall, September, maybe? I'm sure I could get the exact date for you if I were on my computer. As for where I have no idea. Did you show those to Charlene, Dr. Caron's wife?"

"Yes."

"Oh my God, that poor," she said, unable to finish her sentence again.

"Were you aware of Dr. Caron's unusual sexual tastes?"

"Oh my God, NO! This is just sick," she looked like she may vomit at any moment just thinking about it.

"Ok, I'm sorry, no more questions for now."

A relieved expression crossed Rebecca's face. "Thank God," she sighed heavily. "That was awful."

"I'm sorry, Rebecca, but you have been very helpful."

Having finished his interviews with the staff and seeing the CSI team had things well in hand, he left and called DA Wydman.

"What ya got for me, Theo?" the DA asked, using the Inspector's shortened first name.

Just as DA Wydman had a sensitivity to the mispronunciation of his last name, Thelonious Adams never got comfortable with his given first name – a gift from his father who revered the great jazz pianist Thelonious Monk. The DA was one of the few people in the world who knew Adams' full first name and one of the few who could use his shortened first name without peril. It was their first meeting that sealed their friendship. Inspector Adams had pronounced the DA's name as Weedman, and the DA called him Thelonious. Both erupted in unison "My name is" and then erupted in laughter, recognizing that they shared similar maladies.

"The blondes' name is Margo. She's a pharmaceutical rep with AlzCura."

"Jeezum, here we go again. What do we know about her?"

"Not much. She was here once last Fall as a fill-in for the regular rep. The staff didn't like her."

"Dr. Caron apparently did," the DA exclaimed sarcastically. "How did the wife react to the news?"

"She puked when I told her he was dead and didn't believe it when I told her that he hung himself."

"How did she react to the pictures? Did she know Margo?"

"She was devastated, and no, the Office Manager told me the blondes' identity."

"Was the wife angry?"

"No. In fact, she was concerned about her husband's reputation and didn't want me spreading the pictures all around."

"So, this was a complete surprise to the wife."

"Yeah, kinda hard to puke on-demand and react the way she did if she was somehow involved."

"Did the wife share anything about the good doctor's sexual proclivities?"

"No. She said they had a normal sex life."

"Maybe the good doctor had an itch that his wife wasn't scratching?"

"Maybe, but I didn't get any indication that there were any marital problems."

"What about the office staff?"

"They respected him. He wasn't a joy to work for by any means, but it didn't look like anyone had an ax to grind."

"What about Dr. Caron's mood?"

"Neither the wife nor the office staff could believe he would take his own life. They all said he seemed more at ease and productive over the last week - like he had something to live for."

"So, we're back to Margo."

"Yep."

"I'm sure AlzCura will be as forthcoming assisting in this investigation as they have been in the Darius Scott investigation," he said cynically.

"Listen, perhaps we don't have to go directly to AlzCura."

"What?"

"I met with Dr. Caron, Jackie Deno, and Curt Barnes last week to discuss our investigation and their concerns about AlzCura."

"Really?"

"Yeah, and now I'm worried that AlzCura may have found out about our meeting, and perhaps Dr. Caron's death is related. Someone has also put a scare into Curt Barnes."

"But doesn't Jackie work for AlzCura?"

"She did work for AlzCura. They cut her loose a couple of weeks ago on some trumped-up allegations of impropriety with a client. Meanwhile, her husband may have died from complications caused by the Alzheimer's vaccine her former employer manufactures."

"No, shit."

"Listen, instead of calling her, I'll plan on having you join us when we meet in the near future. You calling her out of the blue might spook her. I mean, she doesn't know you from Adams."

"Oh, you're just a laugh a minute Will."

"Sorry, Theo, I couldn't resist. Don't call AlzCura just yet. I don't want to tip them off until we have to."

CHAPTER 11

D
r. Myron David Muckland, or "M.David," as he preferred to be called, was AlzCura's Medical Director for their Northeast Regional Lab in Buffalo. He was a seasoned and presumably competent pathologist whose disgusting and quirky personal habits had commonly resulted in abbreviated stints with previous employers. In addition to chronic spittle that would accumulate at the sides of his mouth, he insisted on wearing a lab coat that looked as if it hadn't been washed in years and contained samples of every specimen he ever examined. He carried a sandwich in his coat pocket and would take bites from it throughout the day, regardless of whose company he may be in or the task he was performing. If he ever washed his hands, the staff had never noticed. His last employer dismissed him after finding a dead skunk in a plastic bag in one of the lab freezers. He had a habit of bagging roadkill on his way to work and preserving it until he could take it home for only God knows what reason. What he lacked in social polish, he more than made up for in terms of being able to polish lab data that could potentially harm AlzCura's interests. Armed with the latest data on the Recallamin trials, he picked up the phone and called his boss, Dr. Sheridan.

"Asa, we're starting to see a pattern that's a bit concerning," Dr. Muckland said ominously.

"What's that, M.David?"

"I see more AST and ALP elevations on Liver Function Tests."

"Can you attribute them to factors other than Recallamin?"

"In some cases, but it's much harder with the Recallamin 3 trial patients."

By protocol, physicians were to perform standard Liver Function Tests periodically on patients they entered into Alz-Cura's Recallamin research trials. An elevation in AST and ALP levels was indicative of liver failure. While many things can contribute to liver failure, one of the complications that were more prevalent than expected in AlzCura's first two Recallamin trials, were the symptoms of liver failure. Since these patients' were often of advanced age, suffering multiple medical conditions, and taking numerous medications, the incidence of liver failure symptoms couldn't be directly attributed to the Recallamin vaccine. Creative patient selection and de-selection, as well as Dr. Sheridan's "help" when Principle Investigators tried to determine causation, magically made this adverse symptom appear to be only as prevalent in the trials as it is in the normal population. However, Recallamin 3 trial patients were significantly younger, and Dr. Muckland was finding it much harder to sweep the results under the carpet.

"What do you suggest?" Dr. Sheridan probed.

"Lower the dose of vaccine for Recallamin 3 participants."

"Changing the dose in the middle of the study will raise red flags. That's not a good option."

"Then how about opening a secondary research arm? Say you want to research what the smallest effective dose is. It will not only improve our net profit per dose but also make us sound safety-conscious."

"That could work. How will that help with the data, though?"

"We give the normal dose to patients who have factors

that are likely to lead to liver failure like heavy alcohol use, frequent use of acetaminophen, history of hepatitis, and congestive heart failure. They will have a higher proportion of liver failure symptoms, but they would be expected to have a higher proportion of liver failure. Then we give a smaller dose to those without these health-risk factors and hope that they don't exhibit this complication at a higher rate than the control group. If the normal dose group starts to show significantly more liver failure than the control group, then we may have to apply the lost to follow-up strategy for a few participants. Worst-case scenario, we shut that research arm down and continue with the low-dose arm."

"That's brilliant, M.David."

"Yeah, but do it quick. I can only scrub this data so much."

"Will do."

As Dr. Sheridan hung up the phone, Cheryl Baker appeared in his doorway.

"Ya got a minute?" she asked.

"For you, always."

"I just spoke to Anthony about Jackie's house."

"And what did he learn?"

"Not much, but he left her a message that I think will guarantee we won't have to worry about her anymore," Cheryl replied.

"And Barnes?" Dr. Sheridan asked.

"I'm pretty sure he's shitting bricks by now worried for the safety of his kids."

"Do you think the State of Maine investigators will give us any trouble?"

"Oh, I'm sure they will try to follow up on Margo. But since she doesn't work for us anymore, we don't know where she is and can only provide them with her position with the company and her dates of employment. Relax, Asa; we've got this under control."

"Yeah, well, I just got off the phone with Muckland, and we have a problem with liver failure in our Recallamin 3 patients."

"Oh well, he's a creative slime bucket. I'm sure the two of you can come up with a solution."

"We already did."

"See? You know, if you don't start to relax, you'll give yourself a heart attack, and then what good will you be?"

"Did Alexis catch her flight to Paris?"

"Yes, why? Do you miss her already?"

"No, well, yes, but I just wanted,"

"I know what you want, Asa. Just keep it in your pants, and tonight Alexis' mommy will take care of you."

"Is there anything else we need to do to make sure this goes away?"

"What do I always say, Asa?"

"Just sell the drug."

"Good boy. We can't get side-tracked by a few malcontents."

"I'm worried about the liver failure. Eventually, some of the research participants we disqualify or that supposedly get lost to follow-up may put two and two together and implicate us. And what if there's another Darius Scott incident?"

"Asa, you worry enough for the entire world. You need to balance your perspective. Just think of all the people that are benefiting from Recallamin. Yeah, it may not be perfect. What drug doesn't have its share of unintended adverse effects? For every adverse effect, there are many more that are recovering their past and being able to enjoy their lives and their families again."

"I suppose you're right."

"Of course, I'm right. Eventually, the impact of Recallamin will force half of the Alzheimer's units to either close or find a new service to deliver. Just think of all the families who won't have to deplete their life savings to pay for a loved one in an assisted living or memory care unit? And not that I give a shit about the government, but you wait, eventually AlzCura will be heralded as a company that single-handedly and dramatically cut the government's healthcare costs. Heck, the President will probably invite us to the White House. Don't lose your focus. We're doing great things."

"I knew I hired you for a reason."

"Oh, I can think of a few reasons you hired me," she winked and turned to exit the office.

CHAPTER 12

C urt opened his eyes and wondered if someone had dropped an anvil on his head. Barely able to lift his head off the pillow, he struggled to recall the previous evening. His head felt disproportionately heavy and unbalanced. He couldn't focus. He rolled out of bed and weaved towards the bathroom, bracing every step with a hand to the wall. His mouth felt like a desert. Cranking the cold-water faucet, he cupped his hands under the stream and alternated between splashing his face and slurping it up to revive himself. Instead, the water felt like a rolling bowling ball in his gut, and he struggled to keep it down. He hadn't felt this hung-over since the day after his binge at The Lost Loon, which now felt like years ago. He turned on the shower and almost fell over when his foot failed to clear the tub wall stepping in. Once safely in, he assumed a wide stance and braced his hands at the side and front of the shower stall, and allowed the warm water to pelt his aching head. Slowly the concerns of the previous day bled back into consciousness. The person who impersonated his brother and called the school, the note left on his door, his fear, and his decision to end the crusade.

"No, wait, didn't I talk with Will last evening?" He asked himself as the train of his thoughts hit a snag.

"What did we talk about? "

Suddenly, like a flash, it reappeared. He had agreed to continue the crusade and agreed to call Jackie.

"Did I call her?"

He searched his faulty memory bank and could not recall any conversation with Jackie. Surely, he would have remembered talking with her.

"No, I didn't." He answered himself in his head and made a mental note to call her later in the day.

A knock on the bathroom door interrupted his internal conversation.

"Daaaaaaaad, are you going to take us to school?" wailed Caitlin.

"Yeah, I'll be out in a minute."

"Can you make me a bowl of cereal?"

"Can't you get it yourself?"

"No, I want you to make it."

"Alright, in a minute."

"Me too," chimed Cade.

Curt ended his shower therapy only slightly more together than when he had stepped in. Dousing his bloodshot eyes with eye drops, swishing around some mouthwash, rolling on some antiperspirant, and dragging a comb through his hair was all the renovation he could muster. Throwing on some jeans and a t-shirt, he padded to the kitchen, where Caitlin and Cade sat expectantly at the kitchen counter.

"You know, it wouldn't hurt you to fix yourself breakfast every once in a while," he said as he filled their bowls and poured the milk.

"But Daddy, we like it when you feed us," Caitlin pouted like a child half her age.

"Yeah," echoed Cade.

"I know, I know. And I like to feed you too," he conceded.

He knew he was spoiling them, but he always rationalized that it was better than being a deadbeat Dad. Besides, didn't he have to show the care and compassion of two to make up for their mother not being there?

As the kids wolfed down their cereal, Curt fixed a cup of coffee, hoping the black elixir would help him shake the cobwebs and the dull ache in his head. They drove to school in blessed silence, as the kids seemed more interested in pointing out school friends waiting at the bus stops along the way than blasting the radio. As they pulled around to the front of the school, Principal Taylor emerged. Caitlin and Cade gave Curt quick hugs and kisses, and with backpacks in tow, they made their way towards the entrance. Principal Taylor waved to Curt once the kids had crossed the threshold, and Curt waved back, acknowledging he had received the Principal's silent message.

As Curt navigated his way back home, his anticipation for talking with Jackie grew. He forced himself to pick up around the apartment first, thinking that eight a.m. was a bit too early to call. By ten a.m., the apartment was in order, and he reached for his phone. Before he could punch in her number, his phone sprang to life with an incoming call. He almost dropped the phone from the surprise. The screen read: "Jackie."

"Jackie, you won't believe this. I had just picked up my phone to call you."

"Oh Curt, I'm so glad you answered. I have so much to tell you."

"Well, I have a lot to tell you too."

"Really?"

"You won't believe it, but why don't you go first."

As Jackie proceeded to tell Curt about the break-in and the message left in Ashley's room, his resolve to stay in the game began to melt. Added to Dr. Caron's death and the ominous events of the previous day, he was starting to believe he might be better off changing his identity and moving to some distant land. As Jackie cataloged how her fears were suddenly transformed by her vision of Stu encouraging her onward, Curt felt the pull of Jackie's resolve and commitment. His eyes shifted to the wedding photo he kept on the dresser of him and Calli with Lake Campion in the background. Something about Calli's eyes that he had never noticed before seemed to speak to him at that moment. He picked up the photograph and looked closer as Jackie continued her saga. As if a bad joke, there was a fire and a determination in Calli's eyes. Was she sending him messages from the grave just as Stu had sent Jackie?

"So, what do you have to tell me?" Jackie concluded, and Curt realized that his thoughts had drifted.

"Are you sitting down?" he asked, putting the wedding picture back in its place.

"Yes."

"Good, because we're in a war, Jackie, and what I have to tell you will be disturbing."

Jackie found it hard to reconcile the devastation she felt when Curt told her about Dr. Caron. Perhaps it was because she had misjudged him. Maybe it was that he held most of the evidence against AlzCura, and they now may not learn the full truth. It was crippling information for their case, and she couldn't quite fully understand the tears streaming down her face. When Curt launched into his story about the impersonator and the note left on his door, Jackie realized that all of this must be a coordinated response to the threat they posed to AlzCura. Jackie, oh my godded through Curt's account, and when he finished, she asked the only question that came to mind.

"What are you going to do, Curt?"

"I don't know, Jackie. At first, I wanted to call it quits. Then I spoke to Will, and he changed my mind. Then your story had me questioning myself again until the part when Stu visited you. I'm a mess. I don't know what to do."

"We can't stop," she stated simply.

"Why not?"

"Because they won't stop, because people are getting hurt, because we owe it to Stu and Calli, and because I have to believe our chance meeting was more than coincidence. It happened for a reason, Curt."

Jackie's powerful barrage left little doubt in Curt's mind about his stance on the matter.

"You're right, Jackie. I guess I lost track of all that. I'm sorry."

"Don't be sorry, Curt. I have my doubts too. I'm sure there will be times you will have to support me. Will you do that for me, Curt?"

DA Will Wydman had asked Curt to keep Jackie in the game, but here she was holding him in the game. Instead of feeling weak, something in the way Jackie spoke strengthened him.

"Of course, I will, Jackie. Thank you for helping me. What are you going to do about your house?"

"I'm in it right now. I'm going to clean it up and get a security system installed. I'm not going to let them scare me out of my house. What about you? What are you going to do about the impersonator?"

Following Jackie's courageous lead, Curt improvised.

"I'm going to do everything in my power to hunt him down. I already spoke to Will, and he is going to help."

"How's Will doing?"

"Well, he's up to his eyeballs investigating Dr. Caron's death. He suggested that we might want to get together to regroup and reload."

"That's probably a good idea. Let me know when you want

me to come up."

"I wish you didn't have to make the trip, but it's probably unreasonable to expect Will to make the trip down there."

"That's OK. Once I get the security system installed and know that Ashley is safe with my parents, I can take a couple of days out of my schedule. I'm sure the weather up there is getting pretty nice."

"Well, it's mud season, and the black flies are pretty bad, but in a week or two, it should be nice. Maybe you could bring Ashley with you. Caitlin and Cade haven't stopped talking about you, and they would love to meet Ashley."

"That would be nice. I would love to see them again and have them meet Ashley."

"I'll talk with Will and see what works for his schedule."

"Sounds good, Curt. I hope to hear from you soon."

"You will, Jackie. Thanks again for clearing my head."

Curt's hangover was gone, replaced by clarity and purpose that Jackie had inspired. Instantly she converted his fear from the previous day into a steely resolve to fight back. He bagged the impersonator's note and punched in Will's phone number.

"Will, Curt, I just spoke to Jackie," he rat-a-tat-tatted.

"And?"

"They broke into her house while she was up here and spray-painted a threatening message in the baby's room."

"Those bastards. So, I imagine she's out."

"Hardly, she's in big time."

"Really? She's quite a woman."

"You're telling me."

"And you? Are you still having cold feet?"

"I was until I spoke to her."

Will laughed, "So the news about Dr. Caron and your situation didn't scare her away."

"Not at all."

"Did you speak to her about a meeting?"

"Yeah, and she's game. Just let me know when is good for you and I will tell her. I guess we'll have to rename ourselves the Table for Three."

"Not so fast, cowboy. I'm going to invite Inspector Adams. You haven't met him, but he was the inspector on the Darius Scott case, and he's also investigating Dr. Caron's death. We need to round up the wagons. It's still Table for Four."

"And when should we have this little soiree?"

"How about in two weeks? We should have some information from Dr. Caron's autopsy. I've already requested the phone records from your kids' school, and if you get me that note, perhaps we can piece together some information and a plan."

"Sounds good. How about Friday, May 8th?"

"That works. Six p.m. at our secret meeting place?"

"We'll be there. And I'll drop off the note at your office this afternoon. Are you going to be in?"

"Unfortunately, not. Just give it to my assistant, Julie. I'll let her know to expect you."

Curt hung up and quickly called Jackie back.

"Hi Curt, geez, it's been a long time. Where have you been?" she said sarcastically.

"I know, but it's such a pain talking to you. I can only take you in small, very intermittent doses," he gibed back.

She laughed, and Curt felt his stomach flutter like some lovesick schoolboy. He was unprepared for this visceral reaction and tried to bring his mind back to the reason for the call.

"I'm hurt. I thought you liked me?" Jackie pouted.

His stomach flipped again, and he could almost picture her pouty lips and those captivating eyes. He tried to transition from playful banter to business.

"I'm sorry, you're just not my type. Against my better judgment, Will has asked me to invite you up for a meeting on May 8th."

"I can do that. Can I bring Ashley, or does your disdain for me extend to my daughter too?"

"No, the little brat can come. Better you have her here rather than have you go into histrionics being apart from her."

"You're too kind, kind sir. How can I ever repay you for such selfless generosity?"

Their playful repartee felt natural and exhilarating. What Curt intended to be a brief call extended to over an hour as both took turns backfilling each other's knowledge of one another's past. It was as if both were starved for a comfortable conversation.

"This conversation has been an unexpected pleasure, given I'm not your type," Jackie prodded.

"Maybe I was a bit hasty in my assessment."

"So, if I fly up May 8th and stay the weekend, you won't experience any ill-effects?"

"Well, I can't promise that."

"Okay, I'll let you know once I make arrangements for the flight, car, and hotel."

"You don't have to rent a car. I can pick you up. It will save you a little money."

"Are you sure?"

"It would be my pleasure."

"My, how your tune has changed. What's gotten into you?"

"Perhaps you have woven some magical spell on me. Are you a good witch or a bad witch?"

"Ah ha ha ha ha, wouldn't you like to know?" Jackie cackled in her best witch voice.

"I'll take my chances. Let me know when to pick you up. The kids are going to be so excited."

"I can't wait to see them. And you too."

"And I can't wait to see Ashley. Oh, and you too."

Jackie laughed, causing Curts' stomach to do another flip. He didn't want the call to end.

"Thanks for calling Curt. This has been so refreshing. I almost hate to hang up," she said as if they were experiencing some kind of long-distance Vulcan mind-meld.

"Me too, Jackie. I guess I like you after all."

"Let's talk again soon."

"OK."

Curt and Jackie hung up and, unbeknownst to each of them, breathed a simultaneous sigh followed by a smile. The phone call was not just healing but transformational. Curt fed off Jackie's strength, and their playful tête-à-tête buoyed Jackie's spirits.

Curt grabbed the zip-lock bag containing the impersonator's note and bounced down the stairs and to his car to make the trek to Will's office. Meanwhile, Jackie picked up the roller brush and put the first coat of paint over the words on Ashley's wall that she was determined to erase from her memory.

CHAPTER 13

A big, burly guy with a leather jacket, 3-day beard, flattened nose bent from multiple breaks sauntered into Cheryl Baker's office. Despite looking out of place, he plopped himself into the chair across from her desk like he owned the place.

"What you got for me, Anthony?" Cheryl said without looking up from whatever she was reading.

"She's moving back into the house, and I think she's planning another visit to Maine."

"That stupid bitch. How do you know?" she sighed in exasperation and looked up.

"Surveillance cameras and microphones I planted in the house. She was talking to Barnes yesterday, and she said something about visiting the weekend of May 8th."

"Well, you sly dog. What about Barnes?"

"Andrew's watching him. He went to the DA's office yesterday."

"So, it looks like our little scare tactics didn't work."

"Nope."

"How unfortunate. What do you suggest?"

"Crank up the stakes. Show them we mean business."

"Maybe, but we need to be careful. If we get too aggressive

or careless, we could have the FDA, FBI, and every other fucking government acronym crawling up our butts."

"So, what do you suggest?"

"We wait and watch. With Dr. Caron out of the way, they can't have much of a case. Assuming the State's investigation of Caron's so-called suicide doesn't turn up anything peculiar, perhaps all this goes away on its own."

"What about Alexis AKA Margo? Won't they eventually identify her and try to figure out how she was involved?"

"Not necessarily. Caron wouldn't be the first man to have an affair and off himself to avoid the shame and embarrassment of being exposed. If we get a call from the State about her, then we know they're snooping around. If we don't, then we know they've bought the suicide."

"Yeah, but waiting and watching ain't any fun."

"But it's prudent, and what are you complaining about? I'm sure you're getting a peep show from Jackie with those cameras you installed, you perv."

"She is pretty fine," he answered lasciviously.

"Ugh, sometimes you disgust me. Well, don't be playing with your joystick on company time."

"I won't, Mom," he chuckled.

"Get out of here."

"Love you, Mom."

"Love you too, Anthony."

CHAPTER 14

She had just finished the second coat of paint in Ashley's room and was about to restore order to her bedroom when her phone rang.

"Ms. Deno, this is Dr. Jacobson. Is this a good time to talk?"

It had only been a few weeks since she had met with Dr. Jacobson, but it felt like years since she had spoken with him.

"Dr. Jacobson, hi. Yes, this is a good time," she replied while moving some clothes off a chair to make room for her to sit down.

"I got the Lab results back, and unfortunately, nothing definitive was found."

"So, you can't determine why Stu had liver failure and a brain bleed?"

"I'm afraid not, but the toxicologist did find a substance in the tissue samples that he described as 'suspicious but inconclusive.' I spoke to him, and he has seen a few cases like this, but not enough to help him identify the substance. He suspects it might be a rare genetic condition."

"A rare genetic condition?" Jackie questioned.

"Yes, something that the usual lab tests and physical examinations wouldn't typically pick up."

"What about the other cases. Did they die too?"

"I didn't ask, but by definition, yes, this toxicologist only examines samples from autopsy cases."

"So, this condition could have caused Stu's death?"

"Neither he nor I can say."

"So, I'm left with suspicious and inconclusive?"

"I'm afraid so. I'm sorry."

"Is there anything more we can do? Is there any way to find out whether those other people and Stu may have anything in common? I mean, does my baby have this genetic condition? Do I?"

"I understand your anxiety, Ms. Deno. Unfortunately, if the Chief Toxicologist can't piece the puzzle together, we're out of luck. Perhaps if he starts to see more cases like this, then he might be able to establish causation."

"What about other Regional Labs? Did he consult with them on his findings? Maybe he only has a few cases, but there are more at other Regional Labs?"

"I'm sure the Regional Labs have linked databases and that he probably consulted them. I know this is hard for you, but Stu appears to have had a rare condition that may or may not have caused his death. Even if you and your baby were to get genetic testing and find this suspicious substance, there is no guarantee that it will result in early death. Furthermore, since they don't know what it is, there is no identified treatment. I would suggest you not worry yourself sick over this. The reality is that sometimes young, seemingly healthy people die."

"Alright, Dr. Jacobson, thank you," she resigned.

"I'm sorry, Ms. Deno, I wish I could have given you more definitive results. I will send you a copy of the Regional Lab report. If you have any more questions, don't hesitate to call me. I wish the best for you and your daughter."

"Thank you, Dr. Jacobson."

The inconclusive findings knocked the wind out of Jackie's sails, and she no longer felt the energy to tidy up around the house. She scrolled through the contact list on her phone and selected the one person who she knew could brighten her outlook.

"Hi Sunny."

"How are you doing, girl? I've been thinking about you."

"You wouldn't believe the half of it, Sunny."

"Well, I've got time. Talk to me."

For the next hour, Jackie filled Sunny in on being let go from work, Stu's autopsy results, the decision to fight AlzCura, the suicide of Dr. Caron, the break-in, and Ashley's latest developmental milestones.

"Jeez, Jackie, all that has happened in the last few weeks? I guess I've been living life in the slow lane in comparison. You should fly out here with Ash for a vacation."

"Tempting, but I have so much to do in the next two weeks. Maybe after I return from Maine, we can plan a trip."

"Well, unless you like temperatures over 100 degrees, you better get your pretty little butt out here soon. June thru August is hotter than you know where."

"I'll call you in a couple of weeks, OK?"

"It's a date. Take care of yourself, Jackie. I miss you."

"Miss you too, Sunny."

A dose of Sunny was just what she had needed to refocus and reenergize. She called the Security Company, who said they could have a guy come out later that afternoon. In the meantime, Jackie worked her way from room to room, putting back in order the disheveled mess caused by the intruder. She had left Ashley with her mother, not wanting to expose her to the noxious paint fumes. She realized that she had yet to come clean to her parents about her job and the crusade that undoubtedly caused the break-in. She began an internal debate about just what to tell them if anything. She settled on telling them she was taking a week off from work to put the house in order. She would then take another "business" trip to Maine. She reasoned that if she could find a job closer to home in the next few weeks, then she wouldn't have to ever worry them about all the sordid details of her tenure with AlzCura.

With the house in reasonable order and an hour before the Security guy would arrive, Jackie fired up her laptop and started to scan the employment sites. She found a couple of public relations/marketing jobs in and around Nora. She updated her resume, and as she was applying to the last job posting, the doorbell rang, announcing the Security Company's arrival.

"Good afternoon Ms. Deno. I'm Jerry from the Security company. May I come in?"

"Hi Jerry, call me Jackie," as she opened the door and motioned for him to enter.

"I understand you want to install a security system."

"Yes, I had a break-in last week, and I want to try to prevent it from happening again."

"Understandable. Do you have any idea what kind of system you want?"

"l have no idea, Jerry. What are my choices?"

Jerry took out a brochure and handed it to Jackie. "That will summarize your choices. Perhaps if you could tour me around, I can get an idea of the layout and potential vulnerabilities and let you know what I recommend."

"That sounds great. I'd be happy to."

Jackie escorted Jerry through the house and then outside. Along the way, Jerry ticked off items on a checklist. After their tour, they returned to the dining room.

"Would you like some water or a soda, Jerry?"

"Yes, please, water would be great."

As Jackie went to the kitchen for the water, Jerry examined his checklist. Seeing Attic was unchecked on his list, he called to her from the dining room.

"One thing I didn't check off my list is an attic. Do you have an attic?" Jerry queried.

"Oh, we walked right by it," she called. It's upstairs in the back hallway."

"If you don't mind, I should pop my head into the attic."

"Go right ahead," Jackie called from the kitchen.

Jerry bound up the steps. Jackie had never bothered to go into the attic and didn't even know how Jerry would get up into the attic.

"Do you need a ladder?" Jackie called from downstairs.

"Nope, the attic door has one of those pull-down ladders. Thanks, though."

Jackie sat down at the dining room table, twisted the cap off her bottle of water, and took a long draw. The cold water hit her empty stomach, and it growled as if rudely awakened. She realized that she had worked through the day without stopping to eat or drink. The attic ladder groaned and squeaked, announcing Jerry's ascent into the attic. A short time later, she heard him descending the ladder followed by creaks and a thump as Jerry closed the attic door.

"Did you know that you have a wireless surveillance system?" he declared upon re-entering the dining room.

"What?"

"Yeah, there's a router up there."

"Are you saying that my house already has a security system?"

"Looks like it. I didn't see any cameras on our tour, but perhaps they're hidden. I have a device out in the truck that can help me determine if there are any cameras and their location."

"I can't believe this. Is there a chance the system recorded the break-in?"

"It's possible. The router is on, but let's check for cameras first. Let me go out to the truck."

As Jerry made his way to his truck, Jackie started looking around the dining room for potential cameras. Not seeing any, she walked into the living room. Jerry returned with a device that looked like a small TV remote with a telescoping antenna.

"What's that?" Jackie asked.

"It's a Radio Frequency Detector. Since the system is on, as I sweep the rooms, it will tell me if there are any cameras or listening devices."

"Listening devices?"

"Yeah, it's not uncommon now for cameras to have built-in audio, but I'll check for separate listening devices as well."

Suddenly Jackie got a sense of foreboding. The previous owners were an elderly couple that had lived in the home for 40 years. They certainly didn't seem the type that would need a security system. Maybe one of their children had done it, concerned about their parents' safety. Then she realized neither the home disclosure nor the home inspection before they bought the house mentioned a security system. Horrified, she realized that the most likely source of the installation was the intruder. They, whoever they were, were spying on her.

"Stop," she shouted.

"What?" Jerry said, startled, stopping mid-pirouette of his sweep of the living room.

"What if the intruder installed this system? "

"Ma'am, do you want me to continue?"

"I don't know. If the intruder did install the system, perhaps there are fingerprints."

"Do you want to call the police?"

"Yes, I should. They took fingerprints after the break-in, but I better call them."

"I can still sweep the house to locate cameras. If the police are going to do any additional dusting for prints, they will need to know where they are."

"Good idea. I'm sorry for startling you earlier."

"Not a problem. I understand your concern."

Jerry continued to sweep the room as Jackie scrolled through her contact list to find Officer Todd's number.

"Nora PD, this is Officer Todd. How can I help?"

"Barrett, this is Jackie. Jackie Deno, the woman who's,"

"Jackie, yes, I remember. How are you doing?"

As Jackie started to brief Officer Todd on her discovery, Jerry's Radio Frequency Detector lit up like a Christmas tree. Jackie watched as he strolled towards the built-in shelving and pointed to a small, well-hidden camera.

Jackie relayed Jerry's find to Officer Todd and asked how to proceed.

"He can continue to sweep the house to identify any cameras but tell him not to touch anything. I will get the officer who took prints at your house, and we will be right over."

Jackie relayed Officer Todd's instructions to Jerry, who then continued his sweep through the house. Jackie started trembling as the realization that someone had been watching her began to sink in. She felt violated.

"I can't believe this," Jackie's voice cracked over the phone as tears welled up in her eyes.

"Jackie, just hold on," he responded, recognizing Jackie was about to decompensate. "We'll be over as soon as possible, OK?"

"OK, thank you, Barrett," Jackie sobbed as she sank into her living room couch.

As Jackie sat zombie-like on the couch, her mind started working overtime. It was one thing to get over feeling violated by the invasion of your home; it was quite another to learn that someone was spying on her. She tried to rewind the last few days in her head, wondering what she had said and done. She realized that whoever was spying on her likely knew all the details of her conversations with Dr. Jacobson, Sunny, and Curt. If the spy was someone connected to AlzCura, they knew the break-in had not deterred her. They knew she and others were continuing their crusade. She shuddered, remembering the warning painted on Ashley's bedroom wall. She had been able to paint over it, but no amount of paint could remove it from her consciousness.

A knock on the front door announced Officer Todd's arrival. Jackie steeled herself against her revelations as best she could and picked herself off the couch. At the same time, Jerry was descending the stairs, having completed his sweep.

Jackie opened the door and welcomed Officer Todd, who introduced her to the Officer that had accompanied him.

"Jackie, this is Officer Dunn. He is the Officer who took prints after your break-in. He will be able to determine if additional dusting for prints is necessary," he said as he placed a reassuring hand on Jackie's shoulder.

Introductions completed, the Officers joined by Jerry forged ahead with the business at hand.

"What did you find, Jerry?"

"Seven cameras and the router in the attic."

"Seven? Where?"

"Yes, seven. Dining Room, Living Room, Kitchen, all three bedrooms, and the upstairs bathroom."

Jackie felt herself getting nauseous as the extent of the spying sunk in.

"Anything outside?"

"No, nothing outside."

Jackie started to sway and swoon, and for the third time in as many weeks, Officer Todd caught her before she crumbled. Postponing their conversation, Officer Todd propped Jackie up on the way to the living room couch while Jerry went to the kitchen and got her a cold, wet towel and a bottle of water from the kitchen.

"Perhaps it's best for you to rest here. Do you mind if Jerry shows us what he found?" Officer Todd asked.

"No, go right ahead," Jackie replied, trying to regain her bearings.

"Jerry, is the router still on?"

"Yes, it is. I needed to keep it on to find the cameras."

"OK, job one, shut off the router. That will make the cameras go dark, right?"

"Right."

Jerry and the two Officers climbed the stairs, and Jackie heard the telltale creaking of the attic ladder. She closed her eyes and tried to block out all the thoughts that were bombarding her, telling her to stop this crusade and pursue a more peaceful, conventional life. Meanwhile, Officer Todd, Officer Dunn, and Jerry continued their work systematically dusting the equipment for prints before removing, bagging, and tagging the cameras and router as evidence.

"What kind of surveillance system is this, Jerry?"

"It's a Network Video Recording system. Unlike a DVR, an NVR processes the video data at the camera and then streams it wirelessly via the router and Internet to a recorder. It uses IP cameras that record video and audio together."

"Is it possible to determine where and who is watching these feeds?"

"That's hard to say. Most systems have encryption and protocols that prevent discovery."

"Most but not all."

"Right."

"So, our tech folks at the station will be able to tell?"

"I doubt it. Whoever is monitoring these feeds knows we discovered the system. As long as they don't turn on the recorder, you won't be able to track the IP address."

The three returned to the living room after completing their mission to brief Jackie.

"OK, Jackie," Officer Todd began. "Officer Dunn dusted all the equipment and only found one partial print on the router. He will bring it to the lab, add it to the other prints we found, and we should have the results in a few days. We've removed all the equipment, so you don't need to worry about anyone spying on you."

"Thank you all," Jackie sighed, addressing all three men. "Jerry, I hope you're not upset. I'm not feeling up to deciding on a Security System right now."

"No problem. I will write up my assessment and put my recommendations together and mail them to you. You can then decide at your convenience."

"Thank you. Do I owe you anything?"

"No, ma'am, our assessments are free. Believe me, if they did cost something, I would have waived it anyway!"

Jackie walked Jerry, and the Officers to the door, thanked them once more and breathed a sigh of relief after closing the door behind her.

Now armed with the knowledge that AlzCura likely knew their plans, Jackie called Curt.

"Curt, it's Jackie," she opened with urgency.

"Jackie, what's up? You sound out of breath."

"I'm upset. I had a security guy over here to install a security system, and he discovered someone had previously installed cameras in my home."

"I don't understand," queried Curt, "why would that upset you."

"It was on! Someone installed the system during the break-in and has been spying on me since."

"My God, AlzCura."

"Exactly," Jackie affirmed, "Curt, we need to change our plans for meeting on May 8th. They probably know about it now. Who knows what they'll do next."

"We have to meet sooner rather than later," Curt recommended, "This is getting out of hand."

"I agree, but what if they have someone tailing me? What if they have someone tailing all of us?"

"Hmmm, you might be right. Let me call Will and see what he suggests. We may need to take our plans underground and fight fire with fire."

Curt couldn't believe he chose that cliché and winced at the realization. Jackie, sensing his pain, sought to help him recover. Despite her earlier reservations about the crusade, something about Curt's vulnerability now strengthened her conviction.

"Curt, I'm sorry. I know this is not what either of us wanted in our lives. We need to be strong for Calli and Stu's sakes."

"Thanks, Jackie. You're right. We can't let what they're doing deter us. If we quit, we not only quit on Calli and Stu but potentially on thousands of others."

"You're right. Call Will and let me know what he suggests."

"I will."

"Oh, and Curt?"

"Yes."

"Before you call him, make sure your home isn't bugged."

"I will," Curt responded as he started to scan the apartment for surveillance equipment.

CHAPTER 15

For the second time in a week, Anthony barged into his mother's office unannounced.

"You know it wouldn't hurt for you to knock. What do you want now, Anthony?"

"I've lost eyes and ears on Jackie."

"What are you saying?"

"The surveillance equipment. They found it."

"Who's they?"

"I don't know, some security guy and a cop. They were at Jackie's, and before I know it, they started pulling the cameras, microphones."

"Is there any way they can trace it back to you?"

"No."

"You sure? There is no way to trace the cameras or video feeds back to you? You left no fingerprints on the equipment?"

"Ah, no, I don't think so."

"That wasn't very reassuring."

"I used gloves when I installed the system, and as long as I don't turn the recorder on, they shouldn't be able to trace the IP address."

"Have you destroyed and disposed of the recorder?"

"No."

"What are you waiting for? Hoping to get a few more peeks of Jackie naked in the shower?"

"No."

"Liar. Destroy and dispose of the recorder. Today!"

"I will."

"What is your evil twin Andrew up to?"

"Andrew is still in Maine."

"I thought I told you to tell him to back off and come home."

"I forgot."

"Jesus, why do I waste my breath sometimes," Cheryl exclaimed, exasperated.

Picking up the phone, she called her son Andrew. Anthony and Andrew were Cheryl's twin sons from her first marriage. At 25 years old, both were over 6 feet tall and around 250 pounds of pure muscle. For what they lacked in smarts, they made up with brawn combined with a lack of morals and the willingness to do whatever their mother told them to do. They were ideally suited for the dirty work Cheryl had initially sent them to do, but in some respects, they were like dogs to a bone. It took a little persistence to call them off.

"Andrew, it's Mom."

"Hi, Mom. Guess what?"

"What?"

"I figured out that I can grab that guys' kids at recess and,"

"Stop, stop, stop," Cheryl commanded.

"I want you to come home."

"Why? I thought you wanted me to put a scare in that guy."

"Yes, I did, and you did a good job of calling the school and leaving that note, but things have changed. I need you to get out of there now. Understand?"

"Yeah, Mom," Andrew replied dejectedly. "So, I can't maybe just grab the little girl?"

"Oh my god, what don't you understand about get out of there and come home?"

"It's just that,"

"There is no just that. Leave the little girl and the little boy alone and come home. Now!"

"OK."

"I want to see you back here tonight," Cheryl ended and slammed the phone down.

Looking up at her son Anthony, she exploded.

"You idiot. Because you couldn't follow my simple instructions, your stupid brother was planning to grab that guys' kids off the playground."

"So, you wanted him to put a scare in the guy."

"Oh my god, you're as thick in the skull as your father. Get out of here. And what are you going to do when you leave here?"

"I'm going to destroy and dispose of the recorder," Anthony sighed.

"Good boy," Cheryl coddled her son, who suddenly looked like he was going to cry.

"I'm sorry, Mom. I'm trying the best I can," he sniffled.

"I know, sweetheart. Now go and make mommy happy."

CHAPTER 16

H is resolve buoyed by the call with Jackie, Curt combed the apartment for surveillance equipment. Finding none, he called DA Wydman's office.

"Will, this is Curt. We've got a problem," Curt blurted out.

"Well, good morning to you too, Curt," the DA shot back.

"I'm sorry, Will. I'm a little upset about the news I received from Jackie."

"OK then, spill it."

"Someone installed surveillance equipment in her house during the break-in and has been spying on her ever since. They know about our plans to meet on May 8th. They…"

"OK, OK, take a breath Curt," Will interrupted. "Is Jackie OK, and how did she discover the surveillance equipment?"

"Yes, Jackie's OK. Ironically, she discovered the equipment when she had a Security company come to her house to install a security system."

"And what became of the surveillance equipment after she discovered it?"

"She called the police, and after dusting for fingerprints, they removed the equipment and took it into evidence."

"Good. Now let's talk about the next steps."

Will's attempt to slow Curt down by taking control of the

conversation and dictating the direction worked and oddly gave Curt some comfort.

"I'm sorry, Will. I guess I'm a little amped up with all that has happened."

"Little is not the word I'd have used, but I understand."

Curt laughed, and the anxiety he was feeling melted away. He realized that Will's experience better prepared him emotionally for the unpredictability, deviousness, and survival instincts of the criminal mind. Curt began to realize that he would have to modify his think-the-best-of-people attitude if he was to continue this crusade against a foe he was convinced was culpable for the horror wrought in his life.

"What do you suggest we do, Will," said Curt deferring to the DA.

"The events of the past few weeks were designed to try to scare us off. Surveillance equipment or not, we have to assume they're going to watch us. We need to be much more careful about how we proceed."

"So, we shouldn't meet on May 8th then," Curt advanced.

"Correct, but we do need to meet and develop a new covert strategy. We can't be seen together, so I recommend we teleconference for the time being. And let's do it sooner than later - like tomorrow."

"That sounds good. What time is good for you tomorrow?"

"Let me see here," Will paused to check his calendar. "Looks like we'll have to do it over the lunch hour. Does noon work for you?"

"I can make it work. Do you want me to call Jackie and let her know?"

"Yep, and I will call Inspector Adams and send out the teleconference information to everyone."

"OK. Talk to you tomorrow then. Oh, and Will?"

"Yep."

"Thanks for talking me down off the ledge. I've felt under attack, and I guess I'm not very good at dealing with it."

"Welcome to my world, son."

Laughing, Curt thanked Will again, ended the call, and immediately called Jackie.

"Hi, Jackie. Is this a good time to talk?" Curt opened.

"Yep, I was just getting ready to retrieve Ash from my mother's house."

"OK, I'll make it quick then. Will wants to have a teleconference tomorrow at noon to discuss strategy between the four of us. Does that work for you?"

"Yeah, noon is good for me. I usually put Ash down for her nap around that time."

"Good. Will is sending out the teleconference information. I'll let you go so you can go and get Ashley."

"Wait. What about May 8th?"

"Not going to happen, I'm afraid. Will thinks we need to lay low and not be seen together as AlzCura is watching us."

"Makes sense, but I was looking forward to seeing you, Caitlin, and Cade," Jackie said unhappily.

Curt's stomach did a predictable flip-flop. From the time Curt first met Jackie, she had a visceral effect on him. He felt it for the first time when the hostess at the Farrisport Inn mistakenly thought they were a family of four, and Jackie had agreed to have dinner with him and the kids.

"Yeah, I'm disappointed too, Jackie," he replied.

For a moment, neither Jackie nor Curt spoke, and after a long pause, Curt continued.

"Are you doing alright, Jackie?"

"Thanks, Curt, I'm OK. This is all so hard. I haven't told

my parents about losing my job. The break-in, the spying, and now having to watch every step I take. It's stressful."

"I know, Jackie. Will just had to talk me off of the ledge when I called him."

"Really?"

"Yeah, I think we're both in the same boat and both having trouble rowing."

"Boy, doesn't that hit the nail on the head," Jackie chuckled. "Thanks, Curt, somehow that makes me feel better."

"We will get through this," he said, trying to end on a hopeful note.

"We will," Jackie confirmed, "Talk to you tomorrow, Curt."

"Take care, Jackie."

While neither knew it after the call ended, both silently reflected on the dinner that had magically rescued them, both wishing they could reprise that evening.

Meanwhile, as Curt and Jackie were talking with each other, DA Wydman had called Inspector Adams, anxious to put things in motion for their teleconference the next day.

"Hi, Theo, anything new on the Dr. Caron investigation."

"Hey, Will, not much, but we have all the evidence secured, and Forensics is doing their thing. There's a lot to go through. I've never seen so many stacks of folders. It doesn't seem that Dr. Caron was much for technology or a stickler for organization, either."

Have you heard from Dr. Corpisen? Any results yet from the autopsy?

"No, but I'm expecting to get the results soon."

"OK, thanks. Oh, before I forget, I want to set up a teleconference call tomorrow at noon for Jackie, Curt, you, and me. Are you available at noon?"

"I should be. I have an appointment with Rebecca, Dr.

Caron's Office Manager, in the late morning, but we should be done by noon."

"Great. I'll send you the invite. What are you and the Office Manager chatting about tomorrow?"

"We're going to cross-reference the patient names we found on all of those folders in Dr. Caron's office with the office's electronic patient registry. That should help us determine whether any files are missing."

"Were Darius and Elvira Scott's files amongst the evidence you collected from the office?

"No, but I don't want to assume they don't have their records stored elsewhere."

"Good point. So, you may have some news for us on tomorrow's call?" asked DA Wydman.

"Hopefully."

"That would be good. The sooner we can confirm or refute foul play, the sooner we can determine the next steps. I'd also like to know if some of the patient files that can help our investigation of AlzCura are still available.

"I'll do my best," chimed Inspector Adams.

"I know you will. Talk with you tomorrow, Theo."

CHAPTER 17

Rebecca met Inspector Adams in the parking lot of what had been Dr. Caron's main office in Dracut-Campion, which now stood vacant except for their two cars.

"Good morning, Rebecca. Thanks for agreeing to meet with me. I know this must be hard for you."

"Good morning, Inspector Adams. Yeah, I can't get used to this parking lot being empty," she replied as they walked towards the office.

Rebecca, by force of habit, reached in her pocket for the office keys but did not find them. Then she saw the front door still adorned with crime scene tape and remembered that she had previously surrendered her keys to Inspector Adams for the investigation.

"You're right, this is hard," as tears began to form.

"We can do this another time if you'd like, Rebecca."

"No, no, I have to do this. I want answers just as much as you do," she replied, regaining her composure.

Inspector Adams removed the tape, unlocked the door, and turned on the lights illuminating the waiting room. Rebecca then took the lead, switched the lights on in the back office area, and led the way to her office. As Rebecca took a seat at her desk, Inspector Adams outlined the objectives of their meeting.

"We compiled a list of patients from the file folders found in Dr. Caron's office," he said, holding a two-page list. "We hope that you will be able to help us cross-reference the list with your records to determine what if any records are missing."

As Rebecca settled herself at her desk and fired up her computer, she reiterated what she had told Inspector Adams over the phone when they set up this meeting.

"That shouldn't be a problem. Our electronic master patient index should help us make quick work of it," she said confidently.

"One question," he queried, "Why so many paper records? Aren't most patient records all computerized now?"

"Yes," Rebecca confirmed, "All of the information and data on our regular office patients are entirely electronic. However, our computer system is not set up to capture all of the idiosyncratic information required for our clinical trial patients. For those patients, we need to keep paper records."

"Couldn't you scan the paper records into the electronic records?"

"Yes, we do, but only after the patient has completed all phases of the clinical trial, which could take as long as two years in some cases."

"Wouldn't it be easier to scan paper files daily?"

"With the volume of clinical trial patients we have, we would need to hire someone just to scan records and manage files. While the paper records would be quickly accessible in the electronic record, it's more costly than batching the work and paying an outside service to scan the paper records periodically."

"How do you manage the clinical trial records at your other three offices?" he continued hoping to understand the process better.

"We don't. All clinical trial patients are centralized here in our main office. It's a bit of an inconvenience for some patients but prevents us from having clinical trial records spread across four offices."

"So, if I'm a patient who goes to your Ramsey office and I'm interested in being considered for one of your clinical trials, I have to come here?"

"No. If you're at the Ramsey office, the staff can start the necessary paperwork to enroll you in a clinical trial. Then they make a file and have a courier deliver the file to this office. For any subsequent visits related to the clinical trial, you would have to come to this office."

"OK, that makes sense," he responded but continued to dive deeper into the process. "So, before that courier delivers that file, how would you know that a patient in one of your outlying offices was enrolled in a clinical trial?"

Rebecca was beginning to see why Inspector Adams was an Inspector. He would not be satisfied until he fully understood the process. Rather than be annoyed, she was appreciative and comforted by his tenacious questioning. If anyone could unearth whether Dr. Caron committed suicide or was the victim of foul play, it would be him.

"Our electronic medical record system is shared across all four offices. The staff at the outlying office enter all patients into our electronic medical record system, and note in the electronic record when the patient is enrolled in a clinical trial."

"OK, good," Adams said, at least temporarily satisfied. "Let the cross-referencing begin," he announced, handing over his list to Rebecca.

"I've listed the patients in alphabetical order, hoping that would make it easier," exclaimed Adams.

"It will. I should be able to print off an alphabetized list of our clinical trial patients. The one problem we have is that the files in Dr. Caron's office were not all of the clinical trial files."

"How's that?" Inspector Adams questioned.

"Dr. Caron only had a subset of files in his office. We have all of the clinical trial files in a locked file cabinet. So, after we check off the files you have on your list, we need to manually go through the file cabinet and check off all the files there."

On the one hand, this information gave Adams hope that they may find Darius's and Elvira's files in the cabinet. On the other hand, he was concerned that this would delay the answers he hoped to have for the teleconference meeting.

"How many files are we talking about?" he asked anxiously.

"Let me see," Rebecca paused while the computer produced the list of clinical trial patients, "Exactly 1,445."

"You're joking," he replied, shocked at the number.

"Nope. Dr. Caron has, excuse me, had been in practice here for over four years and had been conducting clinical trials from day one. I would guess that he has had patients enrolled in over two dozen different clinical trials over that timeframe."

"Is there a way to stratify the records by what trial they were enrolled in?"

"I'm afraid not."

Rebecca's response dashed Inspector Adams' hope to have answers for DA Wydman, Curt, and Jackie for their call, which was to start in 20 minutes.

"So, how long do you think it will take?" he asked, almost afraid to learn the answer.

"I planned to make a day of it," Rebecca replied. "If I can't finish it today, I would guess no later than noon tomorrow."

"If you have to access all the records manually, can you flag those that are or were involved in a Recallamin trial?"

"Sure, but it will just take more time."

"That's fine. We will probably want to review all of those records in the future anyway, but for now, flag them so we have a count.

"No problem, Inspector Adams," Rebecca said pleasantly, despite knowing the one day she committed to this project would likely now extend to two or three days.

"Alright, I appreciate you doing this."

"As I said, I want answers as much as you do."

"Rebecca, I have to get to the office to get on a call soon, but I'll have an officer come here. Perhaps he could assist you. He will also have to secure the office when you leave."

"I understand. And Inspector Adams," she added as he was turning to leave.

"Yes?"

"Thank you for what you're doing. This has been a nightmare, not only for me but for all of us who worked with Dr. Caron. We appreciate you trying to find some answers."

"You're welcome, Rebecca," he replied, not used to people voicing their gratitude for his efforts.

Inspector Adams got in his car, called the station to dispatch an officer to assist Rebecca, and made his way to his office for the noon meeting with DA Wydman, Curt, and Jackie.

CHAPTER 18

AlzCura's sales of the Recallamin vaccine were sky-rocketing, and the Board, investors, and most of the Senior Executives in the company were ecstatic. Such was not the case for Dr. Asa Sheridan, however. Not only was Dr. Sheridan nervous by nature, but he was also one of the few in the company, along with Cheryl Baker, who knew about the cracks in their armor. He was brooding and pacing in his office when Cheryl marched in, followed by AlzCura's Chief Legal Counsel Chet Humphreys.

"What's on fire, Asa?" Cheryl barked, having received a 911 text from Dr. Sheridan.

"Sit down," he barked back. "I'm growing concerned about a few things."

"Oh, Asa, when don't you have a concern?" she interrupted.

"Shut up, Cheryl. Just shut the fuck up!" Dr. Sheridan shouted as his face turned crimson.

Unaccustomed to be shouted down or seeing Dr. Sheridan as exercised as he was, she quickly backed off.

"I'm sorry, Asa." She responded like a scolded puppy.

"I've asked Chet to be here because I want anything we talk about to be under client-attorney privilege," looking directly at Chet. "Understand?"

"Yes, sir," both Cheryl and Chet echoed.

"As I see it, we have at least four problems. The State of Maine's continuing investigation of the deaths of Darius and Elvira Scott. The increasing incidence of liver failure in Recallamin3 trial patients that Dr. Muckland recently reported to me. Jackie Deno, who, despite her separation agreement, appears to be on a crusade against us. And finally, Curt Barnes, the aggrieved husband, who seems to have joined Jackie's crusade."

"I have a" Cheryl started but was quickly cut off.

"I'm not finished," Dr. Sheridan spat. "In addition, we have yet to respond to the Maine AG's letter asking for information on Darius Scott, the police continue to investigate Dr. Caron's death, and the bumbling efforts of your two jughead sons failed to scare Jackie and Curt off. If anything, it has only served to motivate them further."

"That's not fair, Asa," Cheryl protested after he insulted her sons. "They were following orders."

"Oh, were they now, " Dr. Sheridan retorted. "Was it your orders for Anthony to install surveillance equipment? Equipment that is now in the hands of the police?"

"No," Cheryl mumbled softly.

"I didn't hear you, Cheryl," he said facetiously.

"No," Cheryl repeated loudly.

"Then maybe I'm right. Unless you want me to start questioning your judgment, is that it? Is it you I should be concerned with, Cheryl?"

Cheryl shrank under his withering attack, and all she could do was avert her eyes and try not to cry. Chet, who had been a silent witness to this browbeating, shifted uncomfortably in his chair.

"OK," Dr. Sheridan softened. "I didn't call you in here to beat you up, but we need to have a plan. We need a bullet-proof plan that addresses all of these vulnerabilities.

"I'm so sorry, Asa," Cheryl cried, no longer able to withhold her emotions. "What could I have done better? I, I," she stammered before disintegrating into tears.

"Pull it together, Cheryl," he said, laying a hand on her shoulder and offering her a tissue. "We'll get through this, and I need you. We've been through tight spots before, and I trust you. What's past is past. Let's move on. OK?"

"OK," Cheryl snuffled while dabbing her tears.

"If I may," Chet piped up.

"Go ahead, Chet," encouraged Dr. Sheridan.

"First of all, I will have a draft of our response to the Maine AG's office for your review in the next day or two."

"That's a start," Dr. Sheridan acknowledged.

"Furthermore," Chet continued, "We hold all the cards. We have all the data. We know all the facts. And unless we're careless or defend ourselves too vigorously, we're Teflon. Right now, there is not enough information out there to make anything stick."

"I like that," Dr. Sheridan brightened. "So you're saying we back off, ignore them, and operate from a position of strength."

"Not exactly. I think we still need to keep an eye on them, but no more scare tactics. Also, we want to keep them from escalating their concerns."

"What do you mean, Chet?" asked Dr. Sheridan.

"I mean, we play nice and emphasize our good, responsible Corporate partner efforts. If asked for information, for example, we accommodate the request just enough so that there is no reason to file a complaint with the FDA or some other agency that could descend upon us and make life really miserable. We sponsor some high-visibility charitable events. We get Marketing to produce ads with patient and physician testimonials."

"A good defense is a strong offensive," Cheryl summarized, having recovered from Dr. Sheridan's tongue-lashing.

"Yes, exactly," Chet punctuated.

"You're right," Dr. Sheridan chimed, "We have far more positive and hopeful stories to tell, and investing more in charitable events could go a long way. I will meet with Marketing and get them on it. Now how are we going to keep eyes on Jackie, Mr. Barnes, and the DA up in Maine? And please don't utter the names Anthony and Andrew, Cheryl."

"I'm less concerned about Mr. Barnes and the DA," Cheryl replied. "It's Jackie we need to be worried about. Of the three, she has the most insider information and connections the others don't."

"So you're saying we watch Jackie and not our friends in Maine?"

"Yes," Cheryl responded. "As I see it, our problem was a two-headed dragon - Dr. Caron and Jackie. With Dr. Caron no longer in the picture, Jackie is our barometer. If she moves on with her life, I don't think the DA or Mr. Barnes has a leg to stand on. If Jackie continues on her crusade against us, then we may have to re-evaluate our strategies."

"Then who do we get to watch Jackie," Dr. Sheridan asked.

"Let my Department take that," Chet responded. "I have a few people in the Department that do nothing but audit and investigate concerns. Given Jackie's behavior and the terms of the separation agreement, it makes sense for us to assign someone to ensure that she is following the terms of the agreement."

"Good," Dr. Sheridan replied.

"Tell us more about the liver failure issue you mentioned, Asa," Chet asked.

"Oh, Muckland called me, and there's been an increase in

liver failure in our Recallamin 3 trial. We have a plan to open a secondary arm to that trial that will reduce the dose for select patients, which should address that problem. Muckland's good at scrubbing data. I'm sure he'll get it under control."

"What are we doing about replacing Jackie for the Northeast Region, Cheryl?" asked Dr. Sheridan. "I'm worried that if we don't get an adequate replacement, physicians will start yapping at us. I already have had a couple of calls from physicians in Portland."

"I'm working on it. Whoever it is will have big shoes to fill."

"If you don't find someone soon, you will have to jump into the fray yourself."

"That's not a bad idea, Asa. I'll do that. We don't want the natives to get restless."

"OK, I think we've covered what I wanted to cover," Dr. Sheridan concluded. "Thanks for weathering my opening storm."

"Can't have a rainbow without the rain," Cheryl quipped.

"Or fertile fields without the shit," Asa countered, which helped end the tense meeting with laughter.

CHAPTER 19

"Thank you all for agreeing to meet on such short notice," opened DA Wydman as he began the teleconference with Jackie, Curt, and Inspector Adams. "I guess we'll have to rename our group the Teleconference for Four instead of the Table for Four," earning chuckles from Jackie and Curt but not Inspector Adams, who was not privy to the groups' history.

"Before we begin," continued DA Wydman, "I'd like to introduce Inspector Theo Adams. It has been his tireless efforts that have given us any hope of finding answers to past events and continuing this pursuit of the truth. Theo, I'd like you to meet Jackie Deno, former AlzCura Pharmaceutical Rep, and I think you know Curt Barnes."

If Curt had met Inspector Adams, he could not recollect. All the people that interviewed him on the day of Calli's murder and the days afterward were a blur to him. Losing Dr. Caron from the group was a significant loss. However, Curt felt buoyed that Inspector Adams was joining the group as he had intimate knowledge of the event and all that transpired afterward.

"Welcome to the team, Theo," Jackie offered.

"Yeah, good to have you onboard, Theo," Curt chimed in.

"Happy to be a part of the team. Thanks for inviting me,

Will."

"Alright," sighed DA Wydman, "that was the easy part. Now the real work begins."

DA Wydman asked Jackie and Curt to summarize for Theo the scare tactics and surveillance activities that they suspected AlzCura had launched against them. After they updated Theo, DA Wydman outlined his goal for the meeting.

"At the end of our meeting, I hope to have a clear plan for collecting all the evidence to determine AlzCura's responsibility for the deaths of Calli Barnes, Darius Scott, Elvira Scott, and Stuart Deno. Agreed?"

"Agreed," the others said in unison.

"Good! Now ground-rule number one, Theo and I are privy to information that is part of active investigations. As much as we're a team, we will not be able to divulge this information to you in any detail. Ground-rule number two, your safety Jackie and Curt, and the safety of your loved ones are paramount. Theo and I are obligated to stay involved in this process; you are not. You may opt out any time, no questions asked. Understood?"

Jackie and Curt affirmed that they understood the ground rules, and DA Wydman continued.

"Now, let's take stock in where we are. Theo, as I understand, you had a meeting with Dr. Caron's Office Manager this morning as part of our investigation. Do you have anything you can share that doesn't violate ground-rule number one?"

"Unfortunately, not much yet, Will," Inspector Adams replied. "We are still trying to determine if Dr. Caron's death was a suicide or something else made to look like suicide. His Office Manager may have additional information for me later today."

"OK, thanks, Theo. We also don't have the Medical Examiner's autopsy results yet. So, the case of Dr. Caron's death is still very much an open-ended question."

DA Wydman moved on to summarize where things stood in the Darius and Elvira Scott deaths.

"The State continues to be involved in investigating the deaths of Darius and Elvira Scott based on complaints Elvira made to the Office of Advocacy and the National Association for the Mentally Ill. These complaints are a matter of public record, and the Maine media is all over it and anxious for the official autopsy results to be released. I've seen the results, and mindful of the ground rules, I cannot divulge those results. Let me just say we wouldn't be having this meeting if there weren't some lingering questions about the results," he ended tantalizingly.

"Will," Curt opened, "I'm assuming then that AlzCura never responded to your letter requesting information about Darius and Elvira, correct?"

"Correct," DA Wydman affirmed. "To clarify for the group, it was our Attorney General Talcott who sent the letter to Alz-Cura, but to date, we have not received a response."

"And the letter you asked me to write to AlzCura recently," Curt added, "I'm assuming that we want to rethink that given recent events, correct?"

"Yes, thanks for reminding me about that. No, we definitely have to adjust our strategy on how, or even if, we approach AlzCura for information. One piece of information I just received this morning, Curt, is a partial print on the letter that was left in your door."

Curt wasn't prepared for this and struggled to make an intelligible response, "Wha..." he croaked.

"I'm sorry to spring this on you, Curt. I meant to call you before this meeting, but my schedule got away from me. Unfortunately, we have not been able to link an identity to the print."

"So, what's next?" Curt asked, finally finding his voice.

"I'm afraid the best we can do is keep it as evidence and hope that we can link it to someone in the future. Not very satisfying, I know."

"Will," Jackie interjected, "I'd like to share what I learned from Stu's autopsy results."

"Go ahead, Jackie."

"I recently met with Dr. Jacobson, the Coroner. The first shocking thing I learned was that Stu had received the Recallamin vaccine. He never told me that he had a genetic test done during his annual exam. When they found he had the Alzheimers gene, they offered him the vaccine. As for the autopsy, they found nothing definitive. The coroner did say, however, that the toxicologist found a substance in the tissue samples that he described as 'suspicious but inconclusive.'"

"Really," DA Wydman exclaimed. "That's very interesting. Jackie, I want to be sensitive to your loss, so if you don't want to continue, I can respect that. If you're comfortable, can you tell us some of the symptoms your husband had and to what the coroner attributed his death?"

"Thank you, Will," Jackie replied, touched by his compassion. "Unfortunately, I was here in Maine when Stu got sick. He had been complaining of a headache the night before I left and still had one when he dropped me off at the airport."

Jackie paused to have a brief internal debate about whether to share with the group Stu's outburst at the airport. Deciding she would, she continued.

"Uncharacteristically, Stu got angry with me at the airport," Jackie paused again, feeling tears well up.

"I'm sorry to put you through this, Jackie," DA Wydman said contritely. "If you need to stop, I'll understand, but what you've told us so far has already convinced me this crusade needs to continue. If you can, tell us more about his anger."

"I'll never forget it," Jackie sniffed. "He just seemed to snap and said, 'You aren't going there for work, I know better. Don't lie to me. You're going to destroy everything.' Then he sped off. Later, when I finally reached him on the phone, he said it was due to his headache."

"Thanks for sharing that, Jackie," DA Wydman added. "What about the cause of death?"

"The coroner said that Stu died of liver failure and a brain bleed. Because Stu was otherwise healthy, he thought it might have been from a rare genetic condition. All I could think about was what Dr. Caron told us that night at the Farrisport Inn," Jackie sobbed.

For Theo's benefit and recognizing that Jackie had reached the end of her emotional rope, DA Wydman summarized what Jackie was referencing.

"Theo, Dr. Caron had told us that AlzCura had hidden and misreported complication data on their Recallamin trials. He indicated that he admitted several of his patients to the hospital with symptoms of liver failure. While he called AlzCura and reported these complications, he never saw these complications reflected in their quality data reports. Furthermore, while AlzCura only wanted him to report these complications by phone, he said he noted these complications and calls to AlzCura in his office records."

"Good to know," Theo replied. "I will look for those cases now that we have files in evidence."

"How are you doing, Jackie?" asked DA Wydman.

"I'll be alright," she replied, having gone off-screen momentarily to retrieve some tissues.

"I think we have our first strategic decision to make," announced DA Wydman. "How do we best pursue the liver failure issue?"

"Will, this is Curt," piping up for the first time since the beginning of the call. "In recognition of ground rule number two regarding our safety, would it be better and safer for us to ask the FDA to investigate this matter?"

"Good question," DA Wydman replied. "The FDA is an ace up our sleeve, but do we have enough evidence to make a compelling case to the FDA?"

"I think it may be premature," offered Theo. "I would want to complete my investigation of Dr. Caron's death first. It could give us and the FDA more ammunition."

"I agree," added Jackie. "If Dr. Caron had these concerns, perhaps other physicians I used to meet with have similar concerns."

"Yes, but Jackie," Curt debated, "How can you approach those doctors safely? AlzCura is watching us, and they won't sit idly by if you start meeting with those doctors. The FDA could, though."

"I have a proposal," DA Wydman interjected. "We wait to involve the FDA until after Theo completes his investigation. Also, I anticipate that Darius and Elvira's autopsy results will go public here in the next few days. If I were a betting man, I'd say the results will set off a firestorm in the media. Who knows what the press will dredge up that might attract the FDA's attention?"

"I like that," seconded Theo as Jackie and Curt nodded their heads in agreement on camera.

"OK, good. Now let's revisit the question about our strategy in communicating with AlzCura. While we don't have definitive proof that AlzCura is behind the recent events with Dr. Caron, Jackie, and Curt, it's hard to believe these are coincidental. I think it behooves us to assume that AlzCura is involved and adjust our strategy accordingly."

"I agree. What do you suggest, Will?" asked Curt.

"Well, before I show my hand on that, I was hoping to get everyone's thoughts."

"Will," Jackie spoke up, "before the break-in and finding the surveillance equipment in my home, I planned to contact an employment attorney to file a wrongful termination suit against AlzCura. My thinking was that this would tie up some of their resources while we built a potential case against them on their Recallamin vaccine. I'm not sure that's the right strategy anymore."

"I would agree," replied DA Wydman. "With Dr. Caron out of the picture, and given what you know about their operation, I'm sure you are AlzCura's biggest concern. If anything, I think it best for you to do things that make them think you've moved on."

"I was thinking about getting a part-time job," Jackie advanced.

"OK, that's a start. But would part-time be good enough? If I'm AlzCura and I'm watching you, I'd be asking myself, what is she doing the rest of the time?"

"I'm taking care of my baby," Jackie challenged.

"Yes, but then I'd ask myself, how is she making ends meet? I don't know. I don't want to get too prescriptive. I just want the target off your back."

"And I appreciate that, Will," Jackie replied. "Let me think about it some."

"That's fair," DA Wydman concluded. "Curt, what are your thoughts about strategy?"

"I'm a fan of still working covertly to find the truth, but letting others, like the media and the FDA, do our dirty work. No offense, but the fact that someone tried to pick up my kids at school and left a note on my door, still has me a bit shook up."

"No offense taken and totally understandable," DA Wydman replied. "Theo, what are your thoughts?"

"Yeah, thanks, Will. As I mentioned before, I'd like to complete the investigation of Dr. Caron's death before we consider going to the FDA. I can appreciate the positions Jackie and Curt are in and admire that you're still in the game, but we need to make AlzCura not only think but believe you're no longer involved."

"Great point, Theo, which brings us to how do we do that? How do we make it look like we've gone on our merry way but still communicate with each other and work towards the goal we agreed to when we started the meeting?"

"Teleconference for Four was a good start," offered Jackie. "We can't be seen together."

Although Curt agreed with Jackie's recommendation, he could feel his disappointment registering on his face and hoped it wasn't apparent on camera.

"What about day-to-day communications between teleconferences?" asked Curt, concerned that he did not lose all contact with Jackie. Their recent calls had not only helped him deal with his fears but had brightened his outlook, as she had when they first met.

"I would recommend text messages when possible and limited phone calls. And if you have to talk, make sure you're not within earshot of anyone," DA Wydman recommended. "Oh, do any of you have landlines?"

When all three indicated that they didn't, DA Wydman explained himself.

"Thanks, I wanted to make sure. If you did, I'd have discouraged their use for fear that someone may bug them. Better safe than sorry. The last question, at least from me, how often should we have these teleconferences?"

"Every other week on the same day and time?" offered Curt.

"Same Bat-time. Same Bat-channel, huh, Curt?" joked DA Wydman.

"Huh," exclaimed Jackie, whose face registered her confusion.

"Oh, I'm sorry, Jackie, you and maybe Theo are too young to remember. It's a reference from Batman, a 1960's TV show. I'm showing my age. Any objections to Curt's suggestion?"

"Not to be paranoid," Jackie replied, "but I'm paranoid. Should we vary the day and time, so if someone is watching us, they won't detect a pattern?"

"Smart thinking," DA Wydman praised. "Once again, rather safe than sorry. How about I vary the teleconference dates and times a bit. If you can't accommodate the time of the invite, just let me know. Does anyone have anything else to discuss?"

Jackie, Curt, and Theo thanked DA Wydman for a productive meeting, and the newly minted members of the Teleconference for Four set off to implement their strategy.

CHAPTER 20

Although it was only 1 p.m. when Jackie signed off from the teleconference, all she wanted to do was join her daughter in a nap. She felt drained from recounting Stu's last days and having to consider getting a full-time job. DA Wydman's characterization of her as Alzura's biggest concern and having a target on her back was also unsettling. All she could think to do to provide her restoration and hope was to go to Ashley's room. Looking down on Ashley's angelic face as she napped offered Jackie a reprieve. Until she realized that repainting the wall in Ashley's room hadn't removed the threat still firmly etched in her head. Unable to shake her concerns or her fatigue, she went to the kitchen to make coffee. While waiting for the coffee to brew, her phone rang. It was her mother, and for a second, Jackie thought not to answer but relented.

"Hi Mom," Jackie answered as brightly and energetically as she could muster.

"Hi Honey. What are you doing, and how is my little grand-daughter?"

"She's taking a nap, and I'm making a pot of coffee. Do you want to come over and have a cup?" she heard herself say but then wondered about the wisdom of that invitation.

"I'd love to. I'll be right over."

Jackie hung up and realized that she still had not told her parents about losing her job. Nor had she divulged the alliance she was in to expose her former employer or the disturbing findings from Stu's autopsy or the surveillance equipment she found in her house. She was withholding an avalanche of information and emotions. While Jackie loved her mother dearly, she wasn't feeling up to her inevitable questions. Although Jackie knew it was only a function of her mother's care and concern, right now, she feared it would feel like an inquisition. She wasn't sure she would be able to hold it together emotionally. Before she had an opportunity to form a contingency plan, her mother was at the door.

"Hi, Mom, coffee's ready."

"I like this treatment. You should take more days off from work," her mother replied, immediately touching on one of the topics Jackie wanted to avoid.

Usually, sitting down to have coffee and a chat with her mother was relaxing and one of Jackie's favorite ways to bond with her mother. That was not the case today.

"So, what have you been up to today?" Jackie opened in a blatant attempt to control where the conversation would go.

"Not much. A little house cleaning," she replied, pausing to take a sip of her coffee. "Mmm, this is good. Is this something different than you usually make?"

Jackie, happy to have the conversation continue on this track, replied. "Yes, as a matter of fact, it's a new Kona blend I got from Wegman's."

"Oh, I love that store," gushed her mother. "I wish it weren't so far away. Of course, you drive right past it on the way to work, I imagine."

"I do," Jackie affirmed.

"Say, I meant to ask you," her mother prefaced, "I saw a Security van outside your house the other day. Was that for you?"

Before Jackie could fumble for an answer to her mother's question, Ashley's whimpering broadcast over the baby monitor.

"Oh, the angel awakes," Jackie sang happily. "Let's go get her and take her to the park, Mom. Then I can tell you about the Security van."

Ashley had temporarily saved her mother from a potentially challenging conversation. Jackie and her mother traipsed up the steps to prepare Ashley for a trip to the park. Although it was a relatively mild Spring day, Jackie bundled Ashley up like it was winter.

"The poor child has so much on she can't even move," Jackie's mother said in a pitying tone.

"She's dressed in layers," Jackie replied. "I don't want her to get cold, and I can always take a layer off."

"You're a typical first-time mother."

"No, I'm an exceptional first-time mother," Jackie corrected her as she lifted Ashley into the stroller.

"You're right, dear. Now, if the exceptional mother doesn't mind, can I push Ash in her stroller?"

"I guess so, but I will be watching you like a hawk."

"You do that, even though I have more experience pushing a baby in a stroller than you do."

"Yes, but that was a quarter of a century ago!"

"Oh, Jackie, that makes me feel so old."

The light teasing conversation between Jackie and her mother was refreshing, and the dread that Jackie initially felt about talking with her mother started to lift. They circumnavigated the park that featured three distinct areas - a softball field, the playground area with basketball and volleyball courts, and an expansive green space punctuated with stands of mature elm trees. As her mother and grandmother chatted, Ashley babbled on and on as if carrying on a conversation with herself. Having completed the circuit around the park, Jackie and her mother claimed a bench near the swingset.

"So, about that Security van," Jackie's mother prompted.

"Oh, yes," Jackie responded, having now had sufficient time to plan her response. "After the break-in, I decided to have a security system installed." Leaving out the part about finding the surveillance system that had been spying on her.

"Well, that's a good idea," praised her mother.

"Yeah, I was lucky that nothing was stolen or damaged. Hopefully, there won't be a next time, but better safe than sorry," Jackie said, reprising a phrase that had been used several times on the teleconference call she had earlier.

"You'll have to teach your father and me about the system since we now have the extra key to your house."

"Yep, I'll give you and Dad the code and teach you how to use it," Jackie replied. She had given an extra key to her parents after the break-in and after she had repainted Ashley's wall.

Ashley had started to fuss in her stroller, and Jackie got up and removed the outer layer of clothing.

"Now, don't get upset," her mother prefaced, putting Jackie immediately on notice that she wasn't going to like what followed. "What are you going to do about your job? Don't get me wrong, I love taking care of Ash, but do you want to be doing all that traveling? Why don't you find something local where you don't have to be gone as much?"

Before Jackie could respond, Ashley's babbling evolved.

"Mama, Mama"

Jackie let out a cry of joy.

"Did you hear that Mom?" she said excitedly, "She said, Mama." Filled with indescribable happiness, she praised and prompted Ashley.

"Ashley, you said Mama. Can you say, Mama? Mama?

Jackie's mother, having now joined Jackie by the stroller, chimed in.

"What a good girl. Say, Mama."

Ashley's eyes tracked from her mother to her grand-mother, with a look that seemed to be asking what all the hoopla and attention were about?

"Mama," Ashley repeated, causing her mother and grand-mother to react with such loud cries of joy that it startled her.

"Oh, we're sorry, Ash," her mother crooned, picking her up out of the stroller and instinctually rocking her gently in an embrace.

As she swayed with her daughter in her arms, her delight changed to despair. Then the floodgates opened, and Jackie disintegrated into tears. Now it was her mother's turn to embrace Jackie, and despite not being fully understanding of Jackie's tears, her mother started to cry too.

"Stuuuuu," Jackie sobbed as her mother tightened her arms around her daughter. "He wasn't here," she cried as Jackie crumbled in her mother's arms.

Ashley's milestone moment shielded Jackie from having to answer her mother's questions for the second time that day. But as joyous as that moment was, it illuminated how bitter-sweet all of Ashley's milestone moments would be without her Daddy there.

CHAPTER 21

After the teleconference, Curt had an appointment to see his counselor, Timothy Darling, LCSW. Their weekly sessions had gradually transitioned to every other week and then to monthly as Curt gained insight into his grief, regained control of his emotions, and reached the acceptance stage of his loss. As he drove to Tim's office, he felt a sense of relief from the teleconference but recognized that it had been difficult for Jackie. If not for the group's agreement to limit phone calls to one another, Curt would have called her immediately after the meeting. He made a mental note to text Jackie later to check on her and offer whatever support one could offer via text.

"How have you been doing?" Tim asked in his typical open-ended style.

"Overall, I've been doing well, but there have been a few ups and downs."

"Tell me more," Tim urged.

Curt proceeded to tell him about the mysterious call to his kids' school and the note left on the apartment door. Over the past few sessions, Curt had briefed Tim on his chance meeting with Jackie and the alliance they had formed to pursue the truth about Recallamin and its potential role in their losses.

"Whoa, that must have scared you," Tim exclaimed. But

rather than respond to Tim, Curt's mind went off on a tangent, as he had forgotten that Caitlin had a riding lesson the following day.

"Curt? You with me?" Tim said, trying to bring him back into the conversation.

"Oh, I'm sorry, Tim. When you said 'Whoa,' it reminded me of Caitlin's riding lesson tomorrow."

"Glad I could help with that," he chuckled, "but now about the call to the school and the note?"

"Yeah, that scared me, and I initially had reservations about continuing to be involved in our little crusade."

So, you believe the person or persons who did this were connected to the Pharmaceutical company?"

Curt proceeded to update Tim on all that had transpired with Dr. Caron's death, Jackie's break-in and surveillance, and the decision by the group to take a more careful and covert approach.

"Wow, you have had quite a month. What have you been doing to take care of yourself?"

Invariably, Tim always got around to that question of self-care. It used to irritate Curt, but that was when he wasn't taking care of himself. As he progressed through the stages of grief, he increasingly recognized the importance of self-care.

"I've found talking to Jackie has helped," Curt said in response to Tim's question.

"You have a lot in common," Tim declared.

"Yes, we do. We both lost our spouse, and we are both raising kids as single-parents."

"And you both seek the truth and justice for your losses," Tim added.

"Yes," Curt affirmed, not knowing exactly where Tim was headed with the conversation.

"How do you feel about Jackie?" Tim inquired.

"I like her," Curt shot back as his stomach did its customary flip-flop when he thought about Jackie or was in her presence.

"Is it different than how you liked Chelsea?" Tim probed further.

A few months back, such a question would likely have made Curt uncomfortable, if not angry. Now he recognized the direction Tim was taking him. Now he knew that placing these two relationships in juxtaposition could provide insight.

"Yes, it's entirely different," Curt led out.

"How so?"

"I was desperate, angry, and lost when I met Chelsea. I was looking for a replacement for Calli, knowing full-well that no one could ever replace her."

"And with Jackie?" posed Tim.

"With Jackie, it was more like she was additive, not a replacement for Calli."

"Tell me more."

"If anything, when we first met, Jackie formed a relationship with Caitlin and Cade more so than with me. I was more of a spectator, and the impact she had on my kids was remarkable."

"And her impact on you?"

Curt paused, knowing full well the impact she had on him on many levels but uncertain that he wanted to give voice to them.

"Curt?" Tim questioned after Curt's pause extended beyond 15 seconds.

"I'm sorry," Curt offered, still unsure if he could provide Tim his answer.

"Is my question difficult for you?" Tim stated the obvious.

"Yes."

"Why do you think that is?"

Curt's face and body language spoke louder than any verbal response he could have provided.

"You're afraid," Tim answered for him.

"Yes," Curt responded, appreciating, once again, Tim's laser observations and skill at uncovering all his emotions, even those he wanted or tried to hide.

"Why do you think that is? Tim repeated, hoping that giving voice to Curt's fear may give him the push he needed.

"I like her," Curt responded, sounding like some sheepish grade-schooler afraid to admit the full extent of his feelings.

"Why do you like her, aside from her positive impact on Cailin and Cade?" Tim probed, knowing full well that Curt was struggling with an emotion far more complicated than liking Jackie.

"She gives me hope like there is something to live for," Curt answered, struggling to put words to all of the thoughts and feelings he was experiencing.

"And why would having hope scare you?"

"Because it means I have to let go of the past," Curt responded as he felt himself approaching the root causes of his fear. Then the floodgates opened, and in a rapid-fire fashion, he replied.

"I'm afraid to have hope because I lost hope when I lost Calli. I'm afraid of hope because I don't even know how Jackie feels about me. I'm afraid of hope because I don't want to lose hope again. I'm afraid of hope because if I lose it again, how will it impact my kids?"

"Are you talking about hope, or are you talking about love?" Tim's insight hit Curt like a lightening-bolt. When Curt failed to respond, Tim repeated Curt's response substituting the word hope with the word love.

"I'm afraid to have love because I lost love when I lost Calli. I'm afraid of love because I don't even know how Jackie feels about me. I'm afraid of love because I don't want to lose love again. I'm afraid of love because if I lose it again, how will it impact my kids?"

"Yes, you're right," Curt conceded. "I was taken with Jackie the moment I met her. So were Caitlin and Cade. Of course, then she was married, so it was different."

"This is your next step in the acceptance phase," Tim summarized as the end of their session approached. "Since you're not stuck in the past, you have to accept the uncertainty of the future."

"And that's hard," Curt admitted.

"It is for all of us, Curt," Tim offered.

"That's life."

"That's what people say," Tim sang in his best Frank Sinatra voice, breaking the tension and magically pulling Curt back together as they laughed.

"I'll see you next month, Curt. Keep up the good work."

"Thanks, Tim. I can't thank you enough."

Curt left feeling somehow lighter despite being turned inside out. As he made his way to pick up Caitlin and Cade at school, he allowed himself to daydream about Jackie. What seemed so difficult to speak to in his counseling session was easy to comprehend. She made him feel alive again. Being with Jackie made him feel like anything was possible, and any problem was resolvable. As he turned into the school driveway, realty ripped him from his daydream and deposited him back to the recollection of a stranger attempting to pick up his kids. It was a gut punch he hadn't fully gotten over. As minutes ticked by, waiting for Caitlin and Cade to exit the school, his anxiety increased. When they appeared, followed closely by

Principal Taylor, he breathed a long sigh of relief.

"Hi Daddy," the kids echoed as they jumped in the car. "Can we play on the playground when we get home?" Cade asked before Curt could even return their greeting.

"Yes, we can…,"

"Yeah!!!" the kids cheered before he was even able to complete his sentence.

Their exuberance was infectious, and the fears that had crept into his mind while waiting for them vanished — replaced by gratitude that his kids were returning to normal. He had hardly parked the car when they jumped out of the car and ran to the playground, joining a half dozen other kids, including Caitlin's best friend, Jordan.

Climbing the stairs to the apartment, Curt stopped to survey the playground from their 3rd-floor landing. As the memory of the note on his door returned, he staved off the fears with a sure-fire strategy.

Taking out his phone, he texted Jackie.

CHAPTER 22

"Inspector Adams, this is Rebecca."

"Hi, Rebecca, how is the project coming along?" he asked hopefully.

"All done. Thanks for sending over Officer Schweikert. He was very helpful."

"No problem. Glad he could assist. What did you find?"

"We're missing three files," Rebecca stated.

Before she could continue, Inspector Adams responded.

"Let me guess. Two of the files are Darius and Elvira Scott."

"Yep. You know you'd make a good detective," Rebecca tried to joke.

Not in the mood for jokes, he pressed forward.

"Could Darius and Elvira's files have been misplaced in the office or outside of the office somewhere, like Dr. Caron's home?"

"No. When we didn't find those three files, we searched every nook and cranny in the office. I also can't imagine Dr. Caron taking any files out of the office. He was not very organized, but he was a stickler for protecting confidentiality."

"What about the third file?"

"The patient's name is Norman Boulanger."

"Was he in the Recallamin trial?" Adams probed.

"I don't know."

"What do you mean you don't know?" Adams asked, starting to get irritated.

"Without his file, I can't confirm," she responded. Knowing Adams was on edge, Rebecca proceeded to provide as much information as she could.

"I can tell you that he was 28-years old, so if he were in the Recallamin trial, it would have been the Recallamin3 trial."

"You said he was 28-years old. Does that mean he died?"

"No, it means that he was 28-years old when we entered him into our registry as a clinical trial patient. He never had any office visits, so we don't have any additional information on him."

"But, you must have an address for Mr. Boulanger, correct?"

"Yes, that I do have."

Rebecca gave Inspector Adams the address and apologized, knowing that she had not been able to provide the depth of detail he had hoped for.

"No, I think I need to apologize to you, Rebecca," he countered. "I shouldn't have gotten short with you. I appreciate the work you're doing. Did you have a chance to flag the Recallamin trial patients?"

"Yes, I did. I found 44 patients in the three different trials. Add Darius and Elvira Scott and Norman Boulanger, and that's a total of 47."

"OK, thanks, Rebecca," Adams replied, happy that the number of cases was only a small fraction of the 1,445 files Rebecca had to comb through.

"That number doesn't include the files you have from Dr. Caron's office," Rebecca added.

"Right, thanks," he responded, having forgotten that he

still had 50 files awaiting his review in the evidence locker.

"You're welcome, but I thought I had a good record-keeping system. Now I know better," Rebecca said dejectedly.

"Good but not perfect. Don't beat yourself up. You've been extremely helpful," he added, trying to make amends for snapping at her earlier.

"Do you think you will still be able to determine if Dr. Caron's death was a suicide or not?"

"Let's put it this way; the information you provided has only served to increase my suspicions, but I still can't say either way definitively."

"That's fair. Let me know if there is anything else I can do," Rebecca offered as they ended the call.

Inspector Adams thanked Rebecca and immediately called DA Wydman.

"Will, I've got the results of the Office Manager's file review," said Adams skipping past a greeting.

"Hi, Theo. What did you learn?"

"Three Recallamin patient files are missing out of the 47 files on-premises. Darius and Elvira Scott's and a patient named Norman Boulanger."

"Well, the plot thickens," DA Wydman said ominously. "I understand why Darius and Elvira's files may be missing, but what do you know about Mr. Boulanger?"

"Not much yet. I have Mr. Boulanger's address, and I'm going to try to track him down. I want to take the 44 files into evidence and review them along with the 50 files we have once forensics is done, dusting them for fingerprints."

"I'll get you a subpoena," DA Wydman offered. "Speaking of fingerprints, do we have any results yet?"

"Not yet, but I'll check with them after our call," he replied. "I'm also going to call Dr. Corpisen and get an update on any autopsy results."

"Three missing files are suspicious, especially since two of them are subjects of open investigations. It's a start, but not nearly enough to prove that the good Dr. Caron may have had help ending his life. OK, Theo, don't let me hold you up."

Theo exited his office to take a short walk to the adjacent building, which housed the forensics lab and the evidence locker. Entering the forensics lab, he tracked down Evan Mercer, a lab analyst, who had all the stereotypical traits of a lab rat - obsessive-compulsive, detail-oriented, inflexible, nerdy, and a bit socially awkward.

"Evan, glad I found you."

"Oh, Inspector Adams, this is highly unusual," Evan replied, his body language communicating he was not at all comfortable.

"Yeah, I know, I usually call," he responded, immediately recognizing from the look on Evan's face that his response was insufficient.

"I was in the office and needed to stretch my legs, so I thought I'd walk over here instead of calling," Adams added.

"Ah, alright, I guess," Evan stammered, not entirely satisfied. "What do you want?" he blurted.

"Do you have any results from the Dr. Caron case?"

"Not officially," Evan replied.

"What do you mean, not officially?"

"I have results, but I haven't documented them in my written report as yet."

"So you have results," Inspector Adams pressed.

"Yes, but until I memorialize them in written form, they're not official."

"Do you anticipate that the results will change between now and the time you memorialize them in your written report?" he stated, trying to maintain a calm demeanor.

"No. I am satisfied that my findings are accurate, and they have been validated by another colleague, who, like me, is a certified examiner through the International Association of Identification."

Inspector Adams had all he could do to not roll his eyes.

"Can you tell me what the results were, Evan?"

"I could, but..." Evan started but was promptly cut off.

"EVAN!" Inspector Adams shouted a little more loudly than he had intended causing a few people in the lab to take notice. "District Attorney Wydman would like an update. I just got off the phone with him. Would you like me to tell him that he will have to wait until Evan Mercer finds the time to memorialize his findings in a written report?"

"No, Inspector Adams, that won't be necessary," he sighed. "Just let the District Attorney know,"

"I know Evan, they're not official," he interrupted again.

"Right," Evan replied and then went silent.

"Evan?" Inspector Adams questioned when it was apparent that Evan needed additional prompting.

"What?"

"The unofficial verbal findings, please," he huffed, feeling as though his head was about to explode.

"We received the prints on," Evan began before being interrupted.

"Evan, please just tell me what you found. I don't need all the details leading up to your findings."

"Oh, OK, if you want," Evan stammered again, registering his discomfort. "I found five sets of unique prints." Evan paused until Adams signaled him to continue by making circular motions with his index finger. "One set of prints belonged to Dr. Caron. Another set of prints we traced to Rebecca

Klatz, the Office Manager. Another set of prints belonging to Jacqueline Deno. At this time, results on the two other sets are inconclusive."

"Inconclusive?" Inspector Adams questioned.

"Yes. The prints are excellent in quality, but we could not find any comparisons. None of the prints matched the other office staff."

"So, did you search AFIS?" Adams asked.

"No, Inspector Adams," Evan replied, rolling his eyes and relishing the opportunity to correct him, "I searched IAFIS. The Integrated Automated Fingerprint Identification System that replaced AFIS about ten years ago."

Ignoring Evan's dig, Inspector Adams thanked Evan, resolving never again to set foot in the Forensics Lab if he needed information from Evan Mercer.

Exhausted from prying information out of Evan, he elected to call Dr. Corpisen from his office rather than visit him.

"Inspector Adams, I was about to call Will, but since I have you on the line, I'll fill you in on my findings from Dr. Caron's autopsy."

"Good timing then," he replied, thankful that getting information from Dr. Corpisen would not be as painful an exercise as his visit to the Forensics Lab.

"Yes, impeccable," Dr. Corpisen added. "For most of the procedure, it looked like your run-of-the-mill suicide," paused the Medical Examiner.

"I sense a but coming," he prompted.

"But," Dr. Corpisen said with emphasis confirming Adams' prediction. "I found Gamma-hydroxybutyric acid in his system."

"GHB? The date-rape drug?" Inspector Adams queried.

"Bingo," the Medical Examiner called out.

"GHB, three missing files from the office, and two unidentifiable sets of fingerprints we still need to investigate. It all seems to be pointing to a suspicious death," Adams posited.

"Not seems, does!" emphasized Dr. Corpisen.

"Thanks, Louie. I will call Will and give him the news."

When DA Wydman heard the news from Inspector Adams, his next steps were readily apparent. He needed to convene a meeting to brief Attorney General Talcott. The restless Maine media was about to get a bolus of information that would surely set off a firestorm.

CHAPTER 23

"Come on in, Chet," Dr. Asa Sheridan called from his office door. "What do you have for me?"

Chet Humphreys, AlzCura's Chief Legal Counsel, took a seat and laid down two files.

"Let's get our letter in response to the Maine AG's office out of the way first," he prefaced, handing Dr. Sheridan the draft. After reading it to himself, Dr. Sheridan looked up with a confused look on his face.

"Is this accurate, Chet?"

"Yes, it is. What concerns you?"

"It says here that Mr. Scott was enrolled in the Recallamin 2 trial but did not take any medications."

"That's right, he was given a vaccine that's technically different than a medication."

"You sly dog," Dr. Sheridan grinned. "It's that easy?"

"We're giving them what they asked for," Chet chuckled.

AlzCura's Recallamin vaccine fell under the regulations of the FDA's Center for Biologics Evaluation and Research (CBER). It thereby was not technically classified as a medication. The Recallamin vaccine, however, was unique as far as vaccines go. Clinical trials indicated that it had preventive properties as all vaccines but also had curative properties more typical of medications.

"Asa," Chet added, "The worst that can happen is that the AG recognizes his failure to include vaccines in his request and subsequently clarifies the request. In the meantime, we look like we're cooperating and delay having to provide any additional information."

As Chet spoke, Dr. Sheridan picked up his pen and signed the letter.

"Send it."

"Will do. Now let me brief you on the surveillance activities of our former employee, Jackie. I know it has only been a couple of days, but since I'm here," he began.

"Before you begin, who did you assign to monitor her?"

"Horst Mangrum," Chet replied as a wry smile came to his face.

"Horse?" Dr. Sheridan responded using the nickname everyone used to refer to their best investigator in the company.

"Yep. When you have an important job to do, you send the very best," Chet announced, sounding almost like a Hallmark commercial.

Horse Mangrum transferred to the main office in Buffalo last year from AlzCura's office in Germany. He immediately elevated the company's success in ferreting out and exposing fraudulent claims against the company and providing compelling information that often limited the company's liability on settled claims. In short, he saved the company millions. He had a reputation as a hyper-organized, punctual workaholic with keen senses and a ruthless, unrivaled determination to succeed regardless of the task. This was no less the case when he was assigned to monitor Jackie's activities.

"So what has that too-smart-for-her-own-good troublemaker been up to?"

"Surprisingly, not much. And what she has been doing seems to have no relationship to continuing a crusade against us."

"Good. So what has she been doing?"

"She's been a homebody at least the last two days. She had her mother over. She took her baby to the park. Shopped at Wegman's. Pretty benign stuff.

"Any sign that she's secured a new job?

"No, not yet."

"And no travel other than to the grocery store."

"Right."

"Well, it's too early to tell, but I'm glad Horse is on it. Better than leaving it to Cheryl's two sons, Dopey and Goofy!"

As Chet and Dr. Sheridan had a good laugh, Dr. Sheridan's assistant announced Cheryl's arrival via the office intercom.

"Speak of the devil," Dr. Sheridan remarked, causing them to continue their laughter.

"You boys are having way too much fun in here," not knowing that the laughter was at the expense of her and her twin sons.

"Well, Chet here has done a masterful job responding to the Maine AG's office and has sicced Horse on Jackie."

"Congratulations," Cheryl offered, "Has that little hussy been behaving herself?"

"She has," affirmed Dr. Sheridan. "Speaking of hussy's, what do you hear from Alexis?"

"You mean Monique Deuvolet?" Cheryl corrected.

"Sure, Monique then."

"She has those French physicians eating out of her hand. Sales of Recallamin are up."

"I would imagine the French doctors are eating out of

something other than her hand, and it's not only Recallamin sales that are up!" Dr. Sheridan remarked crudely. Which only he and Chet found amusing.

"Joke all you want. She's getting the job done."

"Well, that's good," Dr. Sheridan replied, letting the opportunity to joke about what kind of job she was getting done pass. "I may have to go visit Monique myself and see first hand," seemingly unable to say anything about Cheryl's daughter that couldn't be construed as lewd.

"Well, you're the boss. You can do what you want to do."

"What about you? Have you visited our doctors in Maine, as we discussed?"

"Asa, that was two days ago. No, but I am making plans to visit."

"Chop, chop, Cheryl. Time's a-wastin'. Chet here has already finished what he was asked to do. Recallamin sales are down in Maine, and they're flagging in all the other markets Jackie was in."

"I'm going next week," Cheryl replied, although she had not yet made any definitive plans.

"Good. And are your boys back in town and behaving themselves?"

"Yes, Asa," Cheryl sighed, wondering why he was giving her the third degree.

"So, was there a reason for your visit, Cheryl?"

"Do I have to have a reason, Asa?" she snapped, trying to mask the fact that putting her on the defensive had made her forget entirely the reason she was there.

"Well, I would hope so. If going to Maine the last two days wasn't important enough, then I can only imagine you were involved in something more important," he challenged.

"You know what, Asa? I can see this is not a good time," as

she marched out of his office before she gave him the satisfaction of bringing her to tears for the second time that week.

"You were a little tough on her, Asa," Chet offered after Cheryl had exited.

"Ahh, she can take it. It's good to light a fire under her ass from time to time."

"I'll remember that next time you get after me!"

"Darn, now I've divulged my secret motivational strategy. You better keep that information confidential, or I'll have to sic my lawyer on you," he joked.

"I am your lawyer," Chet parried.

"In that case, my strategy is protected under attorney-client privilege! Nice work this week, Chet."

As Chet exited his office, Dr. Sheridan picked up the phone and dialed Cheryl's office extension.

"Cheryl Baker's office. May I help you, Dr. Sheridan?" answered her assistant.

"I need to speak to Cheryl."

"I'm sorry, sir. Cheryl is on her way to the airport."

"Do you know where she's going?"

"Yes. She is going to Maine. Would you like me to get her a message?"

Dr. Sheridan smiled. "No, that won't be necessary, thank you," he said, hanging up. Leaning back in his office chair and kicking his feet up on the desk, he gloated and said to himself, "See, my motivational strategy does work."

CHAPTER 24

Having returned from their emotional visit to the park, Jackie felt spent. She felt lost and torn between the joy of her daughter's first words and the despair that Stu was not there to witness it. Her mother had returned home, and Ashley, now liberated from her stroller, was crawling along the living room floor, babbling to herself. Jackie folded herself onto the couch with a cup of coffee, trying to stave off the overwhelming desire to take a nap. As she sat watching Ash and replaying her daughter's first words in her head, her phone announced an incoming text.

"How are you doing, Jackie?" read the message from Curt.

She was surprised how this simple question from Curt at that very moment seemed to lift her out of the gloom that had descended upon her.

"Feel like I've been on a roller-coaster," she texted back.

"I know the feeling. I thought you were very brave on today's call."

Brave was the last thing Jackie would have called it. She had felt like a blubbering idiot, and Curt's characterization, so diametrically opposite her perception, gave her pause.

"Thanks. It didn't feel like brave to me."

"Not easy sharing information like that. I don't know that I could have done it."

Before she could respond, Curt sent a follow-up text.

"Where on your roller-coaster ride are you now?"

"Ash said mama today," Jackie wrote, not sure she wanted to get into all the conflicting feelings that she experienced afterward.

"Wow, that's great!"

"Yeah, it was, but," she typed but couldn't get herself to finish the sentence and send it off. After a minute, Curt sent a follow-up text.

"Calli and I always had mixed feelings when the kids hit milestones. Happy for the accomplishment but sad that they were growing up too fast. You?"

"You are very wise," she texted and sent back. Before Curt could respond, she sent a follow-up.

"Devastated that Stu wasn't there to hear her."

Her text hit home with Curt, and for a moment, he lost himself in thought about milestones Caitlin and Cade would achieve in the absence of their mother.

"I'm sorry, Jackie. Again, I know the feeling."

"How do you deal with it?" Jackie questioned.

"I've had help," Curt started, thinking about all the times that Counselor Tim had to pick him up and help him put back the pieces.

"Family?" she wrote.

"Yes, them too, but I've been seeing a counselor. He has really helped."

"Maybe I should consider seeing a counselor."

"I was nervous at first, but now I wouldn't hesitate to recommend it. He saved my life."

"I'm glad you texted me," Jackie wrote, "you may not be a counselor, but this is therapeutic."

Curt's mind drifted to his rendezvous with Chelsea when she had convinced him that visiting her would be more therapeutic than going to see his counselor. Then his mind went to the night he and the kids had met Jackie at the Farrisport Inn. Skipping his counseling session to be with Chelsea had been a mistake. Meeting Jackie and that magical dinner that had seemed to lift Curt and his kids out of their despair had been therapeutic.

"You've been no less therapeutic," he responded.

"How so?" she texted back, surprised that anyone could derive anything therapeutic from her dismal and erratic moods over the last few months.

"Remember our Table for Four dinner?"

"Of course, how could I ever forget?" she replied, thinking back on how that dinner gave her a much-needed reprieve from the gut-wrenching concern and anger she was experiencing from Stu's outburst earlier that day.

"That dinner was a turning point for me," Curt began, not exactly sure how to describe the impact of that evening. "Anger that I was feeling just disappeared, and it was the first time my kids seemed back to normal," he added.

When Jackie read this, she realized that they had both been saviors for one another that night.

"And you and the kids did the same for me. That was the day of Stu's outburst. I think I would have gone crazy if that hostess hadn't made that mistake."

Both paused, fully recognizing for the first time how fate had blessed them.

"Where would we be if we hadn't met?" Curt asked.

"I don't even want to think about that," Jackie replied.

"Let's not then. You going to be OK?"

"Now, I am. Thanks! And you?"

"Yeah, me too. Thanks!"

Curt and Jackie resolved to stay in touch by text, both feeling an injection of hope and energy that wasn't there before their electronic communication. Jackie picked herself off the couch, corraled Ash, who was about to crawl out of eyesight, and committed the rest of the afternoon to search for a job.

CHAPTER 25

DA Wydman finally found a free 30-minutes on Attorney General Lewis Talcott's calendar, and he, along with Inspector Adams, and Medical Examiner Dr. Louis Corpisen, settled around the small conference table in the AG's office.

"Lew, I thought it important that the three of us have an audience with you on recent developments," DA Wydman prefaced.

"Before we get into that," the AG interrupted. "I just received a response to the letter I sent AlzCura requesting information on Darius' involvement in clinical trials."

"Well, it's about time," Will remarked. "What did they say?"

"Not much. They said Darius Scott was enrolled in their Recallamin 2 clinical trial but had not taken any medications."

"What else?" Will asked.

"That was it."

"That was it? But if he was in a clinical trial, wouldn't they have given him something, even if it was just a, what do you call it?"

"A placebo?" offered Dr. Corpisen.

"Yeah, a placebo?" confirmed DA Wydman.

CHRIS BLIERSBACH

"Apparently, they did not feel the need to expound on that," AG Talcott replied.

"I smell a skunk," DA Wydman remarked. "Do you buy that response, Lew?"

"I have to admit, I was surprised by the brevity of the response. But then again, if Darius wasn't given the medication, what else would they be required to write?"

"You've got a point," Will agreed.

"Lew?" Dr. Corpisen interjected. "Did they say "medications" in their response?"

"Yes, why?"

"Did your letter to them ask for medications, vaccines, or both?" Dr. Corpisen asked, answering a question with another question.

"I don't recall," AG Talcott replied. "Let me pull up my original letter."

AG Talcott went to his desk, fired up his computer, and located the file containing the original letter he had sent Alz-Cura.

"My letter just asks about medications."

"Recallamin is a vaccine," Dr. Corpisen informed the group. "Technically, a vaccine is not classified as a medication. Perhaps the brevity of their response is because we didn't ask about vaccines."

Both AG Talcott and DA Wydman rolled their eyes simultaneously, recognizing that even though AlzCura likely knew what they were asking for, their legal department responded to the actual request, not the intent. There was nothing wrong with this, and any reputable legal department would do the same, but the fact that it took them nearly two months to respond left a bad taste in their mouths.

"Thanks, Louis," AG Talcott replied. "That's pretty embarrassing. I guess the only good thing is that you were here to catch my mistake. I'll write another letter, but this time, I'll have you review it before I send it," he said, pointing to Dr. Corpisen.

"Thank you, Lew. Nothing to be embarrassed about. Very few people understand the distinction between vaccines and medications."

"Yes, but it delays one of the many unanswered questions we have surrounding Darius' death. Since I have to rewrite my letter, I guess I can now also ask about Elvira's participation in clinical trials and whether she was given the vaccine."

The three others around the table nodded their heads.

"Now, let's get to the reason you set up this meeting with me."

DA Wydman set the stage.

"We know that two important events converge next week, our meeting with representatives from the National Association for the Mentally Ill and Office of Advocacy concerning Elvira's complaint, followed by the public release of Elvira and Darius's autopsy results. We wanted to have this meeting to make sure we have a game plan for how to handle the questions that will invariably be raised."

DA Wydman, Theo Adams, and Dr. Corpisen took turns informing the AG of the current evidence. All this pointed not only to the potential harm AlzCura's Recallamin vaccine was causing but also the likelihood that Dr. Caron's suicide was staged to hide a murder.

"Still not enough evidence, gentleman," AG Talcott counseled. "Unless we have definitive evidence to bring charges, all this information needs to be considered as work-product of an ongoing investigation, and thereby not available for our response to NAMI or the media."

"We know that, Lew," DA Wydman replied. "Theo will be

completing his review of the 50 additional files in evidence and following up on the two sets of unidentified prints."

"And since I haven't been able to get a hold of Norman Boulanger by phone, I plan to drive over to his home tomorrow," added Inspector Adams.

"What efforts have we made to follow-up with AlzCura to find and speak with the woman pictured with Dr. Caron in compromising positions?" AG Talcott probed.

"Margo," Theo offered.

"Yes, Margo," the AG replied. "Do we have a last name?

"No last name," DA Wydman responded, "but she was filling in for AlzCura's regular pharmaceutical representative, Jackie Deno, who was on maternity leave. I have been in communication with Jackie, who is no longer employed with Alz-Cura. I will see if I can get additional information from her."

"Do that," AG Talcott directed. "Since we don't have any criminal evidence against Margo, she's a person of interest. The best we can do is ask AlzCura to make her available for questioning. One more thing I can add to my letter to them."

"OK, we will try to tie up as many loose ends as possible before next week's meetings, Lew," DA Wydman promised. "But what I'm hearing is that we will likely just dribble the ball down the court some more with NAMI and the media and tell them that these cases are still under investigation. They won't be pleased."

"I know," AG Talcott acknowledged. "The good news about that, however, is that NAMI and our friends in the media will predictably make a big to-do and that often brings things to light that we weren't privy to before."

"Yeah," DA Wydman added, "they have more latitude to throw around allegations and rumors. As much as the media is a pain in my ass, their reporters playing junior detectives and the court of public opinion can sometimes be our friend."

"Unless more definitive evidence comes to light," AG Talcott concluded, "We may need to invite more acronyms to our party."

"Like the FDA?" DA Wydman offered.

"Yep, and maybe even the FBI," added AG Talcott. "If some of our suspicions are true, then this involves many more States than just good ol' Maine."

AG Talcott thanked the group for the briefing and recommended that they reconvene the following week for an update before the scheduled meetings with NAMI and the media.

CHAPTER 26

Inspired from his text communication with Jackie, Curt called from the landing to Caitlin and Cade, who were still playing with friends on the playground.

"Awww, Dad, can't we play a little longer?" Caitlin whined in response.

Anticipating this response, Curt had a trump card.

"Let's go out to dinner tonight," he called back.

"Can Jordan come?" was Caitlin's predictable response.

"Yes. Now get up here and get cleaned up so we can go out."

Caitlin, Cade, and Jordan needed no further encouragement. Their race up the three flights of stairs sounded like a herd of elephants approaching. Bursting into the apartment and breathless, Caitlin sought to influence the dinner plans.

"Dad, let's go to the Farrisport Inn," Caitlin gasped.

"Take a breath, Caitlin. First things first, did Jordan's mom give her permission to join us?"

Caitlin and Jordan were gone like a shot before he had even completed the question, leaving Cade, who was still trying to catch his breath.

"What do you think, Cade? Do you want to go to the Farrisport Inn?"

Cade vigorously nodded his assent, too winded to put his

response into words. Moments later, the approaching storm of footfalls signaled Caitlin and Jordan's imminent arrival.

"She can go," Caitlin gulped.

"OK, wash up, put some clean clothes on. We're leaving for the Farrisport Inn in 15 minutes."

A chorus of cheers erupted as Curt dialed the restaurant to make a reservation. Curt knew why Caitlin had requested the Farrisport Inn - she lived with the constant hope of meeting Jackie there again. Even though the Farrisport Inn was 45-minutes away, and he knew that Caitlin's wishes would not come true that evening, being there would somehow give him comfort. Fifteen minutes later, the kids had piled into the car, armed with toys to amuse themselves on the ride.

"Do you think we'll see Jackie?" Caitlin asked 10 minutes into the trip.

"I don't think so, honey," Curt responded, hoping to manage her expectations.

"If not, we can still leave a bite of our desserts for her, can't we?" asked Cade, referencing a tradition they had started.

"Yes, you can leave a bite of your desserts. Jackie would appreciate that," he said, happy that they seemed to share his desire to relive their first meeting.

Caitlin and Cade were only too happy to fill Jordan in on Jackie, which was a perfect accompaniment to Curt's replaying their recent text communications.

Dinner did not disappoint. Hostess Brittany correctly asked, "Table for Four?" and seated them at "their table" next to the fireplace, allowing Jordan to occupy what was considered Jackie's chair. For dessert, Caitlin ordered her Crème Brulee and Cade his Chocolate Cake with Ice Cream, observing their tradition in honor of Jackie. Jordan, who had never been there, was amazed about everything and couldn't stop thanking Curt for letting her join them. Curt even splurged and let the kids pick out toys at the store adjacent to the Inn. All three kids fell asleep on the trek back home.

Between Curt's communication with Jackie and dinner with the kids, he had forgotten about his emotional therapy session and the momentary fear he felt while waiting to pick the kids up at school. It was a great start to the weekend.

CHAPTER 27

Inspector Adams arrived at his office early Monday morning, ready to dive into the 50 records that had been removed from Dr. Caron's office. If all went as planned, he hoped to complete the record review by mid-afternoon, leaving time for him to drive to Norman Boulanger's home. That Darius and Elvira Scott's files were missing was no mystery. Who Norman Boulanger was and why his record was missing was very much a mystery.

As Adams settled in surrounded by four stacks of records, an office assistant poked her head into his office.

"Inspector Adams. I have a subpoena here."

"Thanks," he said, getting up and meeting the assistant halfway.

"Damn," he cursed, realizing that the subpoena was for the 44 records that Rebecca had identified at Dr. Caron's office.

"Is there something I can do?" the assistant offered, recognizing that he wasn't delighted to get what she had delivered.

"Yes, as a matter of fact," he replied. "Let me make one quick call."

As the assistant waited patiently, Inspector Adams called Rebecca.

"Hi Rebecca, this is Inspector Adams."

"Hi, what can I do for you?"

"I just received the subpoena for those 44 records you identified last week. If I send an officer over there with the subpoena, could you have the files ready for him? I was hoping to review them today."

"Sure, I should be able to have them ready in about 30 minutes."

"Great, thanks, Rebecca."

Hanging up, Inspector Adams instructed the assistant to have an officer deliver the subpoena to Rebecca, assist her in loading the records into the cruiser, and delivering the files to his office. As the assistant made her exit, he sat down heavily in his chair as if carrying the weight of the additional records he needed to review.

Opening the first record, he familiarized himself with its contents which included: a clinical trial screening form, a signed informed consent form, a hefty document outlining in detail the research protocol applicable to the patient, a medication administration record, and handwritten notes that looked like a record of the patient's office visits. Helpfully, the screening form identified the clinical trial the patient was enrolled in. As the file he was reviewing wasn't related to any of the Recallamin trials, he resolved to first sort through the files to identify only those pertaining to Recallamin.

As he rifled through each record, he noticed to his frustration that there was no consistent organization of the information. In some files, the screening form was in the front, other times somewhere in the middle, and occasionally at the end, slowing the progress of his review.

The sorting process took the better part of an hour, after which he had identified 18 records related to Recallamin trials. As he had combed through the files, he noticed that some had additional or different forms. He realized that without knowing what the records were supposed to contain, it would be hard for him to determine if parts of these files were missing or removed. He realized that he would likely need to meet with Rebecca again to get a better understanding of the documentation requirements.

Focusing on the 18 records related to Recallamin trials, he began reviewing the contents of each file in detail. After the third record, he recognized that the research protocol, the most voluminous and time-consuming document to read, was the same in all files. Eliminating reading the research protocol reduced his review time significantly, and within an hour, he completed the review of the remaining 15 files.

Consulting his notes from the review, the only notable pattern that jumped out at him was that 10 of the 18 records contained a Vaccine Adverse Event Reporting System (VAERS) form. While VAERS forms were found across patients in all three Recallamin clinical trials, what was concerning was that the description of the adverse events and their outcomes were all the same. The ten patients all experienced the same symptoms - jaundiced skin and eyes, abdominal pain, nausea, vomiting, severe headaches, dilated pupils, eye pain, and outbursts of aggressive behavior. Box 21 of the form told the haunting story. All had the same three boxes checked - Emergency room/department or urgent care; Hospitalization; and Patient died. Each of these 10 files also included notes from Dr. Caron indicating that he had reported the adverse event to Dr. Asa Sheridan, CEO AlzCura Pharmaceuticals. In addition, each of the 10 adverse events noted that the patient had been admitted to Dracut-Campion Regional Medical Center, giving Adams another source of information. He made a note to remind himself to request a subpoena for the hospital records.

Inspector Adams did some quick calculations on his notepad. So far, he knew of 12 patients in Dr. Caron's Recallamin trials that had died - the ten he just reviewed and Darius and Elvira Scott. Although he still needed to evaluate the 44 records Rebecca was sending over, if none of them died, 12 out of

64 total Recallamin patients represented a 19% mortality rate - nearly 1 in every 5 patients. That seemed high, but he had no reference point upon which to judge. Until he realized he had 32 records he hadn't reviewed that were from different clinical trials.

Although it was nearly lunchtime, he dug into the 32 files. The first thing he noticed when he came across an adverse event form was that it was not a VAERS form but entitled instead MedWatch. He surmised that the different form was related to the fact that these records included trials involving medications versus a vaccine. However, the content of the MedWatch form was comparable to the VAERS form. Within 30 minutes, he had found only 3 records with MedWatch forms, and none of the events had resulted in death. Despite his tabletop comparison, he knew that he would need to re-view his findings with Rebecca and Dr. Corpisen before coming to any conclusions.

As he was debating about taking a break for a late lunch, an officer arrived carrying a banker box.

"The records from Dr. Caron's office?" he questioned.

"Yes, sir," the officer replied. "I have two more boxes in the cruiser."

Inspector Adams accompanied the officer to retrieve the two remaining boxes. He decided against a late lunch in favor of trying to review the remaining files in the hopes of still making his planned visit to Norman Boulanger.

Now well-acquainted with the Recallamin records, he could quickly comb through the 44 files from Dr. Caron's office. By mid-afternoon, he had completed his review and found an additional 4 VAERS forms. These adverse events, however, had not resulted in death, and the reported symptoms were far less severe, resulting only in a visit to Dr. Caron's office. Unlike the prior forms he had reviewed, these had fax cover pages attached and a confirmation page indicating the form was transmitted to the Department of Health and Human Services. Unlike the previous files with adverse events, there were no notes from Dr. Caron contacting Dr. Sheridan. Maybe Dr. Caron only had to report to Dr. Sheridan when an adverse event resulted in death, he surmised. But why didn't the adverse events resulting in death have corresponding fax cover pages and confirmations? With no apparent explanation, he put his questions on hold until he could meet with Rebecca and Dr. Corpisen.

Anxious to solve the riddle, which was Norman Boulanger, Inspector Adams boxed up the records, found a cart, and transported them back to the secure evidence room. On the drive to Mr. Boulanger's house, he called to brief DA Wydman on his findings and plan to review them with Rebecca and Dr. Corpisen.

"Good job, Theo. I'm with you. Not submitting adverse events resulting in death sounds highly irregular, but I'm no clinical research expert. Maybe the calls to Dr. Sheridan resulted in an alternate reporting process managed by AlzCura? I don't know. Go ahead and set up a meeting with Louie and the Office Manager as soon as possible."

"I will. I also faxed you the names of 10 patients to include on the subpoena for Dracut-Campion Regional's records."

"Got it," DA Wydman confirmed, reaching over to grab the fax his assistant had recently placed on the corner of his desk. "I'll take care of this right away."

"Thanks, Will. I'll let you know what I learn from Norman Boulanger."

"Sounds good, Theo."

Inspector Adams knew from Mr. Boulanger's address that he lived in the trailer park on the outskirts of town. It was a rare day when the police did not have to visit the park to respond to some type of disturbance. Although Boulanger was a relatively common last name in the community populated predominantly with people of French descent, he couldn't help but wonder if Norman was from the family who owned a popular bakery in town. Inspector Adams, who had been unable to reach Mr. Boulanger by phone, felt optimism that he might be home as two vehicles and a motorcycle were parked in the driveway.

As he ascended the steps that led to the door, a dog started barking. Inspector Adams could tell by its bark that it was a small dog. When he knocked on the door, the dogs' yapping got even more urgent.

"Quiet, Sophie," yelled a female voice before the door even opened. Her command was to no avail as, after a short pause, Sophie continued her protest.

As the door opened, Inspector Adams was greeted by a petite young woman with distinctive red hair and mesmerizing green eyes, tainted only by an angry, swollen purplish welt under her left eye.

"Sorry about the dog," she said. "Sophie, quiet!" as the 12-pound Bichon Friese continued her onslaught.

"Hi, ma'am, I'm Inspector Adams," he introduced himself, showing his badge and credentials. "I'm looking for Norman Boulanger. I haven't been able to reach him by phone. Is this the correct address?"

As he was asking his question, the young woman's face and body language expressed the pain each word was causing her. Her eye's teared up, and her face became a mask of despair. As Sophie continued her yapping from a safe distance, the young woman crumpled into his arms, sobbing uncontrollably. At a loss for what to do, he helped her back into her home and settled her into the first chair he could find. With the stranger now in the house, Sophie lost her courage, yipped, and in full retreat mode, scampered down a hallway.

"I'm sorry," the young woman sobbed as he searched for tissues or a towel to offer her.

"If this is a bad time, I could…" he began but was promptly interrupted.

"No, no, please stay," she pleaded between sniffles.

Handing her a paper towel he had found in the kitchen, she struggled to compose herself.

"I'm Celeste. Celeste Boulanger. Norman's wife" only able to get one or two words out as she gulped for air between sobs that were slow to subside.

"I'm sorry, Celeste," Inspector Adams began, now focused on her black-eye and what the story was behind it. "Can I get you something?"

To which she replied in a half-laugh half-sob, "I'm supposed to be the one offering you something. No, thank you. I'll be alright."

He waited until she had dabbed away her tears, and the hitches in her breathing discontinued.

"Now, Inspector Adams," Celeste propped herself up, "what can I do for you?"

"I was hoping to speak with Norman. Is there a better time for me to come back?"

"Norman," Celeste began, as she fought off tears, "died last week at DC Regional."

Inspector Adams found himself apologizing to Celeste again and, biased by the record reviews he had just completed, tried not to jump to conclusions.

"How did he die?"

"They said he died of liver failure and a brain bleed."

As he was formulating how to ask her delicately about whether she had an autopsy done, Celeste had questions of her own.

"Inspector Adams, why did you want to talk to Norman? Was he in some kind of trouble?"

"No, no," he assured her, "I am investigating Dr. Caron's death, and I understand that Norman was in a clinical trial that Dr. Caron was conducting."

"A clinical trial? What's that? And I thought Dr. Caron committed suicide." Celeste asked, taken aback.

Adams was surprised that Celeste was unaware that her husband had been involved in a study. He also realized he would have to proceed cautiously so as not to divulge information in the ongoing investigation of Dr. Caron's death.

"A clinical trial is a study of a medication or vaccine to determine its effectiveness," he replied academically.

"Norman never told me about being in a clinical. What did you call it?"

"A clinical trial."

"Yeah, he never said anything about a clinical trial," she said, her face looking as if it was desperately searching for answers.

Inspector Adams felt at a disadvantage. He was sitting in front of a distraught wife who now had questions about her husbands' involvement in a research study but was severely limited in what he could divulge. He tried to steer the conversation towards safer territory.

"Celeste, I know this must be hard for you," he began, but she wasn't through asking her questions.

"I want to know more about this clinical trial. The people at the hospital never could explain to me why Norman had liver failure or his brain bleed. He was 28-years old, rarely drank, and as healthy as a horse. Then all of a sudden, he complains of headaches, a stomach ache, and has outbursts of anger. That's how I got this black eye, Inspector Adams," she said, pointing to her swollen eye with emphasis and then continued her tirade.

"My sweet, gentle husband," she began, tears filling her

eyes. "Who worshipped the ground I walked on during our 5 years of marriage, hauled off and hit me and then said some of the most vulgar and insensitive things anyone has ever said to me,' she sobbed, tears overflowing their banks.

"It was like someone had flipped a switch, and he was a different person," she cried and struggled to continue. "He was like some zombie, and I feared for my life. Literally, I feared for my life, Inspector Adams. He reminded me of that crazy man who lit that poor woman on fire. I ran out of the house and almost called the police. When I came back, he was passed out on the floor, and his skin looked yellow. I thought he was dead and called an ambulance."

"I've been searching for answers, and no one could give me any. Now you tell me that my Norman was involved in a study I wasn't aware of? I have questions, Inspector Adams. No offense, but my questions are more important than yours," she cried, burying her face in the paper towel he had given her earlier.

As Celeste disintegrated in the chair, he tried to find the few words he could offer to try to comfort her. As he pondered, Sophie made her appearance and jumped up into Celeste's lap.

"Celeste, I want to help you understand why Norman died," he began as she withdrew her face from the towel to look at him. "Have you requested a copy of Norman's medical records from the hospital?"

"No," she snuffled, stroking Sophie's soft white curly hair.

"As part of my investigation, I want to request Norman's record from the hospital and have our experts review it."

"OK," she said tentatively. "Will your experts be able to tell me what they find?"

"Unfortunately, that information would be part of an investigation, and we couldn't release the results to you. I'm sorry."

"Then what good does that do me?" Celeste challenged.

"I can tell you that if our experts do find something unexpected or unusual in your husband's care and our investigation results in criminal charges, we would then share our findings with you. Of course, you could always independently request your husband's records from the hospital and have a physician or a lawyer share their findings with you."

"OK, I hadn't thought about that. Thank you."

"You're welcome, Celeste. And once again, I'm sorry to have had to upset you like this."

"I'm sorry I've been such a blubbering idiot," she replied, looking as though she was about to break into tears again.

Handing her his card, he encouraged her to call him with any information. He made his exit, but not before Sophie added her own barking adieu. Once settled in his car, he called DA Wydman and asked him to add Norman Boulanger's name to the subpoena for the hospital records.

CHAPTER 28

C heryl Baker, AlzCura's Vice President of Operations, landed at the Portland Jetport Friday evening, still fuming about Dr. Sheridan's interactions with her that afternoon. That he would even question her commitment and judgment was insult enough. Doing it in front of Chet, Alz-Cura's Chief Legal Counsel, made it worse and made her furious.

While it had been at least a decade since she made physician sales visits, she knew the critical importance of shoring up the Northeast region's Recallamin business, particularly in Central Maine. Dr. Caron had been one of AlzCura's most prolific research coordinators, and finding a replacement who was as ambitious and as flexible would be hard. Filling Jackie's position, their superstar pharmaceutical representative, had also proven to be difficult.

The only news that buoyed Cheryl's spirit was an email from her assistant confirming a mid-morning meeting with Dr. Preston Slack. Dr. Slack was the most senior member of one of Portland's two neurology groups. Her assistant had also succeeded in scheduling a dinner meeting with Dr. Stephanie Mason, the most senior member of the other Portland neurology group. Both had been strong proponents of Recallamin, but Cheryl was uncertain whether they had the necessary attributes that made Dr. Caron successful. Nor was she sure that either group had the desire or bandwidth to expand their practices to Central Maine. The politics of trying to influence physician resources anywhere was always dicey. This was no less the case in Central Maine, where Dracut-Campion Regional Medical Center fiercely tried to protect against losing patients to the Portland and Bangor markets. Asking a prominent Neurology group to expand into Central Maine would be as welcome to Dracut-Campion Regional as a skunk walking backward into a garden party.

Too angry and tired to go out to dinner, Cheryl elected to check into her hotel and order room service. Flipping on the TV and making herself comfortable, she opened the minibar, delighted to find her drink of choice. Pulling two miniature Maker's Mark bottles out, she quickly poured them into the hotel-supplied tumbler and took a healthy swig. Her irritation began to evaporate as the familiar oaky vanilla and caramel flavor enveloped her in its warm embrace. Kicking off her shoes and settling onto the couch, she perused the room service menu. She called to order a cup of lobster bisque and the Sebago Lake Landlocked Atlantic Salmon. Surprised to find her tumbler empty, she grabbed two more nips. While she was admiring the Portland skyline and Casco Bay from her hotel room window, a TV announcer caught her attention.

"The State Attorney General's office has scheduled a meeting next Thursday to brief members of the media on the long-awaited autopsy results of Darius and Elvira Scott," said the buxom reporter standing outside a 6-story officious gray building that Cheryl presumed was where the Attorney General's office was located.

What struck Cheryl first was not so much the information the reporter was conveying but the reporters' wardrobe, which would have looked more appropriate on a streetwalker.

"Jeez, what the hell is she trying to sell?" Cheryl said to herself.

"Leslie," the news anchor interjected, "has the Attorney General's Office given you any explanation as to why releasing these results is so late in coming?"

"Well, Jeff," Leslie said with a smirk, "they have been very tight-lipped about it, and I can only surmise that the autopsy results contain information that they would rather not divulge. As you know, before Elvira Scott's untimely death, she had filed complaints against the Harlow Psychiatric Institute and the Medical Examiner's Office, claiming that her son Darius died due to medications he was given at HPI. Medications that Ms. Scott claimed the Medical Examiner's Office then conspired to cover-up."

"Interesting," the news anchor intoned dramatically, "Well, I know you'll be right on top of it, pumping them for information next Thursday. Thank you, Leslie."

"You're welcome, Jeff. This is Leslie Anderson, senior investigative correspondent reporting to you live for Channel 5 news," she concluded with an air of importance. Before the shot cut back to the studio, Leslie flipped her blond tresses, and the cameraman gratuitously zoomed in on Leslie and her considerable cleavage.

"Well, we won't want to miss Leslie's report next Thursday, will we, Cindy?" Jeff posed to his female co-anchor.

"Absolutely not, Jeff," she responded, her facetious tone and facial expression conveying that Cindy was not a willing partner in Leslie's and the station's soft-porn news approach.

Cheryl would have laughed if she hadn't found the news of the upcoming media event so disturbing. She drained her second drink and debated whether to call Dr. Sheridan. As she weighed the pros and cons, a knock on her door announced room service had arrived. By the time she had enjoyed her dinner and another drink, her decision whether to call Dr. Sheridan was made for her - she passed out on the couch.

She woke up with a start in the middle of the night bleary-eyed as a salesman on the TV extolled the virtues of a robust and waterproof adhesive. Finding the remote buried in between the couch cushions, she turned off the TV, trudged to the bed, and slept another 5 hours.

Waking up with a pounding headache, she found the Tylenol in her purse, drank the entire complimentary water bottle, and called room service for a pot of coffee. Recalling the news from the previous evening, she tried to remember whether she had called Dr. Sheridan. Scanning her recent calls and not finding any to Dr. Sheridan, she made the call.

"Good morning, Cheryl," Dr. Sheridan answered.

"Not really, Asa," she responded.

"Why? Too much lobster and Maker's Mark last night?" he exclaimed, knowing her drinking habits.

"Not that, Asa. The Maine AGs office is briefing the media this coming Thursday on the results of the Darius and Elvira Scott autopsy results."

"Yes, that could be a problem. It's a good thing that Elvira's complaint names that psychiatric hospital and the medical examiner's office as the source of her son's death. That should keep them off our scent."

"I'm just concerned the AG will implicate AlzCura. They know that Darius was involved in one of our clinical trials."

"Yes, and they apparently also know that Elvira was as well," Dr. Sheridan added.

"What?" Cheryl shouted, "How do you know that?"

"I received a letter from the AG's office yesterday. He clarified their original request for information on Darius, adding a request for information on Elvira and asking that we make Margo available."

"Asa, this is not good. What are we going to do?"

"I was going to meet with Chet next week about the letter,

but given the information you just shared, I will call him today. When are you coming back from Maine?

"Tomorrow."

"Good. Let's meet first thing Monday morning."

As they ended their call, room service knocked.

"Good morning, ma'am," greeted the waitperson much more brightly than Cheryl was feeling. "I have your coffee here and a complimentary copy of the newspaper."

"Thank you," she replied stiffly as the front-page headline screamed out what she already knew.

"AG to Release Highly Anticipated Autopsy Results," it read, accompanied by pictures of Darius and Elvira Scott.

Before she could even think to pour the coffee, she skimmed the lead article. Thankfully, it contained mostly a re-hash of information that was public knowledge, with nothing suggesting Darius or Elvira's participation in AlzCura studies. What concerned her, however, was the media's voracious appetite for answers and the difficulty that posed for managing the story and keeping AlzCura out of the spotlight.

A couple of cups of coffee and a long shower later, Cheryl felt more prepared to face the day. Reviewing the file on Casco Bay Neurology Associates in preparation for her meeting with Dr. Slack, she tried to anticipate the types of questions he would raise. She could anticipate questions about Jackie's leaving the company but felt confident that the notice she had sent to all the physicians in the region had likely quelled their concerns. What she was less sure about was the group's experience and opinion of Recallamin. Dr. Caron had been a Recallamin champion and could be easily convinced to follow AlzCura's novel research protocols. AlzCura did not have the relationship or financial investment in Dr. Slack's group as they had with Dr. Caron. Picking up the file for her meeting with Dr. Stephanie Mason, she realized the same could be said for Cumberland County Neurology Partners. Although Cheryl hoped to find a replacement for Dr. Caron, she realized that it was prudent to lower her expectations for what she could accomplish in this brief visit. Reassure them, show them how to improve their bottom line, and thank them, she recited to herself. If nothing else, Cheryl's strength was reducing a complicated conversation down to its essential elements. This skill had gotten her to where she was today, and she wasn't going to deviate from it today.

"Dr. Slack, thank you so much for agreeing to meet with me on such short notice," Cheryl crooned.

"Oh, my pleasure, Ms. Baker," replied the graying but physically fit principle physician of Casco Bay Neurology Associates.

"Oh, please, call me Cheryl," she prompted. "I just wanted to follow up on the letter I sent you recently about Jackie's departure."

"You sent a letter?" Dr. Slack questioned. "I was wondering why Jackie hadn't been back to visit. I got a thank you card from her for the gift we sent for her baby, but then nothing. My staff must have weeded your letter out of my inbox. I never saw it."

"Oh, I am so sorry, Dr. Slack," Cheryl said with as much genuine concern as she could muster.

"Well, that's disheartening," as Dr. Slack's face registered his disappointment. "She's the only pharmaceutical rep I would agree to meet with. All the others that descend upon our practice, I pawn off to my junior associates. I give them strict instructions to listen politely for 10 minutes, feign a patient care responsibility, take their card, and tell them you'll get back to them after speaking with me. No offense, but if I gave every rep as much time as I used to give Jackie, we'd have no practice!"

"I understand. Jackie was an extraordinary rep, and I said

as much in the letter you didn't get. Unfortunately, between motherhood and her ultimate career aspirations, she decided to move on. I'm happy for her, but it's not uncommon for these rep positions to be a stepping-stone to greater opportunities."

"Well, I think I still have her home address from her thank you card. I will have to write her a letter of thanks and good luck in her future endeavors."

To which Cheryl had no comment, hoping Dr. Slack either misplaced Jackie's home address or would be too busy to follow through writing the letter.

"How are your Recallamin patients doing?" Cheryl asked, trying to transition to a safer topic.

"I have a few who are doing really well, but others who are not."

"Tell me more," Cheryl prompted.

"Our older patients, with definitive signs of dementia, are actually doing better than our 40-59-year-old Recallamin 2 trial patients. We've had a few patients in the Recallamin 2 trial with abnormal liver function test results. I have one in the hospital right now that is in restraints after he got aggressive and injured two nurses. I doubt he will make it."

"Have you discussed this with Dr. Sheridan?"

"Yes, and Dr. Sheridan and I are at loggerheads about the disposition of these cases."

Not comfortable discussing clinical matters and too wise to get in the middle of a dispute between Dr. Sheridan and Dr. Slack, Cheryl punted.

"Well, I understand your concern, but I'm sure you and Dr. Sheridan will be able to iron things out. Have you enrolled any Recallamin 3 trial patients?"

"I'm hesitant to do so until I'm comfortable with the safety of the dose for our Recallamin 2 patients."

"Any other concerns?" Cheryl asked, hoping to sound like she was committed to reassuring him of the safety of their vaccine.

"Well, yes. Now that you mention it. Dr. Caron called and left a message that he wanted to talk to me about some concerns about Recallamin."

"Really?" Cheryl responded with surprise but trying not to appear as concerned as she really felt.

"Yes, but he committed suicide before we could ever connect. I just keep on wondering what it was he was concerned about."

"Yes, Dr. Caron's suicide was tragic. It's curious he would call you with concerns. He never expressed any concerns to us, quite the opposite," she lied, hoping to alleviate Dr. Slack's anxiety.

"Hmmm," Dr. Slack pondered, "you know, perhaps I'll just call Dr. Mason and see what her groups' experience has been."

"That's a good idea," Cheryl responded, grasping at straws as she didn't want to sound defensive but had no idea what Dr. Mason's group would say.

Cheryl felt like she had not accomplished any of the three things she hoped to achieve in her visit with Dr. Slack. His surprise about Jackie's departure, even if due to his staff being over-zealous about screening his mail, had gotten the meeting off on the wrong foot. The concerns about his Recallamin 2 patients and being at odds with Dr. Sheridan didn't help matters. Exploring the possibility of his group's interest in expanding to cover the Central Maine region was a giant leap she wasn't about to try to make. Cheryl decided to try to make the best of it.

"I know you may be too busy, but could I take you to lunch?" she asked, hoping he'd appreciate the gesture, knowing and more than half wishing he'd decline.

"Oh, thank you, Cheryl, but I do have patients to see."

"I understand. We do so appreciate you and your group's dedication and support. I promise I will have a replacement for Jackie soon. Until then, you should feel free to call me," she said, handing him her card. "Would you like me to convey anything to Dr. Sheridan?"

"No, that won't be necessary. I'm hoping to get on Dr. Sheridan's calendar soon to, as you say, iron things out. Thank you for visiting, Cheryl. At least now I understand why we haven't seen Jackie."

Cheryl put on her best and brightest disposition as they said their farewells. This, despite the gloom that had progressively descended upon her during the meeting. Not only had she failed to accomplish her mission, but Dr. Slack's concerns and potential for poisoning Dr. Mason's opinion of Recallamin represented a real threat. Not to mention the possibility that he would correspond with Jackie and learn the truth about her dismissal should she fail to observe the confidentiality clause in her separation agreement. Cheryl's hope now rested on Dr. Stephanie Mason's group having a favorable assessment of Recallamin to allay Dr. Slacks' concerns should he call her as he mentioned.

Cheryl held an internal debate as she made her way to the Old Port waterfront for a light lunch. Should she call Dr. Sheridan now to report Dr. Slack's concerns or wait until after she had met with Dr. Mason? Electing to delay her call to Dr. Sheridan, she ventured into a converted ferry boat restaurant. Placed at a table with a view of the bay, she tried to forget the unsuccessful visit with Dr. Slack and lose herself in the quintessential picture-postcard scenery. But her mind was as blustery as the waves buffeting the boats in the bay. Shifting to Plan B, Cheryl ordered a double Maker's Mark straight up to accompany her Lobster Roll. While she waited for her food and the elixir she hoped would work magic, she opened the file on

Dr. Mason to prepare for their dinner meeting.

At first blush, the file on Dr. Mason and her group looked promising. Dr. Mason was a well-trained Neurologist who was half Dr. Slack's age. She had assembled a similarly youthful and well-trained group of physicians, and over the last couple of years, grew the practice so that it was now comparable in size and patient volume to Dr. Slack's group. Cheryl knew that what younger physicians sometimes lacked in experience, they often made up for in ambition and willingness to try new things. Dr. Caron had been the perfect example of this, and she hoped that she might find the next Dr. Caron in Dr. Mason's group. Armed with this optimism and sated from her lunch and the drink, she felt so relaxed that she decided to go back to the hotel for a nap rather than explore the multiple shops that lined the aptly named Commercial Street.

Refreshed from her nap and hopeful that her meeting with Dr. Mason would be more fruitful, she walked to the restaurant just 3 blocks from her hotel. Meeting Dr. Mason at the hostess station, they shared a cordial greeting as the hostess escorted them to their dinner table. The optimism Cheryl felt about Dr. Mason and her group, however, was quickly extinguished and put Cheryl on the immediate defensive.

"Dr. Slack called me this afternoon after your visit with him." Dr. Mason divulged.

"He mentioned that he might do that," Cheryl replied, trying to hide her surprise and concern.

"I have to say, Cheryl, I harbor similar concerns."

With the hope that Dr. Mason may be able to assuage Dr. Slack's concerns dashed, Cheryl once again found herself in an awkward position.

"I'm sorry to hear that. Tell me more."

Before Dr. Mason could respond, a waiter came to take their drink orders. Although Cheryl wanted something stronger, she deferred to Dr. Mason's suggestion to order a bottle of wine. It would be one of the few things the two agreed upon that evening.

While Dr. Mason had received Cheryl's letter about Jackie's departure, she launched into an unexpected direction.

"My biggest concern is about Recallamin, but before I get to that, I also have concerns about Jackie's departure. Jackie was great, and I was not surprised to hear she was pursuing other career opportunities. My concern is for the caliber of her replacement. If she is going to be replaced by that woman that visited during Jackie's maternity leave, that's a problem. My apologies, but I can't even remember her name. She was that forgettable."

"You mean Alexis?" Cheryl slipped, the stress of the moment causing her to forget her daughter's alias.

"No, I don't remember that name," Dr. Mason replied as a confused look crossed her face.

"I mean, Margo," Cheryl recovered.

"Yes, Margo." Dr. Mason confirmed. "She was totally useless, and that infernal ya know phrase like she was some California valley girl. God, she was irritating. One of my physicians even thought that she was coming on to him. Entirely inappropriate and unprofessional."

"I agree, Dr. Mason, and I'm sorry. We fired Margo shortly after that."

"Well, that's good to hear."

"I assure you, we will find a replacement of Jackie's caliber," she promised.

Having somewhat dodged Dr. Mason's first bullet, Cheryl knew that Dr. Mason would bring out the heavy artillery next - her concerns about Recallamin. Cheryl felt like a lamb led to the slaughter.

Before Dr. Mason could continue, the waiter returned with

the bottle of wine. The process of uncorking the wine, pouring Dr. Mason a sample, and having her sip and approve the wine felt like a stay of execution to Cheryl.

Gaining Dr. Mason's approval of the wine, the waiter poured a glass for both women and suggested a couple of appetizers. Typically, Cheryl enjoyed the opportunity to extend physician dinner visits out over several courses. Tonight, she was only too happy to agree with Dr. Mason's declination of appetizers.

"Preston shared his concerns about Recallamin and the abnormal liver function tests," she began.

Her use of Dr. Slack's first name tipping Cheryl off that today was likely not the first time the physicians had communicated with one another."

"And did he tell you that he and Dr. Sheridan were in discussions about his concerns?"

"He did, but discussions or not, lab results don't lie. We've had a few patients in our practice as well. Not as many as Preston's group, but now that I know about his concerns, I'm going to ask Dr. Sheridan to include me in the conversation."

"That's good. I was going to suggest that. Have you had any successes with Recallamin?" Cheryl replied, trying to shift the conversation to a more positive track.

"Oh sure, we've had a few patients do well, particularly our more elderly patients in the original Recallamin trial."

"You know, Dr. Mason, I'd like to congratulate you on steadily and successfully growing your practice here over the last few years. Very impressive. Any thought of expanding into the Central Maine region?" she ventured in an attempt to steer the conversation towards finding a replacement for Dr. Caron.

"Well, thank you. It has certainly not been without its challenges. As for expansion, Preston and I have had initial conversations about merging our practices after he retires. But expansion to Central Maine has not been on my radar."

"I was just asking because I know they're hurting for neurology coverage and thought it might be an opportunity you might be interested in," Cheryl said, careful not to reference Dr. Caron.

"We're actually getting some of Dr. Caron's patients now, and I believe Preston's group has seen some as well. I'm not particularly interested in having a presence there. Too much travel, and in the end, most of the complex cases come to us anyway."

Even though Dr. Mason had invoked Dr. Caron's name, Cheryl was happy she hadn't mentioned receiving any calls from him as Dr. Slack had. She was wary, however, about pushing the conversation much further. Sometimes planting the seed of an idea was the most successful approach in matters of physician business opportunities.

The rest of their dinner meeting conversation avoided any controversial topics. While Cheryl wouldn't have classified the meeting as a rousing success, it certainly hadn't been a failure. She went back to her hotel, liberated a couple of Maker's Marks miniatures from the mini-bar, and tried not to think about what she would eventually have to tell Dr. Sheridan about the visit.

CHAPTER 29

J ackie, Curt, and Inspector Adams' cell phones simultaneously signaled an incoming text which read: "Watch for
meeting invite in your email. Will"

Jackie received DA Wydman's text in the middle of a call
she received from a Human Resource professional from Nora
Community Hospital. She had called to set up a date and time
for Jackie to interview for their Physician Liaison opening. Of
all the jobs Jackie applied to, this one seemed to make the best
use of the strengths she had honed while at AlzCura.

When Jackie first saw the job, she wasn't sure what the
position entailed. After a bit of research, she learned that hospitals increasingly employed Physician Liaisons to ensure that
the hospital is a physician-friendly and convenient place to
practice. She was surprised to learn that most physicians are
independent contractors who have a choice of which hospitals
in which they choose to work. An effective Physician Liaison
is not only good at schmoozing with physicians but is an expert at reducing the physician's hassle factor when it comes to
working in hospitals, which aren't always models of efficiency.
This seemed right up Jackie's alley.

After arranging her interview for later in the week, Jackie
opened her email to find DA Wydman's invitation for the teleconference scheduled for the following day at noon.

Now that Jackie was fully vested in finding a new job and

was taking a more clandestine approach to the crusade, her guilt about withholding the truth from her parents was replaced with relief that she hadn't needlessly upset them. She was also comforted that there had been no further evidence of AlzCura scare tactics or spying.

❊ ❊ ❊

Curt was at Caitlin and Cade's school for parent-teacher meetings when he received DA Wydman's text. Not only were his kids doing well in school, but there were no repeat incidents of anyone calling the school pretending to be a family member.

Curt was also back to work full-time. He hadn't exercised the option of dissolving the partnership to become an independent contractor as he and his partner Sam Jackson had once discussed. LoriBeth was ecstatic to have him back in the office. Life seemed back to normal, and for this, Curt was grateful.

❊ ❊ ❊

Inspector Adams was in the middle of his meeting with Dr. Corpisen and Rebecca when he received DA Wydman's text. Knowing that a meeting was approaching lent weight to the meeting he was in. He planned to visit the hospital that afternoon to pick up the 11 medical records of Recallamin patients that had been admitted to the hospital and subsequently died from liver failure and brain bleeds.

Rebecca and Dr. Corpisen confirmed Inspector Adam's concerns about the Vaccine Adverse Event Reporting System (VAERS) forms that didn't appear to be transmitted to the Department of Health & Human Services (DHHS) as required.

"I can't believe this. He was so diligent about making sure we reported adverse events," Rebecca exclaimed, making reference to Dr. Caron.

"Yes, this is highly unusual," Dr. Corpisen added. "I can't see any reason why he'd complete a VAERS form, notify Dr. Sheridan at AlzCura, and then not send it."

"Do you think Dr. Sheridan took responsibility for reporting these adverse events?" Adams asked.

"I guess it's possible," Dr. Corpisen posited, "but why don't we see evidence that Dr. Caron transmitted the form to AlzCura? How else would they know what to report? And why have two different systems of reporting? One when the adverse event results in something other than death and another for when a patient dies."

Rebecca sat in stunned silence, now recognizing why Dr. Caron took such an active role in managing clinical trial patient records. He had spurned the idea of hiring a research coordinator to assist him. Now it appeared as though this wasn't due to his dedication to the research as much as his need to hide inconvenient facts.

"Rebecca? You OK?" Inspector Adams asked, pulling her out of her trance.

"No, I'm not," she replied after being brought back to the present. "I was responsible for sending VAERS forms to DHHS when Dr. Caron gave them to me."

"Did you know of clinical trial patients dying?" he asked.

"No. Dr. Caron took a very protective, hands-on approach to the research patients. My job was to pull records, file records, and submit VAERS forms when he requested. I suggested several times that he consider hiring a Research Coordinator to help him. I was concerned about him because he often worked late into the evening," she trailed off as tears brimmed her eyes.

"I think we're done here," Inspector Adams declared. After

thanking Dr. Corpisen and consoling Rebecca, he set off to pick up the hospital records.

Winding his way through the hospitals' circuitous hallways and aided by two staff members along the way, he finally arrived at the Health Information Management department. After confirming his identity, he was surprised when they rolled out a cart containing 4 banker boxes.

"Really?" he exclaimed, "This many boxes for 11 records?"

"Yes, I'm sorry," replied Edna, an elderly woman whose hospital badge announced her position as HIM Tech. "Our electronic records don't print out very well. I'm afraid you'll find them somewhat frustrating to review."

Inspector Adam's plans to review the files before the meeting tomorrow waning with each word Edna spoke. As they wheeled the cart to Inspector Adam's car, Edna regaled him with what could only be described as the miseries of working in her department.

"You'd think computerized records would make things easier and more efficient. But no, no one likes these records. Not the doctors. Not the nurses. Definitely, not those of us in HIM!" she emphasized.

Before he could formulate any response, Edna continued her speech.

"Well, maybe the finance and legal staff like them. The only thing these records are good at is capturing hospital charges and protecting the hospital from any liability by entering boiler-plate legal language on almost every page."

"Uh-huh," was all he could manage before Edna continued her rant.

"All this charting by exception has just made things worse if you ask me. In my day, the saying was, 'If it wasn't documented, it wasn't done.' Now, they say, if it wasn't documented, then everything that was supposed to be done was done. That's dangerous if you ask me."

Mercifully, they had reached Inspector Adams' car. After loading the boxes in his vehicle and allowing Edna to unload her prejudices against computerized records, he made his way back to the office in the hopes of making a dent in the voluminous set of files.

As Edna had predicted, Inspector Adam's review of the medical records was slow going. Unlike the computer version of the records that provided tabs by type of document to ease the search for particular information, the paper records offered no such assistance.

He selected Norman Boulanger's record first. Combing through the 4-inch stack of paper took him the better part of two hours - most of it unenlightening. The only benefit to his slog through Norman's record was finding several helpful documents - the history & physical, Dr. Caron's progress notes, and the discharge summary. The discharge summary, in particular, was the only document he could find that summarized Mr. Boulanger's entire hospital course. It was unfortunate that he spent so much time wading through all the other documents to get to the discharge summary. It chafed him some that he hadn't interrupted Edna's tirade on the state of medical records to ask her advice on finding the record's most useful contents. It would have saved him time.

A review of the remaining ten medical records went more smoothly as Adams concentrated on finding what he considered the most essential information. His task was now more manageable. He felt optimistic that he could complete his review and synthesize his findings before DA Wydman's meeting the next day.

It didn't take Inspector Adams long to find what in legal parlance was the so-called smoking gun. In each of the 11 patient's discharge summaries, Dr. Caron had documented the following:

"Patient was enrolled in Recallamin clinical trial, which may have been a contributing factor to the complaints and symptoms that occasioned this patient's admission and their unfortunate disposition. VAERS form completed (see office record) and principle Study Sponsor, Dr. Asa Sheridan (CEO AlzCura Pharmaceutical) notified."

Dr. Caron's notation in the discharge summary was not definitive proof but drew a clean line that the State or the FDA could trace back to AlzCura Pharmaceutical.

He picked up his phone and called DA Wydman. Although they would not be able to discuss this on their call with Jackie and Curt, they agreed to meet with AG Talcott at his earliest convenience.

CHAPTER 30

C heryl flew back to Buffalo on Sunday, feeling like she had failed miserably in her meetings with Drs. Slack and Mason. Not wishing to incur Dr. Sheridan's wrath, she elected to observe a day of rest on the Sabbath. Although no one, including Cheryl herself, would have described her as the least bit religious.

Instead, she elected to call her daughter Alexis, who was now stationed in AlzCura's Paris office.

"Bonjour Monique," Cheryl greeted, using her daughter's latest alias.

"Hi, Mom! To what do I owe the pleasure?"

"That's a loaded question, Alexis! Hopefully, it's the French doctors."

Alexis laughed. "Frankly, Mom, they're pleased, but they're also pigs, ya know. The food and the wine are great, though!"

"I just wanted to see how you were doing. I visited the doctors in Portland this weekend, and they didn't have much nice to say about you."

"So mission accomplished."

"Yes, you did a masterful job as usual, but without Jackie returning to pick up the pieces, that strategy has backfired. Dr. Mason was furious that you came on to one of her junior physicians."

"Junior is right. I think that man had a size 7 shoe, if ya know what I mean."

"Oh, the horror," Cheryl said dramatically as the two erupted in a cascade of laughter.

"Some people just can't appreciate your talents, sweetheart. You doing alright?" Cheryl asked seriously.

"Yeah, despite the doctor's behavior, our sales are up, ya know. When do you think I can come home?"

"I don't know, honey. Things are heating up in Maine. The AG is meeting with the media later this week to release some information that could raise concerns. Better you stay in Paris for at least a few more weeks."

"OK," Alexis sighed dejectedly. "How are you doing, Mom?"

"I've been better. Asa is acting like an ass lately. As usual, he's worried about everything, and the pressure seems to be getting to him."

"Well, that's nothing new. He has a relief valve, ya know."

"You're right, sweetie. I guess he isn't much different than your French doctors."

"Nope, same pig, different accent," Alexis replied, eliciting another cascade of laughter.

"I love you."

"Je t'aime maman," Alexis replied in French.

The call with her daughter brought Cheryl much-needed relief and a renewed perspective about how to approach Dr. Sheridan. Rather than wait until the meeting with Dr. Sheridan the following day, she punched his number on her phone.

"Hi, Asa. I'm back," she said brightly.

"Good. How did it go?"

"How about I come over there, and we can talk about my

trip while I cook you your favorite meal?

"That sounds great. I'll have the wine ready when you arrive."

"And I'll bring the dessert," she purred sensually.

"Wrapped in my favorite red dress?" he asked, confirming that she had successfully found her way to his heart, and it wasn't through his stomach.

"That could be arranged," she teased.

After a wardrobe change and a stop at the store for a few dinner items, Cheryl arrived at Dr. Sheridan's doorstep wrapped in red. She hardly had time to put the fixings for dinner down on the kitchen counter.

"Let's start with dessert," he said, wrapping her in a hug and immediately unzipping her dress.

They never got to dinner or to how her trip to Maine went, but Cheryl knew that she could relax about tomorrow's meeting. Sated from dessert, Dr. Sheridan rolled over and fell asleep. Cheryl quietly thought of her earlier conversation with her daughter.

"Thanks, Alexis. I found that relief valve," she smiled and drifted off to sleep.

CHAPTER 31

D A Wydman welcomed Jackie, Curt, and Inspector Adams to their second call. He prefaced it by stressing its importance for his meeting with Attorney General Talcott and Dr. Corpisen later that day in preparation for the highly anticipated meeting with the media on Thursday of that week.

"Ladies first," DA Wydman announced. "Jackie, what's new with you since our last meeting?"

"I know this doesn't have anything to do with the purpose of this meeting, but my baby said "Mama" for the first time," she said proudly, as Will, Curt, and Theo echoed their con-gratulations.

"On a more pertinent note, I have an interview for a job this Friday."

"That's great," DA Wydman replied. "Doing what?"

"Physician Liaison at Nora Community Hospital."

"Hmm, I'm not familiar with that job title. What does a Physician Liaison do?"

Jackie educated the three men on the role of the position and how it complemented the skills she developed as a Phar-maceutical Representative at AlzCura.

"That sounds perfect for you, Jackie. Congratulations!"

Curt offered his support.

"Well, I don't have the job yet, but thank you, Curt. I'm excited about it."

"Not to be a fly in the ointment, but will a job in a hospital that entails communicating with doctors be something that will comfort or concern AlzCura executives?" DA Wydman challenged.

Jackie had not considered this, and she realized that the DA's question could only be answered one way.

"It will probably concern them," Jackie replied, deflating the optimism and excitement she had about the job.

Curt, having done an internet search on Nora Community Hospital during this interchange, chimed in.

"Will, Nora Community is a small, independent hospital not connected to any of the major health systems in the area. I doubt AlzCura execs will see her work there as a major threat."

"Well, look at the Maine healthcare consultant coming to the rescue," Will replied. "Exactly how does a consultant in Maine know so much about a small hospital in northwest New York?"

"The wonders of an internet search, Will," Curt chuckled.

Meanwhile, amid Will and Curt's repartee, Jackie felt rescued by Curt, and her optimism and excitement about the job returned.

"OK, nice work Curt. And Jackie, my apologies for having to ask the tough questions."

"I guess that's what makes you great at your job, Will," Jackie replied.

"Yeah, tell my boss that," Will joked, spurring all four to laughter.

"In all seriousness," Will continued after their period of merriment, "have you felt safe? Any more concerns about Alz-

Cura spying on you?"

"No, thank you for your concern, Will," Jackie said, sincerely appreciative.

"OK, then let's go to Curt. Other than your mastery of internet searches, what else is new?"

"Thankfully, not much, Will. I'm back at work full-time, the kids are doing great, and there haven't been any more incidents like the ones I reported last time."

"No news is good news then," Will summarized.

"Yep, life is good," Curt concluded.

"That's great. I can't thank you and Jackie enough for your assistance. I was worried about your safety after our last call, and I'm happy that you and your families haven't had any repeat incidences. Let's move on to Theo, who I know has been very busy. What do you have for us?"

"As you know, Will, I've had my nose in a lot of medical records the last few days. What I found in them, combined with some files that remain unaccounted for and a couple sets of unidentified fingerprints, all lead me to conclude that there is something rotten in the state of Denmark," quoting Shakespeare but leaving Jackie and Curt hanging. "I'm sorry, I really can't go into detail without compromising the confidentiality of our investigation."

"So what Dr. Caron told us when we met at the Farrisport Inn was true, Will?" Jackie queried.

"If you're talking about his allegation that they were hiding or misrepresenting the complication data on Recallamin, we may have found evidence to support his claim. However, I have to caution. Our findings are preliminary."

"And the three files that are unaccounted for," raised Curt, "are they files of Recallamin patients, and do you suspect someone took them?"

"I'm sorry, Curt. We are still investigating the answer to

those questions, and I wouldn't be able to tell you even if I knew. Without compromising the sanctity of legal protocol, let me put it this way, I think we are very close to having the evidence we need to consider alerting the FDA as you suggested at our last meeting."

"Then I suspect you also can't tell us if you've ruled Dr. Caron's death a suicide," asked Jackie.

"Yes, I can't comment on that either," Will replied, knowing that a no comment was as good as an admission that there were suspicious circumstances still under investigation.

"I will be discussing the findings from the file review and Dr. Caron's death in detail with AG Talcott and Dr. Corpisen later today. Suffice to say, what AG Talcott elects to say on Thursday at the meeting with the media will be public knowledge and may answer some of your questions."

As frustrating as it was for all parties on the call to dance around the facts, Jackie and Curt understood the need for the legal process to have clear and firm boundaries, particularly if the information the State had resulted in criminal charges.

"And the unidentified fingerprints you found in Dr. Caron's office, did you compare them to the fingerprint you found on the note on my door?" Curt asked, hoping this wouldn't breach the limitations of the investigation.

"Hmmm, Theo, did we compare those?" DA Wydman asked.

"I hate to admit it, Will, but I don't think we have."

"Let's get on that right away, Theo. My apologies, and thanks, Curt."

"No worries," Curt replied. "I'm sure you're juggling a lot of details."

"I'll try to get you an answer as soon as possible. Otherwise, let's plan on another group meeting this Friday at noon," Will suggested. "Does that work for everyone?"

"That might be cutting in close for me," Jackie remarked. "My interview starts at 9 am, and they told me to allow 3 hours."

"OK, how about we make it at 1 p.m. then?"

When the alternative meeting time gained unanimous consent, DA Wydman thanked the team and ended the call.

Shortly after, Jackie sent Curt a text.

"Thanks for saving my job opportunity on the call today."

"That's what friends are for!" Curt responded.

"I would have never known to check on the hospital's ownership. I have a lot to learn."

"I'm sure you're a quick study, but I'll be happy to help orient you to the bizarre and mysterious world of hospitals!"

"Thanks, Curt. I'll take you up on your offer if I get the job."

"When you get the job."

Jackie smiled and sent a smiley face emoji in response.

Two hours after the teleconference, DA Wydman, Inspector Adams, and Dr. Corpisen marched into AG Talcott's office, armed with the information they felt would finally move their investigations of the deaths of Dr. Caron, and Darius and Elvira Scott forward.

"Gentlemen, thanks for accommodating my schedule," AG Talcott greeted, directing them to his conference table. "I'm anxious to hear what you've learned so that I can prepare for my meetings with NAMI and the media."

"I think you'll be pleased, Lew," opened DA Wydman. "Theo, with an assist from Dr. Corpisen, deserves the credit. Theo, do you want to summarize?"

"Sure, thanks, Will. Let me begin with the investigation of Dr. Caron's suicide. Here are the facts," he began, handing AG Talcott a file for review.

Theo proceeded to tick off the evidence, including the date-rape drug found in Dr. Caron's system, the missing office records, the two unidentified sets of fingerprints, Dr. Caron's admission to DA Wydman, Jackie, and Curt of AlzCura's shady practices, and the compromising photos with Margo.

"I believe all of these provide evidence that AlzCura had the motive to blackmail and ultimately silence Dr. Caron," Theo said emphatically. "Not to mention, I will also provide evidence that he was clearly concerned that study patients were dying but was compelled by AlzCura not to report them to DHHS as required. In short, the evidence supports that Dr. Caron was having a crisis of conscience, and AlzCura having everything to lose if he sang, first tried to blackmail him and then took him out."

"Nice work," AG Talcott began. "I tend to agree with your line of thinking. The question is, how do we approach AlzCura to follow-up on Margo's role in this and the unidentified fingerprints?"

"We have some ideas about that," Will replied. "I would like Theo to present the evidence related to Darius and Elvira Scott and the more significant issue of the safety of the Recallamin vaccine."

"OK, shoot, Theo," AG Talcott prompted.

Theo handed AG Talcott another folder that contained VAERS forms, Dr. Caron's discharge summary notations, and a summary table illustrating clearly that Darius and Elvira Scott, and 11 other individuals had suffered the same symptoms and causes of death.

"By my count, 13 patients of Dr. Caron's 65 patients in the Recallamin trial had the same symptoms, and all died of the same causes. One in every five Recallamin patients. A twenty percent mortality rate. To our knowledge, none of these were reported to the proper authorities responsible for evaluating and assuring the safety of vaccines."

As Theo paused, AG Talcott asked, "Other than Darius and

Elvira's autopsies, I don't see any others. Did any of the 11 other patients have autopsies?"

"Not that I could determine from their medical records."

"Louie, wouldn't these 11 cases meet the requirements as a medical examiner case?"

"Yes, I would think they would have met at least one if not two of the 11 criteria."

"Then why didn't your office get these cases?" the AG queried.

"It's the rare hospital that has robust processes for identifying and reporting medical examiner cases, I'm afraid."

"Do we have any recourse?"

"Well, if any of the patients have yet to be buried or cremated, I can order a hold."

"All the patients, except for Norman Boulanger, died months ago," Theo added. "Mr. Boulanger died two weeks ago."

"Theo, check on Mr. Boulanger then. Will and Louie, I know it would be extreme, but do you think we should exercise Section 3029 and have the bodies exhumed?"

The DA and Medical Examiner looked at each other, not having considered this extreme measure.

"I don't know Lew," DA Wydman responded after a long pause. "Let me run the plan the three of us had discussed by you and then reconsider your question."

"OK, what's your plan?"

"Given the facts about Recallamin and AlzCura dragging their feet in responding to us historically, we suggest providing the evidence to the Department of Health and Human Services. At the same time, we call the FBI to facilitate further investigation of Dr. Caron's death."

"Alright, let me play the devil's advocate," AG Talcott began. "What if AlzCura reported these deaths to DHHS? What if some or all of the patients in the Recallamin trial that died weren't given the vaccine? What if Dr. Caron was a playboy who liked to play sex games with GHB, and his death was just a game that went too far? What if we are never able to identify the two sets of unidentified prints or link them to AlzCura or Dr. Caron's death? If I'm AlzCura Pharmaceutical, I'm salivating at the chance to sue the State of Maine and line their pockets even further. Before we call in the calvary and disrupt AlzCura's operations, we need to dot a few more I's and cross a few more T's."

"That's fair. Our concern, if I can speak for Louie and Theo," DA Wydman replied, "is that we have no leverage with AlzCura, and they can stall, or worse yet, destroy evidence based on our inquiry while more patients are harmed or die."

"I hear you. Let me propose a friendly amendment to your proposal," AG Talcott replied. "Let's wait to see how AlzCura responds to my most recent letter asking for information on Darius and Elvira and requesting they produce Margo for questioning. I gave them a firm deadline, and if they fail to respond by the deadline or their response is inadequate, I will call my counterpart at DHHS and discuss our concerns about the adverse event information and the VAERS forms. If they confirm it wasn't provided by AlzCura, then we submit Dr. Caron's VAERS forms to DHHS and consider whether we have sufficient information to contact any of our other friends at the FDA or FBI."

All three heads nodded, recognizing the advantages of AG Talcott's proposed approach.

"As for my message to NAMI and the media," AG Talcott continued, "I'm afraid we still just have to push the ball down the court with the fact we continue to investigate Darius and Elvira's deaths. They'll have more questions than I will have answers, but that's usually the case."

"I'm sure you'll tap dance just fine," DA Wydman added,

causing chuckles all around.

"Thanks, gentlemen. I'll let you know if and when I receive AlzCura's response to my letter." With that, the meeting ended.

After the meeting, Inspector Adams decided to stop in on Celeste Boulanger on his way home. Not only did he want to follow up on AG Talcott's instructions, but he hoped that Celeste would be in a better place emotionally to be able to answer some of his questions.

When Celeste answered the door, this time with Sophie offering her chorus of barking in the background, Adams almost didn't recognize her. Gone were the disheveled young woman with an angry, swollen black eye. In her place now was a woman, so put together and fashionably dressed that she looked as if she had just walked off a model's runway. Adams was momentarily dumbfounded by her flaming red hair framing stunning green eyes, high cheekbones, and dimples like apostrophe signs calling attention to her full-lipped smile.

"Inspector Adams, I was actually about to call you. Come on in."

Still unable to find his words, he nodded and followed her into the trailer, hoping that he would eventually regain his voice.

"Can I get you something to drink? Water? Coffee?"

"Coffee, please," he was finally able to respond. As she made her way to the kitchen, he settled into the chair that he sat in just a week earlier. Sophie stopped barking and sat like a sentry at the kitchen entrance.

"How do you take your coffee?" Celeste called from the kitchen.

"Black, please."

"At least you caught me at a better time this visit," she said, handing him a steaming mug.

"Thank you. I'm glad you're doing better," he replied, his

professionalism stopping him short of commenting on how much better she looked.

"I took your advice and asked the hospital for a copy of Norman's record. They charged me $46.50 for copying costs," she spat indignantly. "I guess the $75,000 hospital bill wasn't enough."

"You're kidding."

"I wish I was. And then, once I get the record, it's over 1,000 pages, and I can't make heads or tails out of all the medical and legal mumbo-jumbo."

He could only nod in agreement, having had a similar experience.

"Celeste, I don't want to upset you, but when I reviewed Norman's record, I didn't see anything about an autopsy. Did you request an autopsy, or do you know if one was done?" as he took a sip of his coffee.

"No, the hospital asked me if I wanted one done, but they said it would cost extra. I told them I couldn't afford it. I mean, the casket for his funeral was $8,000. I also couldn't stand the idea of them cutting him up."

"I understand," he said empathetically despite recognizing that useful evidence may have been buried along with Norman Boulanger.

"Inspector Adams, I know you told me last time you wouldn't be able to share the results of your review with me. If you were in my position, what would you do?" she asked, her green eyes glistening with tears that drew him in and threatened to break his resolve to remain professional.

"Celeste," he began, fighting off the urge to get up from his chair and go to the couch to hold and console her, "I wish I could be of more help to you. I think you need answers. So my recommendation would be that you find a doctor or a lawyer to review Norman's record with you."

"But won't that cost money? I'm already staring at a hospital bill I can't pay off."

"Not necessarily, Celeste. Some lawyers will do the review for free."

"Really? Why would they do that?"

Celeste's naivete and fragility made it even harder for Adams not to get over-involved in her life and her situation.

"Attorneys will review medical cases to determine if the hospital or a doctor did something wrong and whether the hospital or doctor is liable for any harm. If so, they may suggest that they represent you in a lawsuit. If the court rules that a hospital or doctor was liable for the harm, not only could your hospital bill be paid, but you could get additional money for pain and suffering. The lawyer would also be paid out of the legal settlement."

As he explained the legal process, he could see a lightbulb going off in Celeste's head.

"Are you saying I have a case against the hospital? Did they do something wrong?"

"No, I'm not saying that, Celeste. Please hear me clearly. Only an attorney or a doctor is qualified to determine if you may have a legal case, and it isn't necessarily the fault of the hospital or the doctor. In some cases, it could be a medication or a medical device. All I'm saying is that an attorney or a doctor should be able to help you make sense out of the care Norman received."

"Or that clinical trial?" Celeste asked, hitting on the target of Inspector Adams' investigation.

"Yes, that's another possibility," he answered.

He already felt as though he may have said too much. He knew that if he didn't leave soon, he would find it that much harder not to get into deeper water with the fragile fire-haired beauty trembling across from him.

"OK, I'm sorry. I'm just not very smart when it comes to medical and legal stuff."

"You don't have to apologize, Celeste. I hope I've helped."

As he stood to leave, Celeste sprang from the couch, crossed the divide between them, and without warning, wrapped him in a hug.

Sophie, as surprised by Celeste's actions as Inspector Adams, began to bark with urgency.

His arms outstretched at first, slowly folded around her body, now convulsing as she sobbed into his shoulder. She pressed ever more tightly against him as tears began to wet his shirt.

Sophie, sensing the moment, ceased barking and retreated to another part of the house.

Inspector Adams, always the consummate professional, was human and could no longer deny the intensity of her needs or the power of his feelings. Celeste's tears finally began to subside as they remained locked in their embrace. Lifting her head from his chest, she began to apologize.

"I'm sorry, I got your shirt all wet and my lipstick," she trailed off as she pawed at the smudges on his shirt.

"Don't worry about the shirt."

"Why do you always make me cry, Inspector Adams?"

"Theo. Call me, Theo. And I don't mean to make you cry."

"Well, Theo," she said as she finally released him from their hug, "I may look like a wreck now, but your visits have been the first bit of information and hope anyone has given me since Norman,"

She paused, unable to finish the sentence.

"You don't look like a wreck," he said, watering down significantly what he really wanted to say. "I'm glad I've been helpful. But I better be going."

"Will I see you again, Theo?" she asked as she opened the door.

"I don't know. Perhaps if other questions come up in my investigation."

He could tell from the look on her face that this was not the answer she wanted to hear.

"Of course, you do have my card, and if you ever have any questions or want to discuss anything, I'm at your service."

Her face brightened. As he smiled and turned to leave, she said, "Oh no, you don't," and upon turning back towards her, she embraced him in a hug again. "You're not getting away without a proper goodbye."

From Inspector Adams' perspective, there was nothing proper about it, but he didn't resist and didn't complain.

CHAPTER 32

Cheryl Baker and Chet Humphries sat at Dr. Sheridan's conference table with the Maine Attorney General's recent letter between them like an unwelcome centerpiece.

"This one will not be as easily dismissed as the last one," Dr. Sheridan began, stating the obvious as Cheryl and Chet nodded their agreement.

"I'm not surprised by the addition of Elvira Scott, but why do you suppose they're asking to speak with Margo?" Dr. Sheridan continued. "That can't have anything to do with Darius or Elvira."

"It must be related to Dr. Caron's suicide," Cheryl responded. "They must have found the pictures."

"I find it interesting that they don't provide Margo's last name in the request," Asa remarked. "Chet, could we insist they provide a last name?

"I think the problem with that is they identify wanting to speak to Margo, who provided interim pharmaceutical representative services in Maine during the period of Jackie Deno's maternity leave."

"They obviously learned something new since that first lame letter they sent us," Asa concluded.

"Yes, and they also put a deadline on this one," Chet added.

"However, they didn't state what they would do if we were to miss the deadline. That may give us some latitude."

"Listen," Cheryl interrupted, "the Margo issue is easy to dispense with. We tell them we fired her, and we don't have any additional information on her whereabouts. There's a reason the AG didn't give us the last name - she never used one."

"What if they come back and request her Human Resource file?" Chet asked, trying to anticipate the AGs response to Cheryl's suggestion.

"Well, let's see," Cheryl pondered the options. "Maybe we lost it, or better yet, we purge the files of interim staff who we don't intend to rehire and only keep basic information about when they were here."

"That could fly," Chet replied.

"What I am worried about," Cheryl continued, "is what I learned this weekend in Maine. Between the AG releasing Darius and Elvira's autopsy results to the media this Thursday and our Portland physician's concerns about liver failure complications, this could quickly become a powder keg."

"Physicians?" Dr. Sheridan questioned. "I knew that Dr. Slack had concerns, and we had a conversation a few weeks ago."

"Yeah, well, whatever your conversation was didn't alleviate his concerns, and now he's poisoned Dr. Mason, who wants in on a follow-up call with you. They both have what they think is an excessive number of patients with abnormal liver function test results."

"Alright, I'll set up a call with them," Dr. Sheridan sighed. "Dammit," he cursed, pounding his fist on the table and startling both Chet and Cheryl. "I told Muckland to fix this liver function test issue," he spat, referring to a previous conversation he had with his Laboratory Medical Director.

"Can I make a suggestion, Asa?" Cheryl asked as delicately

as she could.

"What?" Dr. Sheridan raged, his face turning red.

Knowing she was on fragile ground, she proceeded cautiously.

"It may help if you meet with Dr. Slack and Dr. Mason before the Thursday media event."

"And why is that?" he challenged.

"For starters, they will see that I took their concerns seriously and spoke with you."

"But why before the media event?" he asked impatiently.

"Because, Asa," she replied, putting her hand on his arm. "If the autopsy results indicate liver failure, and the AG even hints that Darius and Elvira were involved in a clinical trial, it will spook them even more. It's scary enough to think about what the media would do with such information. Just think what it could do to our two nervous doctors."

Dr. Sheridan's rage began to dwindle, feeling Cheryl's touch and listening to her explanation delivered calmly and confidently.

"OK, that makes sense, Cheryl. Thank you. So, I'll set up a call with the doctors, but what about responding to the letter?"

"We have until the end of next week," Chet replied. "I don't see any benefit to responding to them any sooner."

"Alright, by then, we will know the details of the released autopsy results. Can we review a draft of your response next Wednesday, Chet?"

"That's doable."

"Do we want anyone in Maine this Thursday and Friday to keep a pulse on the release of information and the media's response?" Cheryl asked.

"Good idea," Dr. Sheridan replied. "Who do you have in mind?"

"Well, that would probably be me since I still haven't been able to fill Jackie's position."

"Maybe you could test the waters in the Bangor area?" Dr. Sheridan suggested. "We don't have a presence up there yet."

"Good idea. I'll do that."

Their plan in place, they adjourned the meeting. As soon as Cheryl and Chet had exited his office, Dr. Sheridan picked up his phone and made a call.

"I thought you were going to fix the fucking liver function test results, Myron!" Dr. Sheridan screamed when Dr. Myron David Muckland, his Medical Director of the Regional Laboratory, answered the phone.

"Asa?" he asked, shocked at both the tone and the use of his first name rather than his preferred "M. David."

"Yes, Asa! What have you done since we talked about this issue a few weeks ago?"

"I, I, I," he stammered, clearly caught off guard and ill-prepared.

"Spit it out, Myron!"

"Please don't call me,"

"Oh, shut the fuck up about your pretentious M. David. Now, what have you done? Because if you've done nothing, consider this your last day as my Medical Director!"

"I've scrubbed the data, as we discussed."

"Then why are my doctors in Maine complaining about too many patients with high liver function test results?"

"I've scrubbed the data for the study results we submit to the Feds. I can't scrub the results the doctors see."

"Why not?"

"You're not suggesting I change the lab results before sending them to the doctors, are you?"

"No, I'm not suggesting it. I'm telling you to do it. I thought that was what you would do after we first talked about this."

"But wouldn't that be fraudulent?"

"And what you're doing now on the back-end by scrubbing the data isn't?" he screamed. "Listen to me. By not scrubbing it before releasing it to the doctors, you are assuring that if the Feds conduct an audit, they will find the inconsistencies. Do you want to replace your lab coat with striped pajamas? Correct the lab results before they go out. Then you don't have to worry about scrubbing it on the back-end or generating inconsistencies that could be found on an audit."

"Do you want me to do it for all high values or just some?"

"What's wrong with you, Muckland? I thought this was your forte?"

"Well, it is, but I'm a little shook up, Asa. I mean, you did threaten my job."

"OK, OK, relax. Just do it on some of the high values. Some high values are to be expected. Just don't let the rates get too high for any of our doctors. Start with Dr. Preston and Dr. Mason's patients in Portland. Go back and fix a few of their patients who had high levels in the last 6 months. Then craft a letter to each doctor informing them of the corrected results. I will call them tomorrow and let them know we found a glitch that erroneously reported high liver function test values. Then make sure they don't see another patient with a high value for at least 6 months. That should change their tune."

"OK, Asa. I'm sorry I misunderstood what you wanted in our first conversation. By the way, were you ever able to create that alternate arm to the Recallamin 3 trial as we discussed?"

"No, I'm still working on that," Dr. Sheridan lied, having forgotten he had agreed to pursue that as part of their first conversation. "We good here now?"

"We are." Dr. Muckland replied despite feeling like a beaten puppy.

"Good," Dr. Sheridan said and ended the call as he had begun it, without the customary niceties of a greeting or a farewell.

Still furious from his call with Dr. Muckland, Dr. Sheridan barked at his assistant thru his office intercom.

"Set up a teleconference with Dr. Slack and Dr. Mason for tomorrow."

"Yes, sir," she replied pleasantly, accustomed to his moodiness and less than polite requests.

While it was only 10a.m. on a Monday, Dr. Sheridan got up from his desk and went to his bar, and poured himself the first of several drinks he would consume that day.

The following day, Dr. Sheridan had his teleconference call with Dr. Slack and Dr. Mason. He thanked them profusely for identifying their concern, allowing them to find the glitch that had erroneously reported high liver function test results in a few of their patients. He assured them the problem had been corrected and that they would be receiving a letter from the Medical Director of the Regional Laboratory, identifying the corrected values.

Dr. Slack and Dr. Mason, seemingly satisfied with this explanation, expressed relief. For good measure, Dr. Sheridan reminded them that up to 9% of asymptomatic patients have elevated liver enzymes and that they should be particularly suspicious of liver function test findings in patients who are pregnant or who exercise vigorously. This information caused Dr. Slack and Dr. Mason to share anecdotes of patients they had in the past who had abnormal lab results caused by something other than disease or dysfunction.

Reasonably confident he had dispelled their concerns about Recallamin, he thanked them again and made a pitch that they consider the Recallamin 3 trial for their younger patients with the Alzheimer's gene. Indicating that they would seriously consider doing so, Dr. Sheridan thanked them for one final time and ended the call.

CHAPTER 33

AG Talcott welcomed Cole Minor, Jr. (Chief Advocate, Maine Office of Advocacy) and Sharon Orendorf (President, Maine Chapter of the National Association for the Mentally Ill) into his office. They had been meeting periodically since Elvira Scott first filed a complaint claiming that Harlow Psychiatric Institute had given her son, Darius, medications that caused his death.

Although Cole Minor, Jr. was born and raised in Maine, his family roots were in West Virginia. Cole, Jr. was named after his grandfather, Cole Minor, Sr., who, as his name suggested, was a coal miner. Cole, Jr.'s parents decided to name their son after his grandfather, who had died of black lung disease shortly before Cole, Jr. was born. Cole, Jr. had aspirations of becoming a lawyer but stopped short of earning a law degree and instead pursued and received a Master's degree in Social Work. He was subsequently employed by Maine's Department of Health and Human Services and, after 15 years, was installed as Maine's Chief Advocate. This role combined his passion for ensuring the rights of individuals with disabilities and his love of law.

Sharon Orendorf, like many members of the National Association for the Mentally Ill, had lost a family member to the ravages of mental illness. In Sharon's case, she tragically lost her son Steven to suicide when he was 16-years old. Sharon, who tried her best to provide her son with the love and support he needed, found the so-called "mental health system" severely lacking, and it did not, by any stretch of the imagination, resemble a system. She was traumatized when she lost her son, but that trauma was only magnified by the frustrating lack of services for her son, compounded by no semblance of coordinated care between the available services. She persevered through her own battle with depression. She eventually converted that trauma and her grief into a tireless crusade to transform Maine's mental health system.

The previous meeting between the three had been quite contentious, and AG Talcott was determined in this meeting to provide them with enough information to satisfy Cole and Sharon's demand for answers and action without compromising what was still an ongoing investigation.

"Sharon and Cole, I was as dissatisfied with our last meeting as I know you were," he opened, trying to disarm them with his admission. "I believe I can provide you with some answers today and additional answers tomorrow when we formally release the autopsy results."

"Well, I think I can speak for Cole when I say, we hope so," Sharon offered, as Cole nodded his head in assent. "What do you have for us?"

"We are confident that HPI did not give Darius medications that contributed to his death. I am going to say that for the record tomorrow in front of the media, and I would ask that you keep that information in confidence until after I announce it tomorrow."

"OK," Cole responded. "How are you so sure?"

"Darius complained of a headache and was given two 500mg tablets of Tylenol once during his stay at HPI. That was the only medication he was given. When I release Darius' cause of death tomorrow, I think you will agree, two Tylenol was not the cause."

"Then what was the cause?" Sharon asked.

"Unfortunately, Sharon, that is the question that I will not be able to answer for you in the detail you want."

"Let me guess. It's part of an ongoing investigation," Sharon replied, rolling her eyes.

"Yes, but not so fast. I started this meeting saying I was determined not to make excuses but to give you some answers, so hear me out. We are investigating a possible connection between Darius and Elvira's causes of death that has nothing to do with HPI."

"Intriguing but still unsatisfying," Sharon responded. "Will we hear more about this tomorrow?"

"Unfortunately, no. This possible connection may involve more than just Darius and Elvira. So, again, I need your patience in this matter and your pledge to hold this in strict confidence. I cannot emphasize enough that the three of us are all on the side of public safety, but I need your support and cooperation. I've said more than I probably should have, but I need you with me on this."

Surprised by his openness and recognizing he was making progress, Cole and Sharon thanked him and provided their assurance they would not disclose the information he had shared. AG Talcott, in turn, thanked and warned them to anticipate that tomorrow's meeting would prompt a period of invasive media inquiries that would test their patience and resolve.

AG Talcott concluded, "I will keep you both in the loop, and when I have something of substance to share with you, I will set up another meeting."

As AG Talcott was feeling optimistic about his meeting, Cheryl Baker was boarding a plane for her trip back to Maine with a fair amount of dread. Not only were there no direct flights from Buffalo to Maine, but she was still stinging from her less than successful visit just a few days earlier. With the potential for a media-feeding frenzy with the AG's release of Darius and Elvira's autopsy results and a cold call to try to sell Recallamin to a physician group in Bangor, Cheryl didn't have high hopes.

That her connecting flight was delayed only intensified her trepidation about her trip. Upon finally arriving at the hotel and anxious to relax with a drink in her room, the insults just continued, finding no hotel bar or mini-bar.

"Oh, hell no," she said to herself, grabbing her phone and searching for the nearest drinking establishment. She finally felt her luck changing as the closest bar was within walking distance. Ten minutes later, she walked into Willy Wacks Tavern, a small rustic bar whose décor consisted of a series of framed Maine-ism words and phrases that the owners probably thought comforting to locals and quaint to tourists.

Taking a seat at one of the many open stools at the bar, Cheryl ordered her go-to drink.

"Maker's Mark straight up. Make it a double."

Settling in, she found herself mindlessly taking an inventory of the bars Maine-isms.

"You can't get there from hee-ah!"

"Ain't that cunnin'?"

"Pahk the cah in the door yahd

"Ayuh"

And, of course, "You're out in the willy wacks," a nod to the inspiration for the establishment's name.

The bartender thankfully rescued her from further study of cultural linguistics, setting a tumbler of liquid gold in front of her. With a bolus of her favorite medicine on its way to her bloodstream, her attention was drawn to the TV above the bar.

"Yes, Jeff," said the buxom blond reporter whose blouse

looked like it was just barely holding on for dear life. "The highly anticipated meeting with Attorney General Talcott tomorrow is expected to draw media attention, not only from the press in Maine but from across the entire Northeast region."

"Not her again," Cheryl said to herself, noticing that all the men in the bar, including the bartender, stopped whatever they had been doing to watch the TV.

"The big questions that have taken way too long to answer are, 'Did the Harlow Psychiatric Institute give Darius Scott medications that killed him?' If not, what did? And what about his poor mother, Elvira? How did she die shortly after making the allegations against HPI? The Attorney General, the Medical Examiner, and the police have been dragging their feet on this, and as far as I'm concerned, the people of Maine deserve better."

"Well, Leslie, we know you will be upfront and center tomorrow, making sure we get the answers we deserve," the anchorman added.

"Thank you, Jeff. This is Leslie Anderson, senior investigative correspondent reporting to you live for Channel 5 news," she concluded with a signature flip of her blond tresses. Once again, the cameraman provided a gratuitous shot of Leslie's best sultry expression, and her endowments barely contained within her tight, protesting blouse as the men at the bar broke into hoots and applause.

Cheryl was awestruck. Polishing off the rest of her drink, she threw a twenty onto the bar and made her way to the exit as the male patrons continued to act like giddy, testosterone-charged adolescent boys. She had had enough and knew that the outlook for the next day wasn't much better.

CHAPTER 34

At a table to the left of the podium sat District Attorney William Wydman, Medical Examiner Dr. Louis Corpisen, and Attorney General Lewis Talcott. All three were busy acting as if they were reviewing their notes, studiously making last-minute additions to keep from making eye contact with the throng of reporters. In the wings stood Inspector Adams and several other law enforcement and government officials. Directly in front of the stage and for 20-feet down the sides of the auditorium stood a phalanx of beefy law enforcement officers spaced every few feet. Beyond this imposing line of sentries were dozens of reporters jockeying for the best seats and creating a din worthy of an excited crowd at a rock concert. Behind the reporters were cameramen representing all the major television stations in Maine, along with a smattering of stations from Manchester, Boston, and New York. In a rare move, the Attorney General had granted permission for the Maine TV stations to broadcast the proceedings live. All elected to pre-empt their regularly scheduled broadcasts. Beyond the cameras was a standing-room-only crowd of interested parties and the public, including Dr. Lang and other representatives from the Harlow Psychiatric Institute, Sharon Orendorf from the Maine chapter of NAMI, and Cole Minor, Jr. from the State Office of Advocacy.

As Attorney General Talcott stood and walked authoritatively to the podium, the commotion amongst the crowded auditorium magically muted. The AG with the flags of Maine and the United States framed behind him paused and looked out over the sea of faces that waited in restless anticipation.

"Good afternoon. I am the State of Maine's Attorney General Lewis Talcott." Turning to his right and extending his arm toward the table, he continued. "I am joined on the stage today by District Attorney William Wydman and Chief Medical Examiner Dr. Louis Corpisen," each nodding as introduced.

"While we anticipate questions and have planned a Q & A session later in the program, I ask that you hold your questions while I read a prepared statement. The text of this statement will be made available to members of the media at the end of today's meeting. During the Q & A session, to maintain order and allow everyone to have their questions answered, we will position the microphone stands in each aisle. We ask that you line up behind each microphone at the appointed time. We will accept one question from each individual and will rotate between aisles. We thank you in advance for your cooperation with these rules."

A murmur arose from the media members that didn't surprise AG Talcott. He had designed the Q & A rules to avoid the free-for-all environment and shouting above one another that was typical when a gaggle of reporters vied for the floor and the attention. As the buzz started to die down, AG Talcott started to read his prepared statement.

After his opening salutation, he took a moment to recognize Maine's law enforcement members. He then launched into a summary of the events that led to Darius Scott's arrest and eventual incarceration and death at the Harlow Psychiatric Institute. Following that, he summarized Elvira's complaints and allegations against HPI and the Chief Medical Examiner's office and her death shortly after that. The media, who were all familiar with these facts, grew restless, waiting for something other than the fodder they had been reporting on over the past few months.

"Before I provide the results of Darius and Elvira Scott's autopsies and our findings from investigating Elvira Scott's complaints and allegations, some of our findings are still a matter of an active investigation. Therefore, I will have to limit my responses so as not to compromise that investigation."

No surprise to the AG, this announcement caused an audible groan from the audience.

"Darius Scott's autopsy revealed," he shouted above the din, pausing briefly to let the crowd come to order.

"Darius Scott's autopsy revealed that he died of liver failure and a massive brain aneurysm, the cause of which is still under investigation. The Chief Medical Examiner's findings, along with a second independent examination by another board-certified forensic pathologist, determined that the two Tylenol tablets administered to Mr. Scott by HPI personnel did not in any way contribute to his death."

A buzz arose in the media pit, and AG Talcott waited for it to die down.

"What did cause the liver failure and aneurysm?" shouted a member of the media.

"As I said, questions will be taken after my statement. Please observe the rules I laid out at the beginning of this meeting. Those who cannot follow my rules will be removed from the auditorium. Last warning," AG Talcott glared at the questioner.

If the AG's withering stare wasn't enough, about two dozen of the questioner's peers also turned to scowl at him.

"Darius Scott's toxicology report did find an unidentified substance in varying concentrations in his heart, liver, and brain. This substance wasn't from any known source, and to date, this finding is described quote, as suspicious but inconclusive, closed-quote."

An even louder buzz hung over the crowd that persisted, but this time no one dared shout out any questions.

"Elvira Scott's autopsy revealed," he continued, pausing until the buzz subsided and he had everyone's full attention.

"Elvira Scott's autopsy revealed that she died of liver failure and a massive brain aneurysm, the cause of which is still under investigation. Similar to her son, Elvira's toxicology report found an unidentified substance in varying concentrations in her heart, liver, and brain. This substance wasn't from any known source, and to date, this finding is described quote, as suspicious but inconclusive, closed-quote."

The fervor in the crowd grew to a fever pitch, and the law enforcement officers tightened ranks in anticipation of a potential disturbance.

"In summary," he paused again, waiting for silence. "In summary, we can definitively say that Darius Scott did not die from the care he received at HPI. Furthermore, independent assessment by a forensic pathologist not associated with the Maine Chief Medical Examiner's office not only confirms the cause of Mr. Scott's death but refutes allegations by Elvira Scott that the Chief Medical Examiner's office was involved in a cover-up and removed evidence that had contributed to Darius Scott's death. Finally, Darius and Elvira Scott both died of liver failure and massive brain aneurysms. They were found to have concentrations of an unidentified substance in varying concentrations in their hearts, livers, and brains. This substance, the source of this substance, and its role in the deaths of Darius and Elvira Scott are still a matter of an active investigation, which I am not at liberty to discuss further."

AG Talcott looked up from his notes, paused briefly, and continued.

"We will now begin the question and," his next words were

drowned out by nearly all the members of the media rushing into the aisles to jockey for position behind the mic stands, which had not yet been put in place.

"Whoa, Whoa, Whoa," AG Talcott said emphatically as the law enforcement officers moved into the aisles to meet the crowd. "Back to your seats, please. Back to your seats."

As the members of the media reluctantly retraced their steps back to their seats, AG Talcott imposed additional rules to impose order.

"We will be placing two microphones in each aisle momentarily. To avoid the stampede that I just witnessed, I will call by row number those who may leave their seats and line up at the nearest microphone. Once again, you will be allowed one question and one question only. Once you have asked your question, please return to your seat."

As the microphones were being placed, one media member broke ranks and pushed her way to an aisle.

"Attorney General Talcott," she yelled as she pushed people out of her way, "the press will not be silenced or forced to subscribe to your rules. I demand"

"Ms. Anderson," AG Talcott interrupted, "It's your choice. Either go back to your seat, or I will have you removed."

The infamous Leslie Anderson paused briefly in her tracks as her media colleagues began to jeer. "Well, I have never," she huffed and stormed back to her seat.

"And for your grandstanding, Ms. Anderson," AG Talcott replied, "I will take your question last after all of your colleagues have had their opportunity."

The media section, except for Leslie Anderson, erupted in a cheer and standing ovation for the AG's actions.

"Now, is there anyone else who would like to break the Q & A rules?"

Their applause turned to laughter, and AG Talcott had done

the impossible. Not only had he controlled the typically un-ruly media, but he had also won them over. All but Leslie An-derson, who sulked in her seat, looking like she was going to cry or explode or both.

As the media members complied with the rules and filed up to the mics in an orderly fashion, AG Talcott answered their questions.

"Nick Simon Channel 4 news. Can you tell us the name of the independent forensic pathologist?"

"Thank you for your question, Nick. One of the principles of peer review is that the reviewer's identity is kept confiden-tial. I can tell you that the reviewer was not from Maine and was an experienced forensic pathologist with exceptional cre-dentials."

"Sharon Scovill, Dracut-Campion Star-Ledger. Since Darius and Elvira Scott died from the same causes, have you ruled out a genetic or environmental reason?"

"Thank you, Sharon. As I mentioned, the cause is still part of an active investigation, we have not ruled out genetic or en-vironmental factors, but we are also looking at other potential sources."

"Abe Rothberg, The New York Times. Darius and Elvira Scott died months ago. Why did it take so long to release the results of their autopsies?"

"Thank you, Abe. We elected to wait until now so that we could report not only the autopsy results but the results of our investigation of Mrs. Scott's allegations. Their autopsies were completed in a relatively timely fashion. However, toxicology results, identifying a competent physician to conduct the peer review, and the peer review process itself, all take time."

"Terrance Hawkins, Channel 3 news. Dr. Steven Caron committed suicide, but the State has not yet ruled it suicide. Why not?"

"Thank you, Terrance. We continue to investigate Dr. Caron's death. Being an active investigation, I cannot comment further."

The parade of questioners continued for 30-minutes, most asking questions that AG Talcott had to deflect as the answers were the subject of their current investigation. One microphone stand stood empty as the reporters had exhausted their questions.

All of a sudden, there was a commotion near the back of the auditorium, and AG Talcott saw a police officer blocking a petite, red-headed woman from approaching.

"I have a question," she yelled. "Please, I have a question."

"Officer," AG Talcott called out, "What seems to be the problem?"

"She's not a member of the press, sir," he yelled as the woman tried to get by the officer.

"Let her through."

The woman approached the microphone, wiping tears from her face. The media members, who had almost lost interest and become numb to the questions that could not be answered, all turned to look at the interloper. They were first surprised that AG Talcott hadn't disciplined the woman, but it was what she said that blew the roof off the proceedings.

"Thank you, Mr. Talcott. I mean Attorney General Talcott," she corrected, blushing with embarrassment.

"No worries, ma'am, I've answered to much worse," he responded, breaking the tension and causing the woman and the audience to laugh. "What's your name, and how can I help you?"

"My name is Celeste Boulanger," which made DA Wydman almost fall off his chair. Before he could react and figure out what to do, she continued on.

"My husband Norman died 3 weeks ago. I came here today

because before he died, he acted crazy, just like Darius Scott. He hit me and said hurtful things to me. I thought he was going to kill me," she stopped talking as she saw a man walk up to AG Talcott.

DA Wydman, finally reacting, had walked up to AG Talcott and whispered in his ear.

"She's a witness in our investigation. We need to stop this and meet with her privately."

"Celeste, I appreciate your coming to speak with us today. We'd like to meet with you privately to answer your questions. Would you be open to that?"

Celeste, looking confused at first, suddenly realized the opportunity and asked the AG when they could meet.

"Right now, if that's OK."

"Yes, that would be fine," she replied.

As the media members rushed towards Celeste, AG Talcott gave directions to the law enforcement officers.

"Officers, please escort Celeste to my office and make sure she doesn't speak to the media."

As the officer who initially tried to detain Celeste now rushed her out of the auditorium, the rest of the officers formed a wall cordoning off the media members' access to her.

This didn't prevent them from yelling out their questions. Nor did it stop Leslie Anderson from making her anger towards the AG heard.

"I was promised the last question, Attorney General Talcott! You can't end this meeting until I have asked my question. Don't you dare leave."

As AG Talcott, DA Wydman, and Dr. Corpisen exited the stage, Leslie Anderson erupted.

"You're a fucking liar Attorney Asshole Talcott," she taunted as she rushed the stage and tried to climb the stairs in pursuit. She was met by two police officers who blocked her ascent, and she predictably turned her anger on them. When she wouldn't back down or stop her profanity-laced tirade, they cuffed her and deposited her kicking and screaming into the back of a police cruiser.

The proceedings, which had been tightly controlled, organized, and respectful, disintegrated into chaos and intrigue. For media executives, this was precisely the chum that created a media-feeding frenzy that would fuel lead stories and headlines for weeks.

CHAPTER 35

Cheryl Baker, who watched the Attorney General's meeting on TV from her hotel room, went from pleased to mortified.

For most of the meeting, the Attorney General's release of information and the media's questions hadn't identified Darius and Elvira as part of a clinical trial or, in any other way, implicated AlzCura. If anything, the press was barking up the genetic or environmental factors trees. That was until Celeste Boulanger made her appearance and characterized her husband as the second-coming of Darius Scott. While Mrs. Boulanger hadn't mentioned anything about her husband being part of AlzCura's clinical trial, three things concerned Cheryl. Norman had been in AlzCura's clinical trial. Celeste was talking with the authorities, and they might make the connection if they hadn't already. The media's curiosity had been peaked, and they would dig into and report the story of Norman Boulanger with vigor. None of this was good news, and she immediately called Dr. Sheridan.

"Asa, we're in trouble," she began bluntly.

"What happened?"

"Everything was pretty vanilla until Norman Boulanger's wife made an appearance and spilled the beans about her husband in front of almost every media outlet in the Northeast."

"Did she mention us or the clinical trial?" he asked anxiously.

"No, but she's talking with the Attorney General in private right now, and you can bet the media is going to turn over every rock on Norman Boulanger."

"Do you think she knows her husband was in a clinical trial?"

"I don't know. Maybe not, but it would be dangerous to assume that."

"Well, at least we have her husband's record from Dr. Caron's office. So that's one less rock anyone can turn over."

"Yes, but we have no clue what he told her or what the hospital's medical record may contain."

"What about silencing Mrs. Boulanger?"

"It may be too late, and it would be hard now that she will probably become the media's darling."

"We need to do something. Our strategy needs to change. Find out what opportunity there may be with Mrs. Boulanger."

"What do you want me to do about visiting the Bangor physician group?"

"Screw them. Mrs. Boulanger has to be our focus. Then get back here. I want to meet with you and Chet tomorrow."

Cheryl hung up, made a quick call to her son Andrew, and then called the airline to change her flight back to Buffalo.

* * *

Curt, having watched the fiasco on TV, immediately picked up his phone and texted Jackie.

"Media meeting just ended. All I can say is WOW!"

"Wow, good or wow bad?"

"Good, I think. Darius, Elvira, and Stu all died from the same causes, but that wasn't the most interesting thing."

"I'm sitting on the edge of my seat," she texted, wishing they could just call and talk to one another.

"A woman named Celeste announced that her husband had died and behaved aggressively just like Darius before his death. The AG didn't let her continue but said he would meet with her in private. Then chaos erupted."

"Do you think she was just some basket case?" Jackie texted.

"I don't think so, but I guess we may hear more from DA Wydman at tomorrow's meeting."

"I can't wait. I wish I could have seen it."

"I wish we didn't have to text each other."

"Me too. Let's ask Will to lift the ban tomorrow."

"Good idea."

❊ ❊ ❊

Celeste Boulanger looked like a frightened little bird perched in the chair surrounded by Attorney General Talcott, District Attorney Wydman, and Medical Examiner Dr. Corpisen.

"Can I get you something, Mrs. Boulanger?" AG Talcott asked, recognizing her nervousness. "Coffee, tea, water?"

"Water, please," she said, trembling.

As AG Talcott went to retrieve a bottle of water, DA Wydman tried to make her more comfortable.

"Mrs. Boulanger," he began.

"You can call me Celeste," she interrupted.

"Ok, Celeste. I can see that you're nervous. You can relax.

We're all on the same team here, and we want to be able to answer any questions you may have."

"I thought I did something wrong," she replied. "And then all those people started rushing me and asking all sorts of questions. And the cameras and the police officers. It was scary."

"I'm sure it was, but you didn't do anything wrong," he replied.

AG Talcott returned with bottles of water for all.

"Thank you," Celeste said meekly, accepting the water.

"You're welcome, Celeste," the AG responded. "The reason we asked to meet with you here is that the circumstances of your husband's death are part of our ongoing investigation. That being the case, we want to keep the details of our investigation confidential. You may have heard me say this during the meeting."

"Yes, I did, but I guess I didn't know I was part of that investigation."

"Well, you are because you have information that may help us understand why your husband acted as he did and why he died. We are as interested in understanding these things as you are. Until we know those answers, though, we don't want information about our investigation getting out."

"So I did do something wrong," she lamented as tears welled up.

"You didn't know, Celeste. Now you do." AG Talcott consoled, reaching for a box of tissues and passing it to her.

"I guess I should have known," she said, dabbing her eyes with a tissue. "That nice Inspector Adams visited me, and he was so helpful. He told me you were reviewing Norman's medical record but that I wouldn't get to find out the results."

"We're glad to hear that Inspector Adams was helpful. As for our review of Norman's record, we can't share the results of our review unless we determine a crime has been committed."

"Oh, yeah. I guess Inspector Adams did say that. Has a crime been committed?"

"We really can't tell you that, Celeste. Norman's death is part of our investigation to determine whether a crime has been committed. You mustn't talk about this to anyone except us and, of course, Inspector Adams."

"OK, I won't."

"I'm afraid, now that the media is aware of Norman's death and the similar behavior he exhibited to Darius Scott, you will have more attention than you'd like."

"I hadn't thought about that. Is that why those people all rushed me in the auditorium?"

"Exactly. And they will find out where you live and where you work and follow you wherever you go. They will try to get information from you, and you will have to resist their efforts. It would be helpful if you had another place to stay for a while."

"I have a sister who lives in Ramsey."

"OK, but it would be preferable if it were a friend. Someone not in your family. The media folks are resourceful. They will find out you have a sister and find out where she lives."

"I really can't think of anyone. I have a dog, so that complicates things too."

"Would you be opposed to us having officers patrol the area around your home periodically?"

"No, that would be fine."

"And if the media folks don't observe your privacy or get too obnoxious, you can call us, and we'll send someone over."

"OK, I can do that."

"Now, do you have any questions for us?" AG Talcott asked.

"Inspector Adams mentioned that Norman was involved in a clinical something or other," she blushed. "I can never remember what the term is."

"Clinical trial," Dr. Corpisen chimed in.

"Yes, thank you. Clinical trial. Is that what you think may have killed my husband?"

"I want to help you, Celeste, but that question puts me in an awkward position," AG Talcott said, shifting uncomfortably in his seat. The best I can do is tell you that we are investigating that, along with other things, as the possible cause of your husband's death."

"And you'll tell me if you think a crime has been committed?"

"Yes."

With that, the meeting ended, and AG Talcott had a police officer drive Celeste back to the auditorium, where they found a group of reporters surrounding Celeste's car. After shielding her and getting her safely into her car, the police officer escorted her home only to find another group of reporters on her lawn. Celeste's dog, Sophie, was apoplectic, barking incessantly from behind the living room window.

Celeste's police escort shielded her from the surge of reporters and cameramen as they hurled their questions at her. Once in the trailer, having survived the swarm of reporters who resembled a school of piranhas, she collapsed on her couch and tried to console Sophie. She had gone to the Attorney General's meeting to find answers to her husbands' death only to return a prisoner in her own home.

When Sophie finally settled down and curled up in her lap, Celeste fell apart and began to cry.

CHAPTER 36

J ackie rushed into her parent's house carrying Ashley, who uncharacteristically had been fussy and now was in a full-throated wail.

"Mom, could you please take her? I can't be late for my interview," she huffed frantically.

"I was wondering what was taking you. I almost called."

"Oh, she's been a handful this morning. I fed her and had her all ready to go when she threw up. I had to change her."

"Well, thankfully, she didn't throw up on you. You look nice, dear."

"Thanks, Mom. I don't feel nice right now. If I go into this interview all harried like this," she paused as her mother took Ashley from her.

"I've got her now. You can relax, and I'm sure you'll do just fine. Now go. Go," she said, shooing Jackie out the door.

Once in her car, Jackie took a few deep breaths to calm herself, then started the car and headed towards Nora Community Hospital for her interview. As she mentally rehearsed answers to questions she anticipated they would ask, she didn't notice the car following her. Nor did she see it follow her into the hospital's parking lot.

All of Jackie's anxieties about the harried start to her day and interviewing melted away during her meetings. She first met with the Chief Medical Officer, a venerable surgeon in the community who had recently retired from practice to accept this administrative leadership position. Jackie then met with a panel of physician leaders representing some of the major service lines in the hospital, including cardiology, obstetrics, hospitalists, critical care, emergency medicine, general surgery, and orthopedics. Jackie's previous experience with physicians made the first two hours of her interview a breeze. Based on her interviews, she quickly realized that the role of Physician Liaison was very similar to her previous job, just broader in context. Instead of focusing on pharmaceuticals, this role would introduce her to many other aspects of medical practice. She found the idea of expanding her knowledge and experience without having to travel invigorating.

Her final interview was with the Chief Executive Officer of the hospital - the person who would be her boss if hired. To this point, Jackie felt confident that she had made a very favorable impression on the physicians she had met. As she waited outside the CEO's office, she started to get nervous. Her mind rewound to her last meeting with Cheryl and how quickly and unceremoniously she had gone from AlzCura's star performer to persona non grata. It didn't matter that she knew she had been working for leaders that were ethically challenged. Getting let go from a company and a job you dedicated years of your life and effort to didn't sit well.

As Jackie began to try and focus on something more positive, the CEO's door opened, and a confident middle-aged woman strode towards her.

"You must be Jackie. Hi, I'm Tara Newman," she said, shaking Jackie's hand firmly. "Come into my office."

Tara Newman had been Nora Community Hospital's Chief Executive Officer for two years. Before being named the CEO at Nora, she had successfully turned around a smaller beleaguered hospital 50-miles south of Nora. She had earned a reputation as a charismatic leader with an uncompromising dedication to excellence in patient care. While many CEOs are well-spoken, she was an uncommonly effective communicator and listener. Not only did she block off 2-hours a day to round on and listen to patients, family members, and employees, but she personally published a one-page electronic newsletter every Friday highlighting a patient story or a staff member who went above and beyond the call of duty.

Although her leadership style rarely required her to get sharp with anyone in a demonstrable way, when she had to, her words could just as quickly eviscerate as they could encourage. The few people who had to endure such uncomfortable occasions and remained in the organization secretly called her "Tara Someone a New One." In most cases, it was just the attitude adjustment the individual needed to improve their performance. While the moniker they gave her was not kind, they universally respected and thanked her for their transformation. In some cases, it jettisoned employees that had been toxic baggage to the organization for too long.

"I need a coffee," Tara announced as Jackie seated herself in a comfortable corner chair. "Can I get you one?"

Already captivated by the CEO's energy and palpable enthusiasm, Jackie couldn't help but accept.

"Yes, I'd love one. Black, please."

"Oh, I can tell I'm going to like you," Tara responded. "Only real coffee drinkers drink it straight up," she remarked as she exited her office to fetch the caffeine pick-me-ups.

While Tara was out, Jackie scanned a wall filled with frames. To her surprise, the frames contained letters of gratitude or photos from patients or their families that she had received. Missing was the usual and customary things executives mount on their walls, like diplomas and awards.

"Here you go," Tara said, handing Jackie a mug of coffee.

"Thank you," Jackie replied and took a sip.

"I have to tell you, Jackie. I have never had so many physicians visit my office immediately after interviewing someone."

Wondering if this was a good or a bad thing, the CEO didn't leave her hanging long.

"I usually like to spend a good hour with candidates, but based on the rave reviews I received from the docs, this may be short and sweet."

"I'm pleased to hear that. I very much enjoyed meeting with the physicians."

"It shows. Your experience at AlzCura obviously paid off."

"It did," Jackie replied, as her roller-coaster relationship with Dr. Caron all of a sudden revisited her consciousness.

"Tell me about your time at AlzCura?

Jackie had been rehearsing her response to this question, and her answer, which focused on the positive aspects of her tenure, was well-practiced.

"That's great, Jackie," Tara commented, "now tell me what wasn't so good at AlzCura and why you left."

Jackie was not as rehearsed for this question, and before answering, she took a long sip of her coffee, trying to find some time to formulate her answer.

"I guess I learned some things about the company with which I wasn't comfortable," she finally responded, hoping that this would be sufficient.

"Tell me more," Tara urged.

"I learned of some practices I thought were wrong and maybe unethical. When I raised my concerns to my boss, she didn't do anything about it, and I was offered a separation agreement."

The moment it was out of Jackie's mouth, she felt that she

had failed the interview, and Tara would cast her as a trouble-maker best avoided.

"Good for you!" Tara congratulated her. "And I assume the separation agreement obligates you to confidentiality, so I won't ask you any more questions about it. Standing up to ethical concerns is hard, and I admire that you did. Do you have any questions for me?"

Jackie asked a few questions about what Tara expected out of the Physician Liaison role and, after answering Tara, concluded the brief interview.

"Jackie, excellent job today. Are you interviewing anywhere else?"

"No, but I have applied for a few other jobs."

"Good. I'd like to offer you the Physician Liaison position. Do you have time to meet with Human Resources right now?"

Jackie's face registered her shock.

"Yes, I just said that, Jackie. I'm offering you the job."

"I'm shocked. I'm happy, but I wasn't expecting,"

"I do things a little differently, Jackie," she interrupted. "Great people are hard to find, and I'm still trying to get my Human Resource Department to be as responsive as we need. The era for waiting for anything as a patient in our hospital or as a job candidate is over."

Since Jackie's meeting with Tara had only lasted 30 minutes, she had 90-minutes before the teleconference with DA Wydman.

"I'd be happy to meet with Human Resources. Thank you, Tara," Jackie smiled and stood to shake Tara's hand.

"I'd like you to start as soon as you can. If you have a problem with what Human Resources offers you for a salary, ask to speak to me."

"If everything looks good, I can start as soon as next week,"

Jackie replied.

"Super. Unless I hear differently from you, I expect to see you bright and early on Monday then."

Jackie felt like she was walking on air as she made her way to Human Resources. An hour later, she had completed the necessary paperwork, agreed to her salary, and set up an appointment for a health screening the following day to start her new job on Monday. Driving home, her excitement about the job and her admiration for her new boss distracted her from recognizing that the same car that followed her to the hospital was following her home.

Arriving home with 15 minutes to spare before the teleconference with DA Wydman, Jackie called her Mom to tell her the news about her job and asked if she could keep Ashley for another hour or two.

"Of course, I can. She's taking her nap right now anyway," Jackie's mother replied.

"OK, I will be over later to pick her up."

* * *

"TGIF," DA Wydman welcomed Jackie, Curt, and Inspector Adams on the call. "It's been an exciting week, and I'm anxious to hear from all of you. But first, Theo called me earlier, following up on a question that Curt raised on our last call. I'll have Theo tell you what he told me.

"Thanks, Will. Curt, the fingerprint on the note that was left on your door matches one of the unidentified prints in Dr. Caron's office. We still don't have a way to identify the individual, and as with all fingerprints, we have no way of knowing when that print was created."

This ominous finding had Curt speechless.

"Curt?" DA Wydman asked.

"I'm sorry, Will. I'm a little stunned that someone who was in Dr. Caron's office also tried to pick up my kids and left me a note. As you're still investigating whether Dr. Caron's death was a suicide, I can't help but think that there's a chance that print belongs to a person who may have killed Dr. Caron."

"I understand, Curt. Perhaps I should have asked you to come to my office this morning to break the news. I'm sorry."

"No apologies necessary, Will. I'm glad I was able to help put some evidence together for your case."

"Well, we appreciate your help, believe me. Since we started the meeting with you, Curt, do you have anything new to report since the last meeting?"

"No news is good news, Will. I'm anxious to hear from Jackie. As I recall, Jackie, you had an interview this morning."

"You're right, Curt. Thanks for remembering. And I have great news. I got the job!" she announced with glee.

The three congratulated and applauded.

"When do you start, Jackie?" DA Wydman asked.

"First thing Monday."

"Well, you don't waste any time, do you?"

"Nope. I'm really excited."

"And we're excited for you," DA Wydman replied. "So, I'm assuming you haven't had any more incidents of AlzCura spying or threatening you."

"No," Jackie replied, suddenly recalling the concern DA Wydman had expressed on their last call.

"That's good. Anything else to report?"

Before Jackie could respond, Curt chimed in, adding to DA Wydman's question.

"Yeah, how is Ashley doing?"

"Thanks for asking, Curt. Other than this morning, when she was fussy and threw up, almost making me late for my interview, she's been great."

"Sounds like she was trying to keep her mommy from leaving," Curt said half-jokingly, knowing how as babies Caitlin and Cade could often sense when he or Calli was about to leave them.

"I never thought about that. I was kinda in a rush."

"Kids and even babies do seem to have an innate sense and connection to their parents."

"And to our wallets," DA Wydman chimed in. "Mine are in their 20's, and it seems like every time they call, I'm reaching for my wallet." As the group chuckled, Jackie continued.

"Well, I can see I have a lot to learn as a new mom. Thanks for the education Curt and Will. I have nothing else to report, Will. I'm just looking forward to getting back into a regular routine."

As Will proceeded with the meeting, it took Jackie a moment to return to the meeting mentally. She found herself unable to shake what Curt had said and now questioned how her new work schedule was going to affect Ashley.

"I'd like to update you on the meeting I had with AG Talcott last week," DA Wydman began. "We discussed getting DHHS, and potentially the FDA and FBI involved, but to make a long story short, he wants to wait until AlzCura responds to his most recent letter before considering that option."

"And when will that be? Do they have a deadline to respond?" Curt asked.

"Yes, the deadline is next Friday. I know you have been pushing for this, Curt. I think between Theo's investigation findings, which I'm not at liberty to discuss, and the AG's rationale to wait for a response to his letter, all will contribute to a much stronger case for their involvement. If and when we decide to engage our federal partners, that is."

"I understand, Will. It's just my concern that every day we wait represents another day they have the opportunity to harm or kill someone."

"Point taken. All I can say is that there is light at the end of the tunnel, and that end could be as early as next Friday. Now let me get to yesterday's meeting with the media. I know you were there, Theo. Were you there, or did you watch it on TV, Curt?"

"I watched it on TV."

"Good, then much of what I am about to say is for your benefit, Jackie. I don't assume you had a way to watch it."

"No, but I'm anxious to hear. Curt did text me some highlights from it."

DA Wydman summarized the meeting agreeing to email Jackie a copy of AG Talcott's prepared statement.

"I'm sure Curt must have texted you about Celeste Boulanger."

"He did, but texting isn't the easiest way to communicate."

"True. Perhaps we can revisit allowing phone calls," DA Wydman replied, sensing her frustration. "Celeste lost her 28-year old husband a few weeks ago, and before he passed, he uncharacteristically became aggressive towards her. I'm sure that story sounds familiar to you, Jackie."

"It does. That poor woman," Jackie said, feeling an immediate affinity for her.

"Turns out, Theo here has met with her a couple of times. By the way, Theo, I forgot to tell you, but Mrs. Boulanger had very nice things to say about you when AG Talcott, Dr. Corpisen, and I met with her."

"Thanks, Will," Theo responded, feeling himself blush.

"As I was saying, Theo had met with Celeste, and since

she and her husband Norman are part of our investigation, AG Talcott had to interrupt her during the meeting so that she wouldn't compromise our investigation. We met with her afterward, and now she has to contend with the media constantly hounding her. I don't think she knew what she was getting into."

"I imagine like Curt and me, she was just trying to look for answers anywhere she could find them," Jackie replied.

"That's exactly what she said to us. I can't tell you much more, but she and the circumstances of her husband's death are important to our case. Judging from the headlines in our newspaper this morning, she will have to endure constant scrutiny and efforts to squeeze information out of her."

"Are you giving her any protection," Curt asked.

"We have patrols making frequent visits to her neighborhood and have offered to station an officer there if she feels the need."

Concerned that this was inadequate, Curt made a pitch to DA Wydman.

"With all this publicity, I'm sure AlzCura execs will catch wind of her if they haven't already. Based on Jackie and my experience, you should consider stationing someone there round the clock."

"I agree," chimed Investigator Adams, "she was very fragile emotionally and naïve about legal matters when I met with her. Now her appearance at yesterday's meeting has only called unwanted attention to her. I think she probably does need more protection."

"Good points. I'll speak with the Chief of Police in Dracut-Campion and see if we can work something out. Anything else we need to discuss?"

"How about lifting the ban on phone calls between us?" Curt offered.

"I'm good with that, providing we make and receive the calls in secure surroundings, and there is no further evidence of AlzCura snooping around in our lives," DA Wydman responded.

"Deal," Curt replied.

"Good. How about we have a call next Friday?"

"I'm not sure what my work schedule will look like," Jackie replied. "I know it might not be popular with the rest of you, but can we make it on Saturday?"

As all three agreed they could accommodate Jackie's suggested meeting on the following Saturday, they ended the call.

Jackie, torn between picking Ashley up and calling Curt, decided to send Curt a text.

"Have to go pick up Ash and tell Mom about the job. Can we chat later on a REAL phone call?"

"ABSOLUTELY!!!" was Curt's emphatic one-word response.

Jackie sent a smiling emoji, left her home, and walked to her mother's house down the block. On the way, she didn't notice the non-descript sedan that had been following her earlier in the day now parked across the street.

CHAPTER 37

"OK, good news, bad news, as I understand it." Dr. Asa Sheridan prefaced his Friday afternoon meeting with Cheryl Baker and Chet Humphreys.

"First, the good news. I was able to get Muckland to work some lab magic, and Dr. Slack and Dr. Mason are now, not only reassured, they are considering expanding their support to our Recallamin 3 trial."

"Well, that is good news, but I'm afraid I have the bad news," Cheryl added. "And it is very, very bad."

As Cheryl gave an account of the AG's meeting with the media, she could tell that Dr. Sheridan was growing increasingly anxious and angry.

"The only silver-lining as I see it," Cheryl concluded, trying to put a positive spin on it, "is that even with that woman's unexpected appearance, and the media's fascination over her husband's behavior and death, there was no mention of us or that they were involved in our clinical trials."

"Well, to me, what may be your silver-lining, is my shit sandwich," Dr. Sheridan exploded. "There is nothing good about the media attention that split tail fire crotch skank is getting. She's pictured in full-color on the front page of the New York Times and Boston Globe. If they haven't done so already, she'll soon be on every podunk paper in the Northeast, including our Buffalo News. And believe me, they won't drop this story until they milk it for all it's worth."

"What do you suggest we do, Asa?" Cheryl replied. "There was no way to anticipate this."

"I want her taken care of. We can't afford to have her out there shooting off her mouth. We scared off Jackie and Curt Barnes. I say we do the same with that bitch," he spat.

"Well, Asa, not so quick," Chet replied. "I got some news from Horse today that I don't think you're going to like."

If Dr. Sheridan wasn't about to explode before Chet's comment, he was now. His face turned red, and the veins in his forehead and neck began to protrude and throb. He was beyond the ability to speak.

"Jackie went to Nora Community Hospital this morning. Horse thinks she was there for an interview."

"That's not good news," Cheryl responded, seeing Asa decompensating further. "I will get my boys to address both Celeste Boulanger and Jackie. OK, Asa?"

Still unable to find words, Dr. Sheridan nodded and then stood up, walked over to his office bar, and waved Cheryl and Chet out. As they exited his office, they heard him roar, followed closely by a crash of glass later learned to have been a bottle of bourbon that had met its sudden demise against his office wall.

Not the first time he had taken his anger out on his stocked bar, and without having to go in to inspect, his assistant called their cleaning service to come in over the weekend.

CHAPTER 38

Inspector Adams called Celeste Boulanger's phone after the meeting with DA Wydman, Curt, and Jackie. When the call went to voice mail, he left a message, only to receive an immediate return call.

"Hi Theo, this is Celeste. I'm sorry, I've been screening my calls. The reporters must have gotten my number somehow."

"Hi, Celeste. I'm sorry they are bothering you."

"It's awful. I have been blocking numbers left and right, but they keep calling. I had to put Sophie in the back bedroom because she was going crazy with all those people in the front yard and my phone ringing every few minutes."

"I figured they would do this. That's one of the reasons I called. I wanted to see how you're holding up."

"Just barely until you called. I really messed up going to that meeting."

"Don't be so hard on yourself. You were just looking for answers. By next week, the media will have something else to focus on, and you'll be old news."

"I hope so. You said one of your reasons for the call was to see how I was doing. Was there another reason?"

"Yes. I wanted to see if I could come over and talk to you about a meeting I just had with my boss."

"I'd like that, Theo. I'm afraid you'll have to fight your way through a crowd."

"Oh, that won't be a problem. I have ignored their invasive questions and techniques for so long they hardly bother anymore."

"Can I put a pot of coffee on for you?"

"That sounds great, Celeste. See you soon."

At 33 years old, Theo Adams had never been able to cultivate a lasting relationship. They typically failed for one reason - he was married to his job. The few women he dated never felt like they were number one in his book. When their efforts to supplant his dedication to his career failed, they invariably ended the relationship in frustration.

Inspector Adams was happy that Curt raised the concern for Celeste's safety and hoped that DA Wydman would quickly arrange to have a detail stationed at her house. After what had happened to Curt and Jackie, he didn't want the same to happen to Celeste. He knew that his feelings towards the recently widowed, red-headed beauty complicated his role as the investigator on the case. Despite his unassailable professionalism up to this point in his career, he could not deny that he cared for her. Maybe it was her vulnerability or her naivete, but whatever it was, he wanted to care for and protect her. He wrestled with these feelings in his mind, knowing full well that she was his kryptonite.

As Inspector Adams entered the trailer park, he could already see the impact of Celeste's newfound notoriety. News station vehicles and vans, some with telescoping broadcast antennas extended, were lined up as he approached Celeste's trailer. Unable to find a place to park near her trailer, he was forced to park a distance away and suffer the inevitable attention from a gaggle of approximately 20 reporters and cameramen stationed in Celeste's front yard.

As reporter's questions came rapid-fire and cameras swung

toward him, he went into media avoidance mode. This consisted of walking at a brisk pace, with a determined I-have-somewhere-else-to-be look on his face while holding his arms out with palms forward to block the cameras and microphones being thrust at him. This technique and an unshakable commitment not to respond to any questions had been his recipe for success. And today, the results of media avoidance mode were no different.

Successfully navigating the sea of reporters, he approached Celeste's front door. He didn't even have to knock. Celeste had heard the reporters' voices crescendo on his arrival, and as he approached, she opened the door. Safely inside, Inspector Adams could see that Celeste had added extra window coverings for privacy. Although it was mid-afternoon on a sunny day, you would have thought it was nighttime. Only soft light from a corner lamp and a couple of candles illuminated the living area. It was oddly serene amid the chaos he had just left outside. As his eyes adjusted, Celeste was in his arms.

"Oh, Theo, I'm so happy you're here," she said, desperation in her voice as her arms encircled him.

Her body against his, the smell of her perfume, the candle-lit room, her need, his want, and the risk of the media outside the door suddenly attracted them like magnets. Their lips met in a long, passionate kiss. Their greeting transitioned to her, laying in his arms on the couch, unloading the emotional baggage that she had been carrying. How Norman's behavior had scared her. How his death had left her lonely and confused. Her suffering job performance as a cashier at a local grocery store. How her effort to find answers only caused her more problems. How he had provided her with answers and compassionate support. Celeste's catharsis only entangled Theo deeper into the miasma between his role as a professional investigator and her personal savior.

Inspector Adams, having liberated Celeste's cascading concerns, albeit most unconventionally, finally was able to speak to her about the plan for her security.

"Celeste, we'd like to have an officer stationed here round the clock."

"Well, if that's you, then I'm all in favor of that plan," as she tightened her embrace and kissed him.

"I'm serious, Celeste. It wouldn't be me, and we're concerned for your safety."

"Why? They're just reporters and cameramen. You even said they'd probably move on by next week."

"It's not the media folks we're concerned about, although they have been known to do some brazen things to get a story."

"Then, who?"

"We don't know for sure. We do know of people in your situation who have had incidents of having their house broken into and being spied on. Others have had threats to their safety or the safety of their children."

"Because their spouse died?"

"Because their spouse died, and their spouse or the person who killed their spouse were involved in the same clinical trial."

The weight of what Inspector Adams was saying sunk in, and she started to tremble in his arms.

"So you're saying that someone from the pharmaceutical company that is doing the study is doing this?"

"No, I can't say that, but someone has done this, and we're trying to find out who."

"Would the officer be in my house?"

"No, he or she would be stationed outside."

"I guess that would be alright."

"My boss is working with the Chief of Police to set something up. I don't know when it will start, but I'm hoping fairly soon."

"Wanna have that coffee now?" she asked, hoping to extend his stay.

"Thanks, but I better not. I'm sure the reporters out there have me on a timer. Raising their suspicions would not be a good thing."

"Well, then I can't wait until they're no longer out there."

He smiled and indulged himself in the thought of being with her outside of his role as an investigator. He was in dangerous territory, and he knew it.

"Are you going to be alright?" he asked.

"As long as I have you."

His effort to gently start an exit process failing as she kissed him deeply and pressed her body into his. Five minutes later, they were finally able to tear themselves away from each other. After assuring his hair and clothes didn't look like he just had a torrid session of consoling the lonely, distraught widow on her couch, he opened the door and waded into the storm of reporters and cameramen. Once again employing his trusty media avoidance mode, Theo was soon safely back in his car, leaving the reporter's questions and their camera's prying eyes in his rearview mirror.

✳ ✳ ✳

Jackie's visit with her mother had been a perfect accompaniment to the great day she was having. Her mother was ecstatic that Jackie would be working locally. That grandma would also get to care for little Ashley every weekday didn't hurt either. It also relieved Jackie of the guilt she had over not telling her parents about how she lost her job or the sinister threat spray-painted on Ashley's bedroom wall. She could move on, and she had spared her parents of the fears and anxieties she endured.

As the two sipped coffee and snacked on homemade cookies, Jackie spoke animatedly about her interviews and how much she liked her charismatic new boss. As if choreographed, Ashley stirred from her nap just as Jackie finished her coffee and finished answering her mother's questions about her new job. Retrieving Ashley and placing her in her stroller, Jackie hugged her mother and made the short walk home with her daughter babbling all the way.

No sooner had Jackie arrived home and placed Ash in her playpen when her phone rang the screen announcing Curt was calling.

"Hi, Curt," she answered brightly.

"Are you in a secure spot to talk? I wouldn't want to break Will's phone call rules," he joked.

"Hold on a sec, I have to put earplugs in Ash's ears. I wouldn't want her repeating our secret conversation," she said, playing along.

"It's good to hear you so happy, Jackie."

"It's good to be happy. Thank you for remembering that I had an interview on the call today."

"No problem. I know the last few weeks have been a rollercoaster for you."

"It has, but it finally feels like I'm moving on."

"Yeah, our role in the investigation really feels like it has shifted away from us, and Will, Theo, and the Attorney General seem to be working a good plan. I just wish we'd call in the Feds already."

"I feel so sorry for that woman who spoke up at the meeting. She did not know what she was getting herself into. I'm glad you pushed Will to get her protection," Jackie empathized.

"I almost suggested that we include her in our calls. While Will and Theo can't share much information, being able to speak to them, and knowing you have gone through a similar hell as I have has helped."

"That's a great idea, Curt. You know, I don't care what all the others say. I think you're a really thoughtful and caring guy," she jabbed playfully.

"Glad I've fooled you," he replied as the two laughed.

"Now that you've worked your magic with Will on the phone calls, do you think you can get him to agree we should all meet in person again?"

"Wouldn't that be nice? Rarely a week goes by without either Caitlin or Cade asking me when we're going to see you again."

"Really?"

"Oh, you have no idea. Do you know what they do when we go to the Farrisport Inn for dinner?"

"No, what?"

"They ordered the same desserts they had when we had our dinner together, and they each leave a bite for you."

All Curt heard in response was a muffled sniffle, and then finally her response.

"That is so sweet," she cried as tears streamed down her face.

"I'm sorry I've made you cry."

"That's OK, they're happy tears. What about you?"

"Me?"

"Do you leave me a bite of your dessert?"

"No, I eat it all and lick the plate clean," he said in mock selfishness, hoping to hear her laugh.

"I take my previous compliment about you back," she said,

laughing.

"I love hearing you laugh," he said and immediately worried his admission may be more intimate than she may be comfortable with.

"Awww, you must like me," she pouted sweetly.

"Guilty," he pleaded, laughing.

"Well, I love hearing you laugh too."

"So then, you must like me," Curt asked.

"Guilty as charged, but I'm not into handcuffs," Jackie replied, taking the conversation to a whole different level.

When Curt was caught speechless, Jackie's laughter broke the silence, and he laughed with her.

"Had you worried there, didn't I?" she chuckled.

"Worry was not the word I'd use," he said in a scandalous tone.

Now Jackie was speechless, and Curt had to break the silence.

"Had you worried there, didn't I?" he laughed.

"If only Will knew what important things we've had to talk about," she laughed.

"Yeah, he'd probably ban us from calling each other."

"This is fun, Curt. I really miss you and the kids."

"And we miss you."

The two talked about their weekend plans and agreed to chat again on Monday night after Jackie's first day of work. After the call, Jackie basked in what had been her best day in many months. She hoped it was the start of a happier and brand new chapter in her life.

CHAPTER 39

C hannel 5 senior investigative correspondent Leslie Anderson was livid as she walked out of a holding cell at the county jail on Friday afternoon. For her antics at the AG's media meeting, she was charged with disorderly conduct and ordered to pay $500. They waived any jail time but made sure she was aware that they could have extended her stay at the jail for up to six months. What irked her, however, was not the threat of incarceration or the fine she had to pay. It was the overnight stay in the holding cell, which prohibited her from being on camera to report on the most significant news event since Calli Barne's murder. This did not prevent her from eventually putting an indelible mark on the media firestorm created by Celeste Boulanger.

Although late to the party, Leslie was used to employing unconventional and occasionally legally questionable techniques to outwit her media colleagues. She noted that the horde of reporters in front of Celeste's trailer had not gained access to Celeste or broke any stories of note during her incarceration. She decided to choose a different path. While all of her colleagues wondered when the infamous Leslie Anderson would make her appearance, she plotted her strategy.

❅ ❅ ❅

DA Wydman arranged for an officer to be stationed at Celeste Boulanger's house with the assistance of the Dracut-Champion's Chief of Police. He called Inspector Adams on Saturday morning to inform him.

"Theo, we have a detail that will be stationed at Mrs. Boulanger's house starting on Monday."

"Not until Monday?"

"Yeah, they couldn't put the coverage together until then. Can you let her know? She might not understand why it's necessary, so do your best to get her cooperation without spooking her."

"I already met with her to let her know we were working on this. She's fine with it, but I'll let her know it will start on Monday."

"I should have figured you'd be one step ahead of me."

"Just doing my job," he said, as images of laying with her on the couch danced in his head.

"OK, have a good weekend, Theo."

"You too, Will."

As soon as the call disconnected, Inspector Adams called Celeste.

"Hi, Theo," she answered.

"Hi, Celeste. I just wanted to call to let you know that we won't be able to have an officer stationed at your place until Monday."

"OK, that's fine. I'm not planning on going anywhere until my shift at work tomorrow afternoon. Do you want to come over?"

"What I want and what I should do are two different things," he replied. "I really can't come over as much as I'd like to."

"I understand," she said sadly.

"When's your shift tomorrow?"

"From 2 p.m. to 10 p.m.," she replied.

"OK. Maybe I will have to go grocery shopping tomorrow afternoon."

"I'd like that, but I might be really slow in scanning your groceries."

"I won't mind that in the least."

Ending the call, both looked forward to their plan to see each other briefly at the grocery store the next day.

* * *

Curt buoyed by his call with Jackie Friday afternoon, had made spontaneous arrangements to surprise the kids and Jordan with a weekend trip to a Dude Ranch.

At 6a.m. on Saturday, he sprung the surprise on Caitlin and Cade. But rather than doing it himself, he had arranged for Jordan to come over and wake them up and break the news. It was a resounding success. The kids were out of their beds like a shot. An hour later, the foursome was on the road for the 2-hour drive to the Dude Ranch. Curt was energized and felt like a super Dad. The kids were excited even though none of them had ever been to or heard of a Dude Ranch. The two hours passed quickly as the kids asked endless questions.

"What's a Dude Ranch?" Cade asked.

"It's a working ranch where people go to experience what it's like to be cowboys and cowgirls," Curt replied.

"Why do they call it a Dude Ranch if boys and girls can go?" Jordan asked.

"That's a good question, Jordan. I don't know the answer to

that one." Before Curt knew it, Jordan had searched the internet on her phone for the answer.

"Here's what it says on the internet," Jordan announced. "Cultured socialites, arrogant and rich, were called "dudes" when they came out West to see what life was like for the "other half." Guest ranches in the Old West quickly earned the nickname "dude ranch" to refer to the type of patrons they attracted."

"Does that mean we're arrogant and rich, Daddy?" Caitlin asked.

"No, honey, it just means we don't typically live on a ranch, and we're just going there to see what it's like."

"What kind of things do they do there?" Cade continued the interrogation.

"Well, there's horseback riding, and we will have a cowboy dinner tonight by a campfire. You'll have to wait and see."

Wait and see was never a popular answer, especially for Cade, who always wanted to know about things in advance.

"Where will we sleep?" Cade fast-forwarded through his father's wait-and-see instructions.

"We're staying in a cabin."

"Will I have my own room?"

"I don't think so, Cade," to which Curt could see Cade's anxiety bubbling up. Before he could protest, Curt tried to short-circuit his concerns. "It will be fun, you'll see."

While Cade didn't respond and didn't offer any additional questions, Curt knew his son was stewing over whether the sleeping arrangements would meet with his approval. While Cade perseverated, Caitlin and Jordan played with a selection of horses from his daughter's now immense Breyer horse collection. A break in questioning allowed Curt to replay his recent conversation with Jackie in his head.

An impressive ranch gate with pillars built from native granite and an ornate wrought iron arch welcomed them to the Downeast Dude Ranch. As Curt turned into the driveway, the kids' attention shifted to a vast pasture containing horses, the number, types, sizes, and colors of which dwarfed Caitlin's toy horse collection. The long, straight driveway and open field gave way to a tree-lined winding section that traversed a stream, which finally opened up to the ranch compound. There, nestled at the foot of an elevation blanketed by pine trees, were a massive main building, corrals, a barn, a dozen cabins, and several other buildings. Interspersed across the grounds were a rock climbing wall, a disc golf course, archery targets, a fire pit, horseshoe pits, shuffleboard courts, cornhole boards, a swimming pool with a towering slide, and a roping area with hay bales equipped with dummy steer heads.

Any concerns the kids may have had about whether a dude ranch would be fun evaporated. Entering the main building, Curt registered and got the key to Cabin #7. In the meantime, the kids had explored a good portion of the building, excitedly reporting on their discoveries.

"Dad, they have an arcade," Caitlin gushed.

Cade came back with an ice cream cone, "Where did you get that?" Curt asked.

"It was free," Cade replied, licking the vanilla soft-serve that already adorned his chin and threatened to drip onto his t-shirt. "Come on, I'll show you," Cade said in response to his father's look of doubt.

Lo and behold, there it stood, an ice cream machine with a sign which read: "All the ice cream you can eat for FREE."

Although it was only 9a.m., Curt let Caitlin and Jordan join Cade in his breakfast dessert. Caitlin chose chocolate while Jordan got a vanilla and chocolate swirl.

In addition to the kids' discoveries, the main building housed the cafeteria, a gift shop, and a wing with hotel-like lodging for those not wanting to lodge in the cabins.

If that was not enough, a ranch map that Curt got at check-in boasted a movie house in one of the outbuildings as well as another building reserved for ping-pong, billiards, and dart game enthusiasts. One-hour horseback trail rides were scheduled every 2 hours throughout the day, and private horseback riding and roping lessons were available for an extra fee.

Add about two dozen other kids of similar age to the mix, and Curt had everything he could do to corral the kids. After they reluctantly helped unpack the car and claimed their respective beds in the cabin, they ran off to make new friends and partake in the dizzying array of entertainment choices. As they excitedly talked about what they wanted to do, Curt's suggestion that they all do one thing at a time as a group fell flat. Realizing that there was no way short of cloning himself that he would be able to participate in or supervise their divergent interests, he ceded control. He prayed that the army of teenage volunteers, adult wranglers, and other parents would provide the boundaries and supervision the kids may require.

These were the moments where he missed Calli most. They were a great team when it came to dividing and conquering. Now he was outnumbered, but he didn't want to limit their choices. He had to trust that the principles and values he and Calli had tried to instill in Caitlin and Cade would guide them in making good and safe choices.

As Jordan had proven to be a mature and positive influence on Caitlin, Curt decided to spend most of his time with Cade, who was not as anxious to navigate the ranch or the activities by himself.

What fears Curt may have had at the outset quickly dissolved as, more often than not, the three kids ended up wanting to do the same activities. By 5 p.m., when it was time for the trail ride and Cowboy dinner, they had already engaged in an exhausting gauntlet of activities.

The Cowboy dinner consisted of a one-hour trail-ride by horseback circumnavigating switchback trails cut through the pine-covered elevation to a clearing on the summit. Picnic tables ringed a campfire as a cowboy with a guitar sang cowboy songs. Cowboy and cowgirl chefs cooked steaks, cornbread, and beans on makeshift grills, hewn in the granite outcroppings rimming the clearing. In between songs and before dinner, the singing cowboy talked to the guests about the cowboy life and the role cowboys played in the history of America.

After dinner, the guests were given long-tined forks to roast marshmallows and all the fixings to make s'mores for dessert. Full of food, fresh air, and a newfound appreciation for the cowboy life, Curt, the kids, and the other guests, saddled up and made their way back down the trail. Many of the guests, including Curt and the kids, felt themselves almost falling asleep to the steady rhythmic rocking horseback ride on their descent back to the ranch. As they trudged back to their cabin, any concern Cade may have had about the sleeping arrangements was lost to sheer exhaustion from a full day of fun.

After a fitful night of sleep, the kids sought to make the most of their last day at the ranch. While Jordan and Caitlin feverishly bounced from one activity to the next, Cade was content to spend his time at the arcade and swimming pool with liberal visits to sample the different flavors of free ice cream. Caitlin learned she had an affinity for roping and dragged Curt to the roping arena to show off her newfound skill. Little did Curt know that this would subsequently result in an $85 expenditure at the gift shop, where he bought a rope and dummy steer head for Caitlin to practice her skills at home. By 4 p.m., when it was time to check out, the kids reluctantly piled into the car for the 2-hour drive home. All three were fast asleep shortly after they exited the driveway. It was a quiet but surprisingly turbulent drive home for Curt emotionally. Something about having so much fun with the kids without

Calli there gnawed at him. Simultaneously, he missed Jackie, adding to his stormy emotions.

CHAPTER 40

lthough the horde of reporters and cameramen had thinned considerably over the weekend, Celeste was unprepared for what awaited when she exited her trailer Sunday afternoon on her way to work. With cameras and microphones thrust in her face and a relentless unintelligible mash-up of questions barked in her direction, she felt under attack.

"Please, leave me alone," was all she could manage, cowering as she tried to navigate her way to the 1986 Honda Accord. The car had been a gift from Norman's grandmother after she was diagnosed with dementia and prohibited from driving.

The relief she felt when she was finally safe in her car quickly turned to horror as she realized they were all jumping in their vehicles and following her to work. How would she be able to work? What would her boss say? What if they posed as shoppers and interrogated her when checking out in her aisle?

As she turned into the parking lot in front of the grocery store, she saw two police cruisers. As she parked in a space reserved for employees, the police officers made their way in her direction.

"Ma'am, we're here to escort you in. We will make sure they won't bother you," the officer said while pointing to the growing number of reporters and cameramen.

"How did you know?" she asked in disbelief.

"Inspector Adams tipped us off about your shift today. We will be here until the end of your shift and make sure you get home safely."

As the officers took up places beside her, the members of the media kept a respectful distance but still shouted questions in her direction.

"What if they come into the store?" Celeste asked.

"One of us will be stationed inside the store and the other outside. You don't have to worry."

"Does my boss know?"

"Yes, the store manager is aware."

As her anxiety subsided, and she began to appreciate Theo's thoughtfulness fully, she became tearful upon entering the store.

"Are you OK, Celeste?" her manager questioned, meeting her at the door.

"Yes, for once, these are happy tears," she remarked. "I'm so happy that the officers were here to keep those reporters away from me."

"I'm sure it has been difficult for you. Do you feel up to working a register? If not, I can try to find something else for you to do?"

"Thanks, but I want to work the register. I am so ready to try to get back to some sense of normal."

"OK. Let me know if you need anything or if anyone bothers you.

With that, Celeste clocked in and took her place at an open register.

Not only did her appearance at the AG's meeting attract media attention, but as she and her manager soon learned, it also drew community members into the store. Fortunately, their interests were more sympathetic, and as her shift progressed, she was amazed at and inspired by all the people who just stopped by to offer their supportive comments and pick up a few grocery items.

As promised, Theo stopped by, and although his visit was brief, it allowed her to thank him for his thoughtfulness and invite him to dinner the following evening. Tempting as her offer was, he gently declined, promising he would take her up on the offer once it didn't represent a conflict with his current investigation. Desperate to feel their connection no matter how fleeting, she grasped his hand as she gave him his store receipt and held it a beat longer than was natural. Her touch, in turn, generated something akin to a pleasant electric pulse that quickened Theo's heartbeat and caused his thumb to caress the back of her hand reflexively. Releasing his hand before customers took notice and before her thirst for his touch was quenched, their eyes met, betraying a mutual and consuming hunger.

By the end of her shift, she started to believe that a return to normalcy and a brighter future was possible. As she was escorted to her car by the police officer, only a few stalwart reporters remained. Seeing her escort, they didn't even bother shouting their questions.

For the first time in her lifetime, seeing the police cruiser in her rearview mirror on her drive home was comforting. Arriving home, with no reporters in her front yard, her walk from her car to the front door was obstacle-free. She waved to the police officer as she opened her front door and immediately let out a scream that the police officer and the neighboring trailer occupants heard.

Her living room furniture was out of place and splattered with blood. A half-naked female corpse lay in a pool of blood from a gruesome neck laceration. Beyond that, in the corner of the room, lay Sophie in her dog bed. But Sophie didn't get up to greet Celeste. The formerly white dog and her white bed were now a sea of crimson.

This was all that Celeste saw before the police officer arrived just in time to catch her as she fainted. Calling for crime scene investigators and additional police backup, the officer put Celeste in his cruiser. Returning to the trailer, he secured the crime scene as neighbors spilled out of their homes.

Having heard the officers call for CSI and back up to Celeste's address on his police radio, Theo feared the worst and immediately sped to the scene. Relieved to find Celeste in the police officers' car, he hugged her, but she couldn't reciprocate. She was in shock, and as an ambulance arrived, he instructed the EMTs to attend to her.

Surveying the scene, Inspector Adams immediately recognized the female corpse as Leslie Anderson, the Channel 5 reporter. Judging from the state in which he found her half-clad body, he surmised that she had been sexually assaulted. Celeste's dog, Sophie, or at least her headless body, was in her dog bed in the corner. As Theo traced a blood trail through the trailer, he found Sophie's head on a pillow in Celeste's bed, like some sick homage to the horse head in the bed from The Godfather movie.

At first pass, the bloody scene and possible sexual assault promised to produce plenty of evidence. What Theo found disturbing, in addition to the grisly crime scene, was why Leslie Anderson was in the trailer. Who could have been in the trailer or arrived at the trailer and killed her while she was there? Could the perp have thought that Leslie was Celeste? Or was this just a random act? It didn't appear anything was taken from the home. So burglary didn't seem to be a motive.

Theo was relieved that Celeste would never have to see what the perpetrator did to Sophie. It could only be construed as someone trying to send a strong message. Then it dawned on him, why send a message if the killer thought he killed Celeste? The killer must have known that the woman lying dead in the living room was not Celeste. Leslie must have been in the wrong place at the wrong time.

This was not a random act, Theo speculated, but a purposeful act designed to either kill Celeste or at least send her a message. While the evidence still needed to be collected and analyzed, his strong suspicion was that someone associated with AlzCura Pharmaceuticals was responsible for this gruesome act.

One thing Theo was sure of, Celeste was lucky to be alive.

As the CSI team and someone from the medical examiner's office arrived, Theo exited the trailer. Finding Celeste was no longer in the police cruiser, he surmised the EMTs had taken her to their rig. As he approached the ambulance, an EMT met him.

"We're treating her for shock. She's asking for you," he said, simultaneously opening the back door.

"Thanks," Theo replied as he climbed into the ambulance.

"Theo," she said with relief as he took her hand. "Sophie?" she implored hopefully.

He shook his head dejectedly.

"Oh, no, my poor Sophie," she cried, shaking her head in disbelief.

He didn't know what to say, so he just continued to hold her hand as tears welled up in his eyes.

"Her vitals are looking better," the EMT who was monitoring her interjected. "She should be good to go when she's ready."

"Do you have a place to stay tonight?" Theo asked.

The look in her eyes told Theo what she was thinking, and he shook his head slightly to discourage the question he knew she wanted to ask.

"I have a sister in Ramsey," she replied, with no real enthusiasm.

"Let's get you out of here and call her, OK?"

When she voiced her reluctant agreement, the EMT removed her IV and the devices monitoring her vitals. Celeste thanked the EMT, and Theo assisted Celeste out of the rig. Putting his arm around her shoulders, he led her to his car.

Once inside the car, and before she had a chance to call her sister, Theo declared, "I'm taking you to my house."

Although she was relieved to hear this, her grief over Sophie was too deep for his words to register any comfort. A deep sigh, placing her head on his shoulder, and shedding more tears were all she could muster.

CHAPTER 41

Early Monday morning, Jackie's phone rang. Seeing it was Curt, she answered even though she was in the middle of getting herself ready for work, and Ashley prepared to go to Grandma's.

"Good morning, Curt."

"Good morning, Jackie. I know you're probably getting ready to go to work, but I wanted to call and wish you a great first day."

"You're so sweet," she replied.

"I try."

"You're succeeding. Even if you don't save me a bite of your dessert," she joked, pulling in a topic from their previous call.

"OK, I'll let you go. Talk tonight?"

"It's a date. You have an awesome day too, Curt."

Fueled by their brief call, both Jackie and Curt felt more prepared to take on the day. Curt dropped Caitlin and Cade off at school and went to work. Jackie dropped Ash off at her mother's and attended a new employee orientation session.

During her lunch break, Jackie called her mother.

"Hi, Mom. How is Ashley doing?"

"She's good. I just put her down for her nap. I'm going to take her to the park this afternoon when she gets up."

"I'm jealous," Jackie remarked, as, over the past few weeks, they had a routine of taking Ash to the park together.

"Only a half-day in, and you're already homesick. Don't you like the new job?"

"No, the job is fine. It's just going to be an adjustment. I enjoyed spending afternoons with you and Ash in the park."

"Yes, it won't be the same without you. Look at the bright side. Isn't it great not to have that commute into Buffalo and all that travel? And how do you expect me to teach Ash how to say Nana if you're always around?" causing Jackie to laugh.

"Oh, I see the bright side, Mom. It took me 4 minutes to get here this morning. If I didn't have orientation today and a short lunch break, I could have come home for lunch."

"I'm so happy you listened to your mother and got that job. See, mother always knows best."

"Yep, you were right, Mom," Jackie agreed, letting her mother believe she took the job on her mother's advice when the entire time, all Jackie could think was - if she only knew the truth.

"Gotta go, Mom. Have a nice time at the park with my precious baby."

"I will. Don't be surprised if you come home tonight, and Ash is saying, Nana."

Jackie couldn't wipe the smile off her face after the call, certain that her mother would indeed be trying to teach her daughter to say, Nana.

Settling into the second half of her orientation, Jackie tried to pay attention and not to let her mind wander. Several times, she caught herself daydreaming about the afternoon at the park when Ashley first said, Mama.

As a parade of hospital leaders marched in and continued to barrage the orientation group with their information, she began to wonder how she was going to retain it all.

As a physical therapist was teaching the group about proper office ergonomics and preventing back injuries using proper lifting techniques, Jackie's cell phone vibrated. Wondering why her mother would be calling her when she knew she was in orientation, she excused herself. She stepped out of the conference room into the hallway.

Accepting the call, all she initially heard was her mother's frantic words so pressured as to be unintelligible. Jackie was beginning to wonder if her mother was having a stroke when she finally said the words clearly enough for Jackie to understand.

"I can't find Ash. She's gone. Someone must have taken her."

The next thing the orientation group heard was Jackie's heart-stopping screams.

"Nooooooo, not my baby," Jackie wailed as she slid to the floor. "No, No, No, Mom."

Ironically, it was the Physical Therapist who ultimately came to Jackie's aid. Observing his own training when helping to lift her back on her feet, he escorted her to a nearby vacant room. She was inconsolable, and within moments the CEO, Tara Newman, arrived.

"Jackie, what's the matter?" Tara asked.

Between sobs, she tried to convey the horror, "Someone has taken my baby."

"Have the police been notified?

"I don't know," Jackie cried as she started frantically looking for her phone. "I can't find my phone."

"Here it is," replied a Nurse in blue scrubs, setting the phone in front of Jackie.

In the chaos, she had dropped her phone in the hallway, and the Nurse had picked it up when the Physical Therapist was assisting Jackie to the room they were in.

Jackie picked up the phone, but in shock, she couldn't even remember why she had wanted the phone.

Recognizing that Jackie was in no condition, Tara took control.

"Jackie, let me have your phone."

Handing Tara her phone, Jackie started to get up from her chair. "I need to go home."

"OK, Jackie, I'll take you home. Just leave your car for now. We'll take mine."

As the Physical Therapist continued his role as Jackie's escort, Tara used Jackie's phone to call the last entry on her phone, which read, "Mom."

When Tara's call was answered, it immediately answered the question that Jackie could not answer.

"Jackie, this is Officer Todd."

"Hi, Officer Todd, this is Tara Newman. I'm with Jackie, and I'm bringing her home."

"Hi, Ms. Newman. I'm with Jackie's mother at the park across from Jackie's house. I just arrived and am starting my investigation. Why don't you meet us here."

"Will do. We'll be there shortly."

As the Physical Therapist assisted Jackie into Tara's car, she graduated from inconsolable sobbing to a near-catatonic state with a mile-long stare. As they arrived at the park, Tara navigated towards Officer Todd's cruiser. Jackie's mother was sitting on a bench with the baby stroller next to her.

Jackie sat up and suddenly came to life.

"Did they find her? Look, it's her stroller."

For a minute, Tara joined Jackie in her hope, only to have those hopes dashed when they walked down to her mother and saw that the stroller was empty. Jackie sat down on the bench and hugged her mother, igniting another round of tears.

As they consoled one another, they saw Officer Todd returning from speaking with someone near the basketball court. Arriving back at the bench, Officer Todd introduced himself to Tara Newman and addressed Jackie, who was still grieving.

"Jackie, I've taken your mother's statement, and as I can see, you're both still very upset. It might be best for me to give you the details. Are you comfortable with that?" he asked, directing the question to both women.

Nodding their approval, Officer Todd continued.

"Mrs. Selaney, please feel free to correct or amplify anything you think I may not address accurately," he prefaced.

"Mrs. Selaney reported that she came to the park with Ashley at approximately 2:45 p.m. At the time, she estimated that there were 8-10 people in the entire park - two other adults with their 2 children in this particular area. At approximately 3:00 p.m., a woman approached Mrs. Selaney frantically, claiming to have lost her son. She asked Mrs. Selaney if she would try to help her find him. Mrs. Selaney briefly assisted the woman, and she estimates that this diverted her attention from the stroller for two to three minutes. When the woman called to Mrs. Selaney from outside the men's bathroom claiming she found her son, Mrs. Selaney returned to this area to find Ashley missing from her stroller."

"She asked me to check the women's bathroom while she checked the men's bathroom," Jackie's mother introjected. "That was the only time I was unable to see the stroller. It couldn't have taken me more than 30 seconds," she said, provoking another round of tears.

Officer Todd thanked her for the clarification and continued.

"I interviewed the two adults who were in the area at the time, and neither of them was aware of the alleged lost child, nor did they see anyone take Ashley from her stroller."

"Did you get a description of the woman?" Tara asked.

"Yes," Officer Todd confirmed. "Mrs. Selaney described her as a petite woman about 5 foot 3 in her 20's with brunette hair dressed in a white t-shirt, jeans, and sneakers. She was wearing sunglasses, so Mrs. Selaney was unable to provide an eye color. She didn't have any distinguishing marks or tattoos that Mrs. Selaney noticed."

"What about the other people in the park?" Tara questioned. "Were you able to speak to them?"

"Yes. I spoke to three other people. A couple was having a picnic on the other end of the park. They didn't see anyone fitting the description of the woman and no one with a baby. The other person was shooting hoops at the basketball court. He also didn't see anything."

While Tara and Officer Todd dialogued back and forth, Jackie sank deeper into an abyss, more bottomless perhaps than the chasm created when she lost Stu. That hole only got deeper when Officer Todd made his next statement.

"Jackie, I think that this might be related to the threat painted on your wall after the break-in and the surveillance equipment we found. Do you have any idea who may hold such a grudge against you?"

Jackie could not have scripted a worse time for Officer Todd to reveal the secret she had been keeping from her parents. That it occurred in front of her new boss made it even more humiliating.

All her mother could say was, "Jackie?"

Tara, recognizing the gravity of the moment, gave Jackie a temporary reprieve.

"Jackie, I know you're devastated. Who wouldn't be? Take all the time you need. Don't worry about the job. Call me if you need anything. Family first, OK? Give me your car keys, and I'll have someone from the hospital bring your car home."

"Ok, thank you, Tara," Jackie managed, handing her the car keys.

Tara hugged Jackie, offered consolation to Jackie's mother, thanked Officer Todd, and marched off towards her car.

As Jackie watched Tara leave, her mother amplified her previous question.

"Jackie? What have you been keeping from me?"

She couldn't avoid it any longer. All she could do is postpone it. And postpone it, she did.

"Can we discuss this at home, Mom?"

Officer Todd, recognizing that his question had put Jackie in an awkward spot with her mother, apologized.

"I'm sorry, Jackie. I didn't know."

"That's OK, it's my fault. I should have told my parents. I didn't want to upset them. I think that my former employer, AlzCura Pharmaceutical, may be behind the break-in, the threat, the surveillance equipment, and now this," unable to even consider uttering the phrase kidnapping her daughter.

Somehow admitting this to Officer Todd rather than directly to her mother made it easier, at least until her mother interrogated her when they got home.

"Anyone specifically at your former employer I should speak to?"

Realizing that Officer Todd wanted to contact AlzCura in follow-up and that he would be going in without the full story, she added to her previous admission.

"No one specifically, Barrett, but before you or anyone else tries to contact them, I need to tell you the whole story. I am working with law enforcement in Maine to investigate Alz-Cura for possibly contributing to my husband's death and the deaths of many others. It's complicated. Can you hold off on contacting my former employer, and we can talk about this tomorrow when I'm in a better frame of mind?"

Jackie's mother's head was spinning, and frankly, so was Officer Todd's.

"Yes, absolutely, Jackie. I will have to take the stroller in case the person who took Ashley left any evidence. Shall I call you in the morning?"

Jackie nodded.

"Oh, and your mother already sent me a picture of Ashley. An Amber Alert should be broadcast soon."

Jackie stood and gave Officer Todd a hug. "Thank you, Barrett. Please find my daughter," she pleaded as tears ran down her face.

"I will do the best I can, Jackie." Officer Todd thanked Jackie's mother and donned gloves to take the stroller to his cruiser.

"Come on, Mom," Jackie urged, giving her mother a hand getting up from the bench. While their destination was Jackie's home, only 150 yards away, it felt like the longest and most difficult walk the two had ever taken.

CHAPTER 42

The news of Leslie Anderson's murder was sensational by itself. That her half-naked body was found in Celeste Boulanger's trailer only added to the intrigue. While media personalities made a point to mourn and publicly renounce the despicable act, most privately licked their chops for the opportunity to wrestle away market share from Channel 5 due to their misfortune. Leslie Anderson may have been popular with male viewers, but she was almost universally despised by her media colleagues.

While facts about Leslie's murder were in short supply, this didn't prevent the media from publishing lurid articles that fueled increased newspaper readership and television viewership. A widespread but implausible story was that Leslie and Celeste were in a lesbian relationship that went south after Celeste stole the spotlight from Leslie at the AG's meeting with the media. These fantastical tales, which were blatantly designed to stimulate readers' imaginations more than report the facts, always gave careful attention and detail to the women's physical attributes. Celeste was often described as the comely, petite, fiery redhead, while Leslie was the brash buxom blond. Although there were no real photos of the two ever in proximity to one another, several media outlets used photo technology to mix and match available pictures of the two women to make it appear they were together in a conflicted relationship. It was masterful from a technical point of view but pure fiction.

The media machine was good at making up stories for the first few days, but as the week wore on, the well was running dry. The problem was that the Medical Examiner wasn't talking, Leslie was dead, and Celeste could not be found.

With Celeste's trailer off-limits as a crime scene, reporters descended on Celeste's sister's home in Ramsey only to be told she wasn't there. Not believing Celeste's sister, a large group of reporters camped out in front of her house, sure that Celeste would eventually make her appearance.

Another group of reporters camped out in the parking lot of the grocery store where Celeste worked, despite the store manager telling them that she was on a leave of absence for an indefinite period.

The third group of reporters assembled outside of Celeste's trailer park, waiting for her eventual return.

* * *

Celeste rolled over in the bed, wrapped her arm over Theo's chest, and threw her leg over one of his. As he drowsily stirred from sleep and turned his head, her lips met his, bringing him to life. Sliding her body over his, she moved to find the connection that had felt natural and right earlier that morning. Abandoning the previous frenetic pace fueled by her grief and the fire of newness and need, she instead indulged in a slow, sensual, incremental advance and retreat. Advance and retreat. As if her body was a wave crashing into the shore and flow slowly back into the sea as another wave rolled in to collide and withdraw.

Since the two had arrived at Theo's home in the early hours of the new day, their bodies were seldom apart. Celeste, desperate to fill the void from too many losses, needed some-one or something to hold on to. Theo, worn down from years of choosing professional discretion, recklessly caved to animal instinct and a personal desire to protect and save her.

Theo's home was actually a year-round cabin on a small pond about a mile down a bumpy circuitous dirt road that he was forever trying to smooth out without success. The camp had been in the family for years, and Theo inherited it after his father died in an officer-involved shooting now 10 years past. What it lacked in modern amenities and convenience, it made up for in remoteness, privacy, and natural beauty. A perfect haven for Celeste away from the spying eyes and the voracious appetite of the media. That her host was the principal inves-tigator in two active investigations that involved Celeste was more of a problem but one that was unlikely to be discovered.

As Celeste dismounted and left the bed, he watched her heavenly sway as she sauntered to the bathroom to start the shower. Knowing he would be joining her shortly, he reached for his phone.

"Good morning Will, did you hear the news?"

"Yeah, I just heard. Were you on the scene last night?" DA Wydman asked.

"Yeah, I heard it on the scanner and got there before CSI did."

Theo briefed him about what he saw at the crime scene and who he surmised was behind the grisly acts.

"Is Celeste safe?"

"Yeah, she was treated for shock, and then I drove her to a friend's house," which was not entirely untrue.

"Good. Hopefully, she can stay there awhile, and the media doesn't find her. The poor woman has been through hell."

"Yeah, no doubt. I think she will be OK," he declared as he got out of bed and stood watching Celeste's naked form through the steam-obscured shower door as she ran soapy hands over her nubile body.

"I'm sure it was a long night. Hopefully, you got some rest. It's going to be a shit show with the media for the next few days."

"Yeah, I'm good," Theo replied, all the time thinking if only Will really knew how long his night was!

Ending the call, Theo joined Celeste for a shower that only concluded because of the limitations of the hot water heater and his need to get back to the scene of the crime.

"Do you have to go?" Celeste asked as Theo was getting dressed.

"Yes, I wish I didn't have to, but I need to find out who broke into your trailer. Until I do, you'll be safe here. Promise me you won't leave."

"I won't. Can I go for a swim?"

"Yeah, you have the run of the whole place, and no one except lives on the pond except me, so no one will see you."

"So I could skinny-dip?" she teased, dropping her towel.

"Not fair, but yes, you can skinny-dip," he replied, pulling her in for a kiss. "I'll see you tonight."

Jumping into his car, Theo headed back to Celeste's trailer, intent on meeting with the CSI team for a briefing and interviewing her neighbors.

✳ ✳ ✳

Curt had tried to call Jackie Monday evening, but his call had gone to voice mail. After leaving a brief message, he sent a text.

"Just tried to call. Anxious to hear how your day went."

When he didn't receive a response to his text after two hours, he texted again.

"You OK?"

When that text wasn't responded to, and the clock approached 10 p.m., he concluded that he probably wouldn't be hearing from her. As the minutes and hours ticked by, sleep evaded him as his mind cycled all the possible reasons for her silence.

At 5:00 a.m., he finally fell asleep only to be awakened by his phone alarm set for 5:30 a.m. Punky and disoriented, he fumbled to shut the alarm off so he could go back to sleep. When his phone rang again at 6:30 a.m., he answered it bleary-eyed and sporting a dull headache.

"Hello," he croaked, rubbing the sleep from his eyes.

"Curt," Jackie cried, "someone took Ashley yesterday," she blurted out.

Curt, still in a fog, struggled to determine if he was really hearing what he just heard or was he just dreaming it.

"Jackie?"

"Curt, this is Jackie. Did you hear what I said?"

"Yes, Jackie, I'm sorry," he said after a long pause. "What happened?"

As Jackie cried her way through the details as she knew them, the fog lifted, and Curt knew this wasn't a dream but a real nightmare.

"My God, Jackie. I was so worried when you didn't respond last night. I didn't fall asleep until an hour or two ago. I'm so sorry. What can I do?"

"I don't know, Curt. I feel so empty and so helpless. I wish I had known you were awake. I could have called you. I was up all night too."

"We have to tell Will and Theo. This has to be the work of

AlzCura," Curt suggested.

"Could you tell them? I am meeting with the police this morning, and I don't know how often I can talk about this before I go completely crazy."

"I'd be happy to, Jackie. How is your mom doing?"

"She's devastated. On top of Ashley being taken, she didn't know anything about my departure from AlzCura or that I was trying to prove they were responsible for Stu's death. I had to tell her yesterday, and she was so shocked and disappointed in me. All I was trying to do was protect them," she sobbed, unable to continue.

"Jackie, I wish I could be there right now," Curt said, swallowing three words he really wanted to say.

"I wish you were here too, Curt," Jackie sniffled, "I feel so lost."

"You've got me. We're a team, OK? I'll call Will, and we'll talk later."

"Thanks, Curt," Jackie replied, feeling a bit propped up by his reference to them being a team. "I'll call you later."

After their call, and before he could notify DA Wydman, Curt rousted his kids out of bed, fixed them breakfast, and got them on the bus to school.

As he scaled the apartment steps on his way to call DA Wydman, his phone announced that Will beat him to the punch.

"Hi, Will. I was just about to call you."

"Hi Curt, have you heard the news yet?"

"No, what's happened?"

"Leslie Anderson, Channel 5 reporter, was murdered in Celeste Boulanger's home last night. Celeste's dog was also killed. Fortunately, Celeste was at work when it happened."

"Thank God for Celeste, but I don't understand. What was

Leslie Anderson doing there?"

"I have no idea, but she has been known to play fast and loose with the laws in her attempts to get a story. Theo was there, and he thinks this is the work of AlzCura. I just wanted to let you know because I know you had concerns for Celeste's safety, and if Theo is right, I want you and Jackie to be prepared."

"Will, Jackie's baby, Ashley, was abducted yesterday," Curt exclaimed, now starting to worry about Caitlin and Cade.

After Curt fielded Will's questions about Ashley's kidnapping, Will suggested that he assemble the group for a teleconference the following day.

"We can't wait until Saturday. This appears to be a coordinated effort by AlzCura. I will try to find some time tomorrow to have a call."

Before the call, Curt had planned to go to work. After the call, the only thing Curt could think about was his kids. He called Principal Taylor at the school and asked him to pay particularly close attention to Caitlin and Cade's safety. Also, he let him know he would be picking his kids up after school. Instead of going to work, he called LoriBeth and asked her to tell Sam that he would be working from home for the rest of the week.

CHAPTER 43

"There's the little darling," Cheryl exclaimed as she entered her daughter's apartment and saw her trying to hold a squirming Ashley.

"There's the little brat, you mean," Alexis replied. "The little shit hasn't stopped crying or fussing. I barely got any sleep, ya know."

"Oh, you'll survive. Now you know what I had to go through with you and your two brothers."

"Spare me. I was an angel. How long do I need to keep this crying poop machine?"

"At least a few more days. Just long enough to make Jackie think she will never see her baby again."

"Ya know, it's not fair to keep me locked up here like a prisoner in my own place?"

"Well, you could go out and get yourself arrested, ya know," Cheryl taunted, emphasizing the last two words that were her daughter's verbal tic.

"Stop it, I can't help it, ya know," Alexis replied, proving her point.

"Better safe than sorry, honey. Just a few more days, and we'll get you back to Paris."

"Can't I go somewhere else? I hate those stuck-up snob

French doctors, ya know."

"Being stuck-up snobs is not just a condition of French doctors, ya know," Cheryl replied. Unconscious that she had adopted her daughter's irritating favorite phrase.

"See, you do it too. You said, ya know," Alexis taunted. "It's all your fault I talk like this."

Ignoring her allegation, Cheryl replied, "I'll see if we can relocate you somewhere else. We just can't have you here."

"Why do I have to go somewhere else when my dumb brothers get to stay here?"

"Well, dear, you just answered your own question. Your brothers are challenged to tie their own shoes and need me around to tell them what to do. You don't. And if you ever tell them, I said that I'll deny it and make sure you spend the rest of your life visiting slimy doctors in Paris."

At that, Alexis smiled, and for the first time, Ashley stopped squirming and wrapped her little arms around Alexis' neck.

"See," Cheryl pointed, "you're going to make a good mommy someday."

Alexis didn't dare speak. Looking down at Ashley's angelic face, she realized that she had instinctively been rocking her while conversing with her mother. Ashley was about to fall asleep. No words were passed, but Cheryl and Alexis pantomimed their farewells.

Cheryl's next stop was Anthony and Andrew's house. She had purchased the house for her twins when it became apparent they might never leave their childhood home and choose instead to live off of their mother until she died. While buying the house for her sons didn't make economic sense, it preserved Cheryl's sanity. It also ensured that her home would not forever smell like the inside of a hockey player's equipment bag. More importantly, it insulated her from being arrested as an accessory should either one or both of them ever decide to act upon and get caught living out any of their aberrant sexual fantasies.

Cheryl rarely visited her son's home, afraid of what she would find, but the mission she had sent them on and their co-operation in the aftermath were critical. As Anthony opened the door and her olfactory system was assaulted with the odor she hadn't missed, she thought seriously about suggesting they meet elsewhere. As she stepped into the living room, she regretted her decision to meet there even more.

In addition to dirty clothes and dishes, empty beer cans and crumpled-up napkins covered the floor. The walls displayed some of the most profane and disgusting pornography Cheryl had ever witnessed, and Cheryl was not naïve. In fact, she was one of the most open-minded when it came to the spectrum of what people took pleasure in.

It wasn't until she saw a collection of screenshots of Jackie naked that she went ballistic.

"I thought I told you to get rid of any evidence from your spying on Jackie?" she fumed as she began ripping the photos off the wall.

"Aw, Mom, why did you do that? She's so hot."

"And you're so stupid," she spat.

"Andrew even likes them, Mom. And he usually only likes little boys and little girls. I guess he also liked that blond lady in Maine this weekend."

"I don't even want to hear it. Shut up. You're both disgusting," as she started ripping down all the pictures.

Hearing the commotion, Andrew made his entrance and stood aghast at what his mother was doing.

"Mom, those are my pictures, and it's our house."

"Oh, ya? When you start paying the mortgage and all the expenses to live here, THEN it will be your house. Until then, it's my house, and you're lucky to live in it," as her blood pressure increased and her face turned an even darker shade of crimson.

"Do you realize what would happen if the police raided this house? As she glared at them.

Their vacant looks told the whole story.

"My God, you two are hopeless. You'd go to jail. And do you know what happens to people in jail who like little boys and little girls? They get killed."

After ridding the walls of pornography and shredding it, she commanded them to clear space at the kitchen table so they could talk.

"Now, Andrew, tell me what happened in Maine. You were supposed to either eliminate the red-headed girl or send her a message. What did you do?"

"I got there Saturday, and there were reporters at her house round the clock. There was no way I was going to get to her. I did hear a yappy dog though and thought that if she did eventually leave, and the reporters followed her, I might get a chance to break in," he paused.

"So then, what did you do?"

" I waited all day Saturday and most of the day Sunday before she finally left. Anthony man, you should have seen her, flaming red-hair, rocking little body, I wish I could have,"

"Stick to the story, Andrew," Cheryl interrupted before he could go any further.

"OK," he said, upset he wasn't able to share his little fantasy. "So I waited until it got dark, put on my gloves, and broke in. Her little dog was barking like crazy, but I caught it and killed it. I don't think anyone heard the barking," he said in a self-satisfied tone.

"How did you kill the dog?"

"Oh, you're going to love this," he replied with enthusiasm. "Remember that scene in The Godfather when that guy wakes up with the bloody horse's head in his bed?"

As his mother and Anthony nodded their heads, he continued. "I cut Fluffies little head off and put it on her pillow. It was so awesome."

"Go on, Andrew," she said, disturbed that he could do such a thing but also a bit impressed by his creativity. "Then what did you do?"

"While I was in the bedroom, I heard someone in the living room. I thought maybe that redhead had come back, but when I went to check, it was this blond chick. She screamed and tried to run out, so I grabbed her by the hair and pulled her down. She was like a wild cat, scratching, screaming, and kicking. I punched her and knocked her out. Then I slashed her throat."

"Wait, that's not the story you told me," Anthony protested. "You told me you fucked her up the ass, you liar."

"Andrew, tell me the truth."

Andrew looked down and didn't say anything.

"Tell me, Andrew."

"I can tell you, Mom," Anthony chimed in, "he told me everything."

"Andrew, if you don't tell me, I will have Anthony tell me."

"She was pretty. I started to take her clothes off, but then she started to wake up, so I slashed her throat."

"So, you didn't fuck her then?" Cheryl questioned as Anthony protested again.

"Mom, he showed me a picture on his phone. He fucked her."

"You took a picture?" Cheryl said, flabbergasted.

"I deleted it, Mom," he said sheepishly.

"Show me your photos, Andrew."

He reluctantly complied, and sure enough, there were no pictures on his phone.

"Now, show me your recently deleted folder."

"What's that?"

"Here, give me your phone."

She scrolled down and opened the recently deleted folder, which displayed not one but four photos of the blond. One picture with irrefutable evidence that her son had sexually assaulted her. She recognized the blond immediately as the TV reporter she had seen twice during her recent visits to Maine.

"You bonehead. It's bad enough you took pictures, but you didn't even wear a condom." Cheryl dropped her head in disbelief, knowing the Medical Examiner would now find DNA evidence. "This woman was a TV reporter up there. Do you realize how much attention this is going to get?" she said as she systematically deleted the photos from the folder.

"Did anyone see you in the trailer or entering or leaving the trailer?"

"The dog and that reporter lady."

Rolling her eyes, she clarified, "Anyone who isn't dead?"

"No, I don't think so."

"I can't believe you, Andrew. You disgust me."

He cowered as though her words hurt him physically. Turning to her son Anthony, she began, "How about your mission? Tell me how it went."

"Me and Alexis drove to that park. I dropped her off, and when she got that lady to leave the stroller, I snuck up, grabbed the baby, put her under my jacket, and went back to the car. Then I drove to the spot where I dropped Alexis off and picked her up."

"Did anyone see you grab the baby or take her to the car?"

"I don't think so."

"Were you wearing your gloves?"

"Yes."

"Did the lady ever see the car you were driving?"

"I don't think so. I parked it on the opposite side of the street like you told me."

"Did anyone see you drop off or pick up Alexis?"

"No, we were quick."

"Good. Did you see anything, or did anything happen that concerned you while you were there?"

"No. It was pretty easy."

"Did you change the license plates on the car when you got back?"

"Yes."

"Good. Now, promise me that after I leave, you'll go to your computer and erase all the pictures of Jackie."

"I promise," he said dejectedly.

"And no more pornography on the walls," she commanded, looking from one son to the other.

"OK, Mom," they replied.

"I need both of you to lay low for a few days. No going out. You understand?"

"Yes, Mom," they said in unison.

Cheryl hugged her boys and exited, happy to take in a long, deep breath of fresh air but dreading the meeting she was about to have with Dr. Sheridan and Chet when she got back to the office.

Her sons had accomplished their missions, but not without at least one serious flaw. What's more, she wasn't sure she could trust them to tell her the entire truth. She couldn't help but feel like the walls would eventually close in on her sons, which in turn could compromise her and potentially the

AlzCura Pharmaceutical juggernaut. If dirty work needed to be done in the future, Cheryl would need to find more reliable henchmen.

CHAPTER 44

After Jackie got off her early morning call with Curt, she tried to get some sleep. She only succeeded in tossing and turning for 20 minutes before getting up, taking a shower, and making a cup of coffee. She restlessly tried to occupy herself while waiting for Officer Todd to call. Not having her usual morning routine of getting Ashley up and dressing and feeding her gnawed at her. Unable to wait any longer and anxious to hear what progress the police may have made, she decided to call Officer Todd.

"Good morning, Jackie."

"I've had better," she replied. "I'm going stir-crazy and couldn't wait any longer. Do you have any news for me?"

"Unfortunately not, Jackie. I have patrols watching the park, as well as your home and your parents' home. The Amber Alert went out yesterday, but we haven't received any leads yet. I have circulated the description of the woman to all precinct offices across the State. I'm afraid looking for a 5 foot 3 woman with brunette hair and sunglasses doesn't give us much to go on. There also weren't any prints on the stroller. I can return the stroller when I come over. Would now be a good time?"

"Yes, the sooner, the better. I haven't slept, and I'm sure I'll start to fade eventually."

"Alright, I'll be over in 15 minutes."

As Jackie waited for Officer Todd's arrival, she poured herself another coffee. She switched on the TV only to see a picture of Ashley as the morning news anchor read the script encouraging anyone with any information to call the local police. While she was glad the media was getting the word out, seeing her daughter on TV made her absence all too real. She didn't try to stop crying until Officer Todd arrived, only to continue weeping when she saw him holding Ashley's empty stroller.

She opened the door, welcomed him in, and, as he had on several other occasions, caught her as her emotions overwhelmed her and made her swoon.

"I got ya," he said as she collapsed in his arms. "I can't imagine how hard this must be, Jackie. Let me get you over to this chair," navigating her to the chair by her coffee cup.

"I'm sorry," Jackie wept. "I'm always such a mess when I see you."

"Unfortunately, I don't get to make many housecalls that are for happy occasions," he replied.

Recovering slightly, she asked if he would like a cup of coffee.

"I see it. I can get a cup. You stay put."

"Some host I am!"

"Nonsense, that coffee is all ready, and I'm sure it will be much better than the dishwater they make at the station."

"I don't know if I'm up to telling all the sordid details about my past employer again. Telling my parents yesterday nearly killed me. They were so upset and disappointed that I hadn't told them."

"Yeah, once again, I'm sorry I made that painful discussion necessary."

"No, I shouldn't have kept it from them. If I had told them, my mother probably would have been more careful. It's my fault, Ashley's gone," the stark truth of her statement spurring another bout of tears.

For the next 45 minutes, Jackie detailed her time at AlzCura and the cascade of events and circumstances that occurred, culminating in her separation agreement and crusade against the pharmaceutical company. She described how she had been meeting with Maine law enforcement and Curt, not only to unearth potential evidence AlzCura was hiding unfavorable data but their possible involvement in Dr. Caron's death.

"I'm glad you gave me this background. I could have really stepped in it if I had just cold-called AlzCura. I'll have to talk to my Chief and see how he thinks we should proceed, but I think that the Chief and I might want to coordinate our efforts with our Maine law enforcement colleagues."

"I'm sure they'd be open to that. I could call them and give them your number."

"Let me talk to my Chief first. If he's good with that plan, I'll text you."

As it was apparent that Jackie was fading fast, Officer Todd thanked Jackie for her time and the coffee. She thanked him for catching her again and for his efforts to find Ashley.

"Get some sleep, Jackie," he called as he navigated down her porch stairs towards his cruiser.

"I hope to," she replied, seeing another cruiser on the other side of the park and one in the vicinity of her parent's home.

The coffee she had was no match for the exhaustion she felt from lack of sleep combined with the relief from finally unburdening herself from the stress of hiding information from her parents and the local police. Five minutes after Officer Todd's departure, she was fast asleep.

Six hours later, her phone sprang to life, pulling her out of her deep sleep.

"Hi Curt," she greeted sleepily, still disoriented as to date and time.

"Did I wake you? I'm sorry," he replied.

"What time is it?"

"2:30 p.m.. I thought I'd call you before I picked up Caitlin and Cade," he said.

"I must have fallen asleep after Officer Todd's visit."

"I'm sure you needed it. How did the visit go with Officer Todd?"

"Alright. I told him all about AlzCura, and he's going to talk to his Chief about potentially speaking with Will and Theo."

"Do they have any information on Ashley?"

"No, unfortunately. The stroller didn't have any fingerprints, and the Amber Alert didn't produce any leads, at least not as of this morning."

"I spoke to Will. You're not going to believe this."

"What?"

"Celeste Boulanger's dog and a TV reporter were killed in her trailer last night. Celeste was at work at the time."

"I'm confused. What was the TV reporter doing in Celeste's trailer?"

"I don't know, information is pretty spotty right now, but Will did say that Theo thought it was likely AlzCura was involved. I'm not exactly sure why, but I'm sure more information will come out soon. I told Will about Ashley, and now he thinks it might be a coordinated effort by AlzCura."

"Are Caitlin and Cade alright?" Jackie asked urgently.

"As far as I know. I called the school principal this morning, so they're on alert, and I'm going to be leaving soon to pick them up. I've decided to work from home this week, so I can transport them to and from school."

"Good idea."

"Will is going to try to set up a call for tomorrow. Be watching your email."

"Thanks, I will."

"Jackie, ever since you told me about Ashley, all I've wanted to do is be there for you. I don't know if that would be helpful, and I wouldn't be able to do it unless I brought the kids."

"Oh, Curt, you're so sweet. I would love it if you came down, but I understand completely about the kids. I just don't know if it would be the best thing for the kids. What would we tell them with Ashley gone?"

"Yeah, that's where my thoughts got stuck all day today."

"If circumstances were different, there is no question I'd want you here in a heartbeat. It's just not good timing right now."

"I know, you're right," his deep disappointment evident in his tone.

"The fact that you want to be here with me is enough, Curt. I don't know what I'd do if I didn't have you in my life right now."

"I can say the same for you, Jackie. I, I," he stuttered and sniffled as tears came to his eyes, and he swallowed once more the words he so desperately wanted to say to her.

"Oh, Curt, you're so special to me. Don't cry."

"I love you, Jackie," he said, finally realizing that if nothing else, their lives had taught them that life was too short to withhold one's feelings.

"Oh, I love you too, Curt. Thank you. I really needed to hear that. Now I really wish you were here

"I am," he replied.

"I know. I can feel it."

They finally gave voice to feelings that had bloomed be-

tween them, the seeds to which were planted at their serendip-
itous first encounter, germinated through their mutual personal tragedies, and sprouted from the pact they had formed
against their common nemesis. They would not allow darkness cast by AlzCura to extinguish their light.

CHAPTER 45

C heryl marched into Dr. Sheridan's office a few minutes late for the luncheon meeting with Chet. Unnoticed by all was the fact that the office bore no hint of the smell or scar on the wall caused by Asa's rage the previous Friday when the bottle of bourbon he threw met its shattering end.

"Well, I'm glad you could find time for us, Cheryl," Dr. Sheridan said facetiously.

"Oh, can it, Asa," she replied, in no mood to be his whipping post as she took her seat where the last plate of salmon and salad sat.

"Kidding, Cheryl. Relax," he tried to recover. "Judging from the local media, it looks like Anthony and Alexis did a masterful job."

"Yeah, their mission was flawless as far as I can tell. Andrew, on the other hand," she paused to roll her eyes and take a bite of her salad.

As news of Andrew's handiwork had not yet reached the Buffalo media outlets, Cheryl felt it prudent to forewarn Asa and Chet about what would eventually become public.

"Andrew couldn't get to Mrs. Boulanger. There were too many reporters still following her around. Once she and the reporters left her home, he was able to break in and left her a very graphic message."

"Oh, don't pussyfoot around the details, Cheryl. What was the message?"

"He recreated The Godfather scene leaving her dog's head on her bedroom pillow."

"How deliciously depraved."

"Yes, I thought that was very creative of him. However, we have a problem."

"What's that?"

"While he was in the trailer, that blond reporter I told you about inexplicably walked in, and he ended up killing her."

"One less ditzy TV reporter is like one less attorney, cause for celebration. No offense, Chet."

"Yes, but my dear degenerate son decided to have an unprotected party in her derriere."

"After she was dead?"

"No, apparently before he killed her."

"So, he screwed the pooch without really screwing the pooch!" Asa laughed, pleased with his clever use of the idiom.

"Not that we know of, at least," Cheryl replied, shuddering at the knowledge she couldn't put anything past him based on the pictures she tore off her son's wall just an hour earlier.

"Well, he doesn't have a record yet, right?"

"Right," Cheryl confirmed.

"So hopefully, there is no way for them to trace the DNA back to him."

"Yes, but as much as I'd like to think my boys will never get arrested, I'm a realist."

"Good point. It probably is only a matter of time."

As Asa and Cheryl were carrying on their conversation, Chet was getting increasingly anxious.

"Chet, the way you're squirming in your seat, I'd say you,

like the reporter, must have something up your butt."

"Thanks for that visual, Asa," Chet remarked. "I agree that we needed to send a message to Jackie and that red-head in Maine, but now I think we have to consider a strategy to throw law enforcement off our scent. I have a plan that you might find counter-intuitive, but hear me out."

"Alright, sounds intriguing, shoot."

"We start by responding to the State of Maine recent letter before the deadline. We tell them that Darius did not receive the vaccine and that Elvira did. We also produce Margo for questioning."

"Have you lost your mind, Chet?" Asa said, flustered.

"No, quite the opposite. Think about it. If we tell them Darius didn't receive the vaccine, then his behavior and actions in murdering Calli Barnes and subsequently dying can't be blamed on the vaccine. That, in turn, makes Mrs. Boulanger's revelation that her husband acted like Darius, not a matter of the vaccine. They'll write it off as just another case of a husband who probably drank too much and liked to use his wife as a punching bag."

"Hmmm, that does make a certain amount of sense," Asa pondered.

"It makes a whole lot of sense to me," Cheryl chimed in.

"But what about Elvira? Why say she did receive the vaccine?" Asa questioned.

"For the sake of making our response believable. If we say that neither she nor Darius received the vaccine, it looks more like we might be trying to hide something. If we admit she received it, that suspicion goes away."

"And her death?"

"More likely to be genetic as her son died of the same thing, and since he didn't have the vaccine,"

"Their deaths can't be attributed to the vaccine," Asa finished Chet's sentence. "Elegant. I see your rationale for them, but producing Margo? How does sending Alexis into the lion's den make sense?"

"We know the State has not certified Dr. Caron's death as a suicide. We can only assume they have some evidence otherwise, but not strong enough to make a definitive judgment. We send Margo in to weaken their case further."

"How does she do that," Cheryl asked.

"I assume they probably have the pictures of Margo with Dr. Caron. They may have also found the GHB in his bloodstream. We send Margo in to say that Dr. Caron had some unusual sexual tastes. He liked to be dominated. He liked asphyxiation sex. He had supplied her with the GHB because, as a doctor, he was able to procure it. He wanted to play a game where she would dose him and take him to a sleazy motel and take pictures of her dominating him, etc., etc."

"Yeah, but who took the pictures?"

"Oh, good point," Chet paused. "Check that, he wanted it videotaped, so they video the dirty deed. And now that video is digital, the pictures could have easily been generated from the video."

"So, where's the video and the camera now?" Asa challenged.

"Not Margo's or our problem, really."

"You're pretty good at this. Maybe I have to take back my comment about lawyers earlier," Asa admitted.

"Then the coup de gras," Chet continued. "Dr. Caron wakes up with Margo the next morning feeling guilty, distraught, and talking about killing himself. She consoles him, but she's not sure she succeeds."

"OK, there's one problem with this," Cheryl raised her hand. "I sent a letter to all the doctors in the region telling them we fired Margo. So how can we now produce her?"

"I doubt that will be information the State will have. If they do raise that question, Margo can admit she was suspended and subsequently reassigned to our Paris office on probationary status. Worse comes to worst, we admit we made an error in describing the actions we took with Margo."

"OK, but Margo in Paris is Monique Deuvolet. How do we address that?"

"Easy. No one knew Margo's last name while she was covering for Jackie, right?"

"Right," Cheryl confirmed.

"Margo is Monique Deuvolet's middle name, and she likes to go by Margo instead of Monique. We change her ID badge to reflect Monique Margo Deuvolet."

"You ARE good at this, Chet," Cheryl exclaimed.

"Oh, I'm not finished."

"There's more?" Asa said in disbelief.

"Well, you do pay me to protect you and AlzCura, right?" he asked rhetorically. We send this letter overnight, so they get it tomorrow, two days before the deadline," as he shoved the letter in front of Asa. "It contains everything we just discussed, including our willingness to produce Margo."

Cheryl looked over Asa's shoulder as he read the letter. After finishing, he looked up at Cheryl, who nodded her head, adding, "Looks good to me."

Asa pulled out his pen, signed it, and instructed Chet to send it as he recommended.

"What else do you got for us, Chet?"

"We return Ashley to Jackie tomorrow morning."

"Why so soon?" asked Asa.

"The law of diminishing returns. We accomplished sending the message to Jackie. Keeping her baby another few days will only allow law enforcement to expand their investigation. Also, Horse reports that Jackie met with a police officer this morning. If we don't return her kid, it is only a matter of time before she tells law enforcement about her concerns that we may be involved, if she hasn't already."

"And how do you suggest we go about returning the baby?" Cheryl asked. "I'm sure the cops are crawling all over the place, especially in Jackie's neighborhood."

"You're right. I pulled Horse out of there this morning for that exact reason. Instead, I had him look for a safe place to drop the kid."

"So, we're not going to keep surveillance on Jackie anymore?" Asa questioned.

"I don't see the point. Horse is good, but we can't afford to have him there with the police on high alert."

"Has he found a safe place to return the baby?" Cheryl asked.

"Yes, but it wasn't easy. Almost everywhere you go these days, there are cameras. He recommends we drop the baby at St. Paul's Church, which is a few miles from Jackie's house."

"The church doesn't have cameras?"

"Yes, it does, but only at the front doors and at the altar. There is a side door that leads right to a devotional area with votive candles and the statue of the Virgin Mother Mary that would be perfect."

"So when do you recommend we make the drop?"

"The church has a daily mass every weekday at 8:00 a.m. The priest unlocks the church doors at 7:00 a.m., and parishioners generally start arriving at 7:30 a.m. Horse recommends we act in the 15-minute window between 7:10 and 7:25 a.m.."

"And who does Horse suggest make the drop?"

"Horse didn't make a recommendation, but I'd recommend

him. We definitely don't want Alexis in the area, and your boys Cheryl,"

"Don't have to say it, Chet. They'd probably get struck down by lightning if they set foot in a church," causing all three to laugh.

"We swaddle the baby up, tight as a bug in a rug, and Horse enters through the side door, place the baby at the feet of the Virgin Mother, and skedaddles. Fifteen minutes later, when the good little Catholics start filtering into Church, someone is bound to discover the baby. They'll think it must be the second coming of Jesus, only to realize that it's the missing baby and hallelujah, it's a miracle, Jackie gets her baby back, and Father has a heartwarming story for his Sunday sermon!"

"Well, as a Jew who has never stepped foot in a Catholic church, I probably can't fully appreciate your plan. You really earned your keep today, Chet," Asa exclaimed.

"Oy vey, kvetch, kvetch, kvetch. You vhant I should schlep baby to temple?" Chet replied, adopting his best Yiddish accent.

Asa and Cheryl chortled heartily.

"No, Rabbi," Asa replied, "good work, mazel tov!"

After another round of laughter, Asa continued.

"Cheryl, if you're good with Rabbi Chet's plan, let's set the wheels in motion."

"I'm supportive. I will let Alexis know. She is going to be delighted. Not only is she not ready to play mommy, but she will be ecstatic not to have to go back to Paris right away."

The three finished their lunches, and Chet's bold plan to throw law enforcement off of AlzCura's scent was underway.

CHAPTER 46

Clara Himber was a fixture at St. Paul's Church in Nora and, at 80-years old, still found the stamina to walk to church and attend daily mass.

Clara and her husband Max emigrated to America from Germany in 1951 after surviving World War II. Steaming into New York Harbor and seeing the Statue of Liberty on a blustery day in October was one of the most glorious days of Clara and Max's young lives.

Their years in Germany had been difficult at best and, at times, horrific. Max was raised Catholic by his Catholic father. However, his mother was Jewish, and in the Nazi's book, that made Max a Jew. As a result, Max, a strapping 18-year old, was torn from his home and placed in a forced labor camp. Conditions in the camp were brutal, and many who entered strong and healthy died from mistreatment and malnourishment.

Clara was a pretty 16-year old girl when the Russians invaded Berlin in the final stages of the war. One day Clara was in the wrong place at the wrong time, and a group of Russian soldiers took turns beating and raping her. She survived, but to this day still carried the emotional scars.

Had Max not escaped his work camp in 1944, he likely would have died. Instead, Max and Clara met shortly after the war. Clara, cautious about forming any type of relationship with a man, found Max to be gentle, patient, and compassionate. Their relationship grew slowly, and in 1949, they married. Clara, now a seamstress, and Max, a furrier, opened a shop together in Berlin. Fortuitously, their shop opened as the German economy was about to recover and boom. In two years, they had saved enough money to realize their dream of moving to America.

Getting off the boat at Ellis Island, they decided to settle in Nora, where they opened Himbers on Main Street. For forty years, Nora's residents and many from around the Buffalo area would travel to Himbers to purchase Clara's custom dresses and suits and Max's fine furs.

Max died a few years after they closed their shop, and Clara continued to sew custom dresses and suits upon request. She also approached St. Bernadette's, one of the grade schools in town, to ask if she could occasionally speak to the students about her World War II experiences. Clara came to terms with her past and now saw the importance of sharing what she learned with the coming generations. Although it brought her to tears every time she shared her story, she knew her message of perseverance, forgiveness, love, and acceptance made a positive impact on the children.

So as Clara climbed the steps of St. Paul's Church that Wednesday morning, she had no idea that her usual routine would be anything but routine. She was always the first one to arrive for daily mass. She would enter the church, dip her hand in the holy water, cross herself, walk to the alcove where the Virgin Mary statue stood to say a prayer, and light a candle for Max. After praying, she would take her customary seat near the front of the church.

Today, as Clara crossed herself with the holy water, she heard mewling coming from the alcove. Unaccustomed to sharing the devotional space with anyone, let alone someone with a baby, she approached the alcove with curiosity. As she arrived at the dim candle-lit area, the crying had stopped, and she didn't see anyone there. Thinking that maybe she just imagined the sound, she kneeled down to pray. Closing her eyes, bowing her head, she whispered,

"Hail Mary, full of grace, the Lord is with thee; blessed art thou amongst women and blessed is the fruit of thy womb, Jesus."

Ashley then let out a wail that startled Clara. Opening her eyes, she suddenly saw the baby wrapped in a pink blanket at the foot of the Virgin Mary. Rising with some difficulty from her kneeling position, she looked around, confused at how a mother could forget her baby. Seeing no one in the church, she went to the baby, who was now in full-throat, her little face red with exertion. Clara picked her up, held her in her arms, and tried to comfort her with a German children's song her mother used to sing to her.

"Hänschen klein, ging allein, In die weite Welt hinein. Stock und Hut, steh'n ihm gut, Ist gar wohl gamut. Aber Mama weinet sehr, Hat ja nun kein Hänschen mehr. 'Wünsch dir Glück' sagt ihr Blick, 'kehr nur bald zurück!'"

As Clara sang, imitating her mother's animated facial expressions that used to make her laugh, Ashley stopped crying and started to giggle. Little did Clara know how appropriate the song was as it tells the story of a little boy who runs away from home, leaving his mother crying and hoping he'll be safe and come home soon.

With Ashley consoled in her arms and no one else in the church, Clara went off to find Father Woznewski.

"Father?" she called as she approached the front of the church. Afraid to go beyond the front railing.

"Father Woznewski," she called a little louder. When Father did not appear, she decided to cross what she felt was a sacred boundary to the sacristy.

"Father?" she called again from the sacristy entrance.

"Yes?" Father replied. "One moment."

Father appeared at the entrance adjusting his vestments, and was shocked to see Clara holding a baby.

"I'm sorry, Father, but I found this baby lying at the feet of the Virgin Mary."

"Praise, Jesus. No need to apologize, Clara. This is Jackie's baby, Ashley. I baptized her two months ago." When he said her name, Ashley turned her head towards Father and said, "Mama."

"I guess that's proof," Father said, laughing.

"The baby that was kidnapped?" Clara asked, stunned.

"Yes, yes, Jackie will be so happy and relieved. I have to go call her now. Why don't you take Ashley, and I'll call her."

"OK. Should we call the police too?" Clara added.

"Yes, thank you. I'll call them too."

As Father disappeared back into the sacristy, Clara made her way to her usual seat. When people started to arrive for mass, Clara urged them to visit, excited now about her discovery. By the time Father returned, Clara and Ashley were surrounded by a dozen parishioners, all talking excitedly. Ashley, now comfortable in Clara's arms, ate up the attention. As Clara recounted how she found Ashley and had comforted her by singing a song, they asked her to sing it again.

Predictably, Ashley began to giggle again, which in turn caused the congregation to laugh with her. As more people arrived, joined the crowd, and learned the identity of the baby, Clara was asked to make several repeat performances of the song. As they waited joyfully for Jackie's arrival, several parishioners learned Clara's song forming an impromptu choir.

* * *

Jackie, whose sleep schedule had been disrupted, found it difficult to sleep on the second night after Ashley's abduction. When her usual remedy of reading a book failed to bring sleep, she took a melatonin pill. An hour later, she drank some chamomile tea. Tossing and turning, she didn't fall asleep until 3:00 a.m..

Still asleep when her phone rang at 7:35 a.m., she groggily reached over, and not recognizing the number, decided not to answer and rolled over, intent on going back to sleep. Ten seconds later, her phone rang again, from the same unfamiliar phone number. Now irritated and expecting it to be one of the many robocalls she received, she answered the call. Instead, she heard Father Woznewski's animated voice.

"Jackie, this is Father Woznewski. We have Ashley. She's safe."

When Jackie didn't immediately respond, not believing what she just heard, Father repeated himself.

"Jackie, did you hear me? We have Ashley. She's at the church."

"Oh, my God," was all she managed to scream out before half laughing and half crying as she jumped out of bed.

As she celebrated, Father instructed her to come to the church.

"I'll be right there, Father," dropping her phone and frantically throwing on the first thing she could find to wear. She would not remember her drive from home to the church, so intent and focused on seeing Ashley. She came to a halt in a no parking spot in front of the church and ran up the church steps that she had ascended more deliberately on her wedding day.

She wasn't prepared for the scene as she flung open the church door. At least 30 people, crowded near the front of the church, cheered as she made her entrance. Now conscious about her appearance for the first time, she ran her hand through her unkempt hair as she ran down the center aisle. Seeing Ashley in Clara's arms, she forgot all about her appearance, and Clara happily handed Ashley to her mother as another cheer arose from the congregation.

Jackie and Ashley were in their own little world. Jackie unbundled her daughter from the blanket and took an inventory of her tiny body. Finding her whole and happily reaching for her mother, Jackie hugged her.

"Oh, my baby. I missed you so much," she cried. "Thank you. Thank you all," she sobbed, surveying the people who beamed with joy around her. As the reality of the reunion with Ashley sunk in, Jackie started to recover her composure.

"Where did you find her?" she asked.

"Clara found here," Father began.

"She was lying at the feet of the Virgin Mary, dear," Clara added. "I was praying for my Max when she cried out."

Beyond words and feeling a new wave of tears arriving, Jackie hugged and held Clara with one arm. Ashley happily sandwiched in between them. Finally releasing their hug, Father added.

"Clara, you sang her a German children's song to comfort her, didn't you?"

"Yes, she was crying, and the only thing I could think to do was sing a song my mother used to sing to me. It worked. She laughed just like I used to laugh when my mother sang it."

"While we were waiting for you to arrive, Clara started teaching us the song. Would you like to hear it?"

Nodding her head, Clara began to sing. As a few parishioners started to chime in, Ashley turned in Jackie's arms and started giggling. When the song ended, the congregation laughed and cheered.

Jackie touched beyond words, could only cry tears of joy.

"What is the song about, Clara," Father asked.

When Clara described the story, it brought another round of tears to Jackie and several others in the crowd.

"Well, we are all truly blessed today," Father stated. "Praise God."

"Amen," some in the congregation responded.

At that, the bells tolled 8 times, signaling the time and the usual start of daily mass.

Father Woznewski offered a suggestion.

"I think we have all been a party to a miracle this morning. With your permission, I'd like to offer a brief prayer instead of our usual service." As the group nodded their heads and voiced support, Father continued.

"Dear heavenly Father, we thank and praise you for the miracle we witnessed this morning made possible by your infinite love and mercy. May Ashley, Jackie, and all of us continue to put our faith in you, our divine creator, protector, and savior. Bless Clara for being an instrument of your love today. Bless Ashley and Jackie. May their undying love for one another continue, and their union never again be broken. Bless this entire congregation as we lift our voices in praise and glory to your name, almighty God and Father."

"Amen," the congregation said in unison. A few of the parishioners started to sing Clara's song as a recessional hymn. When Clara lent her confident voice, others joined in singing or humming the tune. Ashley's giggles as they ended the song were the perfect punctuation, marking what locally would come to be known as "The Miracle at St. Paul's Church."

As the congregation was about to disband, the front doors to the church opened up, and Officer Todd, accompanied by several other officers, entered. While most of the congregation was allowed to leave, Clara, Father Woznewski, and Jackie were asked to stay. The officers taped off the alcove, where Clara had found Ashley, and started to process the area for potential evidence. Officer Todd met with Clara and Father Woznewski to get the details of Clara's discovery. Jackie, meanwhile, immersed herself in her reunion with Ashley.

When Officer Todd was finished taking Clara and Father's statements, he left briefly with Father. Clara came over to say goodbye to Ashley and gave Jackie a hug before her walk home. Shortly after, Officer Todd returned and joined Jackie.

"I'm so happy for you, Jackie."

"Thank you, Barrett. What a relief."

"I'm sure."

"Do you think you'll be able to track down who did this?"

"I don't know. Father and I just reviewed the video and saw nothing. Whoever did this was smart enough to enter through the side door, which doesn't have a camera. The crime scene team didn't find any evidence in the alcove, either. I don't want to say we won't get any leads, but it's not looking promising at this point. I'm sorry, I wish I had more encouraging news."

"That's OK, Barrett. The most important thing to me is safely back in my arms," she replied, giving Ashley a hug.

"I'll be in touch if I do learn anything. Do you need a ride home?"

"No, thanks, Barrett. I drove. That's my car in the no parking zone out front. Sorry."

"I think we can let that pass, given the circumstances," he joked. "Enjoy your reunion with Ashley," as he took his leave.

Now alone with her daughter, Jackie looked at the large crucifix at the front of the church, and kneeling, said a silent prayer as tears of relief and joy fell freely.

CHAPTER 47

Inspector Adams walked into DA Wydman's office mid-morning on Wednesday to brief him on the status of the Leslie Anderson murder investigation.

"Hi Will, I was just at the Medical Examiner's office."

"What did Louie find?"

"The toxicology results won't be back for a while, but the cause of death was clearly exsanguination from the laceration to her throat. He confirmed she was sexually assaulted."

"Was he able to retrieve any evidence?"

"Yes, he found semen but was unable to find a DNA match."

"Anything else of note in the autopsy?"

"There was evidence of a struggle but no traces of skin under her fingernails as she was wearing gloves."

"Gloves?"

"Yes. We think Leslie went there with the intent to break in, presumably to find some information for a story on Celeste or Norman. However, we found the door unlocked, so there was no evidence of a break-in. The door could have originally been locked. It was the type of lock easily jimmied by sliding a credit card."

"Why am I not surprised that Leslie Anderson would do something like that?" Will interjected.

Theo chuckled. "She was notorious for pushing boundaries. I did interview her boss at Channel 5, and he did not know of her plan to visit Celeste's home that evening. However, he told me that was not unusual as reporters typically don't need to get his approval for their plans when chasing a story."

"What about the CSI team? What did they find?"

"Three sets of prints were found. Celeste and my prints, as well as one set of unidentified prints."

"Your prints? You didn't contaminate the scene, did you?"

"No, you know me better than that, Will. I met with Celeste at her trailer twice last week - once in follow-up to her husband's death and then after her appearance at the AG's meeting with the media."

"That's right, sorry."

"I did find something interesting, though."

"What's that?"

"The unidentified set of prints match prints found in Dr. Caron's office and on the note left at Curt Barne's apartment."

"So potentially we have a perp involved in three different crimes?"

"That's possible."

"Don't you find it odd that one person could leave their prints at the scene of three different crimes and not be in our DNA or fingerprint databases? How likely is that?"

"Unlikely if you ask me. He certainly hasn't been careful, but he has been very lucky. He'd be better off if he played the lottery with that luck."

"Did the neighbors see or hear anything?" Will asked.

"No, not until Celeste screamed after the fact. They said they may have heard the dog bark once or twice that night but couldn't be sure. The dog barking was such a regular occurrence that they had become deaf to it and rarely took notice anymore. They didn't see anyone or anything suspicious that evening."

"What about the sequence of events?"

"The perpetrator likely entered first and killed the dog in the living room. Then he decapitated the dog and took it for display on the pillow in the back bedroom. While the perp was in the back bedroom, Leslie must have entered and surprised him. They struggled, and the perp lacerated her throat from left-to-right."

"So, the perp is right-handed."

"Most likely. He then sexually assaulted her."

"After she was dead?"

"Yep."

"I don't get it. How can someone that depraved not have a criminal record?"

"My thought exactly. If he continues to do things like this, he won't have a clean record for long."

"Anything else?"

"Not at this time. We may get more information from toxicology, but that won't change any of the fundamental facts of the case."

"Thanks, Theo. I have to run. AG Talcott just received AlzCura's response to his last letter. I want to see what they said before our teleconference call with Jackie and Curt this afternoon."

* * *

"Will, I'm glad you could make it over on short notice," AG Talcott greeted. "Surprisingly, we received AlzCura's response two days early."

"That's a shock. What does it say?"

Handing DA Wydman the letter, he summarized, "In short, Darius didn't get the vaccine, Elvira did, and they are going to produce Margo for questioning."

"I wasn't expecting that," said DA Wydman handing the letter back to AG Talcott.

"Nor was I. This puts a brand new light on things."

"It does. Do you believe their response?"

"I don't have anything to refute it, and we still have to interview Margo."

"We do still have those 11 adverse event reports of clinical trial patients that died that didn't appear to be communicated to the proper authorities," DA Wydman reminded the AG.

"Yes, but we didn't ask AlzCura about those patients. Since they appear to be cooperating, maybe I should send a third letter asking them about our concerns about those patients?"

"Lew, I just find it hard to trust AlzCura. We're investigating or know of crimes related to five people who were either participants in their trials or employed with the company. Dr. Caron told me straight out that they were hiding unfavorable data."

"But we have yet to prove that. Based on AlzCura's letter, your count is down to four. If Darius didn't get the vaccine, his actions weren't caused by the vaccine. Dr. Caron's death looks suspicious, but they're producing a person of interest for our investigation that could answer some of our questions. And as far as I know, we don't have definitive evidence to pin Leslie's murder on anyone yet, let alone a perpetrator associated with AlzCura."

"And the threat Curt Barnes received and the abduction of Jackie Deno's baby?"

"I hear ya, Will. But the reality is that kids get abducted every day. What evidence is there that AlzCura is connected to those events?"

"I can't speak to the abduction of Jackie's baby, but Theo just informed me that we now can link unidentified prints at the scene of Leslie's murder, in Dr. Caron's office, and on the note to Curt Barnes."

"So we MAY have one person that MAY be responsible for criminal activity, but I don't see you coming to me with sufficient evidence to press charges. We still have work to do, and given AlzCura's cooperation, I'm leaning towards corresponding with them on the 11 adverse event cases that concern us."

"Do me a favor, Lew. I'm meeting with Theo, Curt, and Jackie later today to get an update. Can we hold off on a decision about the next steps until then?"

"Sure, but I do want you to get Margo here to meet with Theo as soon as possible."

"I can do that."

"Good. Let's connect tomorrow."

DA Wydman left the office understanding AG Talcott's points but couldn't help feeling like they were taking a step backward. He didn't trust AlzCura and couldn't take their letter at face value. Unfortunately, short of going over AG Talcott's head and committing career suicide by going to federal authorities, he didn't know what he could do otherwise. He hoped the combined brainpower of Theo, Curt, and Jackie may produce an answer. He didn't have to wait until the teleconference to get his answer.

When he returned to his office, his assistant informed him of a call she had received while he was out.

"A Woodson Shearlow from the Center of Biologics Evaluation and Research called. He would like you to call him back as soon as possible. I left his number on your desk."

"Did he say what it was about?"

"No, but he said it was, and I quote, imperative that you

contact him immediately."

"Alright then, I'll call Mr. Shearlow."

"Oh, don't call him that. I made that mistake, and he informed me in no uncertain terms that his proper title was Doctor Shearlow."

"I can tell already I'm not going to like this guy. I mean doctor!" he said, leaving his assistant laughing as he went into his office to make the call.

"Office of Vaccine Research and Review, how may I direct your call," asked the female voice in a tone that somehow conveyed she hated her job and didn't appreciate being bothered by his call.

"Ah, Mr., I mean Dr. Shearlow, please."

"Who's calling?"

"District Attorney Wydman from"

"Hold," she commanded before he had finished and then was promptly assaulted by a sudden loud and continuous loop of hold music that made him hold the phone away from his ear.

"Hello, District Attorney Wydman," he greeted, mispronouncing his name Weedman.

"Hi Dr. Shearlow, that's pronounced Wideman," he corrected, trying not to grit his teeth and sound as irritated as he felt. "What can I do for you?"

"I've received a concerning number of Vaccine Adverse Event Reports from Dr. Steven Caron. When I called his office to speak to Dr. Caron, his Office Manager informed me that he had died. She referred me to an Inspector Theo Adams, who told me I needed to speak with you. It's been quite the runaround, as you can tell," he said, obviously annoyed.

"I'm sorry for your trouble," DA Wydman said, biting his tongue, as he wasn't sorry in the least. "The circumstances of Dr. Caron's death are under investigation. I assume that is why

CHRIS BLIERSBACH

Dr. Caron's Office Manager referred you to us."

"That's not my concern. What does concern me is that these reports were not filed promptly by Dr. Caron. That's a serious breach of policy and protocol."

"I understand that may be the case, Dr. Shearlow, but I'm not sure what I can do about that. If the adverse reports you're speaking of have to do with AlzCura's Recallamin vaccine, we do have concerns about its safety," DA Wydman replied, trying to find the topic that would align their mutual interests and extinguish Dr. Shearlow's hostile tone.

"So you were aware of the adverse reports," Dr. Shearlow replied. "May I ask why you didn't feel compelled to submit them to us when you discovered them?"

This question not only threw DA Wydman briefly, but he could feel his blood pressure rising. He didn't like Dr. Shearlow's tone or the implication of his question.

"I cannot answer that question, Dr. Shearlow, as it would potentially compromise information in an active criminal investigation."

"Mr. Wydman," once again mispronouncing his name and failing to use his DA title, "I am the Associate Director for Vaccine Safety, part of the Center for Biologics Evaluation and Research with the United States Food and Drug Administration. Are you saying that your investigation takes precedence over the safety of potentially hundreds of thousands, if not millions of people who have been given the Recallamin vaccine?"

"That's District Attorney Wydman," pronouncing his title and name with emphasis, "and no, that is not what I'm saying. We share your concern about the safety of Recallamin, and we would be happy to work with your agency. I cannot, however, compromise an active criminal investigation that may involve murder. Understand?"

"You needn't take that tone with me, DA Wydman," finally

pronouncing his name correctly. "It just appeared as if you've known about this for some time and were sitting on information pertinent to public safety."

"I can assure you, we weren't sitting on it. Like your agency, we have policies and procedures we need to follow when investigating and potentially prosecuting a crime."

"OK, I'm sorry if we got off on the wrong foot. My Deputy Director, Dr. Elizabeth Harder, and I would like to come to Maine to meet with you and anyone else you need to include. We need to discuss the next steps in follow-up to these adverse event reports. Would it be best for my assistant to contact your assistant to find a mutually convenient date and time?"

"Yes, that would be fine."

"Thank you, DA Wydman," he concluded, once again mispronouncing his name.

"You're welcome, Dr. Shearlow," he replied, passing on the desire of correcting him a third time or calling him Mr. Shearlow in retaliation.

Hanging up, he took several deep breaths to calm himself down before calling AG Talcott.

"Lew, we won't need to send that letter concerning the adverse event reports to AlzCura."

"Why not?"

"I just got off the phone with Dr. Shearlow from the Center for Biologics Evaluation and Research. Dr. Caron's Office Manager sent them the reports. He and the Deputy Director, Dr. Elizabeth Harder, want to visit and meet with us to coordinate a response."

"Great. Make sure I'm invited."

"Will do."

* * *

DA Wydman joined the call with Theo, Jackie, and Curt a few minutes late. As he connected, he was met by unexpected animated conversation and gaiety.

"Will," Curt announced, "Jackie's baby was returned safe and sound this morning!" prompting DA Wydman to congratulate Jackie and join the group in their excitement. After Jackie reiterated her story, DA Wydman announced his exciting news.

"Since we're on the topic of exciting news, I just got off the phone with Dr. Shearlow from the Center for Biologics Evaluation and Research with the FDA. I can't divulge details of why he called, but I can tell you that he and the Deputy Director of that branch of the FDA want to visit to coordinate efforts with us regarding some adverse event reports they have received."

"That's great news!" Curt hailed.

"My apologies, Will," Theo chimed in, "I meant to call to forewarn you that Dr. Shearlow was going to call. He pissed me right off."

"Yeah, he rubbed me the wrong way too, but we finally got to where we needed to get. Hopefully, the Deputy Director is easier to deal with."

"Will, you mentioned that the AG got AlzCura's response," Theo began.

"Yes, thanks, Theo. I met with the AG earlier today, and AlzCura's response was a bit surprising. Not only was it delivered two days before the deadline, but they claim Darius did not receive the vaccine, and they're going to produce Margo for questioning."

"What about Elvira," Theo asked.

"They indicated that she did receive the vaccine."

"That is surprising," Curt replied. "If that's true, then the vaccine didn't cause Darius' actions."

"I can't believe they're going to be able to produce Margo," Jackie commented, "They told me she had been fired."

"What else do you know about her, Jackie," asked Theo.

"Not much except that she has an irritating habit of saying 'ya know' a lot, and she doesn't strike me as the brightest bulb in the chandelier. I heard nothing but complaints about her from my doctors when I returned from maternity leave. I'm sure that Dr. Slack and Dr. Mason in Portland could give you more specifics."

"How is Celeste doing?" Curt asked. "I know you probably can't share much about the murder investigation."

"Celeste is laying low at a friend's house," Theo replied, fighting off thoughts of their morning activities. "Under the circumstances, I think she's doing alright."

"Would it make sense to include her on these calls in the future?" Jackie asked. "I know for Curt and me, these calls have helped us cope with our losses."

"Let me consider that," DA Wydman replied. "It seems to make sense. Theo, you have any thoughts about that?"

"Yeah, I think she can probably use all the support she can get."

"OK, Theo, if you get me her contact information, I will invite Celeste to our next call."

"Will do."

"Does anyone have anything else they would like to discuss?" When no one spoke up, Will continued.

"Alright, I will probably schedule the next meeting for after Theo interviews Margo and after we meet with Dr. Shearlow and his Deputy Director about the adverse event reports."

CHAPTER 48

Shortly after DA Wydman's group call, Curt called Jackie to express just how relieved he was that Ashley had been returned safely.

"You wouldn't have believed the scene when I entered the church, Curt. Dozens of people all gathered around 80-something-year-old Clara Himber holding Ashley. They all cheered as I ran down the aisle. It was magical."

"That sounds incredible, Jackie."

"What was really incredible was the German song Clara sang to Ashley when she was crying. Every time she sang it, Ashley would giggle and laugh. The whole congregation ended up learning it."

"That is amazing. What was the song about?"

"Ironically, it was about a mother who is crying because her little boy runs away from home."

"Sounds like Clara is Ashley's new great-grandmother."

"Yes, I will have to make sure to invite her to Ashley's first birthday in a few months," she said, making a mental note. "Now, I want to hear all about the Dude Ranch you took the kids to."

As Curt gave Jackie a detailed summary of the Dude Ranch, Jackie looked out her living room window to see the mailman walking down her porch stairs on his way to her neighbor's house. Realizing she had not checked the mail since before Ashley's abduction, she got up from the couch, opened the front door, and grabbed the healthy stack of correspondence that had accumulated. Returning to the couch, she started sorting through the pile as Curt continued his weekend saga.

"Really? You bought a fake steer head so Caitlin could practice her roping skills? What a Dad you are."

"You should see her. She's really talented. Yesterday she roped her friend Jordan as she walked in the door!"

Jackie laughed as she picked up an envelope, turned it over, and saw it was from Dr. Preston Slack. Setting it aside while Curt finished his story, she wondered how Dr. Slack had gotten her home address.

"Sounds like the weekend was a huge success."

"It was," Curt replied, "The kids couldn't have been happier. They had a blast and are already asking to go back!"

"You'll never guess what I just got in the mail," Jackie said, picking up Dr. Slack's envelope.

"A sweepstake check from American Family Publishers?" Curt joked.

"No," Jackie laughed, "besides, doesn't Ed McMahon deliver those to your door with one of those gigantic checks?"

"Maybe. I give up. What did you get in the mail?"

"A letter from one of the doctors I used to visit up in Portland. How did he get my home address, I wonder?" she exclaimed as she slid her finger under the envelope flap.

"What did he have to say?"

"I'm opening it right now," she replied, suddenly deducing that he must have had her home address from the thank you note she had sent him for the gift card from Babies "R" Us he had sent while she was on maternity leave.

"I'll read it to you," she announced.

"Dear Jackie, I recently learned that you left AlzCura for greener pastures. I'm happy for you but sad for us. In our book, you were the model for what all pharmaceutical reps should be - bright, energetic, well-informed, ethical, respectful, and caring. If you ever get back to Maine, please don't hesitate to visit us. We wish you and your family all the best. Sincerely, Preston Slack."

"Wow! That's nice," Curt stated.

Jackie was overcome and struggled to find her words.

"That's so sweet," she finally was able to utter.

"You should call him?" Curt proposed.

"Do you know him?" Jackie asked.

"No, but how many people take the time to write a note these days? It's even rarer when a busy physician does it."

"I will call him. Now I'm wondering how he learned I left for greener pastures."

"I imagine AlzCura sent out a notice saying all the right things about you, conveniently leaving out the dirty truth that they got rid of you because you knew too much, and your principles threatened to uncover their lies and deception."

"Wow, Curt, it sounds like you've ridden in this rodeo before. I'm impressed."

"I see what you did there - rodeo, dude ranch. Cute. Don't be impressed. Just the voice of experience. I've seen more than a few excellent individuals in my career unceremoniously led out the door by inept or corrupt leaders. Quickly followed by the disingenuous notice espousing the individual's qualities and accomplishments. It makes me sick."

"Yes, but how do you really feel about it, Curt?" Jackie said facetiously, causing them to laugh. "I will take your sage advice. I'll call him."

"What are you going to do about your job?" Curt shifted gears.

"God, I haven't even thought about that," Jackie admitted. "Right now, I can't even imagine leaving Ashley and going back to work."

"Exactly why I asked. Have you talked to your boss?"

"Not today, but she was actually with me when I learned Ashley had been abducted. I guess I should call her and let her know I have Ashley back."

"She may already know. News of an abducted baby returned safe, and sound is a rare commodity. I'm surprised you haven't been overrun by the media yet. It is quite an incredible story, with Clara and the whole church congregation cheering you on and singing."

"I never thought about that," as she looked out the living room window to check if reporters were descending upon her house. "Here I am in blissful ignorance, just happy to have Ash back, and you've already raised two important things I need to prepare for."

"Just looking out for you since I can't be there right now."

"And I am so happy you are."

"What? So happy I'm not able to be there?"

"No, silly. So happy you're looking out for me."

"OK, just checking," he replied, as both laughed.

The call with Curt opened Jackie's eyes and gently pulled her out of the cocoon she wrapped herself in now that her daughter was back in her arms. Curt's call and his concern for her and Ash also opened her heart, and their playful banter and connection made her revisit feelings she hadn't felt since her relationship with Stu.

* * *

As Theo turned the final corner and his cabin came into view, he saw Celeste swimming in the pond au naturel. Parking facing the pond, he turned the car off and watched through the windshield as different parts of her body peeked in and out from the motion of her strokes. Unaware he was watching, her undulating body dipped and dove below the surface, teasing him as her shapely nether region repeatedly rose up out of the water and disappeared.

Theo exited his car but continued to watch Celeste's peep show as he walked down to the shoreline onto the dock.

"I see you made good on your promise to go skinny-dipping," Theo called to her.

"You're welcome," she said, rolling over on her back and floating to the surface, revealing some of her womanly qualities. "Wanna come in," she asked tantalizingly.

Needing no more encouragement, he took off his clothes, dove in, and met her for a watery embrace and kiss. After they had exhausted themselves and embarrassed any fish that were the only possible witnesses to their aquatic activities, they retired to the cabin. After drying off and dressing, Theo started a fire in a large pit just beyond the cabin porch.

As dusk turned to dark with only the fire and the stars to light the night, Celeste sat in Theo's lap. When they weren't talking, he just held her. She reminisced about Sophie and cried until she couldn't cry anymore. In Theo's arms, they were healing tears.

He told her about Curt and Jackie and how they wanted her to join their calls. Since she had lost everything dear to her in the last two months, she welcomed the opportunity to join the group calls.

Although Theo's relationship with Celeste had clearly crossed a line of professionalism, he was careful not to discuss matters that could compromise the sanctity of his investigations. She was safe, they were happy, and for now, that was all that mattered.

CHAPTER 49

"Casco Bay Neurology Associates, this is Amy. May I help you?"

"Amy, this is Jackie. Jackie Deno?"

"Jackie! Oh my god, it is so good to hear your voice! Where have you been, girl? How is your baby?"

"I left AlzCura, and Ashley said mama for the first time last week!"

"Ahhh," Amy screamed, "that's so awesome. Yeah, I figured you left. Some woman named Cheryl was here a couple weeks ago."

"Hey Amy, Dr. Slack sent me a really nice note, and I was hoping to speak to him. Is he available by chance?"

"Let me check with his medical assistant. Can I put you on hold for a sec?"

"No problem."

Hearing Amy's enthusiasm and remembering how welcoming Dr. Slack and his team had always been made her suddenly miss her old job. At least she missed the practices that managed to be efficient and friendly, like Dr. Slack's practice.

"You're in luck, Jackie," Amy said as she returned to the call. "He is just finishing up with a patient and will be with you shortly. Do you mind holding again?"

"No problem, Amy. Nice to chat with you."

"Take care, Jackie."

The hold music was intermittently interrupted by brief commercials for the services Dr. Slack's practice offered. About a minute in, the music stopped, and Jackie was assaulted by an all too familiar advertisement she had first heard when she met Dr. Caron.

"Do you or a loved one tend to forget things? Do you misplace your car keys? Forget the names of people you meet? Has anyone in your family ever been diagnosed with Alzheimer's disease or dementia? If so, now there is help. I'm Dr. Preston Slack, a board-certified Neurologist specifically trained to treat these conditions. I offer the most effective treatments and participate in leading-edge research that may be the answer to your problems. You may even qualify for a research study, be paid to participate, and get free medication. If you or a loved one are forgetful, or you've had a family history of Alzheimer's or dementia, I offer free screenings at my Portland office."

"Jackie! So nice of you to call." Dr. Slack answered, interrupting her thoughts, which had navigated back to Dr. Caron and her concerns about the ethics of the ad that she eventually learned AlzCura had scripted.

"Dr. Slack, thank you for taking time out of your busy schedule to chat. I wanted to thank you for your note."

"Well, I meant every word. And AlzCura hasn't found a replacement for you yet. Perhaps it's more accurate to say they haven't found someone to fill your position, as I doubt anyone could replace you. And please, call me Preston."

"Aww, you're too kind."

"I felt terrible not sending a note sooner. My office staff apparently weeded out the letter notifying me that you had left your job to pursue a better opportunity. I didn't learn you had left until Ms. Baker visited a couple of weeks ago. So what are you doing now? And how is the baby?"

Jackie held a brief internal debate, torn between keeping the call politic and surface-level or telling the truth. She knew that calling Dr. Slack had already violated her termination agreement with AlzCura that forbade her from contacting clients. Hearing that ad again while on hold and now looking with relief at her daughter, who had been abducted, she knew there was only one right decision.

"Preston," she began tentatively, "AlzCura, let me go. I didn't leave for another job."

"What? That's not what Ms. Baker told me. Why in God's name?"

Knowing she had now opened Pandora's box, she had little choice but to continue.

"I'm pretty sure it was because I told my boss, Cheryl Baker, about concerns that Dr. Caron had about Recallamin. He told me some things that apparently AlzCura executives didn't want me to know or didn't want to fix. I knew too much and foolishly thought that if I escalated his concerns, it would prompt a principled response. I was wrong."

"That is deeply disturbing, Jackie. Dr. Caron had tried to call me just shortly before he committed suicide. Unfortunately, we never connected. What kinds of concerns did he express to you?"

"Where do I begin?" Jackie paused as his question caused a multitude of thoughts and experiences she had with Dr. Caron to swirl in her head. "For one, he was confident that AlzCura was hiding or misrepresenting Recallamin's complication data. He was also concerned that many of his patients were admitted to the hospital with liver failure."

"Very interesting. When Ms. Baker was here, I expressed concerns about some of my patients having abnormally high liver function tests. A few days later, Dr. Sheridan called me to say they found an error in the lab results and would send me the corrected lab values, which he assured me were normal."

"Have you received those corrected lab results?"

"Not yet. By the way, Dr. Mason, who I'm sure you know, had similar concerns about her patients and was on the call with Dr. Sheridan as well. Just last week, one of my Recallamin patients was admitted to the hospital and died of liver failure and a massive brain aneurysm."

"Preston, my husband Stu, who had received Recallamin, died of exactly those same causes."

"Oh, Jackie, I'm so sorry. I didn't know. There definitely seems to be a problem with Recallamin that is not being addressed."

"Preston, would you be willing to meet with a group of people who share our concerns about AlzCura and Recallamin? Your experiences and concerns could help save hundreds if not thousands of lives."

"I'm not sure who is in this group?"

"Maine District Attorney Wydman, Inspector Theo Adams, Curt Barnes, and me."

"Curt Barnes? The husband of that woman murdered by Darius Scott? Why is he involved in the group."

"Yes, that Curt Barnes. Darius Scott was in the Recallamin clinical trial and,"

Dr. Preston finished Jackie's sentence, "And he died of liver failure and a massive brain aneurysm. I know, I heard that when the Attorney General released his autopsy results last week."

"And why are DA Wydman and Inspector Adams involved?"

"They are investigating Dr. Caron's death and the recent

murder of Leslie Anderson. All may have connections to Alz-Cura and the adverse effects of Recallamin. Won't you please join us? It could make a big difference."

"Yes, I have to join you. My conscience would never rest knowing now what you've told me about Dr. Caron's concerns and your husband's death."

"Thank you, Preston. I will speak to them and see if we can set up a meeting soon."

"OK. And Jackie?"

"Yes."

"You should speak with Dr. Mason and consider inviting her to the meeting as well."

"I will do that. Thank you, Preston."

"I look forward to seeing you soon then."

Jackie realized immediately after the call that she had just taken a step down a dangerous path from which there was no turning back. Despite the risks, it seemed oddly comforting. She had agreed to take a backseat approach to the crusade when the Table for Four recommended it, but even that failed to protect her or her daughter. If she and her daughter were going to be targeted, she was going to make damn sure to take affirmative and aggressive action against the adversary.

Jackie subsequently called Dr. Mason, who also agreed to join the meeting after Jackie shared the information she had communicated to Dr. Slack. Before the afternoon was over, Jackie had scheduled a face-to-face meeting at the Farrisport Inn to reconvene the Table for Four, which now had grown to a Table for Seven - DA Wydman, Inspector Adams, Curt Barnes, Celeste Boulanger, Dr. Preston Slack, Dr. Stephanie Mason, and Jackie.

She now had the answer to the question Curt had asked about her plans to go back to work at the hospital. She couldn't go back. Instead, she would devote all her time and energy to expose the fraudulent and unethical practices of AlzCura Pharmaceuticals and bring to justice those who were responsible for killing Stu and countless numbers of other people who entrusted their lives to their so-called miracle cure.

CHAPTER 50

In the days leading up to the much-anticipated meeting that she had arranged at the Farrisport Inn, Jackie put her affairs in order. She had learned a hard lesson about keeping information from her parents and wasn't going to make that mistake again. She would not hide from or run in fear of the past. Nor would she let the losses she had suffered diminish her. She had a clear mission, and oddly, it was Cheryl Baker's words and mentorship that had led to her newfound determination and rebirth. "Expose the truth" became Jackie's mantra, as simple and straightforward as Cheryl's "just sell the drug."

After church, she took her parents to Momma's, their favorite brunch destination. There, with Ash happily babbling in a high chair, Jackie laid out her plans to hopefully garner her parent's support. The combination of being in a public place, the carrot cake pancakes, mimosas, and her unswerving resolve, had their intended effect. In fact, her mother, who was typically cautious and over-protective, seemed to have found her fight as well.

"Good for you, Jackie, and I'll be right there with you. When they messed with my granddaughter, they messed with the wrong person," as her mother leaned over to kiss Ashley's cheek.

"And we lost our son-in-law because of those bastards too,"

her father swore.

"Jack! The baby," Jackie's mother scolded.

"Selaney's are fighters," Jackie's father continued. "Just let us know what we can do to help."

"Thanks, Mom and Dad. I'm sorry I didn't,"

"Stop," Jackie's father interrupted her apology. "Water under the bridge. Now we show your former employer what happens when you cross us. We love you, Jackie, and we'll do whatever we can to support you and Ash."

Fresh from her successful meeting with her parents, Jackie went home, put Ashley down for a nap, and called Tara Newman.

"Hi, Jackie. I was so relieved to hear about Ashley's safe return. How are you and Ashley doing?"

"Thanks, Tara. We're doing great, and I so appreciate your patience and support during this time."

"Not a problem, Jackie. I couldn't imagine trying to work if it had happened to one of my kids. So how are you feeling? Are you ready to come back to work, or do you need some more time?"

"Before I answer that, can I tell you about my time at AlzCura? I think my answer to your question will make more sense to you if I do."

Jackie, keeping to her new mantra, briefed Tara on all the things she had experienced at AlzCura and the crusade she was committed to that culminated in her decision not to return to her hospital job.

"Thank you for sharing that, Jackie. I understand and respect your decision. What's more, I want you to know that if there is anything I can do to help you, please let me know."

"Thank you, Tara."

"I mean it. A lot of people say that, and it's a throwaway

line they never anticipate having to fulfill. I admire your tenacity and want to help you. You've chosen a difficult path against a large, powerful company. I have connections that may help."

"Thank you again, Tara. That means a lot to me. I will be sure to take you up on your offer if and when I need it."

"And after you've successfully exposed the truth on Alz-Cura and need a job, look me up. I can always find a place for a person like you."

Jackie had gone into the call with Tara dreading to have to disappoint her short-term boss, and ended the call feeling like she had gained a valuable ally.

* * *

Curt had arranged for Caitlin and Cade to stay with Jordan's mother after school, so he could pick Jackie and Ashley up at the airport Thursday afternoon. He hadn't told them about Jackie's visit, wanting instead to surprise them.

His stomach did flip-flops as he waited impatiently just outside the airport security doors Jackie and Ash would eventually pass through. Their relationship had evolved since they were last together. He wondered if their comfort with one another on the phone would translate once they were together again. As another wave of travelers came through the doors, he spotted Jackie with Ashley in her arms. Curt navigated upstream through the passengers towards them. When Jackie saw him, she broke into the stunning smile that had first captivated him at the restaurant.

"Welcome back to Maine," Curt said as they came together in a half hug, Jackie kissing him on the cheek.

"Sorry, you deserve a full hug, but I kinda have my arms full," she commented, nodding in Ashley's direction.

"I'll take a rain check. So this must be Ashley," Curt said, turning his attention to Jackie's daughter. "You are just as beautiful as your mother," he exclaimed, as Ashley looked warily from Curt's face to her mother, her lips trembling as she broke into a full cry.

"Oh, Ash," her mother cooed and tried to comfort her, "it's alright. I don't know what's wrong with her. She used to love it when new people paid attention to her, but not lately."

"There's nothing wrong with her," Curt replied, "she's what, 8 or 9 months old?"

"She just turned 9 months."

"She has stranger anxiety. It's a good thing and completely normal. That or I'm just scary, ugly."

"Well, since you're definitely not scary ugly, what is stranger anxiety, and why is it a good thing?"

"I didn't know you traveled all this way, just to learn about childhood cognitive-developmental phases."

"Humor me."

"In short, it means she's bonded with you, and she's starting to be able to discriminate between familiar and unfamiliar things. She's learning to be cautious around new people. It happens around the same time infants develop object permanence."

"Object permanence?"

"That will have to be tomorrow's lesson."

As they made their way to baggage claim, Ashley's wariness diminished as her mother and Curt talked and laughed.

"Oh, I forgot to bring Ashley's car seat," Jackie stated as they approached Curt's car.

"No worries, I pulled the kids' car seat out of storage. We're all set. Let me see if Ash will let me put her in the car seat."

"You want to experiment with my child?"

"No, I just want to be sure it's not because I'm scary, ugly."

As Jackie tentatively handed Ashley to Curt, he gingerly placed her in the car seat and strapped her in.

"Boop," Curt said in a baby-talk voice while lightly touching Ashley's nose. When Ashley giggled, he did it again, with the same results.

"Amazing," Jackie remarked, looking on from outside the car.

"I guess I'm not scary, ugly," he said as he shut the back door and smiled at Jackie.

"Time to redeem that rain check," Jackie replied and wrapped both her arms around Curt in a long, full hug that naturally transitioned to their first kiss. If Curt's stomach was doing flip-flops before, it was now tumbling like an Olympic gymnast. The power of their connection and the relief they both felt in each other's arms brought them both to tears.

"Only five minutes, and you've already made me and my daughter cry," Jackie laughed through her tears.

"Just wait until you've been with me an hour!"

On their 30-minute drive to the Farrisport Inn, Curt and Jackie continued their animated conversation, and Ashley fell asleep. After checking in, Jackie put Ashley down for a nap and freshened up in her room while Curt went shopping in advance of the group dinner scheduled for 2 hours hence.

Jackie, who had organized the meeting, made it a point to be in the lobby early to greet the participants as they arrived, especially Dr. Slack and Dr. Mason, who weren't acquainted with the group. Waiting with Ashley in her arms, she toured the room decorated in things quintessential to Maine - a lobster trap and buoys, paintings of Mount Katahdin, Camden Harbor, Casco Bay, and Acadia National Park, and of course, the mounted moose head.

Once the members of the party arrived and introductions

were made, the group moved to the restaurant, where hostess Brittany greeted the group and led them to the private dining area. Jackie had asked DA Wydman to facilitate the meeting but asked that he let her give an opening statement.

"Thank you all for coming here tonight," Jackie began as Ashley sat in a high-chair next to her, more interested in her sippy cup than what her mother had to say. "About six months ago, DA Wydman, Curt, Dr. Steven Caron, God rest his soul, and I met here. It feels like years ago now. We met because all of us had an interest in or a relationship with AlzCura Pharmaceuticals and a vaccine called Recallamin that they marketed as a miracle cure for Alzheimer's. While we all shared concerns about the safety of Recallamin, it was the allegations and brave and selfless confessions of Dr. Caron that started us on a crusade to expose the truth about AlzCura's unethical practices and their campaign to misrepresent and hide complication data - specifically the prevalence of patients with liver failure."

That Jackie would be here today praising Dr. Caron's instrumental role in the crusade was a far cry from how she felt about him when he first joined the group that evening. Something about voicing the importance of his contribution to the group made her choke up with tears. Pausing, she dabbed her tears with her napkin and took a sip of water.

"I'm sorry. That evening we formed a pact to work together to expose the truth about AlzCura and Recallamin. Since then, Dr. Caron has committed suicide. Someone tried to pick up Curt's children and left a threatening note on his door. My house was broken into, and a threat was spray-painted on my daughter's bedroom wall, and surveillance equipment was installed to spy on me. Most recently, someone abducted Ashley, and as you can see," she said, gesturing towards her daughter, "I was fortunate enough to get her back," her voice cracking as another wave of tears came over her.

Jackie once again paused to compose herself while her

audience sat in silent, rapt attention. Curt and Celeste were also wiping away tears as Jackie's impassioned statement had them reliving their horrors.

"I'm sorry. This is hard," she confessed. "I know that each of you has your story to tell, and I hope you will share that story with us tonight. I also know that DA Wydman and Inspector Adams have limitations in what they can divulge about active criminal investigations in which they are involved. We need to respect that limitation and recognize that it will be their efforts and processes that will ultimately help us achieve our goal. I have made the personal decision to dedicate myself full-time to this crusade. My mantra is, expose the truth. It hasn't been easy, and I have certainly had my share of doubts and fears. I hope you will join me. Thank you again for coming. I hope that we can all eventually look back on this night and say this was when we took action that spared thousands of others from suffering the losses that Celeste, Curt, and I have had to endure at the hands of AlzCura Pharmaceutical."

Jackie's opening statement received an unexpected and unique ovation. DA Wydman, Inspector Adams, Dr. Slack, and Dr. Mason stood clapping as Curt and Celeste continued unsuccessfully to stop their tears, and Ashley, startled by the applause, began to wail. Order was restored when Jackie picked her daughter up, and the applauding group abbreviated their ovation in deference to Ashley.

A natural break in the meeting occurred as their server took drink orders. This gave those around the table time to process Jackie's message and build up the emotional fortitude that would be necessary for the remainder of the meeting.

"Thank you, Jackie. You're a hard act to follow," DA Wydman began after their server had left. "Jackie has asked me to facilitate tonight's meeting. As she has already told you, Theo and I may not be able to contribute information that is part of our active investigations, but what you share with us tonight can definitely help to save lives and potentially bring AlzCura to justice. I'd like to propose two things. First, let's take a few minutes to review the menu. Second, I'd like to go around the table and ask that you each share your story, as Jackie mentioned. Ashley, I will give you a pass," causing everyone except Ashley to laugh.

The group perused their menus, and after a few minutes, their server returned. After delivering their drinks and taking their appetizer and dinner orders, the server exited, and the meeting continued.

"Priding myself on being a gentleman," DA Wydman said, "ladies first. Celeste, are you comfortable beginning?"

"Thank you," Celeste replied, "I don't know that anyone could be comfortable sharing what I have to share, but I know it's important that I do. Before Jackie's opening statement, I didn't think I'd be able to talk about this. I really admire you, Jackie," she said as tears began to flow.

Jackie got up from her chair and went and gave Celeste a hug. You could see Celeste regaining her composure and visibly gaining strength from Jackie's embrace.

"Thank you, Jackie," Celeste continued, wiping away remnants of her tears. For the next 10 minutes, Celeste recounted the last few painful days with her husband, Norman. How his aggressive behavior and sudden death left her with nothing but questions. How Theo had helped her discover that Norman was involved in one of AlzCura's clinical trials, and most recently, how someone broke into her home and killed her dog and Leslie Anderson.

"Now, after losing everything dear to me, I can't even live in my own home. I have to hide, not only from whoever may want to kill me but also from all the reporters and the cameras," she concluded, descending into tears.

Several in the group, including Curt, Theo, and Jackie, offered words of support to Celeste. In contrast to the others, who seemed to be struggling to digest the horrors she had experienced over the last two months.

Appetizers were delivered and passed around, giving the emotion-laden meeting a much-needed intermission.

Dr. Mason and Dr. Slack subsequently shared their experiences with AlzCura and their concerns about the safety of Recallamin. They summarized Dr. Sheridan's recent admission that high liver function test results were in error and were being corrected. During their presentations, DA Wydman and Theo exchanged numerous glances, recognizing that the physicians had information that would clearly strengthen their case against AlzCura.

Dinner was served, and as the meeting was going into its third hour, DA Wydman moved it along.

"I know that some of you may still be finishing your dinner, but given the lateness of the hour, I would like to ask Curt to share his experiences and then end by outlining the next steps."

Curt, whose story had been splashed across the newspapers for months, touched only briefly on the events involving Darius Scott and his wife's murder. Instead, he commiserated with Celeste, sharing how his wife's death, the emotional scars his children suffered, and the more recent attempt by someone to pick up his children from the school had left him living in fear.

"I don't know that I would have survived if I hadn't met Jackie, quite by accident, in this very restaurant last year," he said, looking at Jackie as his eyes glistened with tears. "She was my salvation then, and our friendship and this crusade continue to give me hope that there are brighter days ahead. Days when I don't have to live in fear. Days when no one will be harmed by AlzCura and their greedy and deceitful practices."

"Thank you, Curt," DA Wydman added. "While neither Theo nor I can share much with you, I can tell you about two promising things on the horizon. AlzCura has indicated that they will produce Margo, a person of interest who we wish to question concerning one of our investigations. Also, a branch of the FDA has contacted us about working together to investigate a series of unreported adverse events."

"Will," Jackie interjected, "this may not be possible, but could I listen in on Margo's interview, like from one of those rooms behind a one-way mirror? Like on those TV detective shows?"

The group chuckled.

"Interesting suggestion. Why do you ask?" DA, Wydman replied.

"Well, I know Margo, and I may be able to tell you whether she is telling the truth, especially about AlzCura."

"For that matter," Dr. Mason chimed in, "both Dr. Slack and I are also acquainted with Margo, and based on our experiences, we didn't find her to be very helpful or ethical." As Dr. Slack, who was sitting beside her, nodded his agreement.

"Well, before we invite a crowd in to watch Margo's interview, let me suggest this. "Theo will set up a time with all three of you to catalog your experiences and concerns about Margo. Once we have that information, I will reconsider the question as to whether we need you to witness her statement."

"That sounds reasonable," Jackie replied as Dr. Mason, and Dr. Slack nodded their assent.

"My meetings with Dr. Mason and Dr. Slack may even help when we meet with the FDA representatives," Theo added. "If you're willing to identify Recallamin patients who have had adverse events, I can get a subpoena so I can review the files in your office."

"I'd be happy to do that," Dr. Slack responded.

"Me too," Dr. Mason added.

"OK, I think our next steps are pretty well laid out," DA

Wydman summarized. "Is there anything else we should consider?"

"Will," Jackie replied, "do you think involving law enforcement from New York may help? I know that Officer Barrett Todd was very helpful to me after the break-in and Ashley's abduction. He is going to speak to his Chief about potentially working with you."

"Well, I can't see how that could hurt," DA Wydman replied. "Since AlzCura is based in New York, it would be good to have boots on the ground there. Keep me posted if Officer Todd's Chief wants to move forward. Anything else?"

With no more suggestions from the group, DA Wydman thanked them and adjourned the meeting. Several stayed behind to finish their desserts or chat with others. Jackie and Curt got together with Celeste to share hugs and give her their phone numbers. Ashley had fallen asleep in her highchair long before the meeting adjourned. Jackie carefully lifted her out of the chair, and after stirring briefly, fell asleep in Jackie's arms. After they made the rounds to say their farewells, Curt escorted Jackie and Ashley out. Returning to the lobby and in the shadow of the moose head, Curt hugged Jackie.

"Thanks for saving my life, Jackie."

"Thanks for saving mine," she replied, both releasing their hug enough to end the night with a long, gentle kiss.

"Pick you up tomorrow afternoon at 4 p.m.?" Curt asked.

"It's a date," Jackie replied, turning to ascend the stairs to her room.

As Curt drove home, he reflected on the evening's events and the plans he and Jackie had made for the weekend. It gave him hope that the brighter days he had spoken of during the meeting were just on the horizon.

* * *

Thank you for reading Dying to Recall, the second book in the Table for Four series. Enter web address below into your internet browser to purchase Memory's Hope, the final book in the series.

https://www.amazon.com/dp/0463395131

ACKNOWLEDGEMENT

My parents both died from complications of Alzheimer's Disease. Before their downward spiral from this devastating disease, they lived long, productive lives. They endured unimaginable hardships growing up, yet survived and emigrated to America to build a better life for themselves and their children. They instilled in me values for which I will be forever grateful. Thanks, Mom and Dad. This book and the entire *Table for Four* series are for you.

A portion of the proceeds from this book and the other books in this series, including *Table for Four* and *Memory's Hope*, will be donated to the Alzheimer's Foundation of America (AFA). AFA's mission is providing support, services, and education to individuals, families, and caregivers affected by Alzheimer's disease and related dementias nationwide and funding research for better treatment and a cure.

BOOKS IN THIS SERIES

Table for Four
A 3-book series about a Pharmaceutical Company's discovery of a cure for Alzheimer's disease that has unforeseen and ominous consequences.

Table For Four: A Medical Thriller Series Book 1

A blockbuster Alzheimer's cure. A murder and unexplained deaths. Two aggrieved parties meet by chance. Will they expose the truth, or die trying?

Dying To Recall: A Medical Thriller Series Book 2

A suicide, a break-in, an ominous warning. Is it a coincidence? Or have Jackie and Curt unleashed the wrath of vengeful pharmaceutical executives?

Memory's Hope: A Medical Thriller Series Book 3

The case against AlzCura intensifies until the FDA's shocking response to the data. Will the guilty parties walk, or will they be brought to justice?

BOOKS BY THIS AUTHOR

Table For Four: A Medical Thriller Series Book 1

A blockbuster Alzheimer's cure. A murder and unexplained deaths. Two aggrieved parties meet by chance. Will they expose the truth, or die trying?

Dying To Recall: A Medical Thriller Series Book 2

A suicide, a break-in, an ominous warning. Is it a coincidence? Or have Jackie and Curt unleashed the wrath of vengeful pharmaceutical executives?

Memory's Hope: A Medical Thriller Series Book 3

The case against AlzCura intensifies until the FDA's shocking response to the data. Will the guilty parties walk, or will they be brought to justice?

Aja Minor: Gifted Or Cursed: A Psychic Crime Thriller Series Book 1

Aja has disturbing powers. She feels cursed, but the FBI thinks otherwise. Will she stop a serial rapist and killer or become his next victim?

Aja Minor: Fountain Of Youth: A Psychic Crime Thriller Series Book 2

Aja Minor goes undercover. The target, an international child trafficking ring. When her cover is blown, the mission and her life are in jeopardy.

Aja Minor: Predatorville: A Psychic Crime Thriller Series Book 3

Solving a surge in assaults and missing children is Aja Minor's next test. But when the hunter becomes the hunted, will she get out of Predatorville alive?

Old Lady Ketchel's Revenge: The Slaughter Minnesota Horror Series Book 1

No one truly escapes their childhood unscathed. Especially if you grew up in Slaughter, Minnesota, in the 1960s and crossed Old Lady Ketchel's path.

Hagatha Ketchel Unhinged: The Slaughter Minnesota Horror Series Book 2

Twenty-four years in an asylum is enough time to really lose your mind. And arouse one to unleash the dark and vengeful thoughts residing therein.

Hagatha's Century Of Terror: The Slaughter Minnesota Horror Series Book 3

What does a crazy old lady in Slaughter, Minnesota, need on her 100th birthday? Sweet revenge, of course.

Loving You From My Grave: A Wholesome Inspirational Romance

He ran from his past. She's held captive by hers. Could love set them free, bridge their differences in age and race, and survive death?

Little Bird On My Balcony: Selected Poems

A collection of poems that speak to the love, loss, longing, and levity of navigating young adulthood.

Adilynn's Lullaby: Poems Of Love & Loss

A collection of poems about love and loss that provide hope and inspiration during some of life's most difficult times.

ABOUT CHRIS BLIERSBACH

 Chris Bliersbach is originally from St. Paul, Minnesota, and now lives in Henderson, Nevada.

Follow him on Amazon, Facebook, Goodreads or join his mailing list at cmbliersbach@gmail.com

Made in the USA
Middletown, DE
15 August 2023

36720330R00213